Homeland

CLARE FRANCIS

Homeland

MACMILLAN

First published 2004 by Macmillan
an imprint of Pan Macmillan Ltd
Pan Macmillan, 20 New Wharf Road, London N1 9RR
Basingstoke and Oxford
Associated companies throughout the world
www.panmacmillan.com

ISBN 0 333 90814 7 (HB)
ISBN 0 333 90815 5 (TPB)

Typeset by SetSystems Ltd, Saffron Walden, Essex
Printed and bound in Great Britain by
Mackays of Chatham plc, Chatham, Kent

For Tom

Part One

Chapter One

HE SLIPPED back to the farm in much the same way as he had left it seven years earlier, in the gloaming of an October evening by the drove-road over Curry Moor. The last light lay in blazing bands across the western sky, making fiery ribbons of the puddled cart-ruts, which stretched out before him, rod-straight, to the wetland edge. The drove appeared deserted as far as the metalled road and the stone bridge, but he strode along at a sharp lick all the same, the sooner to escape the exposure of the open moor, for he knew what people would say if they spotted him coming by this route, that he was running true to form, stealing back like a thief in the night. He had judged the risk worth taking nonetheless, for the chance to do his business quickly and get away unseen.

Mounting the ramp to the small arched bridge, he tensed momentarily as a horse and rider rose up over the crown, but it was only a gypsy boy, bareback on a snorting pony, the creature's eyes glinting red in the sunset. Mercifully the river-top path was clear of people, so too was the path that dropped down to the damp stubble of Hay Moor, but he didn't slacken his pace till he was over the rhyne and starting up Frog Field, when an odd discordant sound caused him to pause, his soldier's instincts reaching out into the dusk. Above his head bats darted and fluttered in jerky parabolas, while in the meadow below, cows stood solidly against the dying light. At last the sound came again, and, making out the distant yawling of a dog, he walked rapidly on.

He crossed an orchard rich with the scent of fallen apples,

which bumped and scuffed against his boots. Looping around the back of Old Maynard's farm, he heard the dog much closer, howling and jerking at its chain. A rarely used path kept him away from the lanes and cottages for a while longer, until, meeting the North Curry road, he was forced onto its ringing surface. Hitching his knapsack higher on his shoulders, he stepped out at a smart clip, but if there was anyone to witness his jaunty march he never saw them. A minute later he gained the shadows of the next footpath which undulated across two fields before sloping down towards the dark expanse of West Sedgemoor.

Even before he sighted the inky line of pollards that marked the old rhyne he felt the cool breath of the wetland against his cheek, he heard the faint riffling of the wind in the withies like the rustling of a woman's skirts, he caught the boggy smell of water and overblown vegetation, scents and sounds that brought a surge of memory, unexpectedly powerful, disturbingly sweet.

A place called Sculley Farm lay ahead. He had intended to skirt its southern boundary, but it was getting too dark to attempt the narrow overgrown path along the wetland edge. Instead, he swung across a field and climbed over a stile onto a lane of loose stones which chimed and rattled under his boots. Coming abreast of the farmyard, a shape detached itself from the darkness by the wall.

A scratchy voice called out, 'Who's that there?'

He would have walked on, but the figure lurched into his path.

'Watch out!' he exclaimed sharply.

An old man's laugh, a blast of cidery breath. 'Billy? That you, Billy Greer?'

'For Christ's sake!'

'Let you out then, did they?'

Billy dimly recognised an old fool named Percy Frith, and brushed roughly past him, annoyed at having been identified, and yet more annoyed at letting it show. He was still berating himself as he strode down the track to Crick Farm. Several times in as many yards he renewed his vow to leave the moment he had finished his business, to get clear away and never come back.

The cottage sat low and dark against the wetland; the damp seemed to rise around it like a mist. A glimmer of light was showing in the kitchen, another behind the curtain above. Entering the yard by the latch-gate, Billy's toe caught on a piece of tangled metal that clanged and clattered as he kicked it aside. Underfoot the concrete was soft with a carpet of stripple and mulch, while in the middle of the yard he almost walked into a pile of withies, mouldering by the smell of them. He felt the first creep of foreboding as he came across more clutter around the lean-to porch: a loaded handcart, a cider barrel with sprung hoops, and, propped anyhow against the shiplap, a jumble of scythes and rakes.

The kitchen door opened on uncertain hinges. He called a greeting and heard only the muted tones of brassy dance music trumpeting from a radio upstairs. At first everything appeared unchanged: the draining board scrubbed and bare, plates slotted neatly into the rack above, dishcloths drying on the clothes-horse in front of the range. Then he felt the chill in the air, he saw the stubby candles guttering and no lamps, he saw on the table the remains of a solitary meal, and it struck him that one of them must have died. This thought triggered the apprehension he always felt at bad news, the prick of guilt and alarm, the sense that, however remote the event, however innocent his part, blame would somehow attach itself to him. Only with an effort did he remember that such thoughts belonged to the past, that he had nothing to reproach himself for. That he never did have, except in his own mind.

Overhead, the muffled dance music gave way to a sonorous BBC announcer. Billy picked up a candle and carried it through into the cramped hallway. He called up the stairs and heard an exclamation followed by the shuffle of feet. Uncle Stan appeared on the landing above: a fierce white face over a shadowy body.

'It's me – Billy.'

'For the love of God,' Stan exclaimed.

'How are you, Old Man?'

Stan clomped down the rackety stairs, wheezing like a pump engine, and peered at him through damp eyes. 'So you be back, then.'

'Not for long,' Billy stated rapidly. 'I can't stay.' When Stan made no sign of having heard, he repeated slowly, 'I – can't – stay.'

The old man's face took on the expression Billy remembered so well, closed, stubborn, remote. Billy gave a humourless laugh. 'Same old Stan, eh? Where's Aunt Flor?'

With a small lift of his head Stan indicated the room above.

'How is she?'

Stan's mouth turned down.

'What's wrong?'

But the old man only shook his head and moved away into the kitchen.

Billy followed. 'Is she ill?'

Another silence.

'Well, either she's ill or she's not ill.'

Still nothing. This had always been the old man's way, to use silence as a weapon of irritation, but Billy wasn't going to rise to the bait, not this time round. As the old man moved towards the larder, Billy ducked his head in front of him and repeated tolerantly, 'Well?'

'What's the point in harping on about it?' the old man demanded with a quiver of agitation. 'There ain't nothing to be done.'

'How can I be harping on about it when I've only just arrived? When I don't even know what's wrong with her.'

'It were a stroke, weren't it? A *stroke*.' The old man was trembling.

'All right, all right. Just simmer down.' Billy wasn't sure what a stroke was, whether it was the same as a heart attack. 'Is she bad?'

Turning away, Stan sat down heavily at the table. 'Bad enough.'

Billy felt like asking what the hell that was meant to mean, but managed to hold his tongue. He looked down at the old man indecisively. He hadn't allowed for this, the sag of the shoulders, the air of defeat, the sense that the old man had grown smaller, almost defenceless. Yet even as he wondered if he might be feeling something as unexpected as pity he had a memory of Stan on the withy beds, glaring at him angrily, delivering a stream of scorn, and the feeble impulse to sympathy died.

In the larder Billy found cider, bread and cheese. Sitting in his old place, perched on the chair with the uneven legs, he poured two jars of cider and pushed one across to Stan. 'So, when did all this happen?'

'I told yer . . .'

'You've told me nothing,' Billy stated firmly.

The old man glowered at him, on the point of arguing, only to hesitate and jam his mouth shut. It wasn't a retreat exactly, more a pause for thought, but it was enough to give Billy a small spark of satisfaction. Over the past few months he had rehearsed this scene countless times in his mind – the calm he would show in the face of the old man's provocation, the indifference to any mention of the past, the effortless authority he would impose on the conversation – and had pictured the look of surprise and respect that would creep over the old man's face as it dawned on him that Billy was a very different person from the one who'd left seven years ago. And here it was, sooner than he'd dared hope: the first hesitation, the first glimmer of respect.

'Start from the beginning,' Billy said.

'It was at the victory celebrations,' Stan offered at last, frowning at his glass, taking a sudden gulp. 'The church bells were rung all morning. The whole village turned out, gathered there in front of the George. There were tables set up with pies and cakes, and the landlord selling ale at a penny a pint. Jimmy Summers brought his fiddle along, and everyone were dancing, right there in the lane.' Stan gave a small snort. 'Even old misery guts, the Baptist minister, took to shuffling a bit. Lifting his feet up and down like the ground were a bit hot underfoot. Flor thought it the best thing she'd seen in a long time. Yes, in a very long time.' Stan pulled a packet of Woodbines out of his pocket and lit up before remembering his manners. Still avoiding Billy's eye, he slid the packet a few inches across the table, and watched Billy help himself. 'Flor, she always loved to dance. Her were light on her feet, oh yes indeed, light as a feather. Knew all the steps. Well, there she were, dancing fit to bust, whirling round and round, when all of a sudden she stumbles and grabs my arm. I thought she were just dizzy, yer know, from all the spinning about. But it were the stroke. I caught her just before she hit the floor. Caught her and held her clear. The doctor were fetched, but there weren't nothing he could do. The whole of her right side were gone, face, arm, leg, and some of the left side too. She'd lost the power of speech, and the doctor thought she might've lost some of her understanding too. But she understands everything I tell her all right, and no mistake.'

It had happened over a year ago, he said. There had been no change since.

'You should have told me,' Billy said.

'Didn't know where to write, did I?'

Or couldn't be bothered to find out, Billy thought. It wouldn't have taken more than five minutes to look through the bureau in the parlour where Flor kept the family papers and find his address. She had written to Billy throughout the war, two neatly penned sides sent on the first and fourteenth of every month, regular as clockwork. After Billy's regiment landed in France, her letters had sometimes taken weeks to catch up with him, often arriving in twos and threes. He remembered with a nudge of guilt how he had skimmed through them, indifferent to the world he had left behind. The only letter he'd read more than once was an early one, some six months after he'd joined up. After that, he'd lost interest in the gossip, and his replies had been at best sporadic, a couple of lines on a postcard if Aunt Flor was lucky. When her letters stopped abruptly, he'd told himself it was because the war was over and she no longer thought it necessary to write. If he'd felt the occasional twinge of concern he'd ignored it easily enough, for if his early life had taught him anything it was to expect sudden, unaccountable change.

After a second glass of cider – the cloudy brew slipped down, more bewitching than memory – Billy felt as ready as he ever would be to follow Stan up the narrow stairs to the room that, during his four years at Crick Farm, he had entered only once, to repair the window.

As Stan opened the door the sound of sickly violin music rose up to greet them. The room was lit by a candle standing low on the bedside table. The candle in Stan's hand added a spasmodic flickering glow to the dark side of the room. Aunt Flor lay in the iron bed, propped against the pillows. At first Billy thought she was awake, then he thought she was dead, finally he saw that she was asleep. The stroke had left her face askew, as though a great weight were tugging down on one cheek. The right side of her mouth was dragging and dribbling, while her right eye wasn't altogether closed even in sleep, so that the white gave off a feral glint in the candle beam.

'Who does the caring for her?' Billy asked in a rough whisper.

'Why, myself, that's who,' declared Stan, as if this should have been obvious.

Billy didn't like to imagine what was involved. He would have turned away but his gaze was held by the drooping eye. It reminded him of a girl he and his mates had dug out of a house in Belgium. The girl's eyes had been rolled back under half-closed lids, the whites coated in a film of dust, until she was carried out and dumped in the sunlight when the whites gave off an unearthly, almost sinister gleam. The girl had been pretty, her body unmarked. Except for the eyes, she too might have been asleep.

'I've come to fetch my mum's stuff,' Billy said over the sobbing violins.

Wordlessly, the old man turned for the door.

'Will you tell her that?' Billy said, following him out onto the landing.

'You can tell her yerself,' said Stan, starting down the stairs.

'What, now?'

'When she wakes.'

'When will that be?'

'In the morning.'

'But I've told you – I'm not staying.'

'Please yourself.'

In the kitchen, Billy said, 'Tell me where my mum's stuff is, then.'

'Couldn't say, could I?'

They exchanged a hostile glare, and for a moment it might have been the old days again. Going through to the parlour, Billy made a quick search of the bureau before accepting that he had lost all chance of getting away that evening. He dug out papers and letters of every description, some old, some new, many still in their envelopes; he found birth certificates, mementos and photographs, but nothing belonging to his mother. In a pigeonhole he came across the cards and letters he had written to Flor during the war. They were tied in bundles, placed next to the letters from the son in Canada. Another son had died as a child, while the daughter lived in Plymouth, bogged down by children.

By the time Billy got back to the kitchen it was in darkness and the old man's footsteps were creaking overhead. Picking up his rucksack, he climbed the stairs to his old room under the eaves. Ducking under the lintel, setting the candle on the table, he had a fleeting memory of his first sight of this room, with its sloping ceiling, low-set window, and sturdy oak-framed bed. He was fifteen then and had been living rough for a year. Caught pilfering from a market stall – apples, of all things – he had been 'saved' from the full force of the law by these two relatives he barely knew. The magistrate had told him he was lucky, but Billy wasn't fooled. He knew that it was a punishment by any other name and the sentence hard labour. And nothing about that first night – not the warmth of the mug of malted milk in his hand, nor the fullness in his belly, nor the unaccustomed smoothness of sheets against his skin – had done anything to alleviate his sense of injury. He'd been deceived by a large meal and a soft bed once before when at the age of nine he'd been carried off by his Aunt May to a life of prayer and moral correction in Bridgwater.

Now, all these years later, he could see above the bed the same mysterious bulges in the rose-and-columbine-patterned wallpaper, and on the ceiling the same crusty rings erupting from the whitewash like lichen blooms on rock. There was no getting rid of the damp down here by the moor, and it was only fools who tried. Its fusty fragrance filled the air and misted the wooden surfaces and rotted the curtains. On the bed the starched linen had subsided limply onto the topography of the mattress. He guessed that Flor had made up the bed a long time ago, ready for his return. Well, it was no good, he wouldn't be staying. And the way Flor was now, she wouldn't know enough to care.

The unaccustomed silence kept him awake for some time. When he finally slept it was to be roused at least twice by the hooting of an owl, then, much later, by the banging shut of a door. He had the impression of sleeping little, yet when he woke it was to full light.

He lay back with a sense of indulgence. There'd been no staying in bed in the old days, no missing of the morning. The old man had been a stickler for getting to work sharp at six, winter and summer. But this morning Stan wasn't calling impatiently from the kitchen, 'Let's be seeing you!', he was clumping about in the bedroom opposite, to the muted strains of dance music. Billy shifted indolently on the pillow and watched the sunlight trickling in through the unwashed glass, casting hazy beams over the edge of the battered chest of drawers which had housed all his worldly possessions, reflecting dimly in the wall mirror from whose crazed and mottled glass his uneasy adolescent frown had glared back at him each morning. The only visible remnant of his four-year occupation was hanging on the back of the door, an ancient railwayman's jacket that Aunt Flor had found for him that first winter, bartered from the crossing keeper for two months' supply of eggs. She hadn't thought him worth the expense of a new one, not then.

Getting up at last, he went to the chest and pulled open an upper drawer. His adolescent paraphernalia was still there: fishing hooks, string, cigarette cards, penknife, pencils. And in a lower drawer his old working clothes, neatly folded and smelling of mothballs. He tried on a thick woollen shirt that had always been too big but now fitted quite well. The trousers, though, were tight at the waist, and he had to leave the top button undone and use a belt. Down in the porch he found his old gumboots at the back of a shelf, covered in dust. The rubber was dry and cracked, but there were no obvious holes.

By the time he stepped outside it was almost eight. The yard was a sight. The mound of withies he'd almost tripped over in the darkness was all canker and rot, while the frame that stretched the full length of the yard was stacked with bundle on bundle of withies, which, going by the coating of lichen on the weather side, had been put out to dry a long while back and not touched since.

In the woodshed, amidst another almighty jumble, Billy found a thick layer of coal dust, a scratching of coal nuggets, and some two dozen apple logs. The peg where the axe used to hang was bare. He hunted high and low, shifting sacks, kegs, barrels and a wheelless barrow before unearthing the axe on the floor beside a paraffin drum. Even then it took a good five minutes with the whetstone before the blade would split the wood the way he liked it, clean, in a single stroke.

He rifled the mound of cankered withies for kindling, but gleaned only mulch. The porch offered better pickings: a brittle apple basket, the base frayed and sagging, and a clutch of spraggled withies, ripe for burning.

He was crouched in front of the range, nursing a meagre flame, when he heard Stan's tread on the stairs.

'You're still here then,' the old man said.

They took a fresh gawp at one another.

The light, slanting upwards from the window, revealed fresh crags and fissures in the hillocky landscape of Uncle Stan's features. Born and raised in the last century, too old for the Great War let alone the one just ended, he'd always seemed ancient to Billy, though even now he was probably little more than seventy. Despite a back bowed and calcified by a lifetime's withy cutting and lungs that were clugged up from a steady sixty a day, the old man had always kept an almost impish energy. But now this too had faded; Billy saw it in the labour of his breathing and the droop of his eyes.

'Managed to stay in one piece then?' the old man said.

'More or less.'

'Well, you look well enough on it, at any rate.'

Billy tried to see himself as Uncle Stan must see him: taller by a good inch, broader in the chest, muscled by a steady diet of meat and potatoes. And more worldly. Yes, that would show too.

'I'll just get it warmed up in here, all right? And then I'll be off.'

The old man tipped his head towards the range. 'You'll not get it to draw properly,' he said with a pull of his lips. 'Chimney's buggered.'

'What's the trouble?'

'Jackdaws. Soot. Lord only knows.'

'I'll give it a jiggle then.'

'It'll take a lot more than a jiggle.'

'Haven't lost your sunny outlook then.' But the remark was lost on the old man, as Billy had known it would be. Returning with some willow sticks, he found Stan putting a match to a small Primus stove.

'Is that how you've been cooking then? With paraffin?'

'She can only take porridge or broth. It's good enough for that.'

'Paraffin's not going to warm anyone's bones, though, is it? Not in the cold. What's happened to the coal?'

'There ain't no coal.'

'Well, I can see that, can't I? What's the problem?'

'Officialdom, that's what. Little Hitlers, the lot of them.'

Unbolting the port in the flue, Billy thrust a stick up the chimney and, lashing a second stick to the base of the first, soon came up against the blockage. After a few jabs, a cascade of soot and lumps came tumbling down the flue, filling the range and billowing into his face.

Half an hour later he had the fire drawing, the kettle on the hotplate, and his face and hands cleaned up. By the time Stan came down from giving Aunt Flor her breakfast, he'd made a pot of tea and poured the first cup.

'Don't have tea at this time of the morning,' Stan cried fretfully.

'Well, you're getting some today.'

'But it's rationed. You don't understand, Billy, everything's rationed. We've had to cut down.'

'But you've plenty of tea. The caddy's full.'

'It's the sugar that's short.'

'Ah, and you always loved your sugar, didn't you, Old Man?' Billy said indulgently.

The watery eyes softened a little. 'I did, too.'

'Well, you've got two heaped spoons in there. Make the most of them.'

The old man sat down obediently. 'It's worse than in the war, I tell you – a lot worse. They keep telling us that things'll

ease up soon, but I can't see no end to it, not for a long while
yet.'

'What's the problem then, apart from the sugar?'

'It's the bloody rules and regulations, that's what. Can't
move without coupons and points and permission for this, that,
and the other. The Ministry of Food go and stick their noses in
everything. They went and prosecuted a farmer over Axbridge
way for slaughtering a pig the day *before* his permit allowed
for it. A whole day! I tell you, if you didn't laugh you'd bloody
cry.'

'Is that why you've no coal – trouble with the regulations?'

But the old man was too busy peering at the cigarettes Billy
was offering him. 'Player's,' he said dubiously, but took one
anyway. 'It was different in the war,' he said. 'Oh yes, we
expected to go without. And the rations stretched all right in
those days. We never went short. Your Aunt Flor made sure of
that. A witch with the cooking, she was.' He squinted at Billy
through the smoke. 'You ate all right in the army, I'll be
bound.'

'Can't complain.'

'Which lot did you join then?'

'Fifth Tanks.'

Stan raised an eyebrow.

'Chased the Jerries up through Belgium and Holland and
over the Rhine.'

'Did you now?'

Billy added, as if it mattered, 'I made it to driver-mechanic.'

'Always had a way with machinery, you did.'

It was their first and last conversation about Billy's war.

Billy said, 'You had a quiet time of it then, did you?'

'What, in the war? If you mean did Adolf himself come
marching through the village complete with brass band, well
then, yes, I suppose you could say it was quiet. But we had the
airfields at Churchstanton and Westonzoyland. Planes all night,
every night, buzz, buzz, like blooming hornets. And then we

had the German bombers trying to blow up the munitions factory at Puriton. Never did hit it, thank the Lord, otherwise the whole of Somerset would have known about it, that's for certain.' He gave a brief guffaw. 'One time we had this German bomber drop its load over King's Sedgemoor way. Boom! Boom! Stirred everyone up a fair treat, I can tell you. It was different then, oh yes . . . everyone in the same boat, everyone pulling together. It was a good time. When all's said and done, yes, a bloody great time.'

'Glad to hear it,' Billy murmured drily.

'Oh, don't go thinking it was *easy*,' the old man retorted. 'I'm not saying it was *easy*. No, it was bloody hard work. But we got by. Kept a couple of pigs. Chickens. And your aunt growing vegetables – cabbages and potatoes by the barrowload. And the apples – the merchants were buying our Tom Putts for eating, *eating* mind, not cider, because the city folk had nothing else in the way of fruit. Well, we couldn't believe it. Selling our apples for eating! Had to sort them, of course. Keep the bruised ones back. Bloody hard work. But the cider tasted the best ever. All that rot in it – never better!' The old man gave a deep bronchitic laugh.

'And the withies? You find a market for them too?'

'Oh yes. Nothing like it, couldn't get enough of them. But it's all different now.'

'What, no demand?'

'It's not the demand, it's the blooming labour.' Stan's voice rose on a note of grievance. 'Can't get it no more. They're all too busy feathering their own nests, and to hell with the next man. That's how it is now – every man for himself. I tell you, this war's gone and changed everything, and it ain't for the better.'

But then nothing would ever be for the better in Stan's eyes, thought Billy derisively. He wouldn't recognise progress if it came and stared him in the face.

Going outside again, Billy got a more accurate measure of how the war had been for Stan and Flor. The mess in the yard and the woodshed was only the start. In the willow shed he found stacks of unstripped withies amid a sea of stripple, while in the centre of the floor the magnificent diesel-powered brake that Stan had bought just before the war stood abandoned and encrusted with muck, the drum coated an inch deep. The mechanic in Billy eyed it longingly: less than a day, he reckoned, to get it cleaned up and running again. Moving on, he found a bunch of old hand-operated brakes in a corner of the shed, their prongs rusted and blunt, while along the far wall the gleam of stagnant water reflected up at him from the sorting pits.

Wandering into the vegetable garden, he found plants that were blowsy and bolted or gone to rot, while at the top of the orchard the withy boiler, a retired ship's boiler acquired from a nautical salvage yard, was little more than a barrel of rust. The chicken house contained eight evil-eyed bantams and no eggs, the pigsty was empty of all but muck, and when he delved around the back there was the scuttle and streak of rats.

Pricked by a strange unformed irritation, Billy started down the orchard through tall matted grass run to seed and stumbled over the carpet of rotting apples beneath. The few leaves still dangling from the trees were peppered with black spot. On the orchard boundary, the line of pear trees carried half-formed fruit, feeble and overcrowded on the boughs. Reaching the drove, heading down towards the moor, he saw ten or twelve dairy cows grazing on the meadow. They were big Friesians and he didn't need to read the ear-tags to know they didn't belong to Stan.

At the old rhyne, he found the water clogged with duckweed, frogbit, bur-reed, and sedge, but it was the sight of the withy bed that heightened his strange undirected anger. For as far as he could see, the withies were sprouting every which way from horny untrimmed stocks amid a tangle of weeds. He walked the length of the one-acre bed, counting the damage, and reckoned that one in ten stems, maybe one in eight, would fetch any sort of price, while the rest were good for nothing but hurdles and kindling. This tally might not have seemed so dismal if it hadn't been for the contrast with the neighbouring bed, which contained rank after rank of well-tended withies standing tall and lush and full-blown, not a stem that wasn't top rate.

Taking the drove-road that ran the length of the moor, Billy found an altered landscape. Where there had been a scattering of withy beds on the edges of the moor there was now acre after acre of withies, interspersed by the occasional field of grain, stretching in a wide band along the northern border of the moor. Just as striking, there wasn't a withy bed that didn't look top notch, not till he reached another of Stan's one-acre plots, where he found the crop choked with withy wind, nettle and vetch. With a sense of wasting his time, he trudged another two miles to the last of Stan's West Sedgemoor beds, a series of half- and one-acre plots under the banks of the River Parrett. If anything these beds were even more unkempt than the ones before, with most of the stocks looking half dead.

A van passed on the Langport road. Tracking it for a moment, Billy made out an unfamiliar structure perched high on the banks of the Parrett and realised with the jolt of the obvious how so much of the wetland edge had come to be under cultivation. The sturdy brick building with its industrial chimney could only be a sodding great pumping station. And they had always said that West Sedgemoor, the wettest, soggiest wetland of them all, wasn't worth the effort.

Starting back, Billy's obscure annoyance of the last hour swelled into a blister of irritation. While Stan's problems were none of his concern, the sight of so much neglect still managed to exasperate him, not least because he had put so much back-breaking toil into each and every one of those beds. To let them go to waste was just plain stupid. But then, that was Stan all over. He muttered aloud, 'Stupid old bugger!'

Striding fast along the drove, he spotted a group of figures on the open moor to the south. It was a gang clearing a rhyne and, standing over them, two armed soldiers. Getting a little closer, he made out German POWs. The prisoners were taking every opportunity to dawdle. They cast their ditch-crooks sluggishly, skimming the surface weeds, getting no drag over the lower reaches, leaving the iris and rush more or less undisturbed. They hauled the weeds up the bank in a half-hearted manner and frequently stopped to lean on their crooks until ordered to get started again, when they resumed work with a sullen air.

It had never occurred to Billy that he would see Germans again, and on the moor of all places. He couldn't help wondering if any of them came from Hamburg, because if so they had a hell of a shock waiting for them when they got back. But perhaps they knew that already; perhaps that was why they worked with such open contempt. If in the thick of the war someone had told Billy that he would live to see German soldiers undergoing this kind of punishment he would have felt a savage triumph, an exultant sense of justice, but watching them now he was aware only that they didn't belong here. Their presence was an intrusion. If the authorities had any sense they'd have sentenced them to the far worse punishment of going home.

He took a different route back, crossing the old rhyne by the meads, eventually joining the path that followed Stan's upper boundary. As he came within sight of the track to Crick Farm he heard the roar of an engine in the lane ahead and saw a bright blue tractor approaching from the direction of the village. He quickened his pace, hoping to cut down the farm track before the tractor reached the gate, but it was coming too fast and he realised with a sudden surge of fury that there was no chance of avoiding it, not unless he made a complete fool of himself by turning on his heel and walking back the way he'd come. Worse, he was to be denied any chance of going unrecognised: as the tractor grew closer he made out an older stockier version of Frank Carr.

'Hello there!' Frank shouted above the rattle of the engine as he pulled up in front of Billy. 'Heard you were back.'

With a glare, Billy walked briskly past and turned down the track. Behind him, the engine clattered to a halt and rapid foot-steps sounded in pursuit.

'Heard you were back,' Frank called again as he attempted to catch up.

Billy bristled with an antagonism that had lost none of its heat for stretching back ten years. 'Not for long.'

'You're not stopping then?'

'Not likely.'

'They said you were stopping.'

'Well, they were wrong, weren't they?'

Billy remembered with a cold and deadly heart the scene outside the smithy during his first summer at Crick Farm. He'd been running an errand for Aunt Flor and, coming round a corner, had spotted too late the line of young people sitting on the wall ahead. In snapshot he saw again the turned faces, the curious stares, he heard the hush as Frank's taunt rang out into the silence. The words came back to him with the merciless accuracy of humiliation: *Watch your pockets, everyone – it's Billy Lightfingers.* He remembered with equal clarity the way Frank had continued to bait and chivvy him throughout the rest of that summer, how in typical weasel fashion he had been too cowardly to take Billy on in front of other people but had waited for a dark night to spring out from the shadows and land Billy a crack on the cheek.

Frank was closing the gap. 'You got work elsewhere then?'

'Plenty.'

'Pity.'

'Why's that?' said Billy, quelling the urge to make up for lost time and clout him sharply round the head.

'Your uncle needing a hand.'

'I wouldn't know about that, would I?' With another cold beat of his heart, Billy veered sharply off to the right and, vaulting the fence, strode into the upper orchard. Behind him, he heard a puff and pant as Frank clambered over the fence, then the swish of grass as he began to follow. Frank was shorter than Billy by a good four inches, the untrammelled grass was high and littered with fallen apples, yet somehow he managed to catch up and keep pace, bobbing along at Billy's side.

'I've offered to buy the withies off his Curry Moor beds,' Frank gasped, 'but he won't have it. I've offered a fair price, as fair as any, but he won't see sense.'

'Well, he's the one to speak to, isn't he? Not me.'

'But if I've tried once, I've tried a hundred times, Billy. I warned him he'd never reach his price at auction – I told him time and time again – but he wouldn't listen.'

Billy didn't mean to slow down, still less to flick a quick glance Frank's way, but he did both.

'His were the only withies that didn't sell. Everyone else managed to sell theirs, no trouble at all. And now – well, if he's not careful, he won't get no one to cut them, not till it's too late.'

'I've told you – you're talking to the wrong person.'

'But I thought you were staying.'

Billy gave a savage laugh. 'Why the hell would I want to do that?'

Frank came to an uncertain halt.

Billy turned to take a proper look at him, and saw a burly man with fair wiry hair, soft plump skin mottled pink and white, white lashes and small brown eyes that were still and animal-like. Billy was irresistibly reminded of an overfed porker.

'Didn't get to the war then?' Billy asked.

'Reserved occupation.' If Frank felt the smallest stirring of shame or embarrassment about this, he didn't show it.

'What – withies needed for the war effort, were they?'

'Not at the outset they weren't. Arable and dairy was what they wanted to begin with,' Frank said stolidly. 'We went and worked on arable farms, arable or dairy. But then they went and announced that they wanted withies after all. For parachute baskets and those panniers for the land girls.'

'I knew that,' Billy said quickly, remembering too late that Aunt Flor had told him in one of her letters. 'So, withy men been getting rich, have they?'

'Making a living, that's all.'

You don't say, thought Billy, remembering the bright new tractor.

'So, this price you were offering Stan – good, was it?'

It seemed to him that the little brown eyes betrayed a wily glint before resuming their porcine stare.

'Look here, Billy, there's one thing we got to get straight right at the outset – I can't be taking on the West Sedgemoor beds. Just can't be done. They're too far gone. And it's not just me that thinks so – there ain't no one that's willing to touch them, not even for hurdles. They're not worth the time or trouble, see? They wouldn't bring in enough to pay for the work involved.'

Frank was waiting for a response, but Billy continued to gaze at him as he might gaze at a rather unwelcome object that had landed up on his doorstep.

Eventually Frank went on. 'Trouble is, Stan won't hear of selling off the one crop without the other. Won't let anyone cut the Curry Moor without swearing to take on the West Sedge-moor. But it can't be done, see, Billy? No way. Not without throwing good money down the drain. I keep telling him—'

'Perhaps that's where you're going wrong,' Billy interrupted. 'Telling him.'

'But I'm only trying to help,' Frank proclaimed in a tone of injury. 'I'm only trying to do a neighbour a good turn. It's no skin off my nose either way, you know.'

Billy suppressed a smile. Frank must think he was born yesterday. Had these people always been this simple? he wondered. Or was it only now that he had the eyes to see?

'So, tell me,' he asked in a bored voice, 'what's your price then?'

Frank puckered his lips and gave a heavy drawn-out sigh.

'Well, now . . . It's not as good as I'd like, Billy. Only wish I could offer more – nothing I'd like better – but it's a bit late in the year to be taking on extra work, see? I'd have to hire in another cutter, and there's a terrible shortage of good cutters. All of them's got plenty of work for the winter. Just plenty. I'd have to pay over the odds.'

'So it's a case of beggars can't be choosers, is it?'

Frank's chin drew back into the soft folds of his plump neck. 'Look here, Billy, there's no call for you to take that attitude. It's not as if I *needed* the extra work. Quite the opposite, in fact. And it's not as if there was a great rush to take on Stan's beds. Go and ask around if you don't believe me. You'll find out quick enough. No, you won't get an offer that's fairer than mine, not by a long chalk.'

Billy eyed the broad pink snout in a speculative way, wondering how it would look after a good sharp jab from a quick right. 'It was just a joke. All right? A *joke*.'

Frank's ruffled feathers settled a little. He said with an embarrassed laugh, 'A joke. I see! Yes, a joke . . .'

'So . . . this price of yours?'

Frank lifted his chin. 'For the four acres on the Curry?'

'The four.'

'And allowing for a good proportion having canker.'

'If you say so.'

'Well, let's see . . . Let's see . . .' Frank made a long-drawn-out show of pondering the matter afresh, folding his arms across his chest, chewing his lip thoughtfully.

Waiting restlessly, Billy caught a thrum of powerful wings and a clamour of ragged hoots, and looking towards the west saw a formation of Bewick's swans sweeping low over the apple trees. Following them down to the moor, he had a memory of winter days on the floods, crouched behind a make-shift hide, a gun on his knee, searching the sky for teal and wigeon.

'Well, now,' Frank announced at last, 'I may live to regret

this – I may be biting off more than I can chew – but if I really
stretch things . . . Yes, I might be able to go to a hundred and
fifty the acre. Six hundred the lot. Can't do fairer than that.'

Billy was careful to hold his expression. 'Six hundred?'

'My best price. Like I told you, there's a lot of canker and
nodules. A quarter, maybe more, won't be good for nothing
but hurdles.'

'A hundred and fifty the acre . . . And what would the top
withies be fetching then?'

'Oooh . . .' Frank exhaled noisily. 'Hard to be sure in this
market.'

'Three hundred? Four?'

'Oooh . . . I wouldn't like to say.'

'Five?'

Frank affected a look of shock. 'Never that much.'

But not far off, Billy thought. 'So Stan won't do better elsewhere?'

Frank shook his head firmly.

'All the same, I don't imagine it'll do him any harm to find
out, will it?'

Frank stared hard at him before giving a faint pig-like snort.
'You been away too long, Billy.'

'Oh, have I?'

'You've forgotten the way things are done around here. If a
man can't offer a fair price, then he won't offer no price at all.
Stan won't get no fairer price than mine, not in a month of
Sundays. Yes, you've forgotten the way things are done, Billy.'

'Well, thanks for the reminder,' Billy said with a laugh that
hit just the right note, halfway between scorn and amusement.

Walking away through the orchard, Billy hastily turned the
skirmish over in his mind and decided that, all things considered,
he had come out of it on top. The leap over the fence had been
a mistake, a stupid infantile gesture, luckily overshadowed by
Frank's laughable efforts to catch up. Remembering the puffing
pink face, the bobbing stride, and the laughable attempts to

pull the wool over his eyes, it seemed incredible to Billy that this ridiculous man could have been the fearsome enemy of his youth.

A car was parked by the latch-gate, black and shiny except for a spray of mud over the lower doors. A tin of Fisherman's Friends sat on the dashboard, a fine woollen scarf on the passenger seat.

There was no one in the kitchen, but Billy heard the murmur of voices overhead and the creak of floorboards, and guessed at the doctor.

Taking a sharp knife, he went across the yard to the withies stooked against the drying rack and cut open a bundle from the top layer. Another two bundles and there was no doubt: the withies had been exposed too long to the wet and the wind. Having been soaked and dried out repeatedly, they were shrivelled and brittle, good for nothing but burning. The bundles beneath weren't much better. Only the bundles at the very bottom contained a few stems with a bit of sap and bend in them, though as likely as not they would snap in the basket-maker's hands.

He wasn't aware of anyone approaching until a voice bid him good morning.

'I'm Dr Bennett,' the man added.

Billy acknowledged him with a short nod before turning back to the withies.

'Mr Thorne told me you were here.'

'Oh yes?'

'I'm sorry, but he didn't give me your name.'

'Greer. Billy Greer.'

'How do you do, Mr Greer?'

Billy's second nod was even briefer, so it couldn't be mistaken for a sign of deference.

'You're a nephew of his, I believe?'

'Distant. Of hers.'

'I see.' Dr Bennett was a thin man, with a long bony face,

greying hair with a neat side parting, grave eyes and a soft voice. 'May I ask if you're staying long?' His manner was oddly modest for a doctor.

'Just today.'

'Ah. And have you come far?'

Not trusting the question, Billy didn't answer.

'I was merely wondering if you were likely to be dropping by on a regular basis.'

'No chance. My work's miles away.'

'I see . . .' The doctor lowered his gaze with a frown. Standing there in his long tweed coat, clutching a trilby to his stomach with one hand, gripping a battered medical bag in the other, he reminded Billy of someone else, though he couldn't think who.

'It's just that Mr Thorne seems to be struggling a bit with the farm,' the doctor said. 'Understandable, of course, in the circumstances.' When Billy again offered no comment, he added, 'I wondered if you knew of anyone who might be able to give him a hand.'

Billy shrugged. 'Don't ask me. I've been away in the war.'

'Yes, of course,' the doctor acknowledged rapidly. 'I just thought you might know of a relative . . .'

'Well, I don't.'

The doctor absorbed this with a slow nod. 'Mrs Bentham thought of asking the neighbours for help. But your uncle, well . . .' Bennett swung his hat away from his chest in a gesture that suggested tactical difficulties. 'He didn't seem too keen.'

'No, he wouldn't be.' Billy had no idea who Mrs Bentham might be, but she couldn't know Stan too well if she thought he'd be prepared to accept favours that he couldn't return. 'He could always hire someone,' Billy suggested drily.

'That's the problem – there's a shortage. Quite a few farms are having trouble finding workers. Not enough men home from the war.'

'Just goes to show how much I know.'

'There is another possibility,' the doctor said tentatively. 'This new government scheme which allows farmers to hire Poles from the Resettlement Corps. I was telling your uncle. It could be just the answer.'

'Oh yes? And what would he want Polacks for?'

The doctor gazed at Billy uncertainly. 'Well, they're extremely hard workers.'

'Like the Germans, you mean?' Billy tipped his head towards the moor. 'I've just seen how hard the Germans work.'

'But the Germans are prisoners of war.'

Turning rapidly away, Billy tugged at a binding on some rotting withies.

'Everyone who's worked with the Poles has been extremely happy with them,' the doctor insisted mildly.

'But they'll be wanting to skedaddle back to Poland, won't they, the second they get the chance.'

'In fact . . . most of them are intending to stay here.'

'Are they now?'

'That's the point of the Corps – to help them resettle.'

Billy cut another binding with a quick upward jerk of his knife.

'The thing is, if your uncle did decide to take some, I'd be very glad to start the ball rolling. There's one soldier who could come straight away. I can vouch for him – a good man. And if your uncle wanted a second, there's an airman who used to be stationed at Churchstanton. Once the camp gets up to strength there'll be plenty more to choose from, of course.'

'Camp?'

'At Middlezoy. It opened a month ago.'

'Oh, *that* camp,' Billy said dismissively. 'But soldiers – they'd be bugger all use as withy men. It's skilled work.'

'I would imagine they'd need supervision, certainly.'

'A bloody sight more than supervision. Full-time nannying, more like.'

'But it would be better than nothing.'

'Not if they have to be paid, it won't.'

'They do have to be paid a basic agricultural wage, I believe.'

'More than some people, then.'

'I understood it was to be very low . . .'

'That's what I'm saying,' Billy insisted stubbornly. 'More than some get.'

The doctor gave way with a small baffled nod. 'Maybe so,' he murmured.

'But look, it's not up to me, is it?' Billy offered abruptly. 'It's for my uncle to decide.'

'Yes, of course.'

'What does he say?'

'He's thinking about it.'

'I bet he is.'

The doctor put his hat on, and made to move away. 'Oh, I take it the coal's finally arrived?'

'Not that I'm aware.'

'The range was lit. I thought . . .'

'There's no coal.'

'Oh dear. I know Mrs Bentham was looking into it. Has she run into a snag?'

'I wouldn't know.'

'Ah . . .' He gave a doctor's smile, empty, distracted. 'Well, I'll see if I can find out later. Good day, Mr Greer.' He bowed politely and began to walk away.

Something made Billy call after him. 'How's my aunt doing?'

The doctor stopped and turned. 'Oh, as well as can be expected.'

'She's not going to get better?'

The doctor took a few steps back towards Billy. 'I wish I could offer hope of improvement.'

'There's no treatment?'

'I'm afraid not.'

'Why do you come then?'

A sharp pause before the doctor said, 'I'm sorry, I don't quite . . .'

'What's the point in you coming?'

The other man looked taken aback.

'Nothing personal, Doctor,' said Billy, for whom few encounters with authority were anything but personal, 'but I'm thinking of the fees.'

The doctor dropped his eyes for a moment. When he looked up again, his expression was strained. 'It's not just your aunt I call on, Mr Greer. It's your uncle too. And there's no great urgency for my fees, I assure you.'

Billy nodded. 'Glad to hear it.'

The doctor bowed again, solemnly. Watching the tall figure walk away, Billy felt the frustration of someone who realises he has revealed himself in a bad light. He didn't give a damn for what the doctor thought of him – officers, doctors, they were all the same – but he cared for the fact that he had let himself down. He had set himself a target, to be a man apart, detached, calm, slow to anger, a figure of respect, and he had fallen below the standard he had set himself. He had resorted to sarcasm and point-scoring; he had demeaned himself in front of a stranger. It was finding himself back in this place that had dragged him down; the sense of being forced back in time, of being trapped. Everything would be fine once he got away. Nevertheless, he couldn't shake off a niggling sense of self-disgust, which was linked in some obscure way to the man the doctor reminded him of. It had finally come to him as the doctor put on his hat that he was not unlike the priest who'd asked Billy and his mates to help dig the people out of the ruined house in Belgium. The priest had possessed the same air of solemnity, the same bowed shoulders and grave face, the same quiet manner. He had also had an impressive capacity for drink. After the burials the two of them had polished off the best part of a bottle of cognac, but while most men of Billy's acquaintance quickly got roaring drunk, the priest had maintained a steady if melancholy dignity. Speaking broken English that gathered momentum with each glass, he told Billy about the family they had just buried – the girl with the gleaming eyes had been a nurse in the local asylum – and the catalogue of hardships and disasters the village had suffered during the occupation, and the spiritual dilemmas facing a priest in war. He spoke so frankly and listened so intently to Billy's opinions that for a while Billy thought he must have mistaken him for an officer, but when Billy dropped his rank casually into the conversation it seemed there was no mistake. They went on to discuss faith, evil, and the limits of personal responsibility. Afterwards, in the blur of a hangover and a rapid advance under gunfire, Billy couldn't remember every detail of the conversation, only that he'd managed to say quite a few good things, and say them well. This burst of eloquence had taken him by surprise. Maybe his brain, so doggedly championed by his English teacher Mr Margolis, wasn't so dead after all.

The ration books were in the kitchen, propped behind the Golden Jubilee tea caddy on the mantelshelf. Extracting them, he knocked the caddy off-centre and took a moment to realign it in the correct position. He found no coupons for coal, however, just for petrol and food, only one or two unused. In London it was commonly believed that country people were living in clover, that, unconcerned for city dwellers, the farmers were bypassing the rationing system and keeping all the best produce for themselves. If so, there was precious little evidence of it in the larder. He counted two eggs, a scrag end of lamb, some bacon and cheese, and a few onions and potatoes, while on a side shelf were a couple of tins of Spam, some dried milk, and a small bag of flour.

There was no sign of Stan. Putting his head outside, Billy finally spotted him by the chicken shed, bent over the open lid of the nesting boxes. It was as good an opportunity as any to see Flor, though as Billy climbed the stairs and knocked on the door his stomach squirmed with dread.

The room smelt of lavender and carbolic, the radio was belting out 'Begin the Beguine', and the light from the window shone straight on her head, propped high against the pillows. Her bright eyes fixed on him and she tried to smile in a strange lopsided pull of one cheek, a creasing up of one eye. The effect was of an exaggerated wink.

He said, 'Bit of a laugh, eh? Me turning up like a bad penny.' He turned off the music and, pulling up a chair, sat at the side of the bed. She reached out and grasped his hand. Her skin was dry and papery and surprisingly hot.

'But I'm not staying long,' he said. 'I'm only here for the day.'

Because he couldn't think of what else to talk about he told her about his war, or rather the high points – the landing in France, the ride through Belgium and Holland, the civilians who'd showered them with hoarded treats, the contrast when they reached Germany, the sight of Hamburg virtually flattened – and all the time he was aware of her eyes fastened intently on his face and the pressure of the hot papery hand in his. Once or twice he tried to slide his hand away, but her fingers tightened instantly and drew him back.

'Before I forget,' he said at last, 'I need my mum's things. The stuff in the shoebox.'

Letting go of his hand at last, Flor reached across to the side table for a pad and pencil. She wrote left-handed, very slowly, with the occasional letter in block capitals. Following her directions, Billy found the shoebox in the back of the wardrobe drawer.

'Thanks,' he said, holding it up to her. Then, because she was attempting another smile, he added hastily, 'Anything you want? Anything I can get you?'

She wrote laboriously on the pad: *Is house clean?*

He laughed aloud. 'Don't you worry – I'll make sure it's up to scratch.'

She began to write again, a longer message, and Billy sat down again so as not to look impatient. When she finally passed him the message, there was nothing in it to make him laugh. Instead, he got to his feet and said sharply, 'Don't be stupid.' Then, moderating his voice, 'Do you want your music back on?'

Without waiting for an answer he turned the radio up and with a brisk goodbye hurried from the room. What in hell did she want to go and tell him that for? *Money behind wardrobe in satchel. I want you to have some.* She might as well have dangled a wad of money in front of his nose and snatched it away again. He could just imagine what would happen if he was stupid enough to accept it. He'd get accused of taking advantage of Flor when she was soft in the head, or of cheating the son and daughter out of their inheritance, most likely both.

Money was all right while you didn't have to think about it, while you had no choice but to grub around for every shilling like the rest of the common herd. The trouble came with easy money. Easy money got you thinking. Already he was wondering how much was sitting behind the wardrobe, whether it was enough to buy a suit, a car, the deposit on a garage premises . . . Easy money caused ructions with your mates. In Germany Ernie had found some jewellery in the basement of a ruined house. The rule was finders keepers, and trust no one but your mates. But someone must have talked, because during a three-day halt the booty vanished from Ernie's kit. Easy money created suspicion, and suspicion was the last thing he needed just at the moment.

In his bedroom he opened the shoebox and went through the contents with an eye to their resale value. It didn't look good. The green brooch that had sparkled so brilliantly in his memories of his mother was dull and chipped, no more than cheap glass, while the fancy watch she'd kept for best had a tarnished metal strap and water marks on the face. There were two gold rings, though, and a small oval photo frame that had every appearance of silver. He packed the valuables in his knapsack and left the tat in the shoebox along with the bundles of photographs and souvenirs. He glanced briefly at the photograph he'd removed from the oval frame: a portrait of his mother, who'd died when he was nine. The picture wasn't as flattering as he remembered; in fact it made her look rather plain and severe. And that was before she'd married his father, when she took to glaring at any camera that dared to point her way.

Now that his business was done he ran downstairs with a sense of relief, even of generosity. He might find time to split some logs and sort out the woodshed before getting away on the afternoon train.

Striding into the kitchen, he came to an abrupt halt at the sight of the woman standing by the table. The light from the window had the effect of bleaching the colour from her face and for an instant it seemed to Billy that she was both flesh and illusion. She was motionless and her skin was smooth as stone. Only her eyes were indisputably alive, and they stared at him unwaveringly.

'I heard you were back,' Annie Drinkwater said.

Billy forced his expression into something approaching impassivity. 'Not for long,' he said.

'I heard that too.'

Billy felt an unnerving sense of dislocation. She seemed just the same yet quite different, her features unchanged yet drawn with an almost photographic intensity, like a film star's in a poster, all eyes and lips and hair, splashed dramatically across the landscape of white skin.

Aware that he was staring openly, he put on a long lazy grin, only to find that she had turned away to unload a basket of vegetables.

'I was wondering how they managed for veg,' he said, looking past the leeks and cabbages to her ring finger and seeing the gold band there.

'Oh, people have plenty to spare. You know how it is.'

'And you fetch it down for them?'

'It's not far.' She shot him a quick smile that managed to be friendly and impersonal at the same time, and again he was struck by the clarity of her features. She was wearing lipstick which accentuated the pallor of her skin and the darkness of her hair, and her eyebrows were fine-drawn and arched. The overall effect was one of sophistication; though perhaps it was just the fashion; perhaps he was just out of touch.

'Good of you to do it, though.'

Shrugging this off lightly, she picked up a bundle of leeks and took them to the sink.

'Hang on,' he said. 'You wouldn't be Mrs Bentham, by any chance?'

'That's right.'

'I'd no idea it was you.'

She ran the tap at full blast. 'Well, you've been away, haven't you?'

'You can say that again.'

He waited expectantly for the question about his war, but it never came.

'Been firing a few rounds at the Jerries,' he said, and winced inwardly, it sounded so crass.

Shutting off the tap, barely turning her head, she gave a short nod, polite but distant. This gesture, like everything else about her, made him feel uncomfortably off-balance. He took a slow breath and relaxed his voice. 'The doctor was talking about you.'

'Oh yes?'

'Well, not so much *about* you. More, what you were doing for Stan and Flor. He said you were sorting things out for them. Like the coal.'

Drying her hands on a towel, she turned to look at him, her head tilted slightly to one side. The appraisal was thoughtful, unhurried, unselfconscious, as if she were making up her mind to ask him something. Her self-possession astonished him. There was no flicker of memory in her face, no acknowledgement of the strong attraction that had brought them together, no shadow of resentment at the way things had ended; in fact no sign that anything had passed between them. Well, he thought combatively, we'll soon see about that. He gave her a foxy lopsided grin and began to shake his head, as if to tick her off for this little charade, only to see her gaze drop distractedly to the floor. For a second or two he might not have been there at all.

'The coal,' he repeated sharply.

'The coal? Oh yes. It was the agricultural permit – Stan forgot to apply for it. And he flatly refused to pay domestic prices. So for a while there was a bit of a stalemate.' Her tone was bright, informative. 'But the permit finally came through yesterday. The order's gone in. The delivery should come tomorrow.'

'Well,' he said, 'thanks for all the trouble.'

Her eyes glittered suddenly. 'The only thanks I need are from Stan and Flor.'

So, it's still there, he thought triumphantly. The attraction or the anger, or both. He grinned. 'Thanks on their behalf, then.'

She accepted this with a minute nod before reverting to a friendly but neutral tone. 'So this is just a quick visit, is it?'

'Afraid so. Got a job waiting in London. Buying and selling cars. Repair work. That sort of thing.'

'Are there any cars? With all the petrol rationing, I mean.'

'Oh, plenty. The garage where I'll be working, it deals in Jags. And people with Jags – well, they don't go and let rationing cramp their style.'

'It's all different in London, then.'

'You can say that again.'

'Is the bomb damage very bad?' She might have been making conversation at a vicar's tea party.

'Bad enough. Though not half as bad as in Germany. We were first into Hamburg and the bloomin' place was flat as a pancake.' Once again, Annie didn't pick up on this. Her lack of interest began to irritate him. 'But in London,' he went on smoothly, 'you don't really notice all the holes. Too busy making the most of what's left, if you know what I mean. Too busy having a good time.'

The mention of good times provoked nothing but a faint

smile and a drift of her gaze towards the floor. 'Well,' she said, 'if any country deserves a good time it's this one, isn't it?'

Feeling he was getting a grip on the conversation at last, he lent nonchalantly against the table and crossed his arms. 'So how about you?'

'Me?' she said lightly.

'You living nearby?'

'At Spring Cottage.'

A vision of the back garden, of waiting for her in the darkness, flickered across his mind. 'Oh yes? With your mum?'

'No. She died – oh, four years ago now.'

'I didn't know. Sorry.'

'Flor didn't write and tell you?'

He made a show of searching his memory. 'No, I would have remembered. But then a whole bunch of Flor's letters never reached me when I was in the thick of it.' Now, her lack of interest in his soldiering could only be deliberate. He asked, 'So how long you been back?'

She paused to work it out. From this angle her hair seemed richer and darker than he remembered, though it might have been the way she wore it, smooth and silky, with a side parting and soft waves over the shoulder. Her skirt and jumper were simple but well fitting. Her poise terrified him.

'Just over sixteen months,' she said.

'And before that?'

'Plymouth. I had a job there till the end of the war.'

No mention of the husband, he noticed. No 'we' plural living at Spring Cottage. He began to wonder if she was like some of the women he'd met in London who in the cold light of peace had got to think better of their wartime marriages. Then she added, 'I lost my husband in the war. It seemed best to come back.'

He said immediately, 'Sorry to hear that,' and he was; though the part of him that was still attracted to her felt the unmistakable itch of sexual opportunity. 'On active service, was it?'

She moved towards him and for a moment he wasn't at all sure what she was going to do, tell him to mind his own business or go to hell, or both. As it was, she gave a small nod before scooping up the basket from the table and taking it through into the larder. As she swept past him he caught a waft of perfume that took him straight back to Belgium and a couple of girls he and Ernie had met in a bar. The memory, like the smell, excited him.

'It was a shock to see Flor,' he called through to her. 'Wish someone had told me.'

'Would it have made any difference?'

'To what?'

She came out of the larder and closed the door. 'To how long you were going to stay.'

He stared at her, then shrugged because he had no answer.

'They could do with some help, you know.'

'Well, that's pretty obvious, isn't it?' he said, bristling suddenly. 'The place is a right bloody mess.'

'You couldn't give them a couple of weeks?' she said. 'Just to get them started.'

'What, and lose this job? They're doing me a favour as it is, holding it for me till I get back. There's a dozen blokes who'd grab it off me as soon as look at me.'

'I hadn't realised.'

Something in her gaze drove him to add, 'Two weeks isn't going to make a blind bit of difference anyway. It'll take a lot more than that.'

'I see.'

'Besides, there's all these Polish refugees he can have. The doctor was telling me he only has to ask.'

'He's not too keen on the idea.'

'No, he wouldn't be, would he? That's Stan all over. Nothing's ever going to be right.'

'He's frightened, I think.'

Billy laughed. 'Him? Frightened?'

'Of strangers.'

'Of people who aren't prepared to put up with his nonsense, more like.'

Annie gave him a tiny frown of rebuke, and for the second time that day Billy had the feeling he had revealed himself in a bad light.

She took her basket and made for the door. 'Best be on my way.' She paused, the silky head swung round. 'I forgot – the shop has dropped off a bag of coal, just to keep things going. It's up by the gate.'

'I'll fetch it now.' He sprang forward and they reached for the door handle at the same time. She withdrew her hand before it touched his. As he held the door for her, he thought he saw her mouth tighten.

She walked quickly away up the yard and he had to stride out to catch up with her.

He said, 'For what it's worth I'll have a go at Stan about the Polacks.'

'Good idea. He's more likely to listen to you.'

Billy scoffed, 'He never did before.'

'Oh, you'd be surprised.'

'I would. All he ever did was yell at me.'

'He just got into the habit.'

'Some habit.'

She had a bicycle by the gate. As she wheeled it out, he said, 'I'd try to stay longer, you know. If it wasn't for this job.'

'Of course,' she said with a bright unreadable smile.

He watched her cycle away up the track. As she turned into the lane, he thought he heard her call out to someone, but she was only singing. The tune wasn't one he recognised.

Chapter Two

As BENNETT turned in through the gates of the convalescent home he met a large military ambulance and had to pull over sharply to let it past. Taking the winding drive between wide lawns and tall specimen trees at a more cautious pace, he spotted an elderly groundsman raking leaves into wind-blown piles, a bonfire venting wisps of smoke, two nurses, but no inmates. Only as he approached the house did he see some pale faces staring gloomily out of the glass-fronted veranda that flanked the west wing.

The house was huge and hideous, the grandiose Gothic boast of an Edwardian sugar baron. Abandoned in the twenties, it had been requisitioned at the time of Dunkirk and adapted in haste, with thin partition walls and copious use of cream paint. Now, more than a year after the end of the war, the paint was the colour of parchment and there was talk of winding the place down, though so far there had been no obvious slow-down in the flow of new patients.

The half-panelled hall was dark and lofty, with high stained-glass windows on heraldic themes which threw a sinister purple and orange light over the notice boards and letter racks. The double doors to the visitors' room stood open, revealing knots of patients and visitors talking in church-like whispers. Bennett didn't bother to check the room; the person he had come to see never had visitors.

Reaching the east wing, he diligently announced himself to the nursing sister, who looked up from her paperwork and gave him a cheery wave. 'What brings you in today, Doctor?'

'Just a quick call,' he said.

The day room was crowded. It had the atmosphere of a railway waiting room on a forgotten branch line. Some men were talking desultorily or reading newspapers; others stared despondently out of the window with the air of people who know that their wait is far from over. As Bennett entered, several pairs of eyes swung his way, only to slide away again. Their awe of doctors was long gone. They knew by heart all the medical pronouncements that dampened their hopes of an early ticket home. And when at long last there was talk of recovery and release dates, they laughed it off, for though they longed for freedom, they feared it too: the shortage of jobs, the changes at home, the girlfriends who, during this endless drawn-out convalescence, must surely have been lured away by healthier men with regular pay packets. While they didn't blame the medical staff for the frustrations of convalescence, they didn't like unnecessary reminders either, and doctors, even part-timers like Bennett, entered the day room on sufferance.

Bennett made for a familiar face, a young gunner with a shrapnel-peppered lung who attended his weekly chest clinic, and asked him if he knew where Malinowski might be.

'The Poles don't hang out here, Doc,' he said. 'You'll find 'em in the reading room.'

Looking around, Bennett realised it was true; there were no Poles in sight.

'Get too fired up,' the gunner remarked affably. 'Drives us barmy. Always jabbering on in that lingo of theirs.'

'Sorry to have bothered you,' Bennett said. 'Will I see you at clinic on Wednesday?'

'Don't have any better invitations, Doc, not at the moment.'

As Bennett stepped into the corridor, he saw the upright figure of Major Phipps, the military liaison officer, emerging from a door ahead. Bennett hesitated for an instant, assessing his chances of escape. The reading room was on the far side of the major, while the one intervening door belonged to a broom cupboard. It was retreat or endure, and as the major glanced up and saw him, retreat was no longer an option.

'Ah, Dr Bennett. Afternoon. What bloody weather, eh?' The major was thin and haggard and bitter because despite thirty years as a regular soldier he'd been passed over for active service. 'Autumn already, and we never had any damned summer.'

'It's stopped raining, anyway.'

'I almost prefer the rain. At least you know where you are.' The major squinted at him. 'Not your usual day, is it, Doctor?'

'No. I came to see one of the Poles.'

'The Poles!' the major declared with a jut of his neat little toothbrush moustache. 'Lucky to find any still here. Matron was all for sending them packing this morning. A bunch of them sneaked off after hours last night and kicked up the devil of a row trying to get back in. Blotto, of course.'

Bennett raised his eyebrows non-committally.

'Matron's not a pretty sight when she's angry, I can tell you,' Phipps remarked with a humourless chuckle. 'We all took cover.'

'I'll bet.'

'But then the Poles aren't making life easy for *any* of us at present.'

Preparing himself for one of the major's litanies of complaint, begrudging the lost time, Bennett responded weakly, 'Oh?'

'The thing is, they're absolutely incapable of making a decision. One of their officers came and explained this Resettlement Corps business to them weeks ago. Told 'em it was that or repatriation. But will any of them sign up? No – they just fiddle-faddle about, blowing hot and cold. And at least five of them are flatly refusing to consider either option. Say they'd rather die, or some such nonsense. Well, it won't do, Bennett. It simply won't do.'

'It's a hard decision for them.'

'That's the thing – it's a decision. They've got to come down on one side or the other. Can't sit on the fence.'

'But they must be allowed time to think it over, surely.'

'They've already had plenty of time. Can't have more. The War Office is quite firm on that. Either they stay and prepare for civilian life, or they go home. Can't carry on as they are. The Polish army has absolutely no official standing, you know. We don't recognise it any more. No one recognises it. Strictly speaking, it doesn't even exist.'

'It existed all right when we needed it.'

'Good God, I'm not saying the Poles haven't done their bit!' the major fired back, looking offended. 'No – brave men, the lot of them. But the war's over now, and it's high time they accepted it. No good them hanging about hoping to get back into the fray, so they can go and settle a few old scores. Can't have a mutinous army.'

'Mutinous?' Bennett questioned mildly.

'Don't know what else you'd call it,' the major retorted in a voice that seemed to ring down the corridors and into the stairwells. 'Their government has told them to stand down and go home, and they're refusing. Can't get much more mutinous than that. Nothing unreasonable about a government wanting its army back, you know – that's what governments do all the time. No' – he glowered at a couple of patients who'd wandered out of the day room into the corridor – 'the best thing the Poles could do is to pack up and go home. Pronto.'

'I'm sure they'd like nothing better, if they felt it was safe to do so.'

'Safe?' The major gave a dismissive sniff. 'I wouldn't believe everything the Poles tell you, Doctor. A great fondness for melodrama, our friends. Can't resist over-egging the pudding. All this talk of getting stick from their own people, of getting *shot* for their trouble . . .' He gave a dismissive snort. 'Stuff and nonsense.'

'Getting stick from those in power, I think they mean. From the new regime.'

'But no regime's going to go and *shoot* its own soldiers, is it?' the major declared. 'Not a whole damned army. No, no, the Poles are spinning you a line, I'm afraid, Doctor. They're devils for trying to tug the old heart strings.'

'I don't think anyone's suggesting the entire army would be shot.'

'And what reason would they have anyway?' the major bashed on. 'Them, Poland, us . . . we all fought on the same side, for heaven's sake.'

'In the war.'

'Of course in the war.'

'I meant only that things have changed since then, that the new regime is an unknown quantity, that the Russians seem to be pulling all the strings.'

Mention of politics seemed to irritate the major. He said crossly, 'Well, if the Poles don't like the way their country's being run, they should go back and sort it out for themselves, shouldn't they? Not our concern. Not our responsibility.'

With the sense of wasting his breath, Bennett argued in a tone of reason, 'But we have a responsibility to make sure we're not sending them back into danger, surely?'

'You talk as though an army has the right to decide things for itself, Doctor. An army must always be the servant, not the master. Otherwise where would it ever end? Anarchy. Chaos. Civil war.' The major gave a satisfied nod, as if he'd scored a bulletproof point.

'Yes, of course . . .' Bennett conceded, because it was easier to do so.

The major ran a finger inside his collar and craned his neck fretfully. 'If it was up to me, I'd have the lot of them packed and on their way by next week.'

It occurred to Bennett that there must be dozens of Phippses in the British army, men past retirement age who, lacking imagination or talent, had been cast into jobs to which they were totally unsuited. Untroubled by doubt, they discharged their duties with a bleak efficiency.

'The one thing they can't do,' the major added brusquely, his moustache shooting forward in agitation, 'is go on as they are. Can't have an army without official standing. Makes a nonsense of the whole set-up.' He made to move away. 'No avoiding a decision, Doctor. Go or stay. No sitting on the fence.' The small defeated eyes refocused on Bennett. 'How's the golf? Getting a couple of rounds in this weekend?'

'I'm not sure I'll have the time,' said Bennett, who never played.

'Well, I hope you don't get caught by this damned weather. What a climate, eh? Never bloody stops.'

With a nod and a last jut of his moustache, the major marched off down the corridor, his heels beating impotently on the lino.

Bennett opened the door of the reading room to a low cloud of cigarette smoke and the babble of Polish voices. He found Wladyslaw Malinowski in a corner hunched over a table, a pen poised motionless in his hand.

'Hello, Wladyslaw. Not disturbing you, I hope?'

'No . . . Please, Doctor.' Wladyslaw sprang to his feet and shook Bennett's hand as if they hadn't met for some time, though it had been less than two days.

'You feel better now, Doctor?'

Bennett smiled. 'I'm meant to ask after you, Wladyslaw. Not the other way round.'

'But you OK?'

'Yes. It was just a spot of bronchitis.'

'Plenty onion, raw – this is good for chest.'

'If you say so.'

'And for the voice too.'

'Oh, it's always a bit croaky,' Bennett explained lightly.

Wladyslaw stood erect, almost to attention, until Bennett had sat down, when the Pole dropped back into his chair. He touched the sheaf of papers he had been working on. 'My sister – I write much to her.'

'It's absolutely wonderful that you've found her again. You must be overjoyed. Where's she living?'

'Lodz. This is in south-western Poland. She is married now. This is why I don't find her before.'

'You must have a great deal to catch up on.'

'Sorry – catch up?'

'A lot of news you want to exchange.'

'Ah yes,' Wladyslaw said with a sigh. 'But I think perhaps I write too much.'

When language difficulties arose, Bennett often found it best to wait.

'We have brother Aleks,' Wladyslaw went on. 'He is murdered with officers at Katyn – ten thousand, you know. But I think it is not good to say this.'

'I'm so very sorry,' Bennett murmured, thinking of the brother.

'Sometimes letters that say too much do not arrive with families in Poland – we know this. And sometimes letters from families don't arrive here with us.' Shaking his head, Wladyslaw leafed through the last few pages of his letter. 'Yes . . . I think I write too many things. I think I make danger for Helenka.'

While Bennett liked and admired the Poles – it was almost impossible not to – and would always defend them against the Phippses of this world, there were moments when he couldn't decide how far their ardent and excitable natures coloured their view of events, particularly those affecting their homeland, for which they had a quite extraordinary passion. It wasn't a question of deliberate exaggeration, as Phipps liked to insist, but of being carried away by strong emotion and intense moral indignation.

'When do you expect to get a reply?'

'I think not before two, maybe three weeks.'

'Well, when you do, I'm sure your sister will let you know if you're speaking too openly.'

'You are right. Of course!'

Wladyslaw gave a sudden smile, open and beguiling. He was slim and energetic, with clear grey eyes, high-boned cheeks and fine features. His moods were like a barometer that switches abruptly from stormy to sunny without transition. He could laugh gaily, sink into gloom, argue forcefully, and pull one's leg, all, it seemed, within a matter of seconds. Beneath these weather shifts, however, a steady intelligence flowed. He looked on the world with an inquisitive gaze that missed little and tolerated much. The only thing he could not stomach was what he described as organised evil. On this score Wladyslaw found little to choose between the Germans and the Russians, a view he was prepared to debate at length with anyone who cared to take him on. He had been at university at the outbreak of war, studying literature, although he had an almost equal passion for philosophy and history. Only the finer points of the English language seemed to confound and frustrate his agile mind.

Watching him fold the letter and slide it into the pocket of his tunic, it seemed to Bennett that, despite the quick smile, he wasn't looking too fit today, that the pale skin was unnaturally tight over the high cheekbones, and that beneath the clear grey eyes the shadows were more marked than usual.

'How are you feeling?' he asked. 'How's the chest? How's the leg?'

'All is good! I feel – how is it? Right as rain?'

Bennett smiled. 'That's it.'

'I learn this from beautiful lady in pub. I learn "right as rain", "tickety-boo" and . . .' Wladyslaw searched his memory. ' "In pink"?'

'In *the* pink.'

Wladyslaw grimaced gently. For him, as for most Poles, the devil was in the definite and indefinite articles. He repeated obediently, 'In *the* pink.'

'I suppose pubs are as good a place as any to learn English.'

'But cider is not good, I tell you. Not good for stomach, not good for head.'

'Ah yes. I heard there was some trouble with Matron.'

Wladyslaw glanced towards the far side of the room where four young Poles were talking volubly in their own language. 'OK, some of our boys, they come back late. They make noise. Just young, you know. Long time away from home. I go to Matron, I say sorry. I ask please' – he pressed his palms together in an attitude of prayer – 'that we are permitted to stay here because in our heart we are all good boys.' He laughed long and easily, before adding in a more reflective tone, 'But perhaps not good for us when boys do this too much. English – they think Poles always make noise, always drink too much.'

Bennett completed the litany to himself: And always charm the women off their feet.

'They get bad idea about us. They think we are good for nothing.'

'They could never think that, Wladyslaw. No, no.' Bennett heard himself give a forced laugh. 'The British are pretty good at letting off steam themselves, you know.'

'Letting off steam?'

Bennett mimed a rush of air from the ears.

Wladyslaw absorbed this with a grin before looking away. When he spoke again, his tone was subdued. 'We left pub quick last night.'

'Trouble?'

'Some English boys, they want to fight us.'

'Something to do with the beautiful lady perhaps?'

Wladyslaw gave a small expressive shrug. 'Maybe.'

They both knew the truth probably lay elsewhere. Following the lead of the trade unions, some of the more hysterical British newspapers had been whipping up fears over the unexpected influx of Poles.

'But you managed to avoid trouble, did you?'

Wladyslaw gave a silent laugh. 'Good soldier – he knows when to run, when to fight.'

'As a nation I'm afraid we have a great talent for xenophobia.' Misinterpreting Wladyslaw's silence, Bennett began to explain, 'Xenophobia is the—'

'I understand this word OK,' Wladyslaw said, his face set at changeable. 'But British government, trade union – we get same story both ways. Poles are bad people now.'

'Nonsense, Wladyslaw! Nobody could ever think such a thing after your fantastic war service. Not *bad*.' Aware that he was protesting too much, Bennett paused abruptly. 'This government's still very new to the job. They're still burning with socialist idealism. Give them a bit more time and they'll see the injustice of it all.'

'You think?' Wladyslaw shifted forward in his chair and fixed Bennett with a hard stare. 'Liaison officer – Major Phipps – you know this man?'

Bennett sighed, 'Yes.'

'OK, I tell you – yesterday he come and say to Poles from Second Corps, why you boys not want to go home? We tell him this is simple – we have no home. Our home is part of Ukraine or Byelorusse now. And he look at us like we're crazy people. Like he not know that eastern Poland is gone now, not part of Poland no more. And this is military man! This is liaison officer!' Wladyslaw spoke with a fervour that, not for the first time, caused Bennett to gaze at him in fascination. 'Then Major Phipps, he says OK, if you not like government so much, why you not go back and get another? And we say, good joke, and we laugh. And he is angry with us. He gets like this' – in a vivid parody, Wladyslaw thrust his chin up, tightened his lips and glared down his nose – 'and he says not laughing matter. And we say, sure, is laughing matter when British understand nothing, when British talk like this to us. Sure – this is funny!'

Bennett could imagine how well this had gone down with Major Phipps.

In a very Polish gesture, Wladyslaw pressed a fist hard against his chest and said passionately, 'This is real deep hurt for us, Doctor. That British not hear what we say. We, who are your real true friends.' The hand swung forward, palm open. 'That you not believe us when we tell you that in all of history Russia is never to be trusted. Not with us. *And*' – he pointed a warning finger at Bennett – 'not with Britain also, although you forget this, I think.'

The thick smoke had begun to irritate Bennett's lungs and he coughed a little. 'I couldn't pretend that history's our strong point, Wladyslaw. But for what it's worth, I think attitudes are beginning to change.'

'But too late for us, I think. Britain, America – they will not fight for Poland second time.'

'No.' Bennett turned aside to cough again. 'What about you, Wladyslaw? Have you had any more thoughts about going home?'

Wladyslaw's passion had subsided as quickly as it had come. He leant back in his chair and said in a tone of gentle melancholy, 'I wait for news from Helenka, but I think it is not good for me to return.'

The coughing took a sudden grip on Bennett's throat and he spluttered helplessly. Springing up, grabbing his bag for him, Wladyslaw ushered him solicitously towards the door. 'Come, Doctor. Come.' He led the way out into the corridor. 'These Polish boys – they smoke too much. They are no good for you.'

'Thanks, Wladyslaw.'

As Bennett's coughing subsided they began to stroll in the direction of the main hall.

'What about your comrades here?' Bennett asked at last. 'Have they come to any decisions?'

'One, two, want to go home. All others, they are too worried that Stalin shoot them damn quick.'

Even allowing for the colourful effect of Wladyslaw's limited vocabulary, Bennett absorbed this with a recurrence of his old uncertainty. While he accepted that the Russians were as capable of brutality as any other nation, he found himself in the somewhat unlikely position of sharing Phipps's scepticism as to the nature of the retribution that awaited the exiled army.

Sensing something of Bennett's doubt, Wladyslaw argued sternly, 'Some men who are gone to Poland already, no one get news from them again. Not ever. Before they go, they fix signal with comrades. Like letter done in pen – is good to follow, letter done in . . .' Losing the word, he resorted to French. '*Crayon?*'

'Pencil.'

'Letter in pencil is *not* good to follow. But after these men arrive home, comrades get no letter, not in pen, not in pencil, not in anything. These men who go home – some are sent to labour camps and some are shot damn quick. Don't make no difference. Result is same both ways.'

Reaching a window to the garden, they paused to stare out into the dusk.

'Mightn't there be safety in numbers?' Bennett asked. 'I heard that a ship with five thousand Poles was leaving for Poland next week. From Scotland, I think it was.'

'Where you read this?'

'In *The Times*, so far as I remember.'

'Russia is not only country good at propaganda, I think,' said Wladyslaw gloomily.

From the end of the long echoing corridor a gong sounded. It was barely five. Bennett always forgot how early the patients were expected to eat in these places. There was the bang of a door, then another, and men poured into the corridor.

'You're not suggesting the report's untrue?' Bennett asked.

'OK, maybe it's true,' Wladyslaw conceded airily. 'But I think it is not whole truth. I think these men come from west, middle Poland. I think they not live under Russians before. I think they not educated people.'

'Lack of education is no bar to judgement, surely.'

Wladyslaw stared at him blankly for a moment. 'I mean, Doctor, it is bad thing to be from educated class in Poland

now. Educated class are bourgeois. They are enemies of—'
Losing the word, Wladyslaw windmilled a hand in the air.

'The new order?'

'Of new socialism.'

Wladyslaw gave one of his sudden smiles, so warm, so
vibrant that the conversation of the last few minutes might
have belonged to another day. 'My friend!' he declared affectionately for no apparent reason.

A little startled but far from displeased, Bennett gave a short
laugh. 'Now, Wladyslaw, I wanted to ask – are you still
interested in taking some work?'

'Ah yes. Good to work, I think. Good to stop being lazy no-
good.'

The laziness had become something of a joke between them.
Badly wounded at Monte Cassino, lucky not to have lost his
right foot let alone the lower half of his leg, Wladyslaw had
been patched together in Italy, only for complications to set in.
After two further operations, he'd been shipped to England to
convalesce. Somewhere along the way he'd contracted pneumonia and septicaemia, from which he'd only just recovered.
One way and another, he'd been in and out of hospitals and
sanatoria for more than two years.

'That job on the dairy farm,' Bennett said lightly, 'I'm afraid
they didn't need anyone after all.'

'No problem.'

Bennett was a poor liar, he could never manage to look the
other person straight in the eye, but he couldn't bring himself
to tell Wladyslaw the truth, that the farmer had flatly refused
to consider a Pole. If Wladyslaw saw through the deceit he
gave no sign.

'There's another farmer I'm trying,' Bennett went on. 'An
old chap with an invalid wife. But I haven't got an answer yet.'

'OK.'

'The farm's in the wetlands,' Bennett added. 'They grow
withies there.'

'Withies?'

'Willow shoots, used to make baskets and hurdles and charcoal.'

'Willow – OK. I know about this. Plenty willow in Poland.'

'I'll try to get a definite answer for you over the weekend. But what about the long term, Wladyslaw? Farm labouring isn't going to get you very far.'

Wladyslaw gazed out through the window. The dying light made his face appear unmarked; but for his wise old eyes, he might have been eighteen and fresh out of school.

'You haven't given any more thought to university?'

'Polish literature not so big in universities here.'

'What about the Scottish universities, though? Apparently they're taking a good number of Polish students. They might well have a literature course.'

'No, Doctor. I am too old to start again.'

He was all of twenty-five. Bennett, at fifty-six, was pain-fully aware of how ancient he must seem to someone like Wladyslaw.

'Perhaps I go to Australia, Canada . . . Or I stay here. Why not?' But he spoke dreamily, without focus.

'Well, if you do decide to go abroad, I recommend you apply for your visa without delay. I believe there's a consider-able backlog.'

Wladyslaw smiled good-naturedly but without interest. Recognising a lost cause, Bennett bent down and took from his Gladstone bag the slim volume he had selected from his shelves that morning.

'I thought you might like to test your English on this.'

Wladyslaw took the book with a small exclamation of pleasure and began to leaf through it.

'I thought you might like to learn about the Somerset Levels.'

Wladyslaw rolled the word around his tongue. '*Levels.*'

'It's the name for the wetlands.'

'I hear this word. And I have seen this place. When I arrive in train, we pass through water. Water everywhere, very wide, both sides. And very close under train. So close that I think train is like a *ship*.'

'That was the Levels all right.'

'And this is where you live, Doctor?' he asked with mock astonishment. 'In water?'

'Not actually on the bit that floods. Our house is on raised ground.'

'Good thing, perhaps.'

'Yes, we rather think so.' Bennett stood up. 'But I mustn't keep you from your meal.'

'This is no big problem. I think I give up on this food soon. *Tapioca* . . . What is this thing, Doctor? For farm animals, I think, not men. *And* . . .' He made an operatic gesture, pressing a palm to his heart with a look of great suffering, and winced expressively. 'This beans in sugar!'

For a moment Bennett couldn't think what he was talking about. 'Ah . . . you mean baked beans. Yes, yes – not to everyone's taste.'

'And not for every stomach either, I think.'

The cooking smells that floated up the corridor did not bode well, a stench of cheap meat and boiled cabbage which fused unhappily with the underlying odour of disinfectant and floor polish.

Bennett said, 'Look, my wife and I are away this Sunday visiting our daughter, but might you be free to have lunch with us the following Sunday? I think we can promise you some decent food.'

'I will like this very much. But I think maybe I am not here still.'

It was an instant before Bennett grasped his meaning. 'You're being discharged?'

'Very soon, they say.'

'But I thought nothing was going to happen for another two weeks at least. Oh dear, this changes everything. Where are they sending you? Do you know?'

'I think I go to my brigade, in north of England.'

'The north of England? Oh dear, oh dear. What about the resettlement camp at Middlezoy? Did you ask about that?'

'For resettlement camp it is necessary to sign with Resettlement Corps.'

'Yes, of course. Yes, you must make your decision, Wladyslaw. In the fullness of time . . . Yes. Such a decision! But oh dear, oh dear. I hadn't realised we had so little time.'

'Listen, Doctor, I thank you for all many things you done for me, OK? I never forget this kindness. I am honoured to have such good friend in England – this is great thing for me.'

Bennett blinked. 'Well, I am honoured to be considered your friend, Wladyslaw. But look here, I'll get on to that farmer straight away and see what can be done about the job, so that if you do decide on Middlezoy . . .'

'Sure.'

Wladyslaw thrust out a hand, and Bennett shook it warmly. 'Thank you also for this book, Doctor. I will study it. I will learn how trains go through water.'

'Goodbye, Wladyslaw.'

'Remember raw onion, Doctor.'

'I'll do my best.' Bennett was turning away when he swung back again. 'I almost forgot. The book – I should explain the word "moor". Normally it describes a high open land where nothing much grows. But hereabouts it means a wetland, low and flat, where they grow withies and graze cattle in summer.'

'High. Low. My God! This language!'

'And there's a word you won't find in the dictionary. Rhyne. It's the local word for a ditch which drains water off the land.' Bennett took the book back from Wladyslaw and, finding an example, pointed it out to him.

'OK. Rhyne.'

'And, just to complicate matters, in some villages they pronounce it "reen".'

'So, spelling – this means nothing?'

'It's not always a reliable guide, no.'

Wladyslaw declared, 'I try Chinese next time. More easy, I think!' With a jaunty wave, he turned and limped away down the corridor.

Watching him, Bennett tried to imagine what was the worst thing about being stranded in England: the lack of any obvious future, the difficulty of the language, or the feeling that, however long you decided to stay, you would never be entirely welcome.

Chapter Three

My dearest sister,

I must tell you that we had a celebration last night in
your honour. Five of us went to a traditional English 'pub'
and toasted your health and happiness in cider (the local
brew of fermented apple juice – to be treated with great
caution). Yet even as your name was being spoken, dear
Helenka, I had to pinch myself to be sure that Tadzio's
letter wasn't just a figment of my imagination, that you
were indeed alive and well. What a miracle.

And married, Helenka! I rejoice with all my heart that
you have found someone to share your life. I have no
doubt he is a thoroughly good fellow with thoroughly
modern attitudes, for you were determined to accept
nothing less. I remember the time you turned down that
Wiktor Solecka character, who thought himself the
greatest gift to all Bialystok, declaring that you would
prefer to remain single than take on the role of a
traditional wife. Forgive me, but a brother is allowed to
remind his sister of her youthful ideals. The fact that you
have overcome your doubts speaks for itself. Tadzio
reports in his letter that your husband's name is Stefan
Malczewski. Please send my sincere greetings to my new
brother, and assure him of my devoted friendship.

The moment I read of your marriage I realised why it
had taken so long to find you. I started pestering the Red
Cross for news of you as soon as I reached Persia in
August '42. They told me they would pass on any

information the moment they received it, but once the war was over the uncertainty became unbearable. I couldn't shake off the feeling that some scatter-brained clerk had simply missed your name off a list. I beat a path to the door of the Red Cross, I drove the liaison staff demented, I wrote letters to everyone I could think of, and then of course I began to wonder if there might be – what are we to say? – special obstacles. But what does all this matter now? The miracle has happened. You have survived.

This prompts an anxious thought – that you might not have received my first hasty note. In this I relayed the simple desolate fact that you and I, with Janina, are all that is left of our beloved family. Father and Mother, Aleks and Krysia, little Enzio – all are gone. I wish I could tell you that their deaths were unavoidable, I wish I could pretend that each met a peaceful untroubled end, but that would be to deny the truth, and in this devious new world where everything is distorted and obscured, truth is all we have left. We must never forget, Helenka. And we must do everything in our power to make sure no one else forgets either.

In recounting what happened, I should say at the outset that I cannot hope to do justice to the love, selflessness and nobility of spirit shown by each and every one of our family in the most desperate of circumstances. They endured so much, Helenka, and with such bravery and forbearance, only for their lives to be destroyed at the whim of madmen not worthy of bowing down at their feet. If God has His reasons, I'm no longer interested in what they might be.

Did you ever get any of our letters during the winter of '39/'40? I have often wondered. Mother wrote regularly during the early autumn, and then I wrote, first to tell you of Father's death, and again in December with the news that Aleks was a prisoner of war. I sent my letters to the medical school, thinking there was a better chance of finding you there, but perhaps they never got through. The last letter we received from you was on, I think, November 14th, and you made no mention of having received anything from us. In a way this was a good thing, because then I could persuade Mother that your subsequent silence was due to nothing more sinister than the breakdown of the postal service.

We heard from Aleks in December. Before then, we had no idea if he was dead or alive. He sent a card: just three lines in Russian to say he was alive and well and 'based in Starobielsk' in the Ukraine. Mother cried with joy at the news. Although he was clearly a prisoner of war, she thought that as a soldier he would be well treated. This – with the belief that you had survived – was a great comfort to her in the terrible months to come. It is a blessing she never knew the truth.

We will probably never know when Aleks was murdered – the late spring or early summer of 1940 seems most likely – but sadly his fate cannot be in doubt, nor the monstrous nature of it. I wish I could tell you otherwise.

I hold a particular memory close to my heart. It is of Aleks's farewell dinner, not only because it was the last time we saw him, but because it was the last time we were gathered together as a family. The end, effectively, of our life at Podjaworka. I remember everything so clearly – everyone's expressions, what they were wearing, what they said – because there was a moment when I thought, will we ever be together again? When I realised I must retain every detail and cherish it. And I did. I sat quietly and watched everyone in turn, hoarding the memories against the dangerous times ahead. The strange thing – though not strange at all – was that I saw Aleks doing the same, looking slowly round the table, absorbing each face, marking it on his memory. He too was taking his last farewell. I feel sure that when he came to stare death in the face it was this picture he carried in his mind, of our family sitting round the table at Podjaworka, in that last sweet summer of peace.

If there is one crumb of consolation, it is that Aleks achieved his ambition to serve his country and his beloved brigade. Did you ever read his letters from his first posting at Lidzbark? I read them when I got home that July, and he was never happier, Helenka, absolutely bursting with zeal and determination to do his best in the event of war. And by all accounts he succeeded in acquitting himself brilliantly. During my time in the Middle East and Italy I always made a point of seeking out men from the Novogrodek Brigade in case they had known Aleks. In southern Italy I had the luck to come across a fellow named Cabut who had not only served with Aleks but been in close company with him during the final retreat. He told me that Aleks had been in the thick of two major actions, the first at Minsk Mazowiecki (were you still in Warsaw then? Perhaps without realising the significance you heard the brigade's guns?), the second during the retreat south, when to save a section of our army from being surrounded the Novogrodek launched a valiant attack on the German line and held it open long enough for large numbers of our men to pour through. Not only was Aleks at the forefront of this attack, Helenka, but in an act of conspicuous bravery he was seen by Cabut to run out under heavy enemy fire and rescue a wounded comrade. But in holding the breach the brigade had forfeited their own chances of escape. They were thoroughly exhausted, without supplies or functioning transport, and forced to rely on horses. Cabut told me that he and Aleks rode up and down the lines trying to keep the men awake, because once they fell off their horses they couldn't be woken again. The column suffered frequent strafing and bombing. They had no food or fodder. And then, incredibly, they engaged and routed a whole German battalion. One can only wonder at the determination and

spirit that took them from the depths of exhaustion to
fight like tigers. But it was all for nothing because within
sight of the Carpathians they were confronted by the
Bolshevik army. According to Cabut, every forest, hill and
valley was swarming with Soviet forces (by previous
arrangement with the Germans of course). Cabut managed
to escape by the skin of his teeth, but he was one of the
few. Aleks, with what was left of the brigade, was
captured.

For over three months we at home heard nothing. Then
came the card I told you about, with a box number.
Mother wrote back immediately, but we never heard from
him again.

You will have some knowledge, I am sure, of what
exactly befell Aleks. I am advised that I must forgo detail
at this point (how restraint goes against the grain!). Suffice
it to say that Aleks will have been with his fellow officers
when he was murdered, that he will have died bravely,
cherishing God, Poland, and us to the last. I only pray that
he rests in peace. For I certainly cannot while this terrible
crime is publicly disowned, ignored, made to vanish as if it
had never happened. Justice and atonement – these, I
realise, are too much to hope for – but some
acknowledgement, some recognition that a terrible wrong
has been done to us – this, surely, we have a right to
expect? Or do I ask too much? Is the world so stupefied by
horror that it has become indifferent to it? I think not. I
think it is more to do with the fact that Poland and all
matters Polish are an irritation to the world in general and
to our allies in particular. We have been shamefully sinned
against, and for this we are not to be forgiven. Our very
existence has become a reproach. After the desperate
sacrifices of our people, after losing family, liberty,
homeland – everything we hold dear – we find ourselves
openly vilified by our allies. Yes, for having dared to point

out the injustice of our situation we are now painted as the villains!

For the most part, the British people are not openly hostile (though they have their moments), but they are woefully ill-informed. They believe everything they are told by their government, who in turn believe everything they are told by their great 'socialist' friend to the east. They believe that we, who fought so valiantly against Hitler, are ourselves 'fascist imperialists' who are refusing to go home because we fear and despise socialist democracy! (Sorry for the ink-blots – my pen is shaking with anger.) You can imagine with what disbelief and dismay we hear such things, and how vehemently we dispute such untruths. But our voices fall on deaf ears. The British believe that their mighty 'friend' is noble and brave, and has sacrificed everything for the cause of – yes, you have it – freedom. They cannot understand why we are reluctant to go home. They grow impatient with us. They tell us there is no future for us here, and reinforce the message by forbidding us all but the very lowliest jobs. But where are we to go, Helenka? We are like fish cast upon the shore, stranded and helpless and pining for home.

Of course when we started fighting our way up Italy we thought we were fighting for freedom. We didn't realise we had long since been betrayed. Even as late as this spring the Corps still believed they would be sent to Germany on garrison duty before returning to Poland as a victorious army. Instead, not only is the Second Corps being ordered to Britain, but it, like the rest of our armed services, faces the bitter and humiliating prospect of being demobilised. Once here, the British urge us to 'go back home' or, if we refuse, to join what they have termed the Polish Resettlement Corps (a good name for a disarmed, disowned and deracinated army, don't you think?), thus taking our first cold step towards permanent exile.

It goes without saying that the final decision is causing me great heart-searching. I want nothing more than to come home, I dream of it constantly, but am I sensible to do so? If I were to start a new life in Poland would it be a life worth having? I've heard that Poles turfed out of the Eastern Borderlands are being resettled in Silesia. But would I have any hope of qualifying? Does one have to be a member of the Communist Party, perhaps? Dear Helenka, I need you to give me your thoughts, to tell me how the land lies (as you see it), to give me your honest opinion on my chances. One hears so many different stories that it's hard to know what to believe. I need the cool judgement of my elder sister.

I have been gone six and a half years now, but the homesickness remains like an open wound. Oh, how it pains me, Helenka! More often than not it is the small things that create an agony of longing. A song we used to sing, a few lines of poetry, a taste of vodka (which is rarer than gold here), some delicious *sledzie*, which a compassionate friend smuggled in for me yesterday. Compassionate, I should explain, because you cannot imagine the food here. I will be generous and suggest it is due to the food shortages, which are still severe, but I rather suspect the English have a liking for this stuff. Example – tripe served plain, not pickled in any way (it's inedible). Having spent the best part of three years with my belly pressed hard against my spine, dreaming only of food, I realise it is the height of ingratitude to criticise such fare, but, Helenka, I only have to think of Masha's *bigos* for my mouth to water and my eyes to grow misty with yearning.

The language is another trial. It is simple enough to reach a level from where one can conduct the basic commerce of life – intentions, actions, deeds – but to master the subtle heights of ideas and abstract thought: this is a very different matter. English has absolutely nothing in common with Polish, and not half as much as it's purported to have with German. The grammar and pronunciation have more exceptions and inconsistencies than a sieve full of water, while the common usage is riddled with idioms and impenetrable slang which varies from region to region, and person to person. Occasionally my smattering of French comes in handy, but for the most part I might as well be studying Sanskrit.

I didn't mean to go on in this way. I meant to tell you more about our family – but, forgive me, I have no stomach for more sadness today. I will write again as soon as I can. If there is a delay it is only because I am on the move, for at long last I am to be discharged from the sanatorium.

Dear Helenka, I can't wait to hear all your news! Please tell me everything about your new life. And of course your opinion on the prospects for a half-qualified ex-student of literature, who sings passably well, rides rather better, and is good for very little that is strictly useful. (The above box number will always find me.)

In the meantime, hardly an hour goes by that I don't thank fate for having spared you.

With loving greetings from your devoted brother,
Wladek

P.S. Last week I managed to acquire a volume of Krasinski. Total joy.

P.P.S. Janina should have got my letter by now and will I'm sure be writing to you herself. But I can tell you she is extremely well. Apparently the baby babbles away in Italian and Polish. Did I mention that they're hoping to take over a café in Rimini?

After supper Wladyslaw settled in a corner of the reading room, intending to go over the letter again and redraft some of it, but the card players were raucous that evening, the radio at full blast, and four comrades from the Italian campaign, embroiled in their nightly argument about the situation in Poland, kept appealing to him for support, information and arbitration, at first lightly and cajolingly, then with increasing emotion. When he stood up and announced he was retreating to his room, the four debaters stared at him, disconcerted at losing their regular mediator, and complained that the evening would be spoilt.

The room Wladyslaw shared with two others was a dispiriting place, especially after nightfall, when a feeble overhead bulb cast a mournful grey wash over the metal beds and dark wooden lockers. There were no reading lamps; reading, like most activities in the convalescent home, was assigned to certain designated areas, and while not actually forbidden in the dormitories was actively discouraged there. The British had a great love for a certain kind of order, Wladyslaw had noticed. The strict routines, the rigid mealtimes, the mania for queuing, the devotion to early nights that left large towns deathly quiet after ten o'clock, the closure on Sundays of anything and everything that might offer the slightest chance of entertainment: all were observed with an obedience that owed less to a love of systems – a vice reserved for the Germans – and more, he sensed, to the demands of equality, a wish to spread the misery of self-denial evenly across the whole population.

Taking a forbidden candle from his bedside locker, he melted the base and stuck it onto a saucer he'd filched from the dining hall on his arrival over three months ago. As the candle flame rose and steadied, he unfolded the letter to Helenka and read it right through to the end. What was immediately clear was that his feeble efforts at obfuscation would fool no one. Any censor with half a brain would object both to the content and the tone. While he might have got away with a few dry facts of family history, his comments were too obvious, too scathing to escape notice. Only the first and last pages could be judged unobjectionable; the rest would be struck out or held in evidence against him.

Despite this, he decided to post the letter exactly as it was. For one thing, he couldn't believe that the secret police had the capacity to check every one of the thousands of letters that must be arriving from Britain daily; there was no reason why his shouldn't slip through. For another, he was damned if he was going to submit to the bitter medicine of self-censorship unless absolutely necessary. He would look for another way first, by getting letters smuggled in, or sending them via Soviet-occupied Germany. One way or another, he would not give in without a fight. There were few enough ways of resisting now that all hope of military and political action was past.

He had written the letter on flimsy copy-paper. Folding it, he ran a fingernail down the folds to make the ten sheets seem less substantial still. Writing the address, he abandoned his ornate literary script in favour of a dull inconspicuous style, though even this gesture, small as it was, constituted a kind of capitulation, a step on the slippery slope to conformity.

He put his name, rank and post-office box number on the back. No need for subterfuge here: the rank of sergeant was suitably proletarian, and his surname common enough not to be immediately identified with the ideologically unacceptable professional class.

After some thought, he drew a flower across the edge of the glued envelope flap, like a lover's seal. Yes: it was a descent into subterfuge. The devil on his shoulder laughed: I'll have you yet!

He put the letter on the locker beside his one photograph of the family, taken when Helenka was about to leave for medical school. He tried to imagine how the years of war and occupation might have changed her, until the throbbing in his leg broke into his thoughts, forcing him to stretch, and, when that failed to do the trick, to pace the room, which, though it did little for the cramp, did at least give him the impression of beating it down with each stride. It was four steps from one side of the room to the other; he counted them off unthinkingly. The far wall was a thin plywood partition, subdividing what

had once been a larger room. As he approached it for the
fourth or fifth time he caught a muffled dirge in monotone
interspersed by a dull methodical tapping.

Three soldiers occupied the next room. One was a music
scholar from the German borderlands whose loyalties were
regarded, probably unfairly, as suspect; the second a wily
country lad from the Carpathians who smiled too much; the
third a fellow called Jozef Walczak, who was troubled and
emotional and roamed the corridors at night.

Wladyslaw hesitated, reluctant to impose on another's misery. Yet the tapping had the insistence of a warning.

In little doubt whom he would find, Wladyslaw went and
knocked on the door. The dirge stopped. Wladyslaw listened a
while longer before putting his head inside. The room was
dark, but in the light from the passage he saw Jozef lying on
his bed, curled up with his face to the wall, his forearm bent
over his head.

'Hello, my friend.' Wladyslaw closed the door and turned
on the gloomy light.

Jozef made no response.

'Troubles?' Wladyslaw went and laid a quick hand on the
bony shoulder. 'I'd be happy to listen if you'd like to talk.'

After a moment, Jozef lifted his head and fastened a fierce
eye on Wladyslaw before dropping his head back onto the
pillow. But if the identification reassured him, it didn't encourage him to speak.

'Anything particular worrying you? Or . . .'

Another silence, and Wladyslaw said, 'What about a drop
of vodka? I've got a bit stashed away, and I'd far rather share
it with you than the ungrateful good-for-nothings in my room.
Wait here,' he added superfluously.

Retrieving the bottle from the back of his locker, he hid it
under his shirt until he was safely back in Jozef's room, when
he pulled it out like a conjuror, with a great sweep of the arm,
a gesture unappreciated by Jozef, whose face remained turned
to the wall.

'It's good stuff,' Wladyslaw assured him, sitting on the end
of the bed. 'Bartered with Jerzy for a Mickiewicz love poem
which I passed off quite shamelessly as my own. But then Jerzy
is so blinded by passion for that nurse of his that it could have
been written by a goat for all he cared.' Wladyslaw took a
quick pull from the bottle and smacked his lips. 'Mmm. A
small piece of heaven . . .'

Another pause, then slowly, stiffly, Jozef levered himself into
a sitting position and, drawing his knees up to his chin, pushed
his knuckles punishingly against his eyes.

Wladyslaw held the bottle out to him. 'Have as much as
you want – feel free,' he coaxed, eyeing the few fingers of
vodka with a touch of anxiety in case Jozef should take him
too literally.

Jozef took a long gulp before swinging his feet slowly to the
floor and reaching into his locker for a handkerchief. He blew
his nose distractedly, then sat hunched and still, gazing at the
floor. He had lost part of his stomach and intestine to a
shrapnel wound at Ancona and was skeletally thin, as though
he had only this moment emerged from a labour camp. His
cadaverous appearance was intensified by the cold overhead
light, which threw an unhealthy grey tinge over his skin and
made a deep hollow of his eye socket.

Beside him on the locker top was a well travelled family
photograph in a bright new frame. Even in his better moments
Jozef wasn't a great talker, and at any mention of home and
family life his silence was positively hostile, but one evening
soon after his arrival, still excited by the move to a new place,
he'd given Wladyslaw a halting, emotionally charged account
of his story.

He was thirteen at the time of the mass deportations.
Lodging near his grammar school some distance from home,
he had escaped the main sweep of February 10th which had
taken his family and all their Polish neighbours away to the
east. Picked up several weeks later, he had been sent to a quite
different camp, and despite numerous appeals to join his family

had never seen them again. He'd later discovered that his father
and eldest sister had died in their camp in the Urals, leaving his
mother and two – no, Wladyslaw corrected himself, *three* –
sisters, who towards the end of the war had managed to find
their way back to Poland.

'Any news from home?'

Jozef's mouth contorted, he glared at the floor, whether
from disappointment or pain it was hard to tell. Wladyslaw
guessed at disappointment and said, 'Well, there's bound to be
something soon.'

Jozef shivered with exasperation, as though Wladyslaw's
remarks were pushing him to the very limits of his self-control.

Searching hastily for another less charged topic, Wladyslaw
said, 'I'm hoping to take honest employment, did I tell you?'

Jozef took a slow shuddering breath, his eyes opened a crack
to stare sightlessly at the floor.

'It's not my dream job, of course,' Wladyslaw went on
lightly. 'But something to keep the wolf from the door. Tell
me, Jozef, what was your ambition? As a kid, I mean?'

Swinging the bottle up high and fast, Jozef took another
swig.

'I dreamt of being a film director,' Wladyslaw said reminis-
cently into the silence that followed. 'I used to go to the cinema
whenever I had the chance. I'd watch every film three times
over. I'd make reams of notes, diagrams of camera angles. Even
rewrite the scripts. My ambition was to put some of the great
classics on the screen – the *Trilogy*, *The Teutonic Knights* . . .
So you see, I wasn't short of ambition or confidence. Some
might even say I was rather too big for my boots. But one has
to have a vision. One has to have some belief in oneself. And it
seems to me that if you don't grab opportunities as they come
along, then some useless fellow with a stunted imagination and
limited talent will get there before you and squander the
opportunity. Yes . . . my ambition was to be a director. I was
young, of course. But I don't rule out the possibility even now.
Far from it, in fact. I believe everything is possible.'

Jozef stuttered, 'Don't be ridiculous.'

Wladyslaw made a gesture of taking this on the chest, and laughed. 'Ah, well, you may be right . . . Castles in the air . . . But one must be allowed one's dreams!' Removing the bottle from Jozef's hand, he took a modest sip, holding the fire in his mouth for a second or two to eke out the pleasure.

'My dream – was to be – with my family.' Jozef's voice came in drawn-out rasps, childishly bitter. 'That was all – I ever wanted. What a joke. What an idiotic joke!'

'But why? You mustn't rule out the possibility of going home, Jozef. Nothing's certain yet. Don't feel you have to rush into a decision. There's plenty of time – and don't let the British try to persuade you otherwise. Listen to your friends.' Even as he said this, it seemed to Wladyslaw that the loneliness in Jozef was like an open wound.

'I was going to work the land,' Jozef stammered. 'I was going to – provide for us all. I had it – all planned . . .'

Wladyslaw wondered what land he had in mind. As if in answer to this, Jozef added, 'I was going to rent a few hectares – keep geese, hens, grow vegetables . . . Sell flowers in the market. I wouldn't have – cared how hard it was. I wouldn't have – minded . . .'

'Farming is a fine life.'

'What a joke. What a joke.'

Like a doctor ministering to a patient, Wladyslaw pressed the vodka back into Jozef's hands and watched solicitously as he took a large gulp.

'Where are they living, your mother and sisters?'

'For God's sake . . .' Jozef whispered. 'What does it matter?'

'Of course it matters. Everything at home matters. To all of us.'

Jozef shook his head impatiently.

'But I'd really like to know.'

Jozef gave in with a furious sigh. 'Wroclaw.'

'And do they have work?'

A shrug which seemed to indicate that they did.

'Well, it's not the same as the country, I grant you. But the
city has its compensations. More opportunities. More people.
Don't rule it out, Jozef. You might like it more than you think.
You might find that—'

Jozef's shoulders hunched, his hand jerked upwards, cutting
Wladyslaw short. 'No – you don't understand. No – they don't
want me. They've told me – they've said – there's no room for
me. They don't want me to come.'

Wladyslaw was momentarily silenced.

'They've – said – I'll get in the way.'

'Ah, but they're just saying that, aren't they, Jozef? So you
won't feel any obligation on their behalf. So you won't feel you
must go back for their sake.'

'No! It couldn't be clearer,' Jozef declared harshly. 'There's
no – misunderstanding. No – my mother couldn't have been
plainer. I'd be in the way. I'm not wanted. So – that's fine. I
understand! I accept!'

'They must have very good reasons for telling you such a
thing. Perhaps life is particularly hard for them at the moment
and they want to spare you the same fate. Perhaps they're
trying to be kind. One way or the other, I'm sure they've got
your best interests at heart.'

Jozef gave a rapid shake of his head.

'Perhaps they're living very simply,' Wladyslaw continued
gently. 'Perhaps they've only one small room between the four
of them, and they worry that there won't be any work for you.
Perhaps—'

'No!'

In the pause that followed, Wladyslaw watched as Jozef
took a long swig of vodka, then another, before upending the
bottle and draining it to the last drop.

Tearing his gaze away from the empty bottle, Wladyslaw
said, 'Listen, Jozef, a mother would never say something like
that unless she wanted to spare you hardship . . . disappointment . . . Unless she believed you had a better chance elsewhere.

And she could be right, you know. Why don't you think about America? Or Canada? Australia? Even England. It isn't such a bad place really, once you get used to it.' Feeling he had ended on a weak note, Wladyslaw added, 'And the girls are nice and pretty.'

Jozef lifted the bottle to his lips again before remembering it was empty. Turning his gaunt, worn-out face towards Wladyslaw, he argued obdurately, 'We're going to – lose our – citizenship if we don't go back. And then we'll have no choice. We'll be cut off for ever.'

'That's only speculation.'

'But they've already started. We're going to be next – they've said so.'

'Have they started? I've only heard of Anders losing his citizenship, but he's a natural target, the commander of our army. The rest of us . . . No, they wouldn't dare. The bullyboys in Warsaw are simply trying to frighten us into hurrying back so that they can boss us around. But we must stand up to them. We must decide our own fate.'

'Our fate is ugliness and horror.'

'Jozef, Jozef . . .'

'Our fate is to be despised, to be left to rot.'

Fishing a clean handkerchief out of his pocket, Wladyslaw pushed it into Jozef's hand and began to intone words of reassurance as a priest might recite the creed, insistently, authoritatively, as a matter of faith. He spoke of time bringing clarity, of no one needing to burn their bridges for a long while yet. He talked about the thriving Polish communities in America and Australia, and gave a glowing, if imaginative, account of the education and work opportunities there; he spoke of freedom and choice, food and good company, huge landscapes and bright sunshine. Then, to be even-handed, he made a case for going back to Poland, for making a new start in familiar surroundings, for meeting undoubted hardship and political changes, yes, but also – he couldn't think of an also, so he talked of the joys of returning to one's own culture, until after half an hour he sensed that a spark of optimism had gained a tentative hold on Jozef's fragile imagination.

'Rest now!' he said at last. 'Let's talk again tomorrow. I'll see if I can't palm off another poem on Jerzy and persuade him to part with some more vodka.'

When Wladyslaw paused at the door, Jozef gave him a slow nod, though whether this indicated belief or doubt it was impossible to tell.

Back in his room, Wladyslaw experienced a bout of misgiving. It was a brave man who dared to hold out hope to another, and a foolish one who promised more than life could reasonably deliver. Already he felt the tug of anxiety that comes from taking on responsibility for another person, the fear that his words would come back to haunt him. It was said that Jozef had lain on the battlefield at Ancona with half his stomach hanging out for several hours before anyone could get to him, and that when they finally reached him he was lying among the bloody, fragmented remains of his closest friend. Wladyslaw didn't pretend to understand the effects of his physical injuries but it seemed to him that Jozef had been suffering from a mental crisis ever since, and that the letters from home were not so much the cause of his troubles as a convenient focus for them. Each soldier arriving in England received a mental health assessment, but this, like the monthly chat with the visiting Polish psychiatrist, had proved absurdly easy to fake or, better still, to subvert by means which could be relied on to provide huge entertainment for the reading room. Despite Jozef's problems he had been as adept as any at bluffing his way through these interviews, and no one, not even those exasperated by his constant gloom, begrudged him his escape from the head doctors. The Polish mental hospital somewhere near London was said to be full of seriously crazy people, and it was an accepted fact that, once inside, you lost all chance of getting out again. As the saying went, you had to be mad to want to see a psychiatrist.

To maintain a hold on one's peace of mind it seemed to Wladyslaw that it was necessary to postpone despair. During the years of deprivation and war he had seen despair sap the will and sour the spirit, and kill as surely as any bullet. Better by far to be carried along by hope, which, given half a chance, would unreel harmlessly before you, just out of reach, effortlessly adjusting itself to all but the most terrible circumstances.

Sitting on the bed, Wladyslaw ran his fingers over the sealed letter to Helenka. Here at least hope had not been in vain. She was alive. His gratitude was still immense, yet subdued by the growing fear that he would never see her again.

It was barely nine thirty. He thought of going for an evening stroll. Though exercise tended to aggravate his leg, he tried to walk for at least an hour a day, either circling the grounds or going into town for a cup of heavy brown tea and what was audaciously termed a sugar bun – the sugar, as Horatio might have it, being honoured more in the breach than the observance. Quite apart from the need to build up his fitness, he clutched at the belief, against much of the evidence, that exercise improved his chances of a peaceful night. Today he had been too busy with the letter to Helenka to walk even halfway round the grounds. And now it seemed he had missed the weather; when he opened the window it was to a stream of damp air and billows of rain chasing across the spill of hazy light.

Reluctantly, he turned instead to his English lessons. He had been working intermittently and with a dispiriting lack of success on, variously, *Hamlet*, *Our Mutual Friend* and *Nostromo*. Now, in expectation of simpler stuff, he picked up the slim volume Doctor Bennett had given him. There were no photographs or illustrations to help him, only small sketches at the beginning of each chapter, variations on a watery theme: a stream from above, with reeds and birds; a stream from below, with eels and fishes; and, angled over the water, with wild flowers at its feet, a stumpy tree with a spiked crown like a giant medieval mace.

He began to read the first chapter at some speed to get the
gist of it, but stumbled to a halt before the end of the first page.
He had been warned about the size of the English vocabulary,
and everything he read seemed to confirm this. There was
nothing for it but to settle down and dismantle each sentence
with the aid of a dictionary. The top of the locker was too
small to work on, so he brought up a chair and, spreading his
books and a pad over the bed, moved the candle closer.

In the heart of the county of Somerset lies a mysterious land
of mist and water, of myth and fable, of worship and mysti-
cism. Here, according to legend, is the land of Arthur and
Guinevere, of Camelot and Avalon, where Balin's Sword smote
upon the water and the knights embarked upon the quest for
the Holy Grail . . .

A door sounded nearby. Catching the murmur of voices
through the partition wall, Wladyslaw strained to listen. He
thought he could make out Jozef speaking lightly, even cheerfully, and felt a fleeting relief. For the moment at least, he could
feel free of responsibility.

Here came early Christians to found a monastery upon the
great tor of Glastonbury, and here, on an island in the midst
of a wide inland sea, King Alfred took refuge from the invading
Danes while he plotted victory over them . . .

On the far side of the partition the door sounded again, and
Wladyslaw realised the voices had ceased. He heard what might
have been a locker door closing and the creak of a bed as
someone got up or sat down. He thought: They've left Jozef
alone again. He cursed them for not making more of an effort.
And yet how could he really blame them? There is nothing that
drains one's capacity for compassion quite so rapidly as unrelieved despair.

The Levels lie at the very heart of Somerset, both geograph-
ically and symbolically, for it is from the wetlands that the
county has gained its name – 'sumer seata' – the land of the
summer people. Until recent times, people retreated to higher
ground during the winter floods, only coming down again once

*the land had dried out, to graze their cattle and grow their
crops.*

*Ten thousand years ago, before recorded time, the Levels
were inundated with salt water, forming a shallow sea of some
250 square miles, rimmed on three sides by hills, corrugated by
low promontories, and dotted with islands, knolls and mumps.
Then as the sea receded, the rain-spill from the surrounding
hills formed a freshwater wetland, and man began his long
struggle to dominate this most stubborn of aqueous landscapes.*

Wladyslaw reviewed his list of new words without enthusiasm. It was hard to believe that 'corrugate' and 'inundate'
would prove useful in general conversation. As for 'mumps', it
– or they – appeared untranslatable except as a virulent disease
dangerous to pubescent boys. He rather wished the doctor had
lent him a modern novel instead, something which would
provide some insights into the English psyche. 'Manners' over
'mumps'.

*It is a battle not yet won, for this is a land caught between
two great watery forces. Firstly, there is the rain which spills
off the mass of the surrounding hills onto the lowlands, where
it is carried sluggishly, if at all, by somnambulant rivers whose
way to the sea is blocked for up to six hours in every twelve by
the tides, causing the rivers to leak, slop, or spill their load over
the wetlands and leave the moors flooded for months on end.
The second great force is the sea itself, which for thousands of
years continued to encroach upon the land at high water, and
can, even now, at the coincidence of a fierce Atlantic storm
with the highest of spring tides make a mockery of the sea
defences and roar in across the Levels for a distance of forty
miles, carrying all before it.*

Wladyslaw had a vision of the Biebrza wetlands, near the
home of his favourite cousins, the Szulinskis. The floods there
had always seemed benign affairs, just a rising and spilling of
water from the Biebrza River's myriad backwaters, pools and
swamps onto the wide water meadows of the flood plain. But
perhaps he had never been there at the time of the spring melt.

Or rain had kept them inside the house. Or the summers had come to blanch out the other memories. The last two summers before the war had been particularly hot, vivid, sun-drenched. He saw again the scorched quality of the light as it fell on the river, he felt the intensity of the heat, he saw again the grave beauty of Krystina as she sat playing the piano late into the evening. Krystina was the third of his Szulinski cousins, a music student two months younger than himself, a pale slender creature with an air of artistic absorption. Most days she preferred to stay in the house practising her music or walking her little dog in the gardens, but one morning her brothers had persuaded her to join the rest of them on a rowing trip. The day was heavy and languid, the branches of the trees bowed almost to the surface of the water by the weight of leaves; all sound was suspended. Krystina lay against the back seat of the skiff under an ancient Japanese parasol. They passed through the shadow of an overhanging branch, she turned her head in profile, and all at once something caught at Wladyslaw's heart, he felt his whole world overturn and found himself irretrievably in love.

His happiness was overwhelming, intense, pierced by an agonised uncertainty that was all too quickly justified when a month after his return to university Krystina sent him a note asking him not to write so often. She wrapped up the message kindly: she said she was too busy with her studies to reply, she was looking forward to seeing him at Christmas when they would surely meet up again, she sent her fond love as a cousin. He thought he would never experience such pain again, though in the end this, like the passion, wore itself out. By the time he saw the Szulinskis again the following spring he was able to greet Krystina with a jovial irony, as though he could look back on the episode as a passing madness.

He wondered if she had survived the labour camps. Picturing the long white slender hands, he thought perhaps not.

Into this battle, man brought his full armoury to bear. For centuries, he ditched and drained the wetlands, he re-routed

*and straightened rivers, he raised and reinforced their banks,
he installed sluices and pumping stations. He built sea defences,
and constructed sea gates, or clyses, across the mouths of the
rivers to hold back the sea at high water. But, despite all his
efforts, he has won a fragile and uncertain victory, for the spill-
waters still flood the most susceptible moors in winter, and
there are no defences that can repel the sea when the forces of
storm and tide conspire to raise it a full five feet above the
coast.*

At ten thirty Wladyslaw closed the book with a sense of,
if not accomplishment, then perseverance. The vocabulary list
was difficult but not perhaps impossible. By the time he climbed
into bed he managed to persuade himself that he was agreeably
tired and had a good chance of an undisturbed night. He had
read somewhere that your dreams are often determined by your
last thoughts, so he fell asleep to images of the Biebrza River.
But the shining water soon evaporated, and he was cast back
to the heat and dust of Uzbekistan and the foul charnel house
that drove his worst nightmares.

Chapter Four

———

BILLY SHOVELLED another load of muck off the hen-house floor and said, 'But why not?'

'They're not going to speak English, are they?' said Stan.

'Nothing to stop you *showing* 'em what to do, is there? A hook's a hook in any language.'

'They'd do it all wrong.'

Maintaining his patience with difficulty, Billy said, 'Yes, maybe they would at the start. But you could put 'em right quickly enough. And it's not as if you've got a whole lot of choice, is it?' He shovelled the last load into the barrow and closed the hen-house door with a bang.

The old man was standing by the chicken run. His lower lip was signalling resistance. 'I don't understand why Frank won't see reason,' he said. 'I told him, if he wants to cut one bed, he's got to cut 'em all. I told him, that's my final word.'

Billy looked sharply away until the impulse to deliver a scathing retort had passed. 'Yes, we know all about that. But Frank Carr's not interested, is he? And nothing's about to change his mind. So forget about him. It's past history. You've only one option now. Either you hire in these Polacks or you let the crop go to rot. Because that's what it boils down to, Old Man. As simple as that.'

'Someone might still take on the cutting.'

'Oh yes? And who would that be? One of the cutters who comes beating at your door each morning looking for work?' He muttered under his breath, 'God give me strength.'

They watched the bantams pecking at the kitchen scraps,

their beaks shooting out like darts, their feet moving delicately over the beaten earth. The old man proffered Billy a Woodbine. His hand was trembling and the packet trembled with it. Fishing out some matches, he then fumbled with the box.

'Give it here,' Billy said gruffly, and struck a light for both of them.

The old man drew on his fag and coughed hard. 'I didn't mean to let things go, Billy. I didn't mean for things to get so bad. But I hadn't reckoned on folk being so busy.'

'Well, they're out to make a living, aren't they?'

'It's the war—'

'Yes, it's the war. And there's not a blind thing you or anyone else can do about it.'

With a slow sigh the old man fell silent and shuffled over to the scrap bucket to scrape out the last of the peelings.

A thin cloud had crept over the sun, a faint breeze was stirring in the orchard, and somewhere close by a magpie gave a solitary screech. Billy looked out over the kitchen garden with its rows of bolted cabbages standing tall and ragged amid a fountain of drooping leaves, and tried once again to make sense of his meeting with Annie Bentham. Her composure still niggled him. Was it suppressed anger that had made her so calm, or plain indifference? Was her opinion of him so low that she'd long since shut him out of her mind, or had this husband been so bloody marvellous that she'd no thought for anyone else? It bothered him that he couldn't work this out, and it bothered him that he should keep trying. He'd never understood what made one woman memorable and another drop from the mind without so much as a ripple. There was the lust factor of course, never to be underrated, but beyond that he'd little idea. He'd known sweet impressionable girls, cheeky girls, good sports, and enthusiastic older women. Sometimes he'd gone for the ones who made him laugh, sometimes for the ones who promised him peace and quiet, but there had never been a pattern as to which, if any, stuck in his imagination. During the war Annie's image had drifted through his mind as often as

any, maybe more than most, usually at the oddest times, sometimes even infiltrating his dreams, to the point where, caught in
a heavy rocket bombardment on the push towards Germany,
witnessing the sight of tanks on either side getting brewed up,
he had sworn in the terror of the moment to go back and find
her. Afterwards he had put the impulse down to the intensity
of his fear, and the choice of Annie to fluke, even a crazy sort
of nostalgia, but now he had seen her again he realised that it
was the power of the attraction he felt for her. It ached in him,
like a hunger.

Stan was back at his side. He said, 'You wouldn't think of
staying yourself, would you, Billy?'

'What?'

'You running the place and me helping out when I could.'

Billy had a brief vision of the place spick and span, making
a tidy profit, but the picture disintegrated when he thought of
the inevitable arguments. He said, 'I've got plans.'

'But the whole place, Billy. Running it the way you like.'

'I told you. I'm heading back to London.'

'Why do you want to go there?'

'Got a job waiting for me.'

'What – better than you'd get here?'

'That wouldn't be difficult, would it?'

'But all them people. All that racket.'

'How would you know what it's like? You've never been
there.'

'If it's money you want, Billy, there's good money to be
made from withies.'

Billy felt a flash of anger, a sudden shiver of heat. He said
roughly, 'Not good enough for me, Old Man.'

'I tell you, best buff and whites been fetching ten bob a
bundle. In the war it was browns they wanted, but now it's
buff and whites. Ten bob – I swear! Frank Carr, he's just gone
and bought himself a spanking new tractor on the proceeds.'

'A bloody fool he looks on it too,' Billy muttered.

Two of the bantams had begun to pick on a third. Stan

banged his hand down on the chicken wire and cried, 'Oy, oy!' but the bullies took no notice and, driving their victim into a corner, pecked viciously at its neck. The victim was small and scrawny, its neck was already raw, and it put up no fight.

Billy said, 'Well, Old Man, if there's so much money in withies you can go and hire as many of these Polacks as you want, can't you? A whole bloody army.' Pinching out his fag and stowing the dog-end in his pocket, he went to the gate in the chicken run and let himself in. Wading through the squawking bantams, he quickly cornered the bloodied victim and caught it at first lunge. He held it up to Stan. 'Dinner or nursing care?'

For a moment he thought the old man had suffered a turn. His eyes had lost focus, his mouth had drooped, his skin had developed a greenish tinge and seemed to hang more pendulously from the bones. Then Billy realised it was resentment that clouded his eyes, and old age that dragged at his skin, and the grey morning light that gave it the colour of death.

Billy made the decision: 'Dinner,' and wringing the bird's neck took it back to the house. When he came out again, he spotted the old man's bowed figure in the vegetable garden, scraping at the weeds with a hoe.

He took another turn around the house, wondering what if anything was worth tackling in the time available. Annie had talked about two weeks to sort the place out, but that would barely see the outbuildings straight, let alone the repairs started and the machinery up and running. Likely she'd picked two weeks because it was the most she thought she could prise out of him in the name of duty. Well, he'd already stayed an extra day; at a push he might stay another, but it wasn't from duty. Disgust, more like. Or pity. He quite liked the idea of pity. Whichever, the most he'd give it was another day. Then last thing on Sunday he would slip away and catch the milk train from Athelney in the knowledge that he was starting his new job with a clean slate.

Ernie Brandon, his best mate from the tank crew, had swung

the job for him. Ernie had been the gunner, perched in the turret above Billy, 'arse by mug' as Ernie described it, 'mine beautiful, yours ugly'. Ernie came from a large family, a confusion of uncles, grans and cousins spread across east London. One of these uncles had done all right for himself with a range of business interests that Ernie described as 'a bit of this and a bit of that', though what these interests were exactly, apart from the Jaguar garage near Euston Station, he couldn't say. The promised job was similarly vague: mechanic or dogsbody, Ernie wasn't too sure, and Billy hadn't been able to find out. On the two occasions Billy had presented himself at the garage at times arranged through Ernie, it was to find the boss out and nobody certain when he was expected back. Nothing, therefore, had been fixed for sure, but Billy trusted Ernie to see him right. In their four-year friendship Ernie had only once failed to deliver on a promise, and that was on the joys of London. During the months they were stuck in Germany waiting for demob Ernie had fed Billy endless tales of the pubs they would drink in, the girls they would sweeten up, the flashy dives they would waltz into. But the London they came back to was drab and dirty, with queues everywhere and empty shops and a dearth of flashy dives open to ex-Tommies without money. For the first week Billy had taken up Ernie's offer of floor space in the room he shared with his brother, but Ernie's family was large, the house cramped, and another brother was expected back from the war at any moment, so Billy had felt obliged to move into the first digs he could find in a dark narrow house that smelt of soot and damp and the acrid fumes from a nearby tannery. When Billy wasn't spending the evening with Ernie, he sometimes went to East Ham to see Johnny, the machine gunner, who lived with his wife and two noisy kids in a back room of his in-laws' house, or to Leyton to have a drink with Crasher, the gun loader, who was working in the family butchery business and newly engaged to his childhood sweetheart. But neither of them could stay out for long, sometimes they couldn't get away at all, and once, in a thick fog, Billy's bus home had taken two hours.

The more Billy thought back to the war, to the months the five of them had spent cooped up in the smelly sardine tin of a tank or dossing down in a succession of verminous billets, the more it seemed to him a time of unparalleled contentment and ease of mind, not because there was anything to be said for war – a sad, dirty, unsatisfactory business – but because the five of them had been the best of mates, part of a team, the best there was, the best there ever could be. Now it struck him with a sharpened sense of loss that those days were gone for ever, that none of them would ever know such freedom again.

The previous day, after Annie had cycled away up the lane, he'd made a start on the yard and the woodshed, oiling, sharpening, sorting, clearing, hauling, burning, stacking. Working on into the evening by paraffin lamp, he'd mucked out the pigsty and laid poison by the rat holes. When he came in for the night, he'd found a pot of chicken and potatoes on the hotplate and Stan gone to bed. He'd slept deeply and without dreams.

This morning he'd gone out at dawn and shot a couple of rabbits close by Owers Meadow, and sawn and split a heap of apple logs, before overseeing the coal delivery and wheeling ten barrowloads down to the bins by the woodshed. He'd spent an hour stacking and burning rotten withies from the drying racks, before deciding his time would be better spent chipping the muck off the hen-house floor.

Now, having made his circuit of the house and finding no job that was more urgent than any other, he decided on a whim to walk over the ridge to look at the withy beds on Curry Moor. He went by the back paths that looped around the side of the village, and crossed the Tone by Hook Bridge. Stan's four acres lay under the banks of the river and were prone to

flooding for most of the winter and often much of the spring
as well, yet he could see immediately why Frank Carr had
wanted to buy the crop. The withies here were in far better
fettle than those on West Sedgemoor, with fine straight stems,
no visible canker and far fewer weeds, as though cattle had
been put on them, bang to order, the moment the land had
dried out, and the second spurt of weeds cut back some time
since, with only the last growth left to run. He reckoned the
yield at nine in ten.

He came back by way of the village. Now that he was
staying on another day he didn't want people to think he was
hiding away. The village was little more than a straggle of
cottages and farmhouses dotted along a lattice of lanes, with
no green, no cluster of shops, no obvious centre. Billy chose
the road that took him past the post office and, some fifty
yards on, the garage. Seeing no one, he took a loop round to
the east, past the chapel and the Rose and Crown, and finally
met three people one after the other. The first called a greeting,
the next waved, and the third stopped to talk. From their
manner he might have been away only a matter of months.

His route brought him up to the George and, just beyond it,
on the corner opposite the church, to Spring Cottage. He'd
meant to walk past but at the last moment turned in through
the gate and knocked. After a few moments he stood back
from the porch and saw in one window a marmalade cat, and
in the other some dried rushes in a blue vase. He knocked
again and, staring at the distinctive wrought-iron boot-scraper,
remembered waiting here once before and seeing Annie emerge
dressed for the May dance in a flowered dress and white shoes.
It was the first time she'd agreed to go out with him and, later
that night, the first time she'd let him kiss her.

After another few seconds he gave up and walked rapidly
back to Crick Farm. He worked on through the rest of the day,
sweeping out the withy shed and pouring oil over the cogs and
axles of the stripping brake. Coming inside at dusk, he lit the
lamps in the kitchen and skinned and paunched the rabbits,

and put them to stew with some onions, carrots and potatoes. He threw the vegetable peelings into the scraps bucket and scrubbed out the sink. Then he swept the floor and passed a mop over the flagstones. Flor had no need to worry about the state of the kitchen while he was around. Cleanliness and order had become something of an obsession with him. It had started as a duty towards his mates, an essential contribution towards the safety and efficiency of the tank, but over time he had come to crave order for its own sake, the security it brought him, the sense of fending off a more personal chaos.

Before supper, Billy popped up to report to Flor on the state of the kitchen floor and managed to make her laugh. After supper, while Stan was busy upstairs, he shaved and washed himself at the sink, the whole business, top to toe. Then, wearing his demob suit and a donkey jacket, hair damped down and combed back, he went up to the village. He had intended to have an ale at the George before knocking on Annie's door, but seeing a light in her window and the curtains undrawn, he gathered his nerve and went straight there.

He knocked and heard silence, then her voice, muffled, but not so muffled that it wasn't apparent she was talking to someone inside the house. The mistake came to him with a lurch, he felt a rush of humiliation, he would have walked away there and then but it was too late, a light had sprung on over his head and Annie was opening the door.

'Billy,' she exclaimed. 'What a surprise.'

'I was just passing,' he said. 'Thought I'd say a quick hello.'

Her hand was still on the door, ready to close it again. 'I thought you'd left,' she said.

'Change of plan. I'm staying till tomorrow night.'

She said brightly, 'That's wonderful.' She was wearing a deep pink lipstick which made her lips seem very full and very wide. Her hair fell to her shoulders in glossy waves. She said, 'Stan and Flor must be pleased.'

'They should be. I've cleared most of the withy shed and half the yard.'

'I meant – pleased that they're getting to see a bit more of you.'

He scoffed, 'I doubt it.'

'You're too hard on them, you know.'

He pulled a frown that went too far and turned into a scowl. It had been a mistake not to get that drink inside him; he would have handled the situation much better.

She had relaxed now, her weight on one foot, her head tilted to one side. She had kept her hand on the door, however, as if to remind him that she wouldn't be stopping long. She was wearing a cardigan that matched her lipstick and small gold earrings. She said, 'They always thought more of you than you gave them credit for.'

'Well, they had a strange way of showing it.'

'Just their own way, maybe.'

Normally he wouldn't have let the remark pass, but he was sharply aware of the unseen presence inside the house, of the cosy scene he had so stupidly interrupted. Did the two of them enjoy a drink or two before going to bed, he wondered? A little chat by the fire? Or was it straight into the sack? The thought brought a coldness over him that was like revulsion.

'Well,' he said, taking a step backwards, 'I'm due at the George, so . . .'

She reached out as if to hold him back. 'I quite forgot – I meant to say before – there's something wrong with the chimney at Crick Farm. It's blocked or—'

'I've cleared it.'

'Have you?' She smiled. 'But of course you have. You were always good at fixing things.'

'Not good enough.'

'How do you mean?'

What he meant was, *not good enough to earn praise*, but he wasn't going to argue that corner now. 'Better be on my way, then.'

The wasp-like buzz of an engine sounded somewhere in the distance and the section of Billy's mind that automatically

categorised anything mechanical marked it down as a motorbike.

'Billy?'

'Yes.'

'Thanks.'

'What for?'

'For doing what you could. For staying on a bit.'

He gave a careless shrug. Then the devil was whispering
irresistibly in his ear, and the devil won. He said in a tone of
exaggerated innocence, 'Sorry to have interrupted your, er . . .
evening.' With a tip of his head he indicated the scene beyond
the door.

'That's all right,' she said.

Feeling he had regained the upper hand, Billy took a couple
of steps towards the gate and said brightly, 'Bye, then.'

'Goodbye, Billy. And good luck with the—' But something
distracted her and she began to speak softly to the person inside
the cottage. Billy took the last two steps to the gate and looked
back over his shoulder, intending to deliver a nonchalant wave,
only to find Annie still occupied with her companion, talking
gently, bending forward a little, aiming her remarks downwards as if to . . . In the instant he registered his mistake, he
heard the high fluting notes of a child's voice and two small
outstretched arms emerged from behind the door and wrapped
themselves around Annie's waist. The child was a girl with
long dark hair and round eyes. She was wearing a pink dressing
gown. Pressing her head close against her mother's side, she
gave Billy a fierce stare.

Billy took a step back towards the door, and said, 'Hello.'

'This is Beth.'

'Hello, Beth.'

He had no experience of children; he didn't know what to
say to them, so he said to Annie, 'She's a beauty.'

'Thank you.' There was pride in her voice, but also a note
of finality.

'I'd no idea.'

'Why should you?'

He wasn't much good at children's ages, but he thought she was about five, possibly six. At this, an astonishing thought struck him. He went very still except for a heavy pulse high in his head which seemed to beat and beat. Six ... Before he could stop himself, he stared incredulously at Annie.

Catching his expression, her smile died, she gave a questioning frown, she shook her head as if she were having trouble believing what she was reading in his face. Finally, she gave a furious gasp. 'My God! You don't change, do you, Billy? Your blooming arrogance. How dare you even think what you're thinking? How *dare* you!'

Billy made a gesture of retreat.

'This is my daughter, the daughter of my marriage – *right*? My God, Billy, you are the absolute limit!'

'No offence,' he said, and tried a sheepish smile.

But she was still a long way from calming down. 'Arrogant doesn't begin to describe you, Billy Greer ... Doesn't even *start*!' Trembling with undischarged fury, she swung away to deal with the child, shooing her upstairs, issuing instructions about bedtime.

When she returned, her face was cold and expressionless; only her eyes held a wealth of anger.

'I wasn't thinking straight,' he said. 'Sorry.'

She shook her head wordlessly.

'I've never been any good at . . .' But it struck him that an inability to judge children's ages might not count for much on the charge of arrogance, rather the opposite in fact, so he shut his mouth and allowed the sound of the motorbike to distract him. The howl was much closer now, and approaching fast. But something about the engine note wasn't right. It was pitched too high and racing even higher, as though the rider were still accelerating.

Billy frowned his concern to Annie, and received an anxious gaze.

He stepped back from the porch and saw beyond the corner

of the cottage a flickering shaft of yellow light piercing the darkness and dancing over the wall of the churchyard, which lay dead ahead on the turn of the right-angled bend. And still the engine was hammering . . .

Suddenly the engine note fell right away and for an instant Billy thought the rider might have throttled back just in time. But then the beam of light sharpened and the bike shot into view, going like stink, and Billy knew the rider hadn't a chance. Too late the headlamp jerked sharply towards the cottage as the rider attempted to over-steer his way out of trouble. But the trajectory, the angle of the machine, above all the crazy speed were carrying the machine relentlessly towards the churchyard wall. In the halo of light around the headlamp Billy glimpsed the contortions of the rider as he flung his weight against the bike's momentum. For a split second it looked as though there might be a miracle, that he might manage to control the skid after all, but then with a graunch of tyres and a scream of brakes, the bike hit the wall sideways on, tyres first, bodywork next, with a dull smack.

In the startled silence that followed, Billy gripped Annie's arm protectively and said, 'Stay here!' before sprinting across the road and half vaulting, half rolling over the churchyard wall. A series of gasps and retches quickly led him to the rider, lying on top of a grassy grave, clutching his stomach and fighting for breath.

Billy dropped down at the man's side. 'Hello there, chum. How're you doing?'

The rider coughed and retched, and sucked in his first proper breath.

'You hurt?'

Through the rasps came a snort or an exclamation.

Billy pushed up the rider's goggles and unfastened the strap of his leather helmet. The rider put a hand to the helmet as if to pull it off, only for his arm to fall heavily when the effort proved too great.

'Take your time. Get your breath.' There was no moon, it

was too dark to make out the man's features, but he seemed tall and gangling.

'Christ . . .' came a hoarse voice. 'Who put . . . that bloody wall . . . there?'

Billy sat back on one heel. 'Not Christ, but you're getting close.'

'So I'm . . . where I think . . . I am?'

'Keeping the dead company all right.'

'A bit sooner . . . than planned . . .'

'Well, you're not dead yet.'

A grunt that was almost a laugh. 'Life's . . . full of . . . surprises . . .'

Annie came hurrying from the direction of the gate. 'Is he all right?'

'Just winded, looks like.'

Annie crouched down beside the rider and asked what, if anything, was hurting. The figure breathed, 'I'm all right. Really.' But Annie pressed a hand to his chest and stomach and ordered him to move each limb in turn before she'd let him sit up. Billy looped the rider's arm around his shoulders and hauled him to his feet. As the other man's head drew level, Billy caught a whiff of alcohol, followed at the next breath by a stronger blast. No wonder the lunatic hadn't broken anything, Billy thought; he probably thought he was flying.

Billy helped him through the graveyard. At the gate the rider said, 'Think I'm all right now, thanks, old chap,' and disengaging his arm limped into the lane under his own steam.

Annie went attentively to his side. She must have been supporting his arm because the rider appeared to lean slightly against her as they started up the lane. Billy went on ahead, intending to look at the motorbike, until he heard Annie laughing softly. Something about the sound made him stop and look back. In the feeble light from the cottage porch he could make out the two figures bending towards each other. It seemed to Billy that the rider's voice, already low, fell still lower as they drew closer. Finally Billy caught a few words: '. . . into a strange country . . .' before Annie replied with another soft laugh, 'Not so strange . . . unless you mean . . .' He missed the rest as her voice also dropped away. Then the rider was speaking in a whisper so flagrantly low, so obviously intended to exclude him, that Billy felt like throwing him back over the churchyard wall.

They fell silent as Billy joined them until, reaching the bend in the churchyard wall, Annie said, 'They've found your bike.'

It was a couple of men from the pub. They had righted the motorbike – it was a Norton 500 cc, Billy noted – and were waiting to offer opinions on the damage. The rider listened to what they had to say before thanking them with elaborate politeness and mounting the machine. As he climbed on, his face became visible in the thin light from the cottage, but it wasn't one Billy recognised.

Annie was saying anxiously, 'You're not thinking of driving, are you?'

He smiled at her. 'Just trying the engine.'

He kicked down on the pedal, and again, until at the third attempt the engine gave an answering roar. He revved it for a few moments before switching it off again. Directing a slow grin at Annie, he lifted an upturned hand, like a gambler who has pulled off a win against the odds.

The men from the pub were wandering off, chuckling. 'You should count your lucky stars that wall weren't no higher,' one of them called.

'And no harder, neither.'

'Thanks for your help,' the rider said, and fastened the strap of his helmet.

Annie said, 'I really do think you should stop for a cup of tea before you go. You might be suffering from shock.'

'You're very kind,' he said, 'but I'm late, you see.'

This time his smile had a blatantly forlorn quality that made Billy's hackles rise. It was the sort of look that made stupid women go soft around the knees and grown men want to vomit. The accent was another source of suspicion. It wasn't quite officer material, and it wasn't quite other ranks either. Billy thought: You're a fake.

'I really don't think we should let you drive,' Annie said, throwing a look at Billy for support and getting none.

'It's his funeral,' said Billy.

The rider gave Annie a last smile before pulling down his goggles. He kicked the bike into life again, and with a careless wave sped off into the darkness.

Billy snorted under his breath, 'Stupid bugger.'

Annie said, 'He's in no state to ride that thing.'

'You can say that again.'

Annie pulled her arms close to her body and shivered.

'You're cold. Here—' As he moved to take off his jacket, she took a deliberate step away from him.

'I'm all right,' she said

'You're shivering.'

'I must get back.' She walked rapidly towards the cottage.

With a shrug, Billy followed her. 'You know that loon then, do you?'

She threw him a puzzled look. ''Course. It was Lyndon Hanley.'

'Hanley?' At first Billy could only remember the father, a dairy farmer with a big place along the ridge. The son took a little longer, but finally and somewhat incredulously Billy connected the motorbike rider with a pasty-faced smart alec who had gone away to boarding school and rarely been glimpsed by the common herd. '*Lyndon*,' he scoffed. 'What sort of a name is that?'

Reaching the cottage, Annie went inside to call to the child before coming back to close the door. 'Good night, Billy.'

He put a hand on the jamb. 'Fancy a walk tomorrow?'

She shook her head instantly. 'Sorry.'

'Not even five minutes?'

'We're busy.'

'What, all day?'

A small frown ruffled the smoothness of her forehead. 'Well – yes.'

'Is it what I said just now? I told you – I didn't mean it. I wasn't thinking.'

She made an effort of memory. 'Oh, *that*. No, no – we're just busy.'

She wasn't going to give an inch then. Well, he thought with sudden heat, we'll soon see about that.

He gave a wide shrug, a sudden smile. 'Just wanted to catch up. Hear what you'd been doing.'

'Another time perhaps.'

'Yes? I'll drop by, then, shall I? When I'm next passing.'

It might have been his imagination but her expression seemed to soften a little in the moment before she closed the door.

Chapter Five

———

IT WAS seven by the time Bennett finished his last call and headed home. As he drove in through the gates, the headlamps briefly illuminated Marjorie drawing the curtains at an upstairs window. She gave him a bright wave and he parked with a sense of good fortune, thinking of the sherry they would enjoy by the fire and the book on the ancient lake villages of Somerset which he was looking forward to reading after dinner. They had come to the village from Bristol four months after the outbreak of war when it became clear that, instead of working towards retirement, Bennett would have to remain in harness for the duration. He had taken over the adjoining practices of two doctors who had volunteered for the army, an option closed to him by dint of age and invalidity. A gas attack on the Somme had left him with recurrent bronchitis and chronic asthma. The Levels were not perhaps the best place for a man with weak lungs, but Bennett had never been prepared to make concessions to his debility. He liked the place, he was intrigued by its history, and though the house was like an ice-box in winter and prone to mysterious attacks of damp in summer, he and Marjorie had fallen for the view across Aller Moor towards the Polden Hills.

'You haven't forgotten that we're going to the Hanleys,' Marjorie said as they kissed.

He had of course forgotten; he always did. 'No hope of escape?'

'None. Their son's just home from the war.'

'Ah yes. What's his name again?'

'Lyndon. He won the Military Cross.'

They had a sherry and a quick supper of soup and cheese before setting off. Bennett was called out to emergencies often enough to be resigned to the loss of his leisurely dinner, but he couldn't help feeling a small pang at having to postpone the joys of his fireside and the long-anticipated book for a gathering from which they would be unable to escape for at least two hours.

They walked to save petrol, wearing galoshes against the mud. Gazing at the stars, Bennett wondered why a farming couple, albeit a prosperous one, should have given their son such an unlikely name as Lyndon. He doubted the idea had come from the wife, a quiet inoffensive creature by the name of – he had to prod his memory – *Janet*. More likely, it had come from the husband, Arthur Hanley, a successful farmer and leader of the local community. Bennett tried not to listen too closely to gossip, yet in such a small place it was impossible to ignore it altogether, and he had heard more than once that Hanley's influence stretched beyond the chairmanship of the local drainage board to the county council itself, and that this influence was not unconnected to mysterious food parcels containing beef, cheese and cider which the county councillors were said to receive on a regular basis. Bennett had always put such rumours down to mischief-making, not only because a man in Hanley's position was bound to attract gossip, but because he found it impossible to believe that influence could be bought by such means.

Janet Hanley opened the door. She was a small shapeless woman with wire-rimmed spectacles, short greying hair held back by a grip, and timid eyes. Barely responding to Marjorie's bright remarks about the weather, she waited anxiously to take their coats and hang them on a peg. She fretted over the galoshes too, placing them on the floor directly beneath the coats, toes pointed neatly to the skirting.

They entered a plain room with lumpy Edwardian furniture, ageing wallpaper and thin rugs over a parquet floor. There

were nine or ten other guests, the men standing in front of the
fire, the women seated around the bay window. There was no
sign of the son.

Arthur Hanley stepped forward. 'Welcome, Doctor. Mrs
Bennett,' he said formally. 'Good of you to come. And what
will you have to drink?'

Bennett's gaze had already fixed on the bottle of Teacher's
standing between the sherry and the Madeira. Scotch was still
a sufficiently rare commodity for him to ask, 'If you can spare
it?'

'Of course.'

Hanley poured a measure that was neither mean nor over-
generous, and it occurred to Bennett that he was someone who
gauged all his actions, large and small, with care.

Marjorie took a sherry and, exchanging a brief supportive
glance with Bennett, moved off towards the other women.

'Good health, Doctor.' Hanley raised his glass. He was a
man in his mid-fifties with a low belly and a pinched face over
hunched shoulders. He wore the tweed suit, checked shirt and
knitted waistcoat of the working farmer, an image reinforced
by his distinctive Somerset burr. He owned the largest dairy
farm in the immediate area, with two hundred acres on the
ridge and another fifty on West Sedgemoor, yet his appearance,
like that of his home, proclaimed a deliberate simplicity and
lack of pretension. He was registered as a patient of Bennett's
but had yet to call on his services. In the normal course of
events Bennett saw him once a week at church, where Hanley,
as churchwarden, read the first lesson in a rich baritone.

'I gather your son has come back with an MC,' Bennett
said. 'You must be very proud.'

Hanley inclined his head modestly.

'Has he been home long?'

'Just a week.'

For once Bennett's memory didn't let him down. 'The East,
wasn't it?'

'Burma.'

'And he got through in good shape?'

'Lyndon's fit as a flea. Always has been,' Hanley declared robustly, with a glance towards the door. 'He'll be here shortly. Been putting his new motorbike through its paces.'

'I say! Lucky chap.'

'Oh, it's not *brand new*,' Hanley corrected him, as though such expenditure in a time of austerity would have been the height of indelicacy. 'I picked it up from an American serviceman in Taunton.'

'Still. A fine present.'

'A small token to mark his homecoming.'

A motorbike was hardly a small token, and Bennett couldn't help thinking that, for all Hanley's show of plain living, he liked people to know he had the means to splash out when he chose to.

'Does Lyndon have any plans yet? Will he be joining you in the dairy business?'

Hanley's slow gaze sharpened. 'It would be a bit of a waste of his education.'

'Ah, yes,' Bennett murmured absent-mindedly. 'Which university was it?'

'Bristol. A first in history.'

'Goodness,' Bennett said admiringly. 'Well, he can certainly pick and choose with a qualification like that. Is he thinking of a profession?'

But Hanley's eyes were back on the door. He said distractedly, 'Come and meet the others.'

Bennett knew two of the men standing by the fire. One was a patient, a retired solicitor, the other a young farmer he'd met somewhere locally. The third, a fortyish man with horn-rimmed spectacles, was introduced to him as John Creasy. From Hanley's manner it seemed that Creasy was a person of some importance, though Bennett didn't grasp in what field. The young farmer was talking loudly about Somerset's performance in the first cricket season since the war. It wasn't until the conversation turned to local matters that Bennett gathered Creasy was a drainage expert.

'Not planning to drain us dry, I trust?' Bennett remarked.

'He doesn't do the *planning*,' Hanley interjected in a firm voice. 'The Drainage Board does the planning.'

'Yes, I—'

'He's an engineer. A feasibility man.'

'Of course. I was just wondering what was possible nowadays from a technical point of view, that was all. I'd certainly miss the floods.'

Hanley exchanged a look with Creasy. 'There you are, John. Got to allow for those that like the water.'

'From our house it's like being on a ship at sea,' Bennett said. 'You feel you're on a voyage without the inconvenience of leaving home.'

Hanley said, 'A rather fanciful view for a scientific man, if I may say so, Doctor. I don't think there's a modern farmer who'd give you tuppence for the appearance of the floods, not when it's his fields that's under water late into the spring.'

'I thought the water had its uses.'

'What, as a fertiliser? You've been listening to the old boys again, Doctor. No, properly drained, with the application of modern chemicals, the land would be twice as productive. Two crops a year. Sheep grazing all winter.'

'Ah. Put like that . . .' murmured Bennett, in no mood for such a dispiriting conversation.

'But we're nowhere near that yet. Are we, John? Too much geography against us, too much rainfall. So I wouldn't fret, Doctor – you'll be at sea for a long while yet.'

The young farmer echoed, with a belly laugh, 'A long while yet.'

Hanley's gaze swung inexorably to the door once again. 'Now where's Lyndon?' he muttered under his breath, and it seemed to Bennett that his mood of anticipation had given way to quiet fury. Small spasms pulled at his mouth, making a bow of his lower lip that rose and fell, flexed and straightened. It was a tic Bennett had noticed before, when Hanley stood at the lectern locating his place for the first lesson.

Looking for something to say, Bennett remarked, 'Demob seems to be speeding up at last. I hear that Mrs Gant's son is home. And the Shepton boys.'

'Mmm? Yes . . . But they've got it the wrong way round, if you ask me.'

'Oh?'

'The authorities – organising demob on the "First in, first out" principle. Got their priorities topsy-turvy. They should have released the men who were prepared to take the vital jobs first, the ones prepared to knuckle down and get the country back on its feet. The sort we're getting now don't want to get their hands dirty. The Gant boy – he used to help us out. But now he's turning his nose up at the chance of dairyman. Says he wants to work for himself. Well, he's in for a rude awakening, I can tell you. They all are.'

'War changes men's aspirations, I suppose.'

'I'd say it muddles their thinking. You can dress it up any way you like, but at the end of the day a man's only worth what the market will pay. And the market's no different now to what it was before the war. You can't suddenly go paying men higher wages if the yield's not there. These boys – they don't know a good thing when they see it. A steady job, a roof over their heads – what more do they want?'

What they wanted, Bennett suspected, was to receive more than the minimum wage and a tied cottage from which they could be evicted at a month's notice, but he thought it unwise to mention this.

'Wouldn't be so bad if they'd send us more POWs,' Hanley sighed. 'Not good for much, the Germans, but at least they keep the rhynes open. The Eyeties were far better of course, but we don't get them any more.'

'Haven't most of them been repatriated?'

But Hanley's attention had wandered again. His eyes flicked darkly over Bennett's shoulder and around the room.

From the window a ripple of laughter rose up. Picking out Marjorie's distinctive chuckle, Bennett turned and watched her for a moment, mildly surprised even after all these years that the fine-looking woman with the pretty smile should be his wife.

Turning back to Hanley, he said, 'If you're short of men, have you thought of employing some Poles from the new camp?'

Hanley muttered, 'Not likely.'

'Why not?'

'Wouldn't work.'

'But many come from farming backgrounds.'

'That's as may be.'

'They're very quick. Very hard working.'

'That's not the point, is it?'

Bennett might have left it there, but something in Hanley's tone stirred his equable nature towards protest. He asked mildly, 'But what would be the problem?'

Breaking free of his thoughts, Hanley brought his full attention to bear. 'Listen, Doctor, I've nothing against them personally, nothing at all, but they don't belong here, and it's no good encouraging them to stay. They need to go back to where they came from.'

'But most of them can't go back.'

'Can't or won't? The trouble is there's no incentive for them to leave, is there? Not when they're getting everything given to them on a plate. Housing, food, you name it. A hundred and twenty *thousand* of them. And that's not counting the wives and children who'll be following them in droves. This is a small country. We don't have room for those sorts of numbers. And we don't have the means to feed them either, not when the country's on its knees, not when our own people aren't getting enough to eat – women and children, men back from the war, going hungry. No – when times are hard, charity starts at home.'

'But the Poles are keen to take on even the roughest work. They'll do anything—'

'And this resettlement camp at Middlezoy,' Hanley hammered on regardless. 'I don't know what the government's thinking of, dumping five hundred of these folk in a rural community like ours, miles from anywhere. What're they going to do all day? How are they going to keep themselves occupied? Well, we already know, don't we? They'll end up roaming the countryside, causing all kinds of trouble.'

'But they're the most delightful people.'

Hanley gave an ugly laugh. 'That's not what I've heard.'

'Well, I can only say—'

'Black marketeers.' Hanley slapped the accusation down like a winning card.

'I only remember one case involving some Poles,' Bennett said patiently. 'About three months ago. Is that the one you mean? I don't believe I've read of any cases since.'

'But for every one that gets caught, there's plenty more that gets away with it, isn't there?' Hanley insisted stubbornly.

'I can only say that my own opinion of the Poles has been entirely favourable. I feel sure they'll fit in very well here.'

Sipping his whisky, Hanley took a hard appraising look at Bennett over the rim of his glass, as if to make out whether the doctor had been a dangerous unconfessed liberal all this time, or was temporarily misguided. 'Perhaps you've been mixing with a rather superior class of Pole, Doctor. Medical men? Pilots from the airfield?'

'I think I've met a pretty wide spectrum.'

Hanley's eyebrows rose in an elaborate show of scepticism. 'Well, according to what I've heard, there's no holding them once they get a few drinks down their gullets. Brawling. Shouting and singing in the streets. Keeping honest folk awake at night.'

Bennett thought it rich to hear drinking singled out for

censure by a resident of Somerset, a county where in the not-so-distant past farm workers had been part-paid in cider, and where even now it wasn't uncommon to see a supine figure sleeping it off under the trees. But he suspected the criticism was aimed less at the drinking itself than the exhilarating effect it had on the already animated Poles.

'Breaking windows,' Hanley added to his list of charges. 'Trampling gardens. Not to mention the way they chase after anything in a skirt, always leading young girls up the garden path. They're real devils for that – everyone says so.' His eyes glittered sharply.

'The Poles certainly aren't faint-hearted where love is concerned,' Bennett said. 'But to suggest they're dishonourable is completely wide of the mark. Most are very correct in such matters. They're strict Catholics.'

'Is that so? I always thought Catholics got to wriggle out of their misdeeds. One visit to the confessional and they start again with a clean slate.'

When Bennett failed to reply, Hanley put on a sudden mechanical smile, as if to correct a faulty mood, and said, 'But maybe I'll be proved wrong.' His gaze, already travelling back towards the door, was diverted by the young woman arriving at Bennett's side. 'Ah, Stella,' he murmured with a marked lack of interest. 'You know my niece, do you, Doctor?'

'Indeed I do. How are you, Stella?'

The fresh young face turned to Bennett and gave him a glorious smile. 'Very fine, thank you, Doctor.' To Arthur Hanley she said, 'Lyndon won't be long, Uncle. He's just having a wash.'

Hanley's mouth twitched and twitched. 'He's back, is he?'

'Yes.'

'You met at the door?'

'No . . . In fact he gave me a lift from home. It's a wonderful bike, Uncle. He really loves it.'

Hanley stared at her soundlessly. When he finally spoke, his voice seemed to come out of the ground. 'What, he just dropped by, did he?'

'On his way back, yes.' Then, as if to admit to the whole truth without delay, she added, 'He took me for a quick spin round the village.'

Hanley's gaze grew opaque, the mosaic of broken veins high on his cheeks flared with colour, and the air became heavy with suppressed anger.

'So, you're all related,' Bennett said brightly. 'I'd forgotten.'

It was a moment before Stella showed her usual spark. 'And how long have you been living here, Doctor?'

'Not long enough, apparently.'

'If you don't remember who's related to who in this place, you can get into serious trouble.'

Bennett laughed. He had always liked Stella. She was a teacher at the village school. He had got to know her during the summer when they had whiled away many an afternoon in front of the cricket pavilion. Stella's father batted at number eight, Bennett at eleven, a position he'd accepted on the understanding that he would never be called upon to defend a wicket. Stella was a good-natured girl, warmhearted, straightforward and outgoing. Despite the age difference, Bennett thought of her as a friend. She was one of the few women he felt he could tease without the slightest risk of being misunderstood. With her open face, broad pink cheeks, blue eyes and coppery hair, she had a beguiling freshness. Tonight her hair was tangled from the wind and her outfit plain, yet he had never seen her looking so pretty, and on a sudden whim he told her so.

She flushed a little. 'Oh, it's just the cold, I expect.'

'No, no. You look radiant.'

She shot her uncle a quick glance then, staring meaningfully at Bennett, did something odd with her eyes. He gazed at her questioningly, but she only repeated the strange eye movements. It wasn't until he felt a tug at his sleeve that he realised she was trying to draw him away.

'Ah,' he said, scouring his mind for a pretext. 'Of course . . . the school . . .'

His little ruse was unnecessary. With a frown at Stella, Hanley was already swinging away, heading back to the group at the fireplace.

'It's Lyndon,' Stella breathed as soon as her uncle was out of earshot. 'He went and fell off his bike and I think he might have hurt himself. Would you have a quick look at him, please, Doctor?'

With a last glance over her shoulder, she led the way out of the room and across the hall to the kitchen, where a young man sat lounging across the table, one hand propping his head, the other holding a cigarette between thumb and forefinger, navvy-style. Seeing Bennett, the young man started to unravel his limbs and clamber to his feet, but Bennett waved him down.

'You took a bit of a tumble, I gather.'

Lyndon settled his angular frame back into the chair, and Bennett saw a sharply sculpted face with a long nose, deep-set eyes, and dark hair flopping untidily over a high forehead.

'I'm fine.'

Stella said, 'He's not fine at all, Doctor. He's got a bump the size of an egg on his head and a twisted knee.'

Lyndon's mouth turned down in an amused way, as though he found her concern endearing but misplaced.

He made no objection when Bennett asked, 'May I?' and examined the lump on his head.

'Headache?'

'Nothing I don't deserve.'

'Oh?'

'I went over a wall and hit a . . . stone slab.' He laughed silently and took another drag on his cigarette.

'Look directly at me, please.'

The dark eyes that lifted to his were glazed and slow moving.

'Is your vision fuzzy at all?'

An infinitesimal shake of the head.

'Feeling sick?'

'No.'

'Dizzy?'

'No.'

Bennett pulled up a chair and sat down. 'Well, there are no obvious signs of concussion, but if you experience any sickness or dizziness in the next twelve hours you should let me know.'

Lyndon humoured him with a mild, 'Of course.'

'Could I look at the knee?'

Lyndon tilted his head back until he could see Stella, who was standing directly behind him. 'Stella Maris?'

'Yes, Lyndon.'

'Be a good girl and get me a whisky, would you?'

'Well, I . . . Doctor?'

'I wouldn't advise it,' Bennett said.

For the first time Lyndon's eyes came alive. 'That's a bit steep, Doctor,' he protested lightly. 'It's not every night a chap finds himself laid out in a graveyard.'

'Alcohol isn't recommended with concussion.'

'But I don't have concussion,' Lyndon argued reasonably with a quick disarming smile. 'You've just said so. And I'd feel a hell of a lot braver about going next door if I had a quick nip.'

Bennett thought: I must be losing my touch, I almost missed it. He's well away already.

Bennett nodded to Stella. 'Just a small one.'

'Thanks, Doc.'

'Now if you'd show me the knee.'

It was swollen and bruised, but nothing appeared to be cracked, broken or torn. 'The swelling should go down in a day or two,' Bennett told him. 'How's the bike?'

'Mmm?' Lyndon was lighting another cigarette, drawing the smoke up over his lip into his nostrils. 'Oh, a dent, that's all.'

'What make is it?'

'Umm . . . a Norton.'

'The 500 cc with the overhead cam?'

But it was clear that Lyndon had no interest in machinery. His eyes sped to the door as Stella reappeared with his drink. 'Thanks, Stella Maris,' he murmured softly.

The whisky was neither small nor diluted, and Bennett realised with a touch of concern that Stella seemed to be unaware of how much Lyndon had already had to drink.

'Is he all right?' Stella asked Bennett.

'Looks like it.'

'Well, there's a mercy!' Sitting down, she gazed happily at Lyndon as he took a gulp of his whisky. She said to Bennett, 'The wild boy went all the way to Bristol and back this afternoon.'

'That's a fair run.'

'And at record speed!' Stella glared at Lyndon in mock disapproval, her eyes dancing. 'We're going to Lyme on Sunday. I'm *told* it'll only take half an hour. I'm *told* I'll have to hang on for dear life. But we'll see about that!'

Bennett scratched the side of his head like a schoolboy summoning his facts. 'Now, let me see – I must have got *this* right at least – you two are cousins.'

'Top of the form!' Stella's face was a mirror for her emotions, and as she threw a shy grin at Lyndon there was no mistaking the strong affection there.

Lyndon took another sip of his drink and, having put it down on the table, picked it straight up again and knocked the rest back in one gulp. 'Dutch courage . . .' he murmured.

'Poor boy,' Stella commiserated, reflecting his mood instantly. 'All these people . . .' She offered this thought to Bennett with a rueful glance. 'It's a bit hard . . . But, Lyndon dear, best to get it over and done with . . .'

'Do I really have to go and change?' he asked gloomily.

She shook her head. 'Too late now. Best go in as you are.'

They all stood up, Lyndon slowly. He was taller than he'd first appeared, and thinner, with wide angular shoulders that seemed to cut into his sweater like wire.

'What am I supposed to talk about?' he asked Stella.

She shrugged helplessly.

He tilted his head to one side as if to beg for a proper answer.

'Well, I . . .' She turned to Bennett in appeal.

'I'm not sure I'm the best person to ask,' he said. 'But rationing's a safe bet, I suppose. And the petrol shortage.'

'Petrol,' Lyndon repeated bleakly.

Scurrying footsteps sounded in the hall. They looked towards the door as Janet Hanley appeared. 'Lyndon, *there* you are!' Her appalled gaze took in the lack of movement or urgency, the cigarette, the empty glass. 'Do hurry, please!' she cried in a voice that shook with agitation. 'Your father's getting so anxious. *Please.*'

'Yes, Mum.'

'You know he can't bear—' Stalling wordlessly, she pushed her hands down at her sides.

'Yes. Sorry.' Lyndon walked to the door and reached out as if to touch his mother's arm, but with a darting bird-like movement she moved rapidly away.

Bennett followed Stella across the hall.

'Oh dear . . .' she murmured under her breath. 'All my fault.'

By the time they entered the living room Lyndon was at the drinks tray, pouring a fresh glass.

Arthur Hanley's voice rose from the other side of the room. 'Lyndon!' It was like a call to arms. 'There you are! Come and meet everyone.'

Lyndon replaced the cap on the whisky bottle and screwed it up tight. In the moment before he swung round to confront the room Bennett saw on his unguarded face an expression of misery.

'He didn't want any fuss,' Stella remarked as they watched him join his father. 'He didn't want a gathering.'

'It was meant well, I'm sure.'

'But he doesn't know half these people. I can't imagine why Uncle asked them. Who's the grey-haired man? And the odd-looking one in glasses?'

'The one in glasses is called Creasy. He's some sort of drainage expert. And the grey-haired man's a retired solicitor from North Curry.'

Stella sighed, 'Oh dear – *useful* people. It won't work. Lyndon will just run a mile.'

Watching Lyndon standing at his father's side, mouth set, eyes hooded, it seemed to Bennett that he had already put himself at a considerable distance.

'What's Lyndon going to do now he's home? Does he know?'

'No idea at all.'

'Well, there's plenty of time.'

A short hesitation before she said, 'He seems very restless.'

'He wouldn't be the first. I couldn't settle at all when I left the army.'

Stella tore her eyes away from Lyndon. 'But weren't you already a doctor then?'

'I was. But I wasn't at all sure what sort of a doctor I wanted to be. I'd always intended to specialise, but when I resigned my commission, well, my health was ropy, our first child was on the way and there weren't any jobs, not for men with dicky lungs just back from the war at any rate. General practice was the only option.'

'What had you hoped to specialise in?'

'When I started out, surgery. But during the Great War I became more interested in lung injuries. Not just because I had duff lungs myself, though that was a part of it of course, but because the whole thing was so badly handled then. Men with burnt lungs, with asthma and chronic bronchitis and all the other things you get from gas damage, were more or less told to go away and get on with it. Not regarded as curable, you see. It was a bad state of affairs, and I wanted to do something about it. When I got home and realised I had very little chance of specialising – well, I got very down. Then Marjorie, bless her, insisted on taking me away on holiday. Bundled me onto a train to Scotland. We hadn't much money so we stayed in this little place in the Highlands and just walked and sat by the fire and talked. By the time we got back, the fog had cleared. I realised there was nothing to stop me from starting a local clinic, developing treatments, corresponding with like-minded specialists. Changing things from below, if you like. And that's what I did. Not huge changes, of course. Not anything that was publishable. But enough, you know. Enough.'

Stella looked back at the men. 'I wish Lyndon could find something like that, something that really interested him. All he's sure about is what he *doesn't* want to do.'

'Well, that's not a bad start.'

'Trouble is, it seems to be everything.'

'Ah.'

A boom of laughter rose from the fireplace. In the ring of jovial, swaying figures Lyndon was still and silent.

Bennett said, 'Why don't you take him away for a bit, Stella?'

She looked up, startled. 'What?'

'Take him right away. It's friends he needs at a time like this, and I suspect he has a fine friend in you.'

She blushed furiously. 'Oh, I don't know . . . I mean . . .'

'Why not?'

'Well, I . . . couldn't leave my work, not in term-time.'

'Christmas then?'

'But . . .' She made a face that implied insuperable difficulties.

'You can't mean that people would notice you were unchaperoned?' he said with heavy irony. 'Well, what about staying in a youth hostel? Or with family friends?'

'I don't know . . . I . . .' But for all Stella's show of indecision the idea clearly excited her. 'Yes,' she said at last, with a small irrepressible laugh. 'Why not?'

'And Lyme tomorrow – take my advice,' said Bennett. 'Make a good long day of it.'

It rained steadily for the next three days then froze hard for two nights running. The succession of wet and cold seemed to unleash the winter's quota of contagious diseases more or less simultaneously. First, two children and three elderly patients came down with high fever, headache, and aching limbs, most probably the symptoms of influenza, though in the children's case Bennett couldn't rule out the possibility of poliomyelitis. A day later, three small children from a single family developed whooping cough. Then, barely two days after that, a child in a nearby village presented with diphtheria. Bennett treated her with penicillin, but the disease was advanced, the child weak, and he didn't hold out much hope. For the patients with flu and whooping cough penicillin could do nothing, and symptomatic relief, quarantine, and strict antisepsis were the order of the day, though as ever these measures offered little guarantee of disease containment or individual outcome. Within two days the child with diphtheria died, followed soon after by two of the elderly influenza patients. At the beginning of the second week three new cases of diphtheria cropped up in the same village, and the whooping cough took off like wildfire, with two to three cases notified each morning. Bennett's days and nights blended into a round of house calls and snatched sleep. Then, just as he began to wonder if the epidemics would ever burn themselves out, two of the children with diphtheria whose lives had been hanging in the balance began to rally, three days went by with no new cases and, apart from the sudden loss of a baby to whooping cough, the worst appeared to be over.

The public health boffins liked to advance a link between high rates of morbidity and poor housing, but here on the Levels it seemed to Bennett that the association was far from proven. Towards the end of the emergency he was called to an old boy of ninety-six who lived in a house under the banks of the River Tone. The place had been flooded so often that a succession of tidal marks embellished the whitewash in ripples of frosted bronze that stretched four feet above the floorboards. Even now, at the end of what might be termed the dry season, the damp seemed to be trapped in the very fabric of the building, as though the river, running close to the back of the house behind tall banks that rose almost to the height of the upper windows, was secretly leaching water into the foundations and up through the brickwork. Yet, apart from a touch of bronchitis, the old boy was amazingly fit, and boasted that he hadn't had a day's illness since catching the influenza in the epidemic of 1918. He lived on a diet of smoked eels, Spam, and vegetables which he grew in the narrow strip of earth between his back door and the slope of the riverbank. He had been born and lived all his life in the house; 'And I shall hop the twig here right enough too!' By contrast, the baby who'd died of whooping cough had lived above the reach of the water in a stone-built house, which though cold was free from damp. Seeing the pallor, lassitude and general sickliness of the surviving children it seemed to Bennett that their susceptibility to disease owed less to their housing than an inadequate diet and the heavy smoking of the parents. But while the parents accepted his recommendation to feed the children chicken broth and fresh fruit, the idea of cutting down on an innocent pleasure like smoking met with stubborn resentment. They did not pay him good money to be preached denial.

While the epidemics ran their course he asked a colleague to stand in for him at the convalescent home. Quite apart from not having the time to go, he was in dread of carrying infectious diseases to men not yet restored to fitness. When he finally judged it safe to resume his Wednesday clinic, it was to find a small package waiting for him in the administrator's office. Inside was the book he had lent Wladyslaw, with a note that read: *Dear Dr Bennett, My request to stay near here is lost, or perhaps forgotten, and now I am sent to join my brigade in Yorkshire. When I arrive there I will request return transfer to*

Somerset again. Forgive me, please, if I ask one more favour. I will be very grateful if you ask administration in Middlezoy Camp to explain I want to come. I would like this farm job still. Until then, I thank you for your great help and friendship, and for this book, which I return with this letter. Wladyslaw

It was two days before Bennett found time to go to Middlezoy. The Polish resettlement camp was spread over three sites just outside the village in overflow barracks which had been thrown up hurriedly in 1944 to house D-Day paratroops leaving from the airfield at Westonzoyland, and abandoned shortly afterwards. Squads of Polish soldiers were working their way through the sites, repairing and refurbishing the bare metal Nissen huts and prefabricated concrete blockhouses. As each grid was completed a batch of new arrivals was installed, and perhaps a quarter of the camp was now occupied. He saw women for the first time, and men in air force uniforms, and heard what he took to be Polish music coming from a wireless.

Bennett was directed to a British liaison officer named Robertson. He was a Scot of about thirty-five, with thick black eyebrows, a shock of white hair, and an air of mild harassment. Armed with a telephone and a battered wooden desk, he had set up an office in the concrete administration block.

When Bennett outlined Wladyslaw's situation, Robertson said immediately, 'I'll gladly make a request. But I can't promise anything. Transfers are strictly an internal matter for the Poles.'

'What are the criteria for a move? Do you know?'

'I'd only be guessing.'

'Is there anyone who might be able to tell me? A senior officer, perhaps?'

'You could try. But you'll have to brush up on your Polish. There's only one of them speaks proper English, and I have the devil of a job getting five minutes of his time.'

'That must make your job interesting.'

The black eyebrows lifted expressively. 'I've resorted to sign language, a great deal of smiling and back slapping, and the imbibing of strong drink at all hours of the day and night. Have to watch it though. They've taken to drinking this firewater from France. Lethal stuff. I don't ask how they get hold of it. It keeps them happy and that's the important thing.' He gave a grunt. 'Not so happy that they don't complain, of course.'

'What about?'

'The food, mainly.'

'Is it bad?'

'Appalling. But as I keep telling them there's bugger all I can do about it.'

'What about getting out and about? Do they go to the village?'

'Oh yes. Middlezoy. Westonzoyland. Even further away.'

'How are they getting on with the locals?'

'Mixed. It's fine when they go around in twos and threes, but they will keep going to the pubs in a huge gang. And you know how it is with Poles, two make a party and ten a riot.'

'There's been trouble?'

'Not in *that* sense, no. But not surprisingly the locals feel a bit crowded out. And not just in the pubs either. In the post offices as well.'

'Why on earth the post offices? Sending a few letters?'

'It's not the letters. It's the bloody great food parcels they send back to Poland every week. Full of tinned salmon and corned beef from the NAAFI – all the things that civilians haven't seen for years. I keep telling them not to make it too obvious, to go in ones and twos, and avoid making a queue – you can imagine the local post mistresses trying to weigh a series of parcels going to Poland. But they don't see the problem. They don't appreciate the need to tread carefully. Here, have you seen this?' He produced a newspaper from a drawer and handed it across. 'The cartoon.'

The newspaper was not one Bennett normally read, but he knew the cartoonist Low by repute. The cartoon depicted a British union official berating a Polish soldier on a horse. The union official was saying: – *and none o' that fancy cavalry riding, picking up other blokes' pay-packets with yer teeth.*

'There've been more in the same vein,' Robertson said.

'I've seen them.'

'Not that I agree with the British brass, advising the Poles to take the flashes off their uniforms before leaving camp – as if people are going to be fooled into thinking they're Tommies. My lot are too proud anyway, say they'd rather take it on the chin. And you know what? I don't blame them. Damned if I'd be prepared to sneak around as if I had something to be ashamed of. There's been a lot of nonsense about luxury living too – the camps being better than the Ritz. The War Office is talking about inviting newspaper correspondents into the camps to show them the truth. It won't be a moment too soon.'

He shut the newspaper back in the drawer with a bang, and stood up. 'This chap of yours' – he looked down at his notes – 'Malinowski. You say he's got a job waiting for him?'

'Yes, on a farm.'

'Have they obtained their Ministry of Labour clearance?'

'I'm not sure about that.'

'Well, they'll need it. Here . . .' He produced a form. 'Take a tip from me. Tell them to say they've been looking for someone to fill the job for months and had no luck at all.'

'But it's true.'

'No harm in spelling it out, though. Otherwise it won't get past the eagle eye of the trade unionists.' Catching Bennett's expression, Robertson said in a wry tone, 'Well, that's what we've come back to, isn't it? The socialists said it all when they came to power. We are the masters now. And they were damn right, weren't they?'

Bennett made a series of house calls to elderly and infirm patients he hadn't managed to see for some time and arrived home just after eight, praying there would be no urgent messages to take him out again that night. He couldn't remember when he had last felt so weary. His lungs were raw and wheezing, always a danger sign.

Marjorie greeted him with a smile and a shake of the head, which meant there were no urgent messages. It wasn't until she had led him into the sitting room and pressed a sherry into his hand that she added, 'But there's someone waiting to see you.'

He gave a faint sigh. 'I was so hoping . . .'

'It's Stella, your cricketing friend.'

'Goodness,' he said in quite another tone. 'Did she say what it was about?'

'No. But it's not urgent. She said she's more than happy to wait in the study.'

The aroma of roasting meat had met him in the hall, a smell he associated with Sunday lunches and family gatherings. Catching it again now, his stomach gave an audible grumble. 'We're not expecting people for dinner, are we?'

'No.'

'But it's a roast?'

'Lamb,' she said innocently. 'I thought we might have a bit of a treat.'

He threw her a look of mild rebuke. 'How did we come by this lamb, may I ask? It wasn't in settlement of a fee, by any chance?'

'Old Mr Pilbeam asked if you wouldn't mind. He said he couldn't manage cash at the moment.'

'Well, I don't suppose I have much choice, do I? But you know how uncomfortable I feel about accepting meat when everyone else is having to scrape by on their rations.'

'But there's no harm in a little barter, surely, darling? And it's not as if we were the only ones. In fact, we must be the last people who still worry about it.'

'I can't believe that.'

'Sometimes I think you walk around with your head in the clouds.'

'You make it sound as though everyone's doing it.'

'Well, I hate to shatter your illusions, darling, but they *are*. Only since the war, of course. It was different while we were still fighting. But now, well . . . people can't see the harm. And I have to say I rather agree.'

If the sherry had warmed Bennett's blood, it had also eroded his energy for argument. He said mildly, 'So we've joined the band of grey marketeers, have we? Spivs, or whatever they're called nowadays.'

'Spivs!' Marjorie cried with a splutter of delight. 'Oh, darling, what a wonderful thought!' Pretending to eye him in a new light, she shook her head, and kept shaking it until her laughter had subsided. 'And if it makes you feel any better, I've given our meat coupons to a family who really need them.'

He would have been very surprised if she had done anything else. They had married in 1916 after a three-month courtship, and spent most of the next eighteen months apart. When he finally returned from the war, in poor health and unable to work, it could have gone terribly wrong. Instead, it had got better and better, mainly because she was the most generous-spirited person he knew, and from witnessing people at every extreme of misery and joy he had learnt that in the currency of human relations generosity had the greatest value of all.

Marjorie took a step closer and examined his face. 'You're looking dog-tired. Shall I put Stella off till another day?'

'No. I'll see her now.'

'I'll put the dinner back in the oven then.'

The study must have been particularly cold because when Stella appeared she was still wearing her coat. 'I'm sorry to disturb you, Doctor,' she said, standing in the shadows by the door.

'Not at all, Stella. Come and sit by the fire. Come on! Can I take your coat?'

'Well, I . . .'

'No, perhaps not. It's not terribly warm in here either, is it? One tries not to be at the mercy of every scare, but with all this talk of a coal shortage we've been keeping the fires to a minimum. Would you like a sherry?'

'No, thank you.'

She sat down stiffly, her back straight, and hugged her arms to her waist.

'Would you like another coat to put round your shoulders?'

'No, I'm fine, than you.' She relaxed her arms self-consciously.

Bennett settled back in his seat. 'So, what can I do for you, Stella?'

She began hesitantly, 'Well . . . I know it's not strictly . . . But I thought that . . . I thought . . .' Then, with a gesture of bringing herself to the point, she said abruptly, 'It's about Lyndon.'

Bennett nodded.

'The thing is . . . well, he's not taking care of himself, for a start.'

'Ah.'

'Not eating properly. Keeping all hours. Drinking too much.'

Bennett prompted lightly: 'When you say too much . . .?'

'Oh, a lot too much.' She gave him an odd frown. 'But I thought you realised, that night at Uncle's house. He's been drinking heavily ever since he got back.'

With this statement it seemed to Bennett that the last of her youthful freshness had dropped away, that she had acquired all the weariness of experience.

'And always away on that motorbike,' she went on. 'For hours and hours. I don't know where – and I don't ask. I don't want him to feel I'm pestering him, not when he's being pestered on every side. Well, not *pestered* so much as . . . given no peace. Uncle's always on at him about this job he's found for him, and getting caught by the police –'

'The police? What for?'

'Having a tankful of petrol. He's already been stopped twice. They say they'll prosecute him next time for certain.'

Bennett had no idea how one went about getting illicit petrol and certainly wasn't about to ask.

Stella's eyes had strayed to the fire, but now they came back to Bennett's with an echo of their old spark. 'I think I might have that sherry after all, if you wouldn't mind.'

'Of course.' Bennett got rapidly to his feet. 'Dry or medium?'

She made an irresolute gesture.

'The medium's probably better.'

While Bennett poured the drink, Stella said in a bright brittle voice, 'Sometimes I wish the police would go ahead and take his licence away, just to stop him from killing himself. It's a wonder he hasn't done it already.' She took the sherry from Bennett with both hands. 'Thank you.' Sipping it, she blinked hard as if it were medicine, which for her it probably was just then. 'Sometimes he goes off late at night and doesn't come back till morning. I can hear the bike from our house – I can hear it even when he goes out of the village the other way – and I worry myself sick when I don't hear it come back again.' The next sip of sherry seemed to go down more easily than the first. 'Uncle jokes that Lyndon's making up for lost time – having a bit of fun, meeting up with friends. Getting back into the swing, he calls it. But it's not like that – Lyndon has no friends round here. It's more . . .' She paused while she tried to pin the thought down. 'It's more that he's frightened of ever stopping and having to face real life.'

Bennett had not credited her with such perception, and he felt the faint surprise one feels at seeing a new side to an old friend. 'What's this job your uncle's arranged?'

'Something at Barton's.'

'The auction people?'

'Yes. On the antiques side. Uncle thought it would tie in with Lyndon's degree. You know – history, dating things. In fact, Lyndon's quite interested in art and furniture and all that, but not on the commercial side. And, you see' – her voice dropped suddenly – 'he'd never want to settle round here. That's what Uncle can't understand. This place is too – *small* for Lyndon. Too set in its ways.'

'He still hasn't any idea what he wants to do?'

She put her glass down on the side table and leant forward.

'That's what I wanted to ask you about, Doctor,' she said. 'You see, he's talking about going back to the East. To Burma. But why on earth would he want to go back there? That's what I can't understand. Of all places.'

'Burma's meant to be a beautiful country.'

She looked at him in puzzlement, as if he had entirely missed the point. 'But the war,' she argued.

'What reason does Lyndon give?'

'He says he can't explain it. He says he doesn't really understand it himself. But I think he does, you see. I think something's troubling him from his time there, something bad, and he can't bring himself to talk about it.'

'I wouldn't be at all surprised. It was a horrible war out there, by all accounts.'

'But to go back – how is that going to help?'

'Only he can answer that.'

She gave a slow nod to show she was giving his views full weight. 'But he won't even discuss it, you see. He won't even talk about it.'

Bennett had the uncomfortable suspicion that he knew where the conversation was leading. 'There aren't many men who can, Stella.'

'Oh, but me and Lyndon – we could always tell each other everything. *Everything.* That was what brought us so close. We never had secrets. Never! And we always swore we never would. Whatever happened. All through our lives.'

The innocence and other-worldiness of the idea momentarily left Bennett at a loss.

'So, you see,' Stella rushed on, 'there can only be one reason for him not telling me. Because he doesn't want to burden me with it. Because he thinks it might upset me.'

Now Bennett was in no doubt as to what was coming. 'You might well be right,' he murmured.

Stella shifted to the very edge of her seat and, resting her forearms on her knees, pressed her palms together in entreaty. 'I was wondering if you would speak to him, Doctor. If you would ask him about it. I know he'll talk to you. I know he'll value your opinion.'

'Stella, I wish I could help, but I can't. I'm sorry.'

She looked taken aback. 'Why not?'

'Because it would be inappropriate. Intrusive. He would have to come to me. I couldn't just ask him what was the matter.'

'I see . . .' She laced her fingers tightly together and took a series of small breaths. 'I see . . .'

'And he's not going to confide in me if the conversation isn't his own idea.'

'No, of course not,' she said immediately. 'I hadn't thought of that. No . . .' She stood up hastily. 'I must go. I'm keeping you from your dinner.'

The mention of dinner brought a hollowness to Bennett's stomach and a rush of saliva to his mouth, but half rising from his chair he held out a staying hand at her. 'Please don't go yet, Stella. Finish your sherry. Please!' He sat down again, and smiled encouragingly as she slowly returned to her seat.

'What about Lyndon's comrades from the war?' he said. 'Does he get to see them at all?'

She rested her shoulder despondently against the wing of the chair and gazed into the poor glow of the fire. 'He said something about meeting up with an army friend in London. David Murray, I think his name was.'

'Well, that might be the best thing for him. Spending some time with comrades who've been through the same experiences.'

'I don't think David Murray's the kind he can talk to.'

'Well, you never know.'

'There was Jim, his best friend at university. They joined up together. But he was killed in Burma. Apart from that . . .' She shook her head distractedly.

With the air of wanting to get his facts right, Bennett asked, 'How long was Lyndon away at the war altogether?'

'Four years – just under. We last saw each other in Decem-

ber '42.' The memory had brought her alive again. She said
with a shudder, 'He phoned from London on his last leave, but
I couldn't get anyone in the factory to cover for me, not till the
next day. And then my train was more than three hours late.
Oh!' She winced at the memory and pressed a hand against her
mouth.

'This was the aircraft factory?'

'What?' Her mind was still on the train journey. 'Oh yes. I
was on night shift.'

'Night shift? I thought you did clerical work.'

'Oh no. I was on the production line.'

'Goodness!' Bennett exclaimed in astonishment. 'I never
realised that. What exactly did you do?'

'Machine-tool operator.'

'Well, well!' Bennett was from a generation where the idea
of young women doing heavy work was still a source of
wonder. 'What made you choose that? Didn't you want to
teach?'

'Oh, there were more than enough teachers around, older
women coming out of retirement. And I couldn't bear to stick
with an easy job. I wanted to do something for the war effort,
and to see another side of life while I was about it.' She gave a
pale smile. 'Didn't see much of anything, of course, working
long shifts. But I made some good friends. And I saw what
Bristol was going through with the bombing.'

'The work must have been very tough.'

'The night shifts were hard – I never got used to them. But
the rest – well, I was glad to be doing something useful at last.
My first idea was to join the WAAF, but they were looking for
typing skills. Then I applied for driving lessons so I could train
for the ambulances, but they were flooded with volunteers. So
I was glad of the chance of aircraft work. None of us minded
the hours and the noise and the hard work, not when we knew
that the plane we were building would be in the air in just a
couple of weeks, when we knew our boys would be flying them
through every kind of danger. How could we mind?'

'Well, well,' Bennett murmured in open admiration.

'I only stayed six months, though. Until Mum got poorly and needed me back at home. When the teaching post came up at the school I thought I'd better take it.'

A last fragment of coal shifted in the grate. The fire was almost out.

Stella shivered a little.

'You're cold.'

'No,' she said, 'I was just remembering that awful train journey.'

'You got to London in the end?'

'For all of half an hour. That was all the time Lyndon had left. We went to the Great Western Hotel for tea but they had no tables free, so we had to sit in the hall. But I didn't mind. It was enough to be together.'

'And you didn't see him again until recently?'

'Oh, we wrote to each other all through the war. His letters were wonderful. He writes so beautifully, you know. He would describe things in such a way – the places he'd seen and the people he'd met and the books he was reading. Yes, in a beautiful way. The censor used to block out quite a bit, of course,' she declared with an odd pride. 'But I knew what he was saying under all that black ink. I knew he was speaking his mind about the war. Things they couldn't allow him to say. And he always expressed himself with such power, you know. I feel sure he could be a writer, if only he put his mind to it. He has such a way with words. Yes . . . they were wonderful letters.'

But were they letters of love or friendship? Bennett found himself wondering. Were the letters eloquent, descriptive, affectionate, but ultimately unrevealing, or did they contain the teasings and anxieties and reproaches of love? For some reason he couldn't immediately identify Bennett had the feeling that Lyndon's affection for Stella was more brotherly than anything else.

Stella looked at her unfinished sherry, then at her watch, and got to her feet again. 'Now I really must go.'

In the porch she gave him a ragged smile. 'I'm sorry to have bothered you, Doctor.'

'I'm only sorry I couldn't have been more help, Stella.'

Watching the beam of her torch strike out into the darkness, catching her figure briefly silhouetted against the pool of light, Bennett found himself wishing he could shield her from the setbacks ahead. But it was a conceit to imagine that one could protect the young from anything, let alone something as inevitable as disappointment.

Chapter Six

⸺•⸺

BILLY ARRIVED to find the market in full swing and some early comers already drifting away. Dealers thronged the cattle pens, while bargain hunters moved along the line of vegetable and second-hand-goods stalls. Above the bellows of the cattle rose the chants of the livestock auctioneers, and from somewhere beyond the pens came the tinkle of a barrel organ.

Billy made a quick circuit of the stalls before cutting through the middle of the pens. With growing anxiety he began a slower round of the stalls, searching the shifting crowd for the shining hair, the vivid features he had come to find. A few families stood watching a Punch and Judy show, others were bunched around the barrel organ, the children laughing at a leaping monkey. But there was no sign of Annie or the child. His anxiety gave way to sharp self-reproach. He should never have left it so late. He'd purposely avoided the early bus because he knew she would be on it and he hadn't fancied sitting apart from her like a stranger or talking to her under the nosy gaze of the other passengers. Now he saw that his caution had been a trap, that it had driven him into wasting a perfectly good opportunity.

He walked up the hill into the main street and looked into a crowded tea room, then an ironmonger's next door and a couple of shops opposite, before returning to the market place by the other road. He stood near the pens and scanned the crowd again, but it was no good – she must have left.

He wandered towards a second-hand-clothes stall with the vague idea of buying himself a cloth cap, then suddenly she was there in front of him, the child at her side.

He halted abruptly.

She gave a broad smile. 'Morning.'

'Morning.'

Her shining hair was partially hidden by a French beret worn at an angle over her forehead. With her tightly belted coat, her intense colouring, she might have been an exotic creature from another land. With an effort he shifted his gaze to the child. 'Hello there.'

The child tucked her chin in and stared at him wordlessly.

Annie coaxed, 'Say hello, sweetheart.'

The child mumbled a shy greeting, and Annie looked up with an apologetic smile.

'What've you got there?' he asked, indicating her basket, which was clearly full of fruit and vegetables crowned by a pineapple.

'Don't even ask what the pineapple cost,' she said. 'It's the first one I've seen since I don't know when. But the rhubarb was dirt cheap.' She added dubiously, 'Oh, and I found some whale meat.'

'Bit slimy, isn't it?'

'I thought I'd fry it up with pepper and onions.'

'A waste of pepper and onions, if you ask me. Why don't I bring you a rabbit instead?'

'But you've brought me enough rabbits already, Billy.'

'I've brought you two.'

'All right – *two*,' she laughed. 'But I wouldn't want Stan to feel I was leaving him short.'

'Plenty more where they came from. But if you'd rather have some mallard, I'll be shooting on the moor later.'

'Well . . .' She rounded her eyes at the child. 'Don't think we could say no to roast duck, could we? Not if you have one to spare.' Reaching into a corner of her basket, she took out a small paper bag and held it out to him. 'Fancy a chestnut? Careful, though – they're scorching hot.'

Taking one, he made a play of passing the chestnut rapidly from hand to hand, and had the satisfaction of seeing Annie smile. He couldn't get over the way she looked. Whenever he imagined seeing her again he half hoped she would seem plain or dull or less attractive, or he would spot some glaring defect that would relegate her to the realms of ordinary women; but each time he saw her, her impact on him was just the same.

He offered the chestnut to the child. 'Here, would you like it? Shall I peel it for you?' The child didn't answer so he peeled it anyway and gave it to her. He did the same for Annie before taking one for himself. 'Where're you headed?'

'We were going to look at the Punch and Judy show.'

'I'll come with you.'

Billy fell into step beside her, the child trailing reluctantly. It might have been his imagination but people seemed to look at them admiringly as they passed. A nice little family. He let the fantasy play over his mind for a couple of moments before pushing it firmly away. He wasn't going to get caught until he was well and truly ready, and ready to his thinking was plenty of money.

When they reached the Punch and Judy booth, the stage was curtained off and a sign announced the next show was at ten thirty, so they went and watched the monkey instead. While the music jangled out, the creature leapt frantically between the organ-grinder's shoulder and the top of the barrel organ, jumping almost but not quite to the limit of its collar chain. When the organ-grinder brought his cap around, the monkey crouched low on the man's left shoulder, its little moon-face and currant eyes darting warily from side to side. As the organ-grinder approached them, Annie pulled out her purse and opened it. She was still delving for a coin when the child reached out to touch the dangling tail.

In rapid succession Billy caught Beth's wrist, the monkey bared its teeth and shrieked aggressively, the child shrank against her mother's arm, and Annie pulled her back with a gasp.

'Best not,' Billy said in a kindly voice intended to reassure Annie as much as the child.

Annie held the child's head close against her side. 'Yes, it might've bitten you, sweetheart. It might've hurt you.'

As they moved away, she breathed to Billy, 'Nasty beast.'

'Can't really blame it though, can you?'

'What do you mean? Why not?'

'Tethered like that. Having to jump about all day. Baited and pestered by people.'

'But fed. Looked after.'

'Food and shelter's not everything though, is it?'

Annie shot him a curious look. 'Well, I'd never have put you down as soft hearted.'

'I'm not. But I could see the animal hated us, and so far as I'm concerned it had every right. Can't blame it for hating. Why shouldn't it?'

'Well, I can't say I'd ever thought about it that way,' she said. 'But, yes . . . I take your point.'

Feeling that he had taken a step up in her estimation, Billy touched her elbow to guide her forward, and smiled down at the child for good measure. They strolled along the line of stalls, stopping to examine some pots and pans and an old willow-pattern teapot, before returning to the Punch and Judy booth in time for the show. The action began with a fight between Punch and the policeman, and continued at the same frenzied pace. Billy didn't find it funny and, judging by the people around him, nor did anyone else. Instead, the audience seemed to be held by a reluctant tension, an uneasy curiosity as to the timing and ferocity of the next fight. To Billy's mind the whole exercise – the endless screaming and bludgeoning, the puppets collapsing over the edge of the platform only to be sucked down into a yawning darkness – had less to do with entertainment than people's underlying fascination with violence.

He stole an occasional glance at Annie. Her expression was solemn, her lips set. After a particularly savage cosh fight, she shook her head a little and looked down at the child's face, then up at Billy's with a questioning frown that spoke of wanting to leave. He gave an answering nod and her expression lifted. The child made no complaint when they moved away, and they left the sound of thwacking coshes and jabbering voices behind with a sense of relief.

'How about a cup of tea and a cream bun?' Billy suggested. Then to the child: 'Or do you like cake best?'

'Cake,' she said.

'Cake it is, then.'

The tea room was busy and they had to wait for a table. The standing area was cramped, everyone bunched up. Taking the opportunity to examine Annie at close quarters, Billy finally found a blemish. On the smooth white forehead, towards the end of one arched eyebrow, was a tiny scar barely a quarter of an inch long and fine as a thread. Far from being a flaw, however, it only went to emphasise the perfection of the whole. She was by far the best-looking woman in the room. It was a miracle she hadn't been snapped up. Even as he thought this, it occurred to him that he couldn't be absolutely sure of that. She'd been widowed at least three years. In that time dozens of men must have asked her out. He'd assumed she had no boyfriend, but the more he thought about it the more unlikely it seemed. She might well be angling for some man she hadn't quite caught, or waiting for a serviceman she'd met on leave who wasn't yet home from the war. As this idea took a firmer grip, he felt a twinge of animosity towards her. She was hiding things from him, she wasn't playing fair.

When they finally sat down and ordered, he said, 'This is on me. I sold fifty bundles of withies yesterday.'

'That's wonderful, Billy.'

'Oh, it was the easy stuff from the withy shed. Already cut and dried. But I got a good price.'

'I bet you did. How about the Polish worker? Any more news?'

'Two to three days, so they say. But there's some sort of permit needed before he's allowed to start, so I'll believe it when I see it.'

'And the job in London? Have you heard? Are they holding it for you?'

He gave a dismissive shrug. 'If it's still there, it's there. If not . . . well, I'll just have to find something else, won't I?'

'But what did your friend say? Couldn't he help?'

'Never wrote in the end. Wasn't worth the bother. Wasn't that much he could have done anyway.'

'Oh.' She searched his face for a moment. 'Well, I hope it turns out all right.'

'I blame the stripping machine myself.'

'Oh yes?'

'Never could resist a bit of machinery, especially when it's in need of care and attention. Worse than women for me, machinery. Much worse.'

She took the remark lightly and gave a short laugh.

Billy added, 'With the bonus that you pretty much know where you are.'

'Ah.' Her smile faded. 'Which you don't with women, is that it?'

He said dryly, 'Far be it from me . . .'

'Perhaps it depends on the kind of woman. Perhaps they need to be chosen with care.' He searched for a gleam of promise in her eyes, a tease in her voice, and found none. Instead, her tone was light, practical, calm; she might have been dispensing advice to a friend.

The waitress arrived with the tea and a selection of cakes. The child chose a fairy cake with a thin dribble of pink icing on top, Annie a fairy cake with a dab of white icing, and Billy took a slice of sponge sandwich that was thin on the jam and not too generous on the sponge either. It tasted all right though. Real butter and eggs. Nothing like the stuff you got in London that tasted of cardboard or worse.

'I tried for a job in Taunton yesterday,' Annie remarked. 'Didn't get it though.'

She had taken him by surprise, both because she hadn't

mentioned it before and because it seemed a strange sort of thing for her to be doing. He asked, 'What kind of a job?'

'Bookkeeping. Same as I did in Plymouth.'

'But why?'

'*Why?*' She threw it back at him with a flash of her eyes and an admonitory snort. 'Same reason as anyone else.'

'You need the work?'

'I could do with the money all right. But it's more than that. It's the work itself. I enjoy it. I only stopped last time because they forced me to. Said the job was wanted for a man.' She pinched her lips together in silent comment. 'Oh, I know men need the work, 'course I do,' she added. 'But all the same. I was good at my job, as good as anyone else. And I miss it. The wages were bad of course, only half what they'd paid before, but it was useful money. And I had my mum-in-law to look after Beth. But this firm yesterday, they turned me down flat when I told them I had a child. Didn't matter that I could have done the job standing on my head. Didn't matter that I had Joan Penny all lined up to keep Beth after school. They got on their high horse. Made it plain they didn't approve of a widow trying for work when other people needed it more.'

'You were paid only half rate before?' Billy asked incredulously.

She nodded. 'I took a peek in the wages ledger.'

'That's a bloody outrage.'

At the swearword the child looked up from her cake and stared at Billy with interest.

'It was the war, Billy. It was that or nothing.'

'I'd rather've starved.'

'You're a man. You'd have had more choice.'

'But wages like that – it's exploitation. It's the bosses paying what they can get away with.'

'Back then I had my share of Alan's army pay, remember. They knew that. They said they weren't about to pay me twice.'

She rarely mentioned the late husband by name but when she did her face showed nothing of her feelings for him.

'But that's not the point, is it?' Billy argued. 'If you do the work, you should get the wage for the job. Anything else is daylight bloody robbery.'

At the repeat of the swearword Annie threw him a half-hearted glance of rebuke and, with an air of going through the motions, briefly covered the child's ears with her hands. 'The way I saw it,' she said, 'I was lucky to get the job at all. Arithmetic was the only thing I was any good at.'

'All the more reason not to sell yourself short.'

'But I never got school cert, Billy. I never got anything.'

'Nor did I. But I didn't let it get in my way. And I'm not about to start now.'

'You went to grammar school, though,' she said. 'You were a clever clogs.'

'But I didn't stay, did I?' he retorted, amazed that she should have forgotten the most significant fact of all.

'I thought you were there for a while.'

'Less than a year,' he said stiffly.

'Ah.' Annie sipped her tea and regarded him calmly over the rim of the cup. 'That was when you fell out with the funny old aunt, was it?'

Startled by how little she had understood of his life, smarting from the sting of old resentments, he glared at her, unable to speak.

'I thought . . .' She made a gesture of uncertainty. 'Weren't you living with the aunt in Bridgwater then? The keen chapel goer?'

A basket bumped against Annie's shoulder and she glanced up to exchange apologies with a woman squeezing past the table. When she turned back, the child was pulling at her sleeve, demanding attention. By the time she looked at Billy again she seemed oblivious to the storm she had stirred up in his mind, her expression friendly, open, unconcerned. The part of Billy that could not bear to be misjudged itched to put her straight, to demolish the half-baked ideas she had picked up about him. But he feared explanations almost as much as he feared disbelief, and the fear won.

'This job you were trying for,' he said at last. 'What sort of a wage were they offering?'

'They didn't say.'

'You should have asked before you went.'

'I don't suppose they'd have told me.'

'Well, you should find out next time. You don't want them thinking they're doing you a favour. You don't want them to get the upper hand.'

'Billy.' Laughing silently, she shook her head. 'You sound like one of those trade union people. One of those . . . what are they?'

'Activists?'

'That's it.'

'Or agitator?'

'Ah. Now that sounds more like you.'

'I might be an agitator already, for all you know.'

She grinned. 'I wouldn't put it past you.'

His mood lifted. He said in a burst of confidence, 'I'll tell you something. You wonder why I felt aggrieved when I left Crick Farm. You wonder why I felt no duty to help out. Well, I'll tell you why. Because Stan never paid me my money. Because when I agreed to stay on he promised me a proper wage and never paid it. Because he strung me along. Used every excuse under the sun. It was' – Billy put on an approximation of Stan's accent – '"Things are a bit tight just now – I'll try to find something next month." Or, "There'll be a good bit waiting for you come Eastertime." But Eastertime came and went, and there was always some reason he couldn't find the money – low prices, the cost of the stripping machine, the cost of coal. Right at the end, when I was going out the door, he gave me ten pounds, and then grudgingly. Said it was all he could spare. When I walked away, you know how much I had to show for all that work? The grand sum of twenty pounds, six and thruppence. And most of that from what I'd managed to save.'

Annie frowned at him without answering, and the defensiveness raced back into his heart. He added coldly, 'Unless you reckon that's fair, of course.'

'Times were very bad then, of course.'

'Not that bad.'

'But if he didn't have the money?'

'He had enough to buy a brand-new stripping machine.'

She gave a troubled sigh. 'Perhaps he was just trying to keep you from leaving.'

'Well, he had a strange way of going about it.'

'Or maybe he was—' She broke off abruptly. 'No . . . Doesn't matter what he thought, does it? It happened, and it shouldn't have, and that's all there is to it.'

She had come down on his side, and he felt a new warmth towards her.

When they got outside, it was raining, ponderous drops that splattered over the pavement and rattled against the ironmonger's dustbins and pails. Heads down, they hurried down the road to join the queue for the bus. When it arrived, they found a bench seat near the back and squeezed in, the child in the middle.

As the bus moved off, Billy made an effort to talk to the child. Not sure where to start, he tried school, which lessons she liked, which teachers. Getting the barest of answers, he scraped around for another topic and could think of nothing until he remembered a barn owl he'd spotted swooping across the orchard at dusk. He told her how he'd tracked it to its roost on a high beam at the far end of the withy shed, how in the daytime it hid itself so well you wouldn't know it was there. The child answered with a solemn gaze that wavered and fell away. Recalling that children were meant to like people looking idiotic, he offered as a last throw the rest of the story, how in trying to catch sight of the owl high in the rafters he'd tripped and almost fallen over a broom. Annie glanced round from the window and smiled, but the child dropped her head and gazed at her lap.

'So, tell me – what is it you find funny?' Billy asked dryly. 'What makes you laugh?'

The child looked to her mother for help.

'What about that time with the dog?' Annie said.

The child grinned a little, and after much prompting finally recounted amid bursts of giggles seeing a man trip over a dog and fall into a watery ditch. Having begun to giggle, the child seemed unable to stop. Alternately bouncing up and down in her seat and throwing herself across her mother's lap, she rolled and writhed with laughter. Recoiling from this sudden frenzy, Billy waited for Annie to tell the child off, and was confused when, far from shushing her, she laughed proudly and pulled the wriggling child into her arms. Watching the two of them, he felt a familiar sense of looking in on a world that he didn't understand.

Billy studied Annie's profile as she resumed her scrutiny of the countryside beyond the window. A strand of hair clung damply to her cheek, and a spot of colour glowed low on her neck where the collar of her coat had chafed it. She was motionless, apparently lost in thought, but he felt certain she was aware of him. It was this awareness that had brought them together in the first place, and it seemed to him that nothing had changed, that it was impossible for them to be within touch or sight of each other without feeling the strong pull of attraction.

The bus ground to a halt to let some people off. Glancing out, Billy realised where they were, realised that beyond a house with a neat garden he could make out the corner of a walled orchard where late in that long-ago summer he and Annie had once made love. The coincidence of thought and memory made him want to laugh, and he searched Annie's face to see if she too was remembering, but just then she lowered her head to talk to the child. Her movements were smooth, her expression untroubled, her mouth tilted by a smile, yet it seemed to Billy that her very calmness gave her away, that she was talking to the child to avoid acknowledging that she had seen the orchard, that she too was remembering.

The bus grumbled up the ridge road and deposited them at the far side of the village. Having eased off, the rain now threatened a fresh shower, and they walked briskly, reaching Spring Cottage just as the sporadic droplets began to sharpen.

Billy carried Annie's shopping through the cottage into the kitchen. It was the first time he had been inside the place; normally she kept him at the door. The kitchen was a lean-to and had the chill of thin walls and draughty windows, but there were bright red curtains and children's drawings stuck to the walls. Through the open door to the sitting room he could see a gypsy shawl arranged over the back of an easy chair, dried flowers in painted pots, and a framed photograph of a man in uniform: husband, father, brother, he couldn't tell.

After seeing to the child, Annie came in and said, 'Thanks.' Then, with a short smile, 'Well . . . I should get started on the dinner now.' It was an invitation for him to leave, and to underline it she moved towards the door.

'Annie?'

She paused.

He came up to her and leant a shoulder against the door frame. 'There's a dance in North Curry tonight. How about giving it a go?'

'I couldn't—'

'Come on,' he said cajolingly. 'A night out, a few hops round the dance floor, a bit of a laugh. I'm a devil at the jive, though being North Curry we might have to settle for the foxtrot.'

She shook her head.

'What, you don't like dancing?'

Her eyes gave a dark glint. 'Sometimes,' she said.

'But not tonight.'

'No.'

'Am I allowed a reason?'

'Well, there's Beth for a start.'

'Can't she stay with a friend?'

'No.' Her tone was pleasant but firm.

He knew what was riling her. He had been half expecting something like this ever since meeting up with her again. He recalled the words he had rehearsed for just such an occasion.

'It was a spur of the moment thing, you know.'

She frowned at him. 'What was?'

'Me leaving. Me walking out. I had a big row with Stan and I just sort of picked up my things and went. I didn't mean to go without seeing you.'

'And you think that's why I won't go dancing with you?'

'Isn't it?'

'No, Billy, it isn't.'

Not convinced, he said, 'I always felt bad – that I didn't explain. That I didn't write.'

She gave a tiny shrug, a lift of one shoulder. 'Doesn't matter how it happened, does it? Not now. Fact is, you left.'

'It seemed the right thing to do at the time.'

'Right for *you*.'

He accepted this with a suitably penitent expression.

'And right for me too, as it turned out,' she declared unhesitatingly. 'You did me a big favour. Got me thinking about moving away and getting war work, and if I hadn't've moved away I'd never have met Alan. I can't pretend I was thankful at the time of course. Thought you were a proper sod. But afterwards – well, I was grateful. More than grateful – Alan was the best thing that ever came my way. I wouldn't have missed our time together, not for the world.'

He thought: Well, what else did I expect? Her words struck at him all the same, and a strange shiver passed through his shoulders. He decided to make a poor joke of it. 'And there I was, thinking you'd missed me.'

'Oh no. Once I got to Plymouth I can honestly say I never gave you another thought.'

He didn't believe her. Her words were too glib, and it was

inconceivable that she hadn't thought about him now and again, if only to hate him. Feeling he had caught her out in an untruth, knowing she had done it out of pride, his confidence flooded back.

'We could pretend to arrive separately,' he said as he followed her to the front door.

She turned on him, ready for anger.

'If you were worried about the gossip, I mean.' He threw it down like a challenge, and she rose to it instantly.

'That'll be the day,' she retorted with a roll of her eyes. 'When you're a widow they talk anyway. They can't believe you're not on the lookout.'

'So being seen with me wouldn't blacken your name any more than it is already?'

He said it to make her smile, and, despite herself, she almost did.

He said, 'So . . . if I paid for someone to mind the child.'

'You don't give up, do you?'

'I'm a born optimist. And I like dancing.'

She was softening, but she wasn't there yet.

'And I haven't got anyone else to ask, have I?'

Now she laughed outright. 'Well, you're honest, I'll give you that.'

Billy made a humorous gesture of entreaty, a turn of the hand, a lift of the shoulders.

She gave in with a wry shake of her head. 'All right. I'll arrange something for Beth.'

He walked into the lane and turned to wave, but she had already gone.

He'd washed and shaved and put on his demob suit. He hated everything about the suit, the cut, the cheapness of the cloth, the way it bagged and bunched, but the only suits he'd fancied in London were displayed in the posher windows of the West End at upwards of ten pounds a throw. As a consolation he'd discarded the demob-issue shirt with its ugly, unfashionable button-down collar and equally hideous tie for a fine cotton shirt and maroon silk tie purchased from a gents' outfitter's near Piccadilly. For the same price he could have bought three shirts from a sweatshop in the East End, but he hadn't come back from the war to subscribe to the national mania for thrift.

When he was satisfied with his appearance he went down to the kitchen for a jar of cider. As he took his first swig he heard the tap of Flor's stick on the ceiling above, her signal that she needed someone to go up to her. Stan was nowhere about, so after another couple of gulps he went instead.

Flor had slipped so low and crooked in the bed that from the door he could barely see her face over the hill of her body. 'What's happened to you then?' he said, lifting her up. 'Got in a tangle, have you?' He puffed up the pillows, and laughed at himself for poncing around like a nurse. 'What were you trying to do – go gallivanting?'

Then he saw what she'd been after: her pencil, which had fallen off the bed onto the floor. He put it back beside her hand, next to her pad.

'So, was it just the pencil you wanted? Or was it the wireless? Battery all right, is it?' He checked the connections between the wireless and the accumulator on the floor beneath, then flicked on the switch to a burst of sound. 'Plenty of juice there, eh? Do you want it left on?'

She shook her head and gestured him to sit down.

'Sorry, old girl. Can't stop tonight,' he said firmly. 'Look at me – I'm going out, aren't I?'

He had learnt to read the half-collapsed features: the twist of the lopsided mouth, the pull of the cheek, the gleam in the eyes; he could see that she was twinkling at him now, she was offering her funny crooked smile.

'All right – five minutes,' he said with a sharp sigh as if she had been pressing him to stay. 'But no more. Just five minutes and then I'll have to be going.'

His offer wasn't entirely selfless; giving up five minutes now

might let him off an hour of tedium another evening. Three
times Flor had roped him into writing letters to her son and
daughter, and he didn't want to be caught again. It wasn't so
bad when the two of them went in for a sort of reverse
dictation, he suggesting what she might like to say and she
signalling yes or no. That way at least they got to have a few
laughs. 'Billy might be shoving off at last,' he threw in, which
caused her to give a pantomime frown. Or: 'Pigs stage mass
escape from market,' which made her giggle. Or her favourite:
'Lady Godiva spotted riding through North Curry.' There was
nothing to amuse him when she drafted the letter herself in her
bedraggled left-handed scrawl and he was faced with the
tedium of deciphering and copying out the news on her health,
Stan's health, the weather, and the latest radio serial.

He pulled up a chair and sat down. 'Well,' he announced
cheerfully, 'I've got nothing to report. Went to the market.
Found nothing I wanted to buy. Came back. Sharpened some
tools, oiled the stripping machine, thought of going down onto
the moor for some duck. Saw the rain and decided against it.
That's it. No such thing as news round here.'

It was the kind of news Flor loved, though. In the old days
no detail had been too small for her, no piece of information
too insignificant that she hadn't chewed it over at length with
Stan in the evenings. Billy couldn't begin to count the hours he
had spent at mealtimes or trying to read a book to the fretful
cadence of Flor's voice as she went over and over the price of
withies or the state of the floods or the rot in the potatoes.

She wrote laboriously on her pad: *When are you leaving?*

'I told you, not till this Polack arrives. In a couple of days,
maybe more.'

She wrote: *Bring satchel.*

This time he didn't argue with her. If she was going to give
him money, then no one could say he hadn't earned it. He
found the satchel jammed tight between the back of the wardrobe and the wall. It was a child's satchel made of battered
leather with worn straps and pitted chrome buckles. He laid it

flat on the bed and opened it for her. She reached inside and pulled out a bundle of five-pound notes folded twice over and held by an elastic band. He tried not to notice how much was there, but it couldn't have been less than two hundred pounds. Using her one good hand, she fumbled with the elastic band.

'Give it here.' Taking the notes, he slipped the elastic band off and put the money back into her hand.

Laboriously she counted off ten of the large white notes, then reached onto the bedside table for a page of her notepad that she must have torn out earlier. She held it out to him like an offering. The message read: *This is owed you.*

'How d'you work that out?' he said awkwardly.

She gave the money a determined push across the counterpane towards him.

'Won't you need it for a rainy day?'

Shaking her head adamantly, Flor pulled open the satchel, inviting Billy to look inside. Craning forward, he saw at least two more bundles of notes, each about the size of the first. He sat back quickly.

'Withies been paying all right then.'

Flor nodded.

'Tell me – is this for then or now?'

It took her a moment to understand. Finally she indicated: *Then.*

'For missed wages?'

She nodded.

'You tallied it up, did you?'

She blinked rapidly before nodding, and he guessed she had done no such thing. Luckily for her, the money was about right, give or take five pounds or so. Yet Billy felt strangely cheated, and he couldn't have said why.

Slowly he folded the money and shoved it into his pocket. 'Well, I'll try not to spend it all at once.'

She reached out a hand to him. Taking it uncertainly, he felt himself pulled towards her and realised she wanted a kiss. He stood up and leant over the bed. First he aimed at her forehead, then, bracing himself, made for her cheek. Her skin felt lifeless under his lips, crêpey and cool and insubstantial, while lurking under the scent of carbolic and lavender was the musty smell of age and decrepitude.

Drawing away rapidly, he indicated the satchel. 'I'll put this back in the hidey-hole, shall I?' He folded the remaining notes and doubled the elastic band around them. Opening the mouth of the satchel to slide them in, he saw that there were not two bundles of notes lying in the bottom but four. By even the most basic arithmetic there had to be a thousand pounds there, maybe more. Suddenly the fifty pounds in his pocket didn't seem so good and his old resentments sprang to the surface, rose over him, until he forced them firmly down again.

When he'd replaced the satchel behind the wardrobe, Flor pointed in the direction of the chest of drawers and tried to say something in her slurred, unbearably slow, and totally unintelligible speech.

Billy shook his head at her. 'No can understand.'

She reached for her pad and wrote: *album*.

He fetched it for her, a large black photograph album, with gold-edged pages, well thumbed. She gestured him to come closer and he shifted his chair until he could see the open pages. They had looked at the album once before, Flor leafing through the pictures with Billy reading out the dates and inscriptions that interested her. Most of the photographs featured her side of the family, a confident bunch from the Blackdown Hills. She had a voluminous memory, and, until Billy cut her short, had started to trace on her pad the outlines of the entire family history: who was related to whom, where they lived, misfortunes, joys, illnesses, children, children's illnesses. The only time Billy perked up was when she came to the members of the family she termed 'unsteady'. There was the maiden aunt who was a secret tippler – *kept hip flask in her skirts*, Flor scribbled; the uncle who had a fancy lady in Taunton – *plump redhead, very loud*, she wrote; and the boot-faced couple, distant cousins, who were dispatched with: *Prudes. No children*, to which Billy had declared, 'Flor!' in a tone of mock outrage.

Billy's side of the family weren't hard to pick out. They had rarely been captured with a smile, preferring to stare, frown, or glare at the camera. Three pages into the album there was a photograph of his mother, aged about sixteen, standing in a scattered family group, squinting into the sun. She was a niece of Stan's, the daughter of his eldest sister. No one had got to know her well, Flor explained, because she had married Michael Greer at seventeen and gone away to live in Taunton and Weston-super-Mare, and possibly Bristol as well. After that, Stan's family lost touch, cards and letters were returned marked 'not known here', until one winter the Greers had turned up again out of the blue and rented a small damp cottage under the Tone at Athelney. Billy was six then, another child was due any day, and Michael Greer was often away, supposedly looking for work on the railways, but by common consent most likely to be found on the racetracks, chancing his arm. Billy was seven when his mother died of influenza along with the baby, and ten when his father gave up his sporadic, increasingly chaotic attempts to take care of him.

Don't mind me telling? Flor scribbled on the pad.

'What – about my father?'

She nodded.

'Lord, no!' he exclaimed with a laugh that sounded strange to his ears. 'There's nothing you can tell me about my father that I don't already know. I lived with the stupid sod, remember?'

We worried about you.

'Oh, I was right enough *then*. I had no troubles – *then*.'

Not a bad man, Flor wrote, missing his point or choosing to ignore it. *Just fekless.*

'That's one way of putting it.' The misspelt word seemed entirely appropriate to describe his father, who throughout his life had managed to get everything slightly but fatally wrong.

Now, as Flor began to leaf through the album once more she missed the point a second time when, pointing to a picture of Aunt May, she misread his silence and looked at him expectantly.

He murmured tightly, 'Don't expect me to talk about *her*.'

Flor stared at him uncertainly before writing: *She meant well.*

The heat leapt into Billy's face, his ears sang, he might have been blind, and for an instant he probably was. 'She meant poison.'

A scribble: *Family thought it best chance for you.*

'Chance of *what*? She ruined any chances I ever had.'

Flor's mouth sagged. She wrote tentatively: *Was it too much religion?*

'Religion?' Billy got abruptly to his feet, sending the chair rocking backwards. 'The only thing she believed in was making my life a bloody misery. That was her religion – to goad and taunt, to belittle and shame. To find any way she could to drag me down to her level.' His throat swelled with old anger, the words dried up, and it was a moment before he could speak again. 'But I wouldn't have it. That's what she couldn't stand – that I wouldn't give in to her. That's why I got away. Because she wouldn't let up, because she never stopped.' He stabbed a furious finger into the air. 'She gave me *nothing*.'

He walked out with a bang of the door and stopped at the head of the stairs, his heart pounding. He saw himself as Flor must have seen him, the furious workings of his face, the shivering rage, and felt the self-disgust of someone who finds he is doomed to repeat his own history.

Chapter Seven

———

Middlezoy,
Somerset,
30 October 1946

My dearest Helenka,

At last I have the chance to finish this letter. For the past two weeks I have been on the move from what seemed like one end of England to the other, only to end up not so very far from where I first started. Such are the ways of the military – or, to be more accurate, the Polish Resettlement Corps. If you have written to me in the meantime, dear sister, your letter will be pursuing me from pillar to post, and will doubtless catch up with me in the next few days. My new home is a camp (again), a temporary residence (one can but hope). It is in the middle of the wetlands of Somerset, many kilometres from the nearest town and convenient for little but long walks. Sometimes I wonder if I'm destined to live in camps for ever, but really I can't complain. Compared to the accommodation in the Soviet Paradise, this is a veritable Grand Hotel.

What follows just below I began in a camp in the north of England, continued a little further south, and now finish in the west of the country. Whatever else, it seems I am destined to be a well-travelled man.

Yorkshire
16 October 1946

Dear Helenka,

Well, I've been sent here to the north of England. Not
at all where I want to be, but I'm hoping to be transferred
back to the south-west again soon.

Now, to the rest of what happened to our family. While
I was convalescing I did in fact write a detailed account of
the whole story, partly to create a proper record for you,
and partly with the idea of writing a book one day – a
novel, I thought, though I haven't yet found a form or
style that would do it justice. But since the account runs to
well over two hundred pages and includes many
descriptive and impressionistic passages it's obviously not
suitable to send through the post. So here's a short version,
which will, I hope, cover everything you want to know.

At the start of the war, as you probably heard, we were
briefly overrun by the Germans. Father was away from
home at the time, searching for his old regiment. He
marched down to the Recruitment Board, rattled his
medals at them, and demanded the necessary mobilisation
papers (you can picture the scene). He got as far as
Ostroleka when the German assault began. I, meantime,
had joined the local Volunteer Corps, but when no arms or
ammunition appeared I realised that the idea of local
defence was a waste of time and went back to Podjaworka
to help Mother, Janina, Krysia and Enzio. Father having
already sent the best paintings to a safe place (they may
still be there), we went about burying the most precious
valuables, leaving a few lesser valuables in place so that, if
the Germans came looting, they wouldn't be frustrated by
the lack of booty. How naive we were! It seems incredible
now.

Having done all I could at home, I then set off to join
the first Polish forces I could find, but just two hours down

the road I met German tanks. It was a terrible shock to
realise how far they had advanced in such a short time,
and I hurried straight back to Podjaworka to do all I could
to protect house and home. The next day a German officer
came and requisitioned stores from the farm, and later that
night two of his troopers returned to demand silver and
jewellery. At the time we branded them thugs, but
compared with what was to come they were almost civil.

When we heard the news of the Russian invasion, we
realised that any hope of rescue by our allies was gone.
Worse, when the Germans withdrew to the far side of
Lomza, we realised that we were to be thrown to the
Bolsheviks. While bracing ourselves for their arrival, we
were attacked by bands of Byelorussian and Jewish militia
(for which read brigands) who came in the night,
threatened us at gunpoint, and helped themselves to
livestock and whatever else took their fancy.

But they were as nothing to the Russians. Wild, filthy,
drunken, they systematically stripped the house and farm
of everything – furniture, clocks, curtains, machinery, tools
– which they piled onto trucks and sent back in well-
organised convoys to Russia (it was all planned, you see).
What they couldn't take they wrecked just for the sake of
it. They burnt all our books, papers, photograph albums.
In a final act of savagery they slaughtered my noble Ishtar
because she refused to let them saddle her. She knew
barbarians when she saw them. She was worth a hundred
of those brutes any day.

I am telling you all this, Helenka, not to add to your
pain, but to leave you in no doubt as to the deliberate and
systematic nature of this destruction. The intention was to
destroy our culture, to crush our spirit, to remove all traces
of Polish civilisation from the ancient soil of eastern Poland.

In the following weeks we made the best of what we
had left – a horse and some chickens, and of course the
sweat of our brow. I may add that our Byelorussian

neighbours remained loyal to us throughout. Indeed they
vouched for us as fair employers and good neighbours, but
as soon as the NKVD began to bully us we advised them
to keep their distance. Only two of them subsequently
turned against us – that young couple who begged Father
for work the previous summer and seemed so grateful.
Nothing, it seems, is so deeply resented as kindness.

In hindsight, we should have thought of escaping to the
German-occupied sector much earlier, while we still had
the chance. But nothing was simple then, Helenka, and by
the time Father returned, the NKVD had gained a firm grip
on the whole neighbourhood. We weren't blind: we saw
the way things were going. But how could we be sure we'd
be better off under the Germans? We were caught between
hell and a fiery place. Even Father, with his deep distrust of
the Bolsheviks, failed to appreciate the extent of their
ambitions, that it wasn't simply annexation and
domination they were after, but the very annihilation of
the Polish people.

The serious bullying began soon after the nationality
referendum (so-called). Sometimes the NKVD came to
Podjaworka in person, sometimes they sent their tame
militias. Father was convinced they were targeting him for
his service in the Bolshevik War. He thought that if he
could escape to the German sector they would leave the
rest of the family alone until he could arrange for us to
join him. It was on the day before he planned to leave that
he went into town and failed to return. Suspecting the
worst, I went to the local NKVD headquarters. At first
they denied all knowledge of what had happened to him,
then over the next few days they gave me a succession of
stories – that he'd been sent to Moscow or executed by a
military tribunal in Bialystok or sent to Siberia. I knew
better than to believe a word. It was risky going into town
(once, I was badly beaten by a gang led by an old
schoolmate, a Byelorussian whom I'd regarded, clearly

with some misjudgement, as a friend – such were the
ruptures in our once-harmonious society), but I refused to
stop asking questions. Finally, a local man told me he'd
seen a group of militiamen dragging Father into the forest.
I went to the spot he described and after much searching
found the shallow grave where Father lay. He had been
shot in the head and would have died instantly. With the
help of loyal neighbours I carried Father's body back to
Podjaworka and buried it in the orchard under the apple
trees. The priest came after nightfall to read the burial
service. The perpetrators of Father's cold-blooded murder
undoubtedly came from one of the Byelorussian militias,
but be in no doubt that it was the NKVD who authorised
the deed. Even at that stage, nothing happened without
their knowledge or approval.

     We continued into the winter under difficult but not
impossible conditions. My first instinct after Father's death
had been to grab what we could and flee to the German
sector, but Mother fell ill with fever (the result of shock,
I think), and Janina was of the strong opinion that, after
Father's murder, nothing worse could happen to us. I have
often blamed myself for not insisting on escape, but there
is no point in self-recrimination. Everything was clouded in
confusion and uncertainty. It was impossible to know what
was right. Even with daily murders and lootings, it seemed
safest to hang on for another day and hope for the best.
Also, as you will remember, the winter was very harsh that
year, deep frosts and the snow very thick.

     In early February we heard a rumour that all young
men from Polish families were to be deported to labour
camps. Immediately, Mother and Janina insisted that I
escape. I felt strongly that we should all go together or not
at all, but they were adamant, so I left late one night and
got as far as Aunt Zofia's in Lomza before I heard that
Mother, Janina, Krysia and Enzio had been seized in the
night, along with thousands of other families, and sent to

Bialystok for immediate deportation. I rushed back to find
Podjaworka inhabited by a militiaman and his family who
promptly tried to kill me. (I escaped by the skin of my
teeth – a bullet grazed my head as I ran away.)

Furious, I went to the NKVD chief and demanded to
know where our family had been taken. For once he didn't
prevaricate but told me straight away to go to the sidings
at Bialystok Station, and there I found a train of cattle
wagons within minutes of leaving. I ran alongside the
wagons shouting Janina's name. The situation was made
all the more astonishing and heart-rending when Nero
bounded up to me from among the hundreds of dogs
seeking their owners. Eventually I heard Janina calling
back. I ordered the guard to open the wagon and
thankfully he did so. There was a crowd inside, I couldn't
at first see Janina anywhere, but when they hauled me up I
quickly found our family together in a corner. What a
reunion it was! We embraced and laughed and wept, to the
mournful sound of the barking outside the wagon. Krysia
was distraught at leaving Nero, but I lied to her, I told her
it wasn't Nero, that I had looked for him and he wasn't
there. In fact he followed us for five days! Running beside
the train and sleeping under our wagon at the stops. Krysia
nearly went mad with worry. Then one day Nero wasn't
there. God only knows what became of him. Hopefully he
was shot.

It took three weeks to reach our destination. The
conditions were grim. There were fifty of us in a single
wagon and the temperature twenty or thirty below. Once,
Krysia's hair froze to the side of the wagon and had to be
cut free. There was one small stove for everyone, no water
except what we could melt from snow collected at the
occasional stops, and a hole in the floor for sanitation. The
old and infirm who died had to be left unburied at the side
of the track. When we reached the Russian border and
changed trains, everyone sang, 'Our free country give us

back, O Lord', and wept and wailed, except for me. I was
too angry, too bent on vengeance to concede that I might
not return.

Eventually we reached Kotlas in the province of
Archangel, where we left the train and started northwards
along the Dvina. For two days we were provided with
sledges, but for the most part we had to walk, until after
seven days we reached a narrow-gauge railway that took
us deep into the forest. From the end of the line we
travelled for another three days on foot and sledge until we
arrived at the work camp.

Thankfully, the regime allowed Krysia and Enzio to
attend the local school, though for the privilege of hearing
that God didn't exist and Stalin was all-bountiful they
received reduced rations. But this, we decided, was less
detrimental than heavy labour on so-called full rations,
which were laughably small. With the rest of the men, I
was set to work felling and logging, while Mother and
Janina were given branch-stripping and loading. The
temperature was thirty or forty below. A month after we
arrived, a log fell and crushed Mother's foot, causing her
great pain. The bones never healed properly and thereafter
she walked with a limp. However, it did result in her being
transferred to the sawmill, which being sheltered from the
snow and wind was a little easier to survive. In general the
work was hard in the extreme, the living conditions vile –
the huts crawling with lice, rats and bedbugs – but our real
enemy was hunger. Have no doubt, Helenka, that
starvation was the weapon chosen to conquer us, the
means by which we were to be subdued and ultimately
destroyed. On leaving Podjaworka, Mother, Janina, Krysia
and Enzio had been given half an hour to bundle clothes,
bedding and food onto the sledge. (Poor Enzio never
forgave himself for grabbing what he thought was a sack
of corn only to discover it was poppy seeds.) At the last
minute Mother had thrown in some of her finest lace and

linen, and it was this she traded for food. It made the difference between quick and slow starvation; we were never less than ravenously hungry. That first Easter, we said prayers over one small egg divided between the five of us. Soon after this, Krysia fell ill with a fever. By selling a gold chain Mother managed to buy extra food and nurse her out of immediate danger, but Krysia remained terribly thin and weak. She could barely drag herself around. Two weeks later she developed another fever and was taken to a hospital many kilometres away. Mother and I managed to get leave to go and see her, only to find she had died half an hour before we arrived. Mother's anguish was terrible. She was inconsolable at the thought of Krysia dying alone and uncomforted. We brought her body back to the *posiolek* and buried her as best we could in the frozen ground, marking her grave with birch twigs and a simple wooden cross. Thus we lost an angel, graced with a serenity and wisdom far beyond her years, imbued with a purity of spirit that shone like a golden beam of morning light.

When summer came, we picked berries and mushrooms from the forest, and, thanks to seeds sent by Aunt Zofia, were able to grow some vegetables. Touchingly, we also began to receive parcels from some of our neighbours from home. Thus for a time our health improved. The mosquitoes and blackflies were terrible, the bedbugs flourished, but for a few weeks we were mercifully free from disease.

In September, however, we were moved to a larger *posiolek* further north where the commandant was much harsher, fining us for the slightest infringement of the rules, stealing our parcels from home, and, most cruelly, insisting that children go to work in the forest. Thus Enzio went to work alongside Mother and Janina. It was useless to object; any complaints were met by a reduction in our already derisory rations.

In the midst of the drudgery came moments of fear. Once, a group of us men were sent to work not far from some Russian prisoners. One of them, a huge, menacing man with a scarred face, demanded bread in threatening tones. I gave him some – I assumed he would take it anyway – and was relieved when we were moved the next day to another part of the forest. Then Mother sent word to me that Enzio was ill with fever and vomiting. I dropped everything and left the felling camp without permission to travel the thirteen kilometres back to the *posiolek*. Enzio later recovered, but I was thrown into the punishment hut, where Russian and Ukrainian criminals immediately stripped me of my clothes. Without doubt I would have frozen to death that same night if it hadn't been for the appearance of the scar-faced Russian, who turned out to be the convicts' leader and who immediately ordered the others to return my clothes (which they did). Thus, against the odds, there were strange unexpected acts of kindness and fellowship in that ghastly place.

Janina also fell ill that winter with pneumonia, but Mother fed her the berries and herbs which she'd stored away for just such an eventuality, and Janina survived. But the lack of nourishment took an increasing toll on all of us – we lost our night vision, our teeth rattled in our heads, and we became covered in boils which refused to heal. That said, we would undoubtedly have been even worse off, by which I mean dead, if it hadn't been for Mother's unceasing efforts to improve our lot and raise our spirits. Her every thought and concern was for us. Countless times she augmented our rations from her own. After a full day's back-breaking work, she would go into the forest looking for lichen or moss with which to supplement our diet, or would offer to clean the administrators' quarters in exchange for extra bread. Where she found the strength is a mystery. However grim the conditions might be, she always radiated love and confidence and a firm belief in the future. I saw her cry only twice: when Krysia died and – secretly – at Christmas.

Then, with summer and Hitler's attack on Russia, came the 'amnesty' for Poles. We were of course overjoyed, though the word *amnesty* stuck in our throats. We had committed no crime that required a pardon! Terminology was anyway irrelevant because the rations dropped again and we were still forced to work – though now it was for the 'glory of the common cause'.

When news reached us in October of the formation of a Polish army in the south it goes without saying that I was itching to join, but, true to form, the commandant found excuses not to issue us with discharge papers. Many men of my age slipped away anyway, but I wasn't prepared to leave without Mother, Janina and Enzio, nor the papers which were meant to provide us with safe passage and guaranteed rations along the way. The wait severely tested my patience. I could see another winter fast approaching while we starved again on the derisory rations. Finally the papers came through at Christmas and we left a week later. We went by sledge as far as the Dvina, then walked the remaining 150 kilometres to Kotlas on foot, sleeping in public buildings or on peasants' floors. Using money from the sale of clothing, we then bought places on a convoy train. (God only knows what happened to those without money – presumably they perished.) The journey was little better than the first: stations crammed with people, severe cold, verminous conditions, long waits for trains lasting days, even weeks, tortuous journeys which often took us back to where we'd started from, and desperate hunger when the promised rations failed to materialise.

Then – it still chills me to write about it – I was separated from our family. It was at Orenburg, near the Kazak border. I leapt off the train to search for food and returned to find that the train had left with Mother, Janina and Enzio still aboard! I had to wait two days for another

train, which was even more crowded and insanitary than
the one before. The journey over the steppes was long and
slow, the temperature scorching in the day and freezing at
night. Typhoid and dysentery were rife. The dead had to
be left at the stops for the Kazaks to bury. Arriving in
Tashkent, I searched for our family everywhere. I made
enquiries of the Polish military and the Soviet authorities,
even of the NKVD – wild men who were arresting and
shooting people at random – but nothing. In desperation I
moved on to Samarkand and Kermine where the 7th
Division of the Polish army was forming. The desert
around Kermine was one huge refugee camp. I searched
and searched, but in the end I was forced to join the army
or starve. Shortly afterwards I contracted meningitis,
which almost finished me off. It was five weeks before I
could regain enough strength to renew my search. Then I
heard that the Soviet authorities had been sending Polish
families without military accreditation to collective farms
scattered over the steppes. But the details were sketchy. It
was only by luck and perseverance that I found an official
who directed me to the region where I was most likely to
find Mamma, Janina and Enzio.

My heart still trembles with cold anger at the memory
of the scenes I witnessed on the steppes of Uzbekistan. Evil
had given way to chaos, and chaos to horror. Polish
civilians not allocated to collectives were camped beside
the railway under tents made of sticks and rags, in a state
of the most abject misery and hunger. They begged for
food, but what could I do? I had precious little myself and
there were hundreds and thousands of them. Their faces
will haunt me all my life. Having survived the cold winds
of Siberia, our brave people were dying like flies of disease
and starvation, their bodies thrown into mass graves
without Christian burial. It was the closest thing I have
witnessed to hell on earth. I hope never to see its like
again.

In growing dread I continued my search for our small family. Eventually I was directed to a collective where my hopes were raised through the roof only to be dashed again. The three of them had been working there until recently, the administrator told me, but were now gone, and he couldn't or wouldn't tell me where. I was at my wits' end when a Polish worker slipped me a message with the name of a small township some twenty kilometres away. Thus it was that I found Mother and Janina lying in a mud hovel on the edge of the steppe, alive but close to starvation. Mother was desperate because Enzio had fallen ill and been taken by some Uzbeks to the nearest town, and she had no idea what had happened to him. Leaving Mother and Janina with blankets, food and water, I went to the town to ask after him, only to discover that he had died two days before. With aching heart, I bore this terrible news back to Mother and Janina. It was the only time I heard Mother berating God. Later, I think she found some comfort in the thought that Enzio's sufferings were over and he had gone to a better place. There could be no doubt he was in a better place. Never have I seen such a godforsaken spot. The hovel was mud-built, the floor a hollow in the ground, the heat, dust and cold extreme. Their only food had been weeds, lizards, hedgehogs, and whatever they could beg from the Uzbeks in the way of grain and rotting fruit. As if this were not enough, their last possessions had been stolen from them while they slept, identity documents, shoes, everything.

I hired an *arba* to carry them to the railway. Thence we travelled to the Polish army in Guzar, where as a matter of course every soldier in the army went short to ensure that none of the families went hungry. We were all skin and bone; but we shared everything.

As soon as Janina regained some strength, she joined the Polish Women's Auxiliary Service and appeared one day looking very proud in a man's uniform that was far too big for her. Mother took longer to recover. I think she was simply bowed down by grief.

For three months we muddled along, the army without arms or the most basic supplies (the Russians not being forthcoming – no big surprise), and everyone hungry. Rumours were rife. One minute we were being sent to the Eastern Front, the next to defend Moscow. So you can imagine the jubilation when we heard that the entire army plus dependants were to be evacuated to the Middle East under the auspices of the British.

At the end of August I left with my regiment on one train, Mother, Janina and the rest of the families following on the next. From Krasnovodsk on the Caspian Sea we then embarked on a ship bound for Pahlevi. The two-day voyage was the last trial in our journey, so overcrowded that it was virtually impossible to move and dysentery rife. The civilians were quartered in another, equally crowded part of the ship so it was impossible to make contact with Mother and Janina, and when we reached Persia we were sent to different reception centres many kilometres apart.

The British had everything organised for our arrival: food, medical treatment, delousing. When they took our clothes away to burn them, we ran naked into the sea and stood in the balmy wind to dry, just a gaggle of bony skeletons, proud and happy to be free at last. The only problem was an ironic one – the danger of too much food landing in our feeble stomachs.

As soon as possible I sent word to the dependants' camp, but before a reply could reach me my unit was sent to a camp near Teheran. Thus it was some days before Janina managed to get a message to me to say that Mama was in hospital in Pahlevi. I arrived to find her grievously ill with dysentery and malaria. Despite the finest medical care, nothing could be done. She slipped towards death as she had approached life, with heroism, unselfishness, and boundless love, thinking only of us. In her last moments

she prayed that you and Aleks were safe. A Polish priest
gave her the last rites and she received a Christian burial in
the Polish Cemetery. When I think of all that Mother did
for us, her tender heart, her generosity and concern for
others, her unquenchable spirit, I know that, even in the
midst of wickedness and despair, goodness can and does
exist. I will carry the memory of her goodness always, as a
standard against which the authors of her misfortune will
be judged.

There is little else to tell. I went with the army to
Palestine and Italy, where I was injured in the final battle
for Monte Cassino. Towards the end of the war Janina
also came to Italy, serving as an army clerk, and it was
here that she met and married Giovanni.

Thus our odyssey came to an end, one journey among
many others. As a family we fared worse than some, better
than others. I suppose we should be thankful to have
survived at all. But I find it hard to feel anything as
unconfined as gratitude when we have lost so much, and to
nothing but the grotesque power struggles of absurd
dictators. When I think of the waste, I can only weep for
the past and despair for the future.

I kiss you goodbye, Helenka, until I write again.

Your loving brother,

Wladek

Wladyslaw put down his pen and stared into the darkness
beyond the candle. It was some moments before he realised the
heavy rain of the night had ceased clattering against the metal
roof and given way to a deep silence, broken only by faint
snores from the next cubicle. He looked at his watch, and then
a second time to make sure he had not misread it. The night
was almost over.

He stretched his bad leg and kneaded the calf before leafing
back through the letter to find the passage covering Enzio's
death. He read it with some misgivings. It seemed to him that

Helenka couldn't fail to spot the glaring omission, particularly when he had been so careful to specify the location and nature of the other burials. Would she comment on it? Or would she realise that his silence was deliberate? And knowing it was deliberate, would she immediately put the worst interpretation on it? On balance he felt he had done the right thing, though he might be accused, not least by himself, of having taken the easy path.

His burden was to have failed to find Enzio's body. His penance was to revisit his failure in his dreams. The dream always began in the same way, mirroring events. The doors of the morgue opened up like a giant maw and he stepped forward into the dark fly-ridden interior, feeling the heat and stench close over him in a noxious cloud. He saw suppurating bodies stretching away into the darkness, laid densely and haphazardly on the floor, shapes that were crudely wrapped or draped in filthy makeshift shrouds from which limbs or faces protruded as if in final appeal. Then the dream diverged from reality: sometimes he searched through the bodies doggedly but illogic-ally, at other times with furious impatience, driven by the dread that Enzio's body would moulder in that terrible place for ever, unclaimed and unburied. Yet however hard he searched he was condemned to failure. Either he found himself back at the door, held immobile by some mysterious force, or, having fought his way through the putrefying limbs to the shadows of the furthest corner, he discovered that the morgue was little more than an anteroom to a whole series of cavernous rooms, ominous and thick with putrefaction.

He could not deny this dream – his failure still weighed on him – but he resented it, not merely for its power to disturb him, but because it overshadowed all his happy memories of the irrepressible Enzio. Awake, he could allow himself the certain knowledge that Enzio was at rest, that his body was buried with the other typhoid victims in one of the mass graves dug by the Uzbeks, and that, then or at some point shortly afterwards, a Polish priest would have been found to say prayers over him. But if Wladyslaw's conscious mind allowed him the possibility of peace, his ungovernable subconscious did not, and in his dreams the guilt sped on regardless like a demon in the night.

He folded the letter and put it on one side. Blowing out the candle, he pulled on his tunic and stepped out of the hut into an uncertain dawn. The first glimmerings of light were muffled by a dense mist, heavy with dew, through which the trees rose and faded as they reached towards an invisible sky. For a moment, it might have been Archangel again.

He walked across grass soft with fallen leaves. A windless hush enveloped everything, bitter-sweet with the scents of autumn. He absorbed the air and its richness, he saw the feathery heads of the trees lifting to the wan light, and suddenly it was a new world after all, vibrant and free. He thought: Yes, I'm grateful to be here. Of course I am!

He came to a narrow sliver of water, blurred with mist, its silken surface speared with rushes and spiky-leaved plants, its banks clustered with dense cabbagy leaves. Along one side, stunted willow trees bent over the water at odd angles, each crown sprouting a giant star-burst of fine stems, while at his feet a string of bubbles pressed lazily against the tight surface of the water before breaking softly. Somewhere in the distance a bird called on a single note, and he thought firmly: Happiness is really a matter of putting one's mind to it. I will be happy here so long as I choose to be.

He walked along the raised edge of the ditch, across heavy wet grass and hillocks and tumbledown fences. Above his head the haze became suffused with brightness and seemed to drift slowly upwards. Ahead, watery colours began to form and he saw through the mist a raised road, a bridge, and a figure slowly walking, like in a Dutch painting. As the mist gently dissolved he made out a long rank of stunted willow trees, and then another, stretching towards an indeterminate horizon. Between them, sudden gates stuck up out of the flatness for no apparent reason, and a hill rose in a perfect dome, like the cupola of a sunken church. Amid the wash of delicate colours a clump of tall frond-like plants formed a velvety block of olive-green. All was damp and soft. Even the ground beneath his feet seemed to yield and quiver, as if water lay just beneath the surface of everything.

Making a wide loop, he came to the village of Middlezoy, which he'd been told about but not yet visited. It stood on slightly higher ground, a low-lying island in the midst of a wide marshy sea. Approaching, he buttoned his uniform properly and ran a hand over his hair, and hoped his unshaven chin was not too obvious.

Stone cottages stood among apple orchards and neat gardens on two diverging streets which snaked over undulating ground. He saw at least one church and one inn, but no obvious centre. He came across an elderly man, followed by a tight-lipped woman. Both nodded at him when he bade them good morning. Then came a girl with dark hair and flashing eyes who grinned and cast a mischievous sidelong glance at him as he passed. He looked back at her and heard a stifled laugh. There was a small post office which was also a shop. He tried the door with the idea of buying some tobacco, but it was closed and he didn't have his ration book with him.

As he reached the end of the village the sun burnt free of the mist and, on a hill ahead, a tall tree retaining a few ragged leaves flamed suddenly with ochre and amber. It was going to be a wonderful day. Walking on with a buoyant heart, he passed an orchard where apples had been heaped into large mouldering piles, then a field dotted with tiny upright huts like sentry boxes where vegetables were growing in narrow strips, then the entrance to Camp A, the first of the three sites which made up the resettlement camp. It stretched across a large orchard only partially cleared of trees, so that the crouching Nissen huts appeared to be sheltering among a tangle of apple branches. He saw washing hanging on a line and smoke rising from one of the communal blocks and heard a woman singing, her voice floating high on the golden air. Camp B, his own, was fifty yards beyond Camp A, spread across a verdant meadow ringed by tall poplars. Camp C, which he hadn't yet visited, lay out of view over rising ground to the north.

Camp B was not yet finished. The building squad was still putting up standpipes and laying paths and slapping white paint over the ribbed interiors of the Nissen huts, which had been dubbed 'barrels of laughs'. Only about sixty people had moved in so far. Happily, there were several families among their number and, since his arrival three days before, Wladyslaw had spent his evenings sitting at a table covered in a clean white cloth, minding his manners and enjoying the enchanting, demanding conversation of women. The families consisted of married couples with grown-up children or elderly parents. There were no young children anywhere, for all the orphans and women with young children who'd reached Persia had either stayed in the Middle East or been sent to camps in India and East Africa.

On the previous evening Wladyslaw had found himself next to a fellow called Grobel who had been separated from his family in this way. With a crack in his voice Grobel had read excerpts from a letter postmarked Masindi, Uganda, describing a life more distant and fantastic than anything he could have imagined in his wildest dreams. Showing Wladyslaw a photograph of suntanned children squinting under a tropical sun, Grobel had marvelled and wept at how much his sons and daughter had grown. He had no idea when or where he would see them again; no transports were scheduled, nor yet proposed. He was finding the separation especially hard to bear now that something approaching normal life was finally possible.

Walking through the camp in the fresh morning light, Wladyslaw saw Grobel again now. Remembering how their conversation had ended, with vodka and tears, Wladyslaw prepared a smile, only to be greeted by a wave like a salute and a brisk enquiry as to whether Wladyslaw was intending to come to the residents' meeting.

'I didn't know any meeting was planned.'

'At ten o'clock in the canteen. No officers or administrators invited.'

'And the purpose . . .?'

'Why, to organise our complaints!'

'Ah.'

'You don't agree?'

'Well . . . if there are valid complaints, then yes – they should be aired.'

'And by us alone.'

'If that's what everyone wants.'

'Of course it is!' Grobel brooded for a moment. 'Valid . . . You think that some of our complaints might *not* be valid then?'

'I meant rather – that all *reasonable* complaints should be put forward.'

'But who is to decide what is reasonable? Are you suggesting it's for others to decide?'

'Not at all.'

' – that it's for administrators and officers to decide?'

'No.'

Grobel eyed Wladyslaw warily. 'But I think you were. I think perhaps that you side with them quite naturally, that you're one of them . . .'

'Hardly.'

'But you're a university type.'

'I don't see what difference that makes.'

'It means that you see only one point of view. Your mind is made up.'

'I very much hope not. In fact – not at all!'

Grobel declared scornfully, 'They'll make you an administrator.'

'Not if I can help it – I hate administration. But isn't that beside the point? Aren't we all in this together? Don't we share the same concerns?'

Grobel glared at him scornfully. 'Where have you been all

this time? Don't you realise this place is riddled with traitors and collaborators? The administrators are throwing them in amongst us without a second thought – men who fought with the Germans, men who secretly sided with the Russians. We can't be expected to live alongside these people. We shouldn't be asked to!'

'Well . . .'

'You don't agree?'

'It's time to draw a line, surely. People were put under intolerable pressure.'

'A traitor is always a traitor!'

'Even when guns are put to the heads of their families?'

'No excuse.' With hardly a pause, Grobel added, 'And it's not just the Nazi types either – what about the Ukrainians? And the Byelorussians? Pretending to be good Poles indeed!'

'But they wouldn't be here if they weren't Polish.'

'Their names . . . their ways . . . How do we know where their hearts really lie? How do we know they weren't conniving with the Russians all along? No – it's an outrage! The administrators sit at their desks, without thought or care. It's us who have to put up with these characters. It's a grave insult. After everything we've been through.'

Wladyslaw adopted a tone of quiet reason. 'Well, if that's your view, I would certainly agree on the need for a careful assessment of the facts.'

Grobel said dismissively, 'There speaks a true administrator. Put everything off till another day. Pretend it's not happening. Oh yes, you'll make your mark all right!'

Wladyslaw wasn't sure if it was the agitation that aggravated his leg, but as he marched back to his quarters he felt the familiar stabbing pains in his calf. He hopped up the steps to the hut door on a leg and a half and limped through the sitting area to his cubicle. Banging open the door he sat heavily on the bed and gave the muscle a violent kneading. There was always going to be a Grobel in every camp, of course, a small man with small ideas who tried to inflate his sense of self-importance by stirring up dissent and suspicion. In the *posiolek* there had been a similarly officious woman who without evidence had accused a family of stealing some food, then gone around boasting about her public-spiritedness; and on the long journey across Uzbekistan a pompous bigot who, having appointed himself spokesman for their wagon, had demanded that a family of Jews travel in a separate section of the train. On both occasions good sense had prevailed, but as always at the expense of much unnecessary tension and argument. In the same way Grobel's ideas would be listened to, discussed and eventually ignored, but not before everyone had been thoroughly upset.

Sitting at the locker which served as his desk, Wladyslaw folded and addressed the letter to Helenka, using the same unschooled handwriting as before and the same flower motif over the seal. He then tidied up. It didn't take long. The cubicle, separated from its neighbours by partitions, was barely large enough to contain the locker, an iron bed, a metal chair, and what the English absurdly called a 'commode' – which, since it concealed a chamber pot that no full-blooded male would be seen dead carrying across a mixed camp in broad daylight to the latrines, was widely scorned and universally derided. When it rained hard, the corrugated-iron roof gave off a deafening clatter like the rattle of small-arms fire, and the insides of the barrel streamed with condensation. The floor was bare concrete and cold underfoot, and the hut's two small stoves looked inadequate for a harsh winter. The thick glass windows at either end of the tunnel-like hut consigned the cubicle to perpetual dusk during the day, and the unshaded lights glanced down over the partitions to create shafts of glare and pockets of deep shadow. in the evening. Yet for all its faults, this space was his own, the first he had had in six years. If he was destined to spend the winter here, he could do worse.

He went to the toilet block to wash and shave, and then to the canteen for breakfast. The place was crowded, the conversation at a roar. He found a seat next to a group of boisterous

young people. A lively corporal was telling tall stories to the
only unmarried girls in the camp, two pretty creatures of
twenty or so. Inevitably, given the fierce competition, the girls
were spoken for, but since the corporal had an Italian bride in
Bologna and the photographs to prove it, no one, least of all
the corporal himself, was taking the flirtation too seriously.

The conversation was fast, the laughter uproarious. Soon
Wladyslaw was laughing with them, though a little self-
consciously. It was a long time since he had been in the
company of well-mannered girls. In Italy most of the good girls
had been kept firmly under lock and key, while in England he
only ever seemed to meet the loud, cheeky, abrasive factory
girls who frequented the pubs. He had forgotten the exquisite
tension one felt in the company of pretty women, the urge
to vie for their attention, the swell of pride one felt at an
appreciative glance. He had forgotten, too, the loneliness that
was the other side of longing, the ache for a love of one's own.

An hour later, on his way back from posting his letter,
Wladyslaw was approached by the upright figure of Major
Rafalski, one of the camp administrators.

'It's Malinowski, isn't it? How are you settling in? Accommodation all right?'

'Fine, thank you, sir.'

'You were transferred to us from the north, weren't you?'

'Yes, sir.'

'Not happy there?'

'It wasn't that. I asked to return to this area because of the
chance of work.'

'Ah. You've had an offer, have you?'

'I believe so.'

'What kind of thing?'

'Farm work.'

The major raised an eyebrow and regarded Wladyslaw
thoughtfully. 'Listen . . .' he said. 'Do you have a moment for
a chat?'

The major's office was in the concrete administration block.

It contained a table, four chairs and a telephone. Papers were stacked neatly on the floor and a large map of Britain hung on the wall.

The major gestured Wladyslaw to a chair and offered him a cigarette. He himself did not take one, but sat upright in his seat, touching his fingertips together in a precise arch. Rafalski was a cavalryman, tall and austere, with highly polished boots and a crested signet ring. He was probably in his late twenties, though his stern face and serious manner made him seem older.

'You joined the army in the Soviet Union?' he asked.

'Yes.'

'You never thought of a commission?'

'No. I was perfectly happy as a regular soldier.'

'But you're an educated man?'

The nature and purpose of education was one of Wladyslaw's favourite hobbyhorses. He liked nothing better than to argue against the trend towards a narrow intensive curriculum in favour of an eclectic, intuitive, meandering path of one's own choosing; though a lively discussion and a worthy opponent could sometimes persuade him to the other point of view for a split second or two. Now, out of old habit, he replied, 'That's an arguable proposition.'

'I beg your pardon?'

'I'm not sure how much real education you get from a formal education.'

The major stared at him uncomprehendingly, and Wladyslaw withdrew the comment with a quick gesture.

'I completed a year at Lublin University before the war, if that's what you mean.'

'And your subject?'

'Literature.'

'Really?' Rafalski murmured appreciatively. Then, on a note of polite conjecture: 'Not many books to be found on a farm, I wouldn't have thought. Nor time to read them.'

'There'll be quite a few winter evenings.'

'But no mental stimulation to speak of.'

'Perhaps not.'

Rafalski was working his way steadily towards some point and Wladyslaw suddenly had an inkling of what it might be.

'You haven't considered a job here on the administrative staff?' Rafalski asked. 'We're recruiting for a number of posts.'

'I'm not your man, I'm afraid. I'm hopeless with paper-work.'

'Ah, but there's a post on the recreational side which might suit you very well. Organising a theatre group, a choir, lectures on British life – that kind of thing.' He added in a despondent tone, 'We need someone who can whip up enthusiasm.'

'Thank you, but I'd prefer to work away from the camp.'

'And on a farm. May I ask why?'

'Well, for one thing I'm determined to master the language. English has to be the most infernal, illogical language on the planet – but so long as the English will insist on speaking it I feel I have no option but to battle on.'

'But what will you learn on a farm? The conversation will be rudimentary, the people uneducated.'

'One's got to start somewhere.'

The major gazed at Wladyslaw in puzzlement. 'You've decided to stay in England then?'

'I'm considering it, yes.'

'But – if I may put it to you – don't you find it demeaning – insulting – to stay in a country where you're treated like an unwelcome intruder? Where you're forbidden to run your own business or practise your profession? Where all work but farming and mining is closed to you? Where doctor, professor, peasant alike are treated as the lowest of the low. Don't you find this – *impossible*? At least here in the Corps you would have a position that commands respect.'

'I'm a born optimist, I suppose. I feel sure that things will change for the better.'

'But the British – you don't find their behaviour objection-able?'

'Not as a rule, no. They have their oddities, of course. But probably no worse than ours appear to them.'

'I meant their behaviour regarding our army,' Rafalski corrected him. 'Aren't you concerned that these people have betrayed us?'

'I prefer not to think of it as a betrayal. More like a mis-judgement.'

Rafalski gave the idea a moment of intense consideration before shaking his head. 'I don't believe that anything so calculated can be termed a misjudgement.' He moved some papers a short distance across his desk and straightened his fountain pen. 'Greater love hath no man than this, that he lay down his life for his friends,' he murmured. 'This is what the British carve on their war memorials, you know. Yet these are the same people who excluded us from the Victory Parade.'

This was one accusation that Wladyslaw didn't try to refute.

'They were only too glad to have us fight some of the bloodiest battles of the war,' the major went on reflectively. 'They made no objection to thousands of Poles laying down their lives at Tobruk and Arnhem and Monte Cassino . . . Yet in victory they ban us from marching at their sides. They turn their backs on us. They betray the memory of the dead.' The major's voice had dropped almost to a whisper, yet beneath the impassive features it seemed to Wladyslaw that his anger burned and burned.

There was a long pause. Finally, the major sat forward in his chair and said crisply, 'I certainly won't be staying.'

'Where will you go?' Wladyslaw asked. 'Have you decided?'

Rafalski had become lost in thought. Emerging slowly from his trance, he murmured, 'I think . . . Paris. I have relatives there. And the way of life, you know . . . the civilisation . . .'

'You speak French?'

'Yes. I learnt it from an early age, along with German and Italian, and a touch of Russian.' Wladyslaw could just imagine the aristocratic household with its private tutors and regi-mented routine. 'The language no one considered of any use,

of course, was English. Consequently I speak not a word.'
From his tone, the major didn't regard this as a great loss.
'German is probably my best language,' he went on. 'In fact
I offered myself for interrogation work during the war, but
the British always preferred to use their own people.' Saying
this, he brought the papers back across the desk and realigned
them with small nudging motions of both hands. 'And your
languages?'

'French. And a bit of Russian.'

'And English?'

'I can make myself understood on a practical level.'

The major gave a slow nod. 'In that case could I ask you to
undertake a small task for me?'

Wladyslaw hesitated. 'If I can.'

'There's a problem in Camp C. Perhaps you've heard about
it? Ten of the accommodation huts have been taken over by
some local people. The British authorities seem reluctant to
move them on, we don't know why. Lieutenant Barut is in
charge up there, but his English is poor and he can't seem to
find out whether these people are intending to stay. Could you
help him out?'

'Well . . . I'll do my best.'

'Would now be convenient?'

'By all means.'

'Oh, and this is not to reach the ears of the British liaison
officer. The British get peeved if things aren't done by the book
– their book, of course.'

At the door Wladyslaw asked, 'When you say local people,
do you mean they come from the immediate area?'

'I've no idea where they're from. By local, I simply meant
English.'

Wladyslaw walked up to the road and a short way along
found the path to Camp C running up a slight hill between a
patchwork of vegetable plots and a broad field. The field had
been ploughed for the winter and a number of small brown
birds with long beaks and delicate legs were picking their way

across the furrows. A breeze had sprung up and masked the early morning sun with a veil of torn cloud, but he could still make out the boundary of an airfield far away to his right and etched against the skyline a lone fighter without a propeller, mothballed or abandoned he couldn't tell.

The third Polish camp was the usual mix of Nissen huts and communal blocks of prefabricated concrete. Unlike the other two camps, however, Camp C had accumulated the detritus and clutter of permanent habitation. Near the first row of huts metal drums lay abandoned alongside odd lengths of timber, and washing hung suspended in long lines, while near a boundary fence rubbish was burning in a smouldering pile. Some civilians were working on strips of land dug up for cultivation, and children were playing football on an open space. It wasn't until Wladyslaw went deeper into the camp that he spotted the first Polish uniform.

He found Lieutenant Barut in the administration block. He was a short jolly man with a quick smile, who raised his hands to heaven and declared undying gratitude for being sent an English speaker at last.

'I'm not the most fluent,' Wladyslaw warned him.

'Believe me – your presence can only be a vast improvement. I've tried French but no one in this country speaks a word!'

Lieutenant Barut led the way along the grid of concrete paths to what he termed the English Quarter. He halted in front of a hut with a yellow door and bright curtains and, propped against one side, a battered motorbike awaiting a wheel.

'His name is *Bank*,' the lieutenant primed Wladyslaw before knocking. '*Len Bank*.'

'Is he their leader?'

'I don't think they have a leader. Not that I'm aware of, anyway.'

The door was opened by a plump round-faced woman of about forty wearing a flowered pinafore. She appeared flushed, as if from the stove, and was wiping her hands on a cloth. At the sight of Lieutenant Barut she offered a tentative smile.

Barut bowed formally. 'Good morning, Mrs Bank,' he said in atrociously accented English.

'Good morning.' She dipped her head in return.

'Friend,' Barut said, indicating Wladyslaw.

'Friend,' the woman repeated, as if they were both attending language class.

Barut waved Wladyslaw forward.

'Mrs Bank? How do you do?' Preserving the formality, Wladyslaw also gave a bow.

She inclined her head again, rather awkwardly. 'It's Banks with an s.'

'Mrs *Banks*, sorry. May I speak with your husband, please?'

She looked from one man to the other. 'Why? What's it about?'

'I wish to ask question. It will take only short time.' Wladyslaw added a warm smile to underline the friendliness of the occasion.

'My husband's not here. What is it you want to know?'

'Ah . . .' Wladyslaw turned to Barut for advice. 'The husband's out,' he explained in Polish.

Barut urged rapidly, 'Well, ask her instead! Go on!'

'Mrs Banks . . . Yes, if you could tell us, please . . . will you stay long?'

Her smile had faded. 'How do you mean?'

'Excuse me – my English is not very good. Will you be remaining for long time in this camp?'

'We'll be staying as long as needs be, that's how long,' she said firmly.

Wladyslaw made a show of absorbing this while he struggled with the concept of *needs be*. 'Excuse me, but . . . you are waiting to go somewhere else?'

'We're waiting to get proper decent housing, that's what we're waiting for. No more, no less.'

'Ah.' Wladyslaw lift a hand in a gesture of understanding before indicating the rest of the English Quarter. 'And your friends? Is it same for everyone?'

'Oh yes. That's why everyone's come. We're all in the same boat.' Then, with a dart of suspicion: 'Why? What's up? They're not going to try and get us out, are they?'

'Excuse me – *they*?'

'The police. The army. Is that what this is all about?' she demanded on a rising note of agitation. 'Because if they're thinking of trying to get us out you can tell 'em we won't be shifting, not for nobody. We'll barricade ourselves in if we have to.'

Wladyslaw threw up both hands. 'No, I swear – is nothing like this. I swear – we know nothing of army, police.'

Lieutenant Barut hissed in Wladyslaw's ear, 'What on earth have you said to upset her?'

'I haven't said anything,' Wladyslaw protested. 'She's just jumped to the wrong conclusions.'

Mrs Banks turned her plump frame sideways, preparing to step back inside. 'You can tell 'em – they won't be getting through this door except over our dead bodies.'

Wladyslaw spread his arms wide then dropped them heavily at his sides in the gesture of an honest man who asks only to be taken at his word. 'I swear – I ask this question only for reason of finding accommodation for Polish people, nothing more. Because if there is not accommodation here, then we must find another place for them.'

'Well . . .' she said uncertainly. 'That's hardly our problem, is it?'

Wladyslaw gave a small equivocal shrug.

'It's only right we should get first call on the housing,' Mrs Banks continued as if he were arguing the point. 'After everything we've been through – it's only right.'

'I see this. Thank you.'

After some hesitation Mrs Banks stepped forward again and said in a voice that had regained its cordiality, 'Look, don't get me wrong. If we'd been looked after all right – well, it would be different, wouldn't it? We wouldn't mind them turning this place over to you people. We wouldn't mind them spending a mint of money fixing it all up. But we've been waiting six years, ever since the bombing, and we're not going to wait no more.'

'I understand.'

'It's the children,' she added, as if this explained everything.

'Yes. Of course.' Wladyslaw made to leave, only to ask lightly, 'And the authorities, what do they say to you?'

'Oh, they *say* they're doing their best,' she scoffed good-naturedly. 'They *say* there's going to be new houses for everyone. Brand new! Well, we'll believe *that* when we see it.'

Wladyslaw gave a small bow. 'I thank you for your assistance.'

'Well?' demanded Barut as they walked away.

'They're dug in for the duration.'

'What – all of them?'

'Looks like it. They're waiting for decent housing, and they're not prepared to move till they get it.'

'And what are the British authorities doing about it?'

'Not much, so far as I can gather.'

The lieutenant gave a fatalistic shrug. 'That's what I thought. Well, we'll just have to make the best of it. You never know, there might be some mutual benefits. They might be able to help us with our English. Anything would be better than the teacher we've been allocated, a harridan with the face of a Gorgon who can't teach to save her life. One can endure any number of irregular verbs if they come with a pretty smile.' Shooting Wladyslaw a mischievous glance, he added, 'The other solution, of course, is to find your own private teacher.'

'Ah.'

'I tell you, if you haven't discovered the local girls yet, you're in for a real treat.'

They were passing down the avenue of Nissen huts that made up the English Quarter. Scattered between the huts were a variety of makeshift shelters harbouring bicycles, prams, stacks of wood and assorted junk. Beside one hut, a car was chocked up on bricks, a man bent under the open bonnet; in front of another, a woman was dabbing paint onto a wooden cabinet. Then, towards the end, they came to a brightly coloured Romany caravan with red-painted shafts, and, busily cropping the grass behind, the horse to draw it. It was a fine caravan, tall, barrel-roofed, with ornate barge boards and elaborate paintwork. As Wladyslaw gazed at it admiringly, the door of the next-door hut opened and a young man in uniform ran down the steps. It was an instant before Wladyslaw realised who it was.

'Jozef?' he called out in astonishment.

Jozef ground to a halt, looking startled.

Wladyslaw laughed, 'It *is* you.'

Jozef's eyes went from Wladyslaw to Lieutenant Barut and back again. Finally, he muttered, 'Wladek . . .'

In the open doorway of the hut, a man had appeared. He had long straggly hair to the shoulder and an unkempt appearance, and his dark eyes stared at them without expression.

Jozef said shyly, 'Hello.'

'I'll leave you to it,' said Lieutenant Barut. With a sharp glance at the man in the doorway, he strode away in the direction of the Polish Quarter.

'How are you?' asked Wladyslaw delightedly.

'Oh . . . all right.' Lost for anything else to say, Jozef's gaze darted rapidly from Wladyslaw to the ground and back again. He was grasping a bundle under one arm, something solid and possibly heavy swaddled in a strip of fabric with a faded pattern.

In the open door of the hut, the unkempt man leant lazily against the door frame and lit a cigarette.

'I'm in Camp B,' Wladyslaw offered. 'I arrived three days ago.'

'Yes?'

'Out of the frying pan into the fire!'

'What?'

'Never mind. It was just a joke.'

'A joke?' Jozef shot him a puzzled glance. 'Ah. I see. Yes . . .'
He was as gaunt as ever, the bones too sharp for the flesh, the
sinews, veins and cartilages of his face revealed in extraordinary detail like an anatomical drawing. Yet his skin seemed to
have shed its grey tinge in favour of, if not a bloom, then a
touch of colour.

Wladyslaw said, 'You've signed up to the Resettlement
Corps then?'

'They promised I could change my mind if I wanted to.
They said I could go back to Poland any time I chose.'

'There you are then. The best of both worlds.' Wladyslaw
grasped his shoulder affectionately. 'So, Jozef, you managed to
escape the doctors?'

'I told them to let me go. I think they were glad to be rid of
me. I only wish I'd done it sooner. This place is heaven by
comparison.' His face lit up briefly.

'You're finding plenty to keep you busy then?'

'Oh yes!' Jozef cried. 'We have music, singing. We go to the
village, the pubs, all sorts of places—' His quick downward
gaze did not entirely conceal the spark of excitement there.

'You've found some friends then?'

'Oh yes.'

Wladyslaw glanced back at the man in the open doorway,
who was now looking at them with something like disdain.
'That's wonderful, Jozef.'

'I've been adopted.'

'You've been *what*?'

'Two ladies.' Jozef added diffidently, 'Perhaps you'd like to
meet them? *Yes*,' he insisted with a sudden burst of confidence,
'you must come and meet them!'

Jozef led the way down a path towards the Polish Quarter.
Reaching a hut near the administration block, he called a
greeting as he pushed the door open. A rich throaty laugh
sounded in reply. 'Jozef! That was quick! Or did you forget the
money?' A woman stepped into the light and peered myopically

at Wladyslaw before raising her hands to one side and clapping
them like a Spanish dancer. 'And you've brought a friend! A
new friend!' She was a square woman, stocky and big-boned,
with a large head and broad features. She wore a faded apron
and loose slippers that slapped against the soles of her feet
as she came forward to greet him. 'Welcome to our humble
palace!'

Her name was Alina. Soon after they had been introduced,
her sister Danuta appeared from the depths of the hut. Another
sturdy woman of indeterminate age, with heavy, almost mas-
culine features, Danuta's looks were redeemed by a sweet,
girlish smile.

Wladyslaw found himself shepherded towards a non-
regulation armchair and pressed to take some refreshment.
'Tea? Or' – Alina laid a square hand conspiratorially on his
arm – 'something more bracing?' She turned to Danuta. 'Don't
you think—?'

'Oh yes! A friend of Jozef's!'

'Yes, this definitely calls for a toast!'

Both women shot Jozef fond glances, which he met with
embarrassment, but not, it seemed to Wladyslaw, displeasure.

Alina unwrapped the bundle that Jozef had brought in and
deposited on the table. Inside were two unmarked bottles
containing a clear liquid the colour of amber. Plucking a cluster
of glasses from a makeshift shelf, Aline unscrewed a bottle and
poured four large measures. 'Can't find vodka for love nor
money. But this stirs the blood quite nicely.'

They toasted friendship, and Wladyslaw suppressed a violent splutter as the firewater seared his throat and flavours
redolent of mouldering fruit and dog's piss exploded at the
back of his nose.

'It takes some getting used to,' Alina said. 'They tell us it's
apple brandy – but who knows? Will you survive?' she enquired
solicitously. 'The best thing is another toast – that'll set you
right.'

The toast to their beloved homeland brought a moment of

reverent silence. This time the firewater passed blamelessly down
Wladyslaw's throat. The two sisters were schoolmistresses from
the Lwow region, they told him. Having survived a camp in
the Urals, they had gone south after the amnesty and spent the
rest of the war teaching at a Polish school in Isfahan. Once
the war was over, they had persuaded the British authorities to
bring them to Britain to teach Polish children. 'Except there are
no children yet!' Alina laughed. Alina was widowed, her sister
had a husband in southern Poland with whom she hoped to be
reunited. Their grown-up children were either dead or abroad.

'Now, Jozef' – turning to him, Alina made a gesture of
regret that was surprisingly elegant, almost balletic, a slow
unfurling of one ungainly hand – 'with all this business, would
you believe it but I've actually run out of cigarettes? And it's
no good' – this to Wladyslaw – 'he knows his Aunt Alina can't
get along without them for long.' To Jozef again, tenderly,
leaning forward to press some money into his hand: 'Dear boy,
if you would be so kind?'

Her lively eyes followed Jozef as he stood up and made for
the door. Danuta, leaning sideways in her chair, craned her
head to watch him to the bottom of the steps, her hand poised
to wave.

'Jozef told us all about you, Wladyslaw,' said Alina. 'Your
kindness to him in the sanatorium. But why didn't they take
better care of him there? How could they leave him so thin?'

'It's the food,' offered Danuta. 'No one can build their
strength on English food.'

'Of course we don't ask too much about the sanatorium,'
Alina said. 'Nor what happened to Jozef during the war.'

Danuta nodded. 'We wait to be told such things.'

'But with someone like Jozef it's not enough to mend the
body,' Alina said firmly, 'one must also tend to the mind and
the spirit. What he needs is to be among young people –
healthy young people.'

'What he needs,' said Danuta, almost under her breath, 'is a
bit of fun.'

'And he finds it here?' suggested Wladyslaw.

'What, with *us*?' Alina declared, deliberately choosing to misunderstand him. She gave her throaty laugh. 'Two women who've seen better days!'

'And that's putting it mildly,' murmured Danuta with a slow smile at Wladyslaw. 'But we've offered ourselves as honorary aunts, haven't we?'

'Godmothers.'

'I prefer aunts.'

'Aunts, then. We try to organise regular events for all the young – social and educational.'

'Recreational too. Walking, dancing, singing.'

'We try to get them out and about. Keep them busy and happy.'

'The trouble, as you know, is the shortage of girls,' Danuta said. 'So we've persuaded the administrators to arrange a bus to take the boys to dances in the local villages on Saturday nights.'

'It's been a great success.'

'I'll bet it has,' said Wladyslaw.

'And then we persuaded Jozef to go up to the local pub, didn't we, Alina?'

'Yes, we virtually walked him to the door and pushed him inside.'

'Quite a few of our boys go there, so there were plenty of people for him to talk to.'

'But then he amazed us by making some local friends.'

'Or *girlfriend*,' Danuta mouthed silently, catching Wladyslaw's eye.

'And now he goes quite regularly to meet them in the pub. And – twice, isn't it, Danuta? – they've taken him out for the day.'

'Yes, he's quite changed. We've noticed the difference already. He's beginning to come out of himself.'

Alina leant her large head towards Wladyslaw and said in a stern tone that sent him straight back to the classroom, 'This talk of going back to Poland is all very well, but for the time being he's far better off here where he can be assured of three meals a day, a roof over his head, and no cares or responsibilities. It's far too soon to talk of going back,' she insisted. 'He's simply not ready.'

'He wouldn't last a minute,' Danuta echoed. 'Not without someone to keep an eye on him.'

Just then they heard footsteps and the three of them turned as one to watch Jozef stride in with Alina's cigarettes.

'We were just talking about you,' Alina said ingenuously. 'We were saying how much better you were looking.'

Before Wladyslaw had the chance to refuse, his glass was refilled and they were drinking a toast to youth and happiness, which prompted the sisters to regale them with anecdotes of their own youthful adventures. As the tales became more convoluted, the misdemeanours more fantastic, Jozef looked up from the floor and shook his head at them, as a child might disapprove of a parent's immoderate behaviour, but for the most part he sat quietly with an expression that if not content was certainly less troubled. Wladyslaw thought with relief: He's going to be all right after all.

It was almost twelve by the time Wladyslaw got away, promising to return the next day. Walking down the line of huts, he passed a group of airmen sitting on a circle of chairs on the grass, laughing and smoking, then wedged in an open doorway a soldier reading a Polish-language newspaper, and on the path ahead two women strolling arm in arm, heads tilted companionably towards each other; and he thought how easy it would be to surrender to this beguiling combination of routine and security, to exist in a cocoon of Polishness for months even years on end, to attend dances and events, slavishly to follow the Polish news, perhaps even to fall in love and marry, all within the confines of the camp. Familiarity would become the mother of inertia. Without the spurs of hunger or fear, there would be little incentive to risk an unknown fraught with language and employment difficulties.

All the more reason, it seemed to Wladyslaw, to make the leap straight away. It wasn't that he felt especially courageous – nothing so noble – more that the dogs of weakness were already snapping at the heels of his resolve. Too long in this place and he feared losing the will power to break away.

Coming into Camp B, Wladyslaw made out the unmistakable figure of Dr Bennett standing by his car, his gaunt form clad in the familiar coat, long and oddly shapeless, and topped by the sort of felt hat favoured by detectives in American films. At his side was a young woman looking away over her shoulder. She was slim, with curly hair the colour of bronze. When she turned towards Wladyslaw, he was struck by a pretty open face with rose-tinted cheeks and bright blue eyes.

Spotting Wladyslaw, the doctor waved cheerfully and came forward to meet him. As they shook hands, Wladyslaw was aware of the girl gazing speculatively at his gammy leg.

'Good news, Wladyslaw. The permit's arrived from the Ministry of Labour. You're free to start work!'

Wladyslaw felt the mixture of anticipation and alarm that comes from having your wishes come true. 'Yes? This farmer – he wants me to come still?'

'I should say so. In fact, he can't wait.' Remembering his companion, the doctor stepped back hastily and stretched one long arm towards her. 'May I introduce Stella Mead? Wladyslaw Malinowski.'

As Wladyslaw brought her hand up to his lips, he caught an impression of eyes that were both exceptionally blue and exceptionally clear, and broad cheekbones that carried the faintest dusting of freckles.

'Stella has kindly volunteered to give English classes to the women in Camp B until the regular teacher arrives.'

'English classes. Ah, this will make everyone very happy,' declared Wladyslaw with his best smile.

But Stella had stepped back and was clasping her right hand in her left, as if to protect it from further assault, and Wladyslaw remembered too late that not all English girls took kindly to hand-kissing. The pub girls treated it as a great joke and, egged on by their friends, were always pleading to have the greeting repeated so they could strike a pose of exaggerated girlishness or play the vamp and fall into paroxysms of laughter. But those were pub girls. This was another sort of girl altogether.

'Stella teaches at the local school,' the doctor remarked. 'I was just saying that she'll find her Polish pupils a lot more attentive.'

'I think so too,' said Wladyslaw. 'And how old are pupils in your school, Miss Stella?'

'Between five and eleven.'

'You teach English to them?'

'Along with everything else.'

'Yes? And what is everything else?'

The bright blue eyes gave him a searching look, as if to gauge the sincerity of his interest. 'Reading, writing, and arithmetic. And drawing and painting.'

He saw now that her hair was not bronze but a glorious, bold copper. It framed her face and shoulders in a sea of Botticelli curls. He said, 'These children, they are very lucky, I think.'

He received another appraising look, which seemed to find in his favour. 'Oh, and movement,' she added.

'Movement? What is this?'

'Moving to music.'

'Dancing?'

'Nothing quite so formal.'

'Formal? Excuse me, please, my English is not so good.'

'We don't teach anything so – *structured*. So definite.'

'I understand now. Thank you.'

'It's more a case of the children learning to express themselves through music. By pretending to be animals. Or plants. Or . . .'

'Fishes?' he suggested, with a sinuous movement of one hand.

Her laughter had a warmth that made him want to hear it

again, but before he had the chance to ask her more the doctor
was saying, 'Wladyslaw, perhaps you can help us. Stella and I
want to find the education officer, one Captain . . .' He dragged
a piece of paper from his pocket and peered at it with a shake
of his head. 'No, it's no good . . .' He handed the paper to
Wladyslaw. 'This one has me stumped.'

'I understand reason for this. This name is long, even for
Polish. And not easy to say, even for long-time Polish speaker
like me!' He grinned at Stella, then read out the name quickly
for effect – 'Stobniak-Smogorzewski' – then slowly for the
doctor's benefit, then a third time with an absurd rhetorical
flourish aimed at Stella, and had the satisfaction of seeing a
giggle rise to her lips.

'You wouldn't know where we could find this chap, would
you?' Bennett asked.

Wladyslaw suggested some likely places. 'But please,' he
said, 'allow me to show you—'

'No, no,' said the doctor. 'No, we don't want to keep you,
Wladyslaw. You must have a great deal to do.'

'But it will be an honour—'

'No, I insist. No . . . you'll want to sort out your discharge
papers. If you can get them issued today, I can run you over to
the farm at about six o'clock.'

Wladyslaw accepted defeat with a rueful smile.

Stella said, 'Goodbye.'

'But we will meet again soon?'

'Well . . .' Stella looked towards the doctor uncertainly.

'I'm sure you'll bump into each other in the village.'

'Bump into?'

'A figure of speech, Wladyslaw. It means to meet by chance.'

'Ah!' Wladyslaw pressed a hand to his chest in mock relief.
'I am glad of this!'

He was rewarded with a broad smile. He would have
offered to shake her hand – minus the kiss – but she was
already moving to the doctor's side, and he gave a small bow
instead. 'Until we meet again, Miss Stella.'

She gave a last smile before turning away. Wladyslaw stood watching the two figures until they were lost to sight behind the chapel. As the coppery head vanished, he felt for a moment inconsolable.

Chapter Eight

BILLY STOOD in the dripping dawn, his breath pluming out before him, and watched the Polack bend to the first row of withies. The rain had been falling continuously for four days. Sometimes it fell heavily under black skies, at other times it drizzled within a globe of dismal grey; but it did not stop and was showing no signs of doing so in the future. On the drove the cart-ruts were like twin rhynes, parallel streams going nowhere; while in the rhynes themselves the water shifted sluggishly, if at all, the level markedly higher each morning, as if the ditches were taking in water surreptitiously during the night. The River Tone, never too accommodating at the best of times, was brim-full with shed-water from the Quantock and Blackdown Hills and could take no more, certainly not from the pump that lifted the rhyne water up from Curry Moor, and had in the last day begun to return the water back to where it came from, dribbling, gushing, slipping its load down onto the moor from a dozen low spots along its banks. The River Parrett, carrying the shed-water from the southern hills, hadn't begun to spill yet, but it could only be a matter of time. There was nothing unusual about the floods – they came virtually every year – but they were meant to come in winter, or even spring, when the hills threw off the postponed wetness of the winter's ice and snow in a mighty rush. They weren't meant to come now, in early November. At this point, the ground should have had some absorbency to it, should have had the capacity to suck the water down, layer on layer, and hold onto the stuff until the cold arrived. November was meant to be the time when withy men could get onto the moor and cut the bulk of their harvest.

Until a week ago conditions had looked good. A single sharp frost had nipped and felled every last leaf from the withies, bang to order, creating a crisp black frost-rimmed leaf-carpet from which the withies rose tall and thin and bare as knitting needles, save for the snarl of withy wind and vetch, which clung to them like tangled wool. But now the withy beds were a glutinous bog, and the leaves had settled into a sodden pulp almost indistinguishable from the surrounding ooze.

Billy brushed the whetstone across his hook with the barest touch; the blade was already razor-sharp. When he judged the Polack to be a good five yards down his row he slipped the whetstone into his pocket and bent to the adjacent row, settling quickly into the familiar rhythm, left hand grasping a cluster of withies, right hand cutting close to the stock in short tapping strokes from the wrist; then at intervals bundling the withies up, tying them off with bonds of green withy and lugging them four at a time across the squelch to the cart, which stood on the relative solidity of the drove. The two of them had been cutting for four days now, ever since the rain had started. Each day Billy gave the Polack more of a head start, and each day he caught up with him roughly halfway along the row, and each day, though he made it a rule to finish well ahead, it was by a tighter margin. The contest was undeclared, the rules unspoken, but the Polack understood the game all right, because as Billy drew closer he would look up from under the hood of his oilskins and smile and call out something in his crazy accent, and, on bringing his final bundles of withies to the cart where Billy was ostentatiously lounging under the tarpaulin with a cigarette, would shake his head with a smile, and say, 'One day maybe, when I am old man from this withies, then I get to light first cigarette.'

Billy's cigarette was largely for show. While waiting for the Polack, he went through the other man's bundles, re-sorting and retying them. It wasn't simply a matter of throwing out the bent, spraggled or otherwise unusable stock, but of getting the finished bundle to the standard girth of thirty-seven inches and ensuring that the bonds of green withy were securely tied. When Billy had started on the beds at fifteen he had found the rose knot the single greatest aggravation among the numerous provocations of that first winter, not the least of which were conditions not unlike this, with biting cold, frequent rain, water-logged ground with the suction of a bog, leaky boots and foot rot. Time and again Uncle Stan had shown Billy the trick of the rose knot, and time and again the blooming thing had slipped its hold and splayed the withies over the ground.

The Polack had more of a knack with knots; most of the bonds were reasonably tight. It was the bundle quality and size he couldn't judge. He missed much of the spraggle, he missed much of the disease, and even when he managed to collect a number of usable withies he tended to make the bundle too small, which wasn't something Billy would care to get noticed at Honeymans' withy works, where payment was strictly by the bundle. Also, while the Polack had learnt to cut the withies good and clean, he tended to cut them a fraction too high, leaving stubs that would produce shorter, heeled withies next time round. But Billy didn't point this out too often for fear of slowing him down. Yield was everything while prices were good and few other withy men were venturing onto the moor.

Thus far, by some miracle, the Polack had avoided most of the pitfalls of a beginner, neither stabbing himself in the ankle, nor burying his blade in a stump, nor breaking the tip on a stone; nor, it had to be said, had he complained of a bad back or griped about the weather, though both were probably only a matter of time.

When the Polack first arrived, Billy had been furious with the doctor for foisting a cripple on him without warning. To make matters worse, Billy had the strong suspicion that Bennett's oversight had been deliberate, a crude attempt to deter protest. This thought so incensed him that he almost rejected the Polack out of hand; but then he remembered how much time had been lost waiting for this man to start and how much money was waiting to be made, and confined his protest to a sharp reminder that the Polack was strictly on trial.

The Polack's attempts to overcome his handicap were almost comical. To haul the cart, he shuffled sideways like a crab, doing a strange hoppity two-step; to cut the withies, he put all his weight on the one good leg, knee bent, and stretched the bad one out in front of him, like a Paddy poised to dance a jig; while to walk at any sort of speed he pitched along like an old tar. The rolling gait solved one problem at least. When the doctor first tried to communicate the Polack's name, it had sounded something like 'Laddy-slaw', which though outlandish was not impossible, but when the Polack himself came to speak it, something different and wholly unpronounceable emerged. For a while, Billy dodged the issue by calling him Polack. Seeing him try to walk, however, watching the heave and dip of the shoulder and the jerky lift of the hip, a far more satisfactory alternative came to him, and he began to call him Long John. The Polack wanted to know why. When Billy told him, he laughed and repeated the word 'pirate' with a grin, and took to clapping a hand over one eye.

After that, Billy just called him Johnnie.

They worked on the withy beds from first light till just before dusk, with a short stop mid-morning and midday for some bread and cheese, a swig of cold tea, and a smoke under the tarpaulin. On these breaks they spoke – or rather the Polack asked questions and Billy proffered a series of answers – about water and floods, about the difference between withies and willows and the uses they were put to, and about the withy man's life.

The Polack offered no information about his own life until one morning when, cigarette jammed in his mouth, he began to pick at the callouses on his palms.

Billy said, 'Not done farm work before?'

'A little. At time of harvest, mostly.'

'So what did you do the rest of the time?'

'Before war? I was student.'

'A *student*,' echoed Billy, in a tone of exaggerated awe. 'And what did you study?'

'Literature. Polish, mostly. But some Shakespeare also. *Hamlet*. You know this play?'

'Now let me think . . .' said Billy, making a show of racking his brains. 'No, I do believe that particular one passed me by.'

'Sure. He write so many plays.'

'Did he now?'

The Polack cast him a watchful smile, as if to assess the spirit in which this had been offered.

With the same exaggerated show of interest, Billy asked, 'So, how many plays was it that old Shakespeare chalked up? Fifty? A hundred? Five hundred?'

'Ah!' the Polack conceded with a quick gesture. 'I don't know this. Too many for this student, that is sure.'

'And remind me,' said Billy, 'is *Hamlet* the one where they all get to kill each other?'

The Polack warmed to the joke. 'Only four or five, I think.'

'Hardly worth bothering with, then.'

'Perhaps not.'

'So, what were you going to do with this literature?'

'Aha! This is question my father asked me often. He hoped I would choose military, law, medicine – something like this.'

'So what would he say if he could see you now?'

'He would say it is good thing to have work.'

'What, even work like this?'

But the Polack wasn't going to be drawn on that one. With an amiable shrug, he drew on his cigarette and looked away into the rain which was falling in a steady curtain.

'You come from a long line of lawyers and doctors, then?' asked Billy, who had no intention of abandoning the subject.

'Some . . . yes.'

'Your father?'

'He was soldier. In Great War, then Russian War. After this, he come home to work land.'

'Russian War? When was that?'

'Nineteen twenty.'

'Blimey. You Poles are gluttons for punishment, aren't you?'

'We do not start this war. It is Bolsheviks. They march in and try to take our land.'

'So who won?'

'Poland. Big time.'

'A touch of David and Goliath, then?'

Maybe the names weren't the same in Polack-speak, because he looked puzzled for a moment. Then as understanding came to him he nodded rapidly. 'Sure. We are David in this war.'

'Then Goliath got his revenge.'

'Yes.'

'Big time.'

'Big time.'

They smoked in silence for a while. Billy watched a heron flapping lazily over the moor, its neck bent almost double, head sunk low on its shoulders, like a fastidious old man. Somewhere close by, a very different sort of bird gave a plaintive call: a teal, unless he was very much mistaken. He remembered long cold days in a makeshift hide next to the floods, waiting for the birds to come to the decoys, and wished he had a gun with him now.

His returned to the conversation with a sense of unfinished business.

'You were brought up on a farm then, were you?'

The Polack hesitated a little. 'Sure.'

'What kind of farm?'

'All kinds. Some animals, some wheat, some fruit.'

'A big place, then?'

The Polack screwed down the lid of the tea jar and gazed at it for a moment. 'Not so big. Most land not so good for farming. Most is forest and lake.'

Billy had a vision of vast acres. He said in an accent of mock refinement, 'Very nice too. Plenty of shooting and fishing then?'

'Sure,' the Polack murmured vaguely.

'So we can send you out to bag us some supper, can we?'

'Sorry?'

'Shoot a bit of game.'

The Polack made a wry face. 'I am not good at shooting. And different animals here, I think.'

'Oh yes? What animals you got there then?'

'In area of Poland where we live – deer, many kinds. And bears, though not so often you see them. And wild – do you say *pig*?'

Billy shrugged. 'Pig'll do.'

'And wild cat, with big ears.' With a hand he fashioned a long tapering ear high above his head.

'Blimey, a real live larder right there on your doorstep. And you didn't shoot 'em?'

'Oh, my father, he liked to shoot. And my next brother also. But I liked quiet time. To ride in forest. I have this horse named Ishtar. Big. Black. Brave. Clever also.' He tapped a finger to his temple. 'She is best horse in my life. She has no fear, not even of wolfs.'

'*Wolfs*,' Billy mimicked. 'Blimey, what sort of a crazy forest you got there, Johnnie? With bloody wolves.'

'But they don't come near. They don't want trouble.'

'Very obliging of them, I'm sure. What, they see you coming, do they, and they just bugger off?'

'Sure.'

'But what if they decide they're feeling a bit peckish that day? What if they decide on a bit of sport, wolf-style?'

The Polack laughed this off as though it was too ridiculous to merit an answer.

'Well?' Billy demanded impatiently. 'What happens then?'

'Listen,' the Polack said equably, 'I tell you this story. One time when I was fifteen, I ride into forest. I go for long time. Two hours maybe. Then I turn to come home again. My mind at this age, you understand it is full of dreams and stories and poetry. I look at trees and sky, but I am not looking at path ahead. So, there is this tree that has fallen across path, like so.' He placed his forearm at an angle. 'There is space to go under this tree if I lie flat on Ishtar's neck' – he ducked his head low – 'but I dream my dreams as always, and I lift up my head again too quick.' He acted this out as well: a throwing up of the head, followed by a grimace of alarm and surprise. 'And too late, I see there is more tree. So *pow*!' He hit the heel of his hand against his forehead and threw his head back in a mime of collision. 'I fall from Ishtar. I know nothing for long time. I am – how do you say – ?'

'Out cold?'

'OK. I am *out cold*. For many hours. When I wake there is no Ishtar. No nothing. Just forest. And my head hurt like hell. Not so good!' he exclaimed with an almost boyish delight. 'Then I hear this silence around me. Animals, you know. And then I see on path in front, maybe just five metres away, six, seven wolfs. But you know something? I have no fear. I know I am safe. They look at me. I look at them. We say hello. And then they are gone. Is OK. No problem.'

When he lapsed into silence, Billy prompted, 'So you *flew* home, did you?'

The Polack dragged himself free of his memories with an effort. 'Excuse me? Ah no. Ishtar, she goes home. She finds Jerzy, who is – I don't know how you call this person – this man who attends horses?'

Billy flicked the last of his cigarette high into the air and watched it arc down onto the withy bed. 'A groom?' he murmured.

'*Groom*. OK. No one is home but Jerzy. Not my father. Not my brother. So Jerzy, he take my father's horse, he take dog with good nose, he take Ishtar also, but it is not dog that find me, it is Ishtar, just like this.' He made an arrow of his hand and sighted along it. 'Not many horses can do this thing. She is best horse ever in my life.'

'Lucky,' said Billy, thinking of the horses and the servants and the acres of forest. 'Surprised you don't want to go back,' he said.

'There is nothing for us now. The Russians take everything.'

'A bit of a change for you, this place, after a big estate, servants.'

There was a pause while the Polack got the measure of this remark. 'We don't have big estate, Billy. Just small place.'

'What, that takes two hours to cross?'

'But forest is not our land. Forest is for – for' – with urgent circlings of his hand the Polack searched for some expression that escaped him – 'for everyone who wish to hunt, to ride, to walk.'

'A sort of park.'

The Polack gave a doubtful nod. 'And servants – I think servant does not have same meaning for us.'

'Oh, I think it has the same meaning everywhere.'

The Polack gave him a narrow stare and looked away.

'Doesn't it?' Billy argued innocently.

'These people, they work for us only sometimes,' the Polack said. 'Other times they work their own land. They choose when.'

'Got it. So, you all muck in together.'

'We help each other, yes.'

'Everyone takes it in turns to act as groom?'

Suddenly the Polack was alive with suppressed anger. 'You wish to say something, Billy? Just say it. OK?'

'I'm not saying anything,' Billy protested. 'No skin off my nose either way, is it?'

'You think we have lazy life or something? You think we do not work?'

Billy shrugged. 'Listen, nice if you can get it.'

Straightening up abruptly, the Polack dragged his hat low over his ears, raised his hood, and prepared to go out into the rain. 'You hear propaganda, I think. You believe bad things in English newspapers.'

'Never read them myself.'

With a gesture of disbelief, a lifting of a splayed hand, the Polack snatched up his hook and, limping over to the withy bed, worked doggedly through the afternoon without looking Billy's way.

For the Polack's living quarters Billy had fixed up the old apple store, which was the only outhouse to have any sort of windows, two small openings set high in the walls, covered in mesh. Billy had replaced the mesh with thick glass cut roughly to size by the smithy and fixed with home-made putty of whiting and linseed oil. He removed the storage racks and accumulated jumble and muck, and limewashed the walls and scraped the peeling paint off the door, and laid a rough covering of flagstones over the earth floor. The doctor loaned a truckle bed, card table and chair, and for heating Billy resuscitated an old paraffin stove from the back of the woodshed.

The Polack made no comment when Billy showed him the room; he merely looked about him and nodded. Next morning, however, he asked if he could put up some shelves, and Billy pointed him towards the tools and the discarded storage racks and said he was welcome to knock up whatever he liked. Later that night as Billy returned from the village he saw a light in the window of the apple store and heard hammering, and, when he went to summon the Polack to work next day, glimpsed through the half-open door two shelves on the wall, not as robust as they might have been, but supporting four or five books and a framed photograph. Billy was turning away when his eye caught a crucifix pinned above the bed. It was small and ornamented and appeared to be hanging slightly off true, but for an instant it might have been the crucifix over Billy's bed at the St Paul's hostel in Bristol where he'd fetched up two days short of his fifteenth birthday. The batty old Christian Brothers who ran the place had taken him in, fed him and found him part-time work. They hadn't asked questions and, apart from the occasional half-hearted admonition to follow a steady path, they hadn't preached either, virtually the only people in that long and troubled year to have encouraged him towards independence. Ordinarily he loathed religious symbols, but the sight of the ornate Catholic crucifix prompted him to feel something like affection.

Before dawn each morning the Polack came into the kitchen to make himself breakfast, and again in the evening to share whatever Stan had cooked up during the day. One afternoon, just before dark, the Polack disappeared into the orchard and returned with a quantity of wild mushrooms which he turned out onto the table with the air of wishing to help out. But Stan wasn't having dubious manure-feeding fungi mucking up his stew and turned them down flat. Mystified, the Polack cooked them up for himself in a separate pot and, defying Stan's predictions, appeared in perfect health the next morning.

Notwithstanding the Polack's foreign habits, the old man made the most of his new audience. In no time he was banging on about the old days on the moor, and the steam-driven pumping engines built in the mid-1800s which, though capable of lifting a devil of a lot of water, still left much of the Levels to flood regularly, until in this last war – the one just gone, he pointed out, so there'd be no confusion – diesel pumps arrived, and a new river, the Huntspill, was carved right across the northern Levels to feed water to the munitions factory at Puriton. As a result, to the delight of the progressive types, a lot more land could be kept dry all the year round. It was only the moors around the Parrett and the Tone that still flooded every winter, he declared with pride. And some years at other times too, because the Tone went nowhere except into the Parrett, and the Parrett had no fall in it and almost no flow, you could drop a leaf into it and watch the damn thing shift all of three or four inches in the time it took to smoke a cigarette; and when the Parrett got past Bridgwater it got too wide to be closed off by a clyse or any other contraption known to man; in fact in its last ten miles it turned into a blooming great estuary – he'd seen it for himself some twenty years back – so that when the wind and tide were high, as often as not you got the flood water right *back* again. Sometimes the water would take weeks – *weeks*, he cried – to travel to within yards of the sea, only to be pushed all the bloody way back again in no time flat. Bloody useless river, he guffawed. Nothing like it.

Every time Billy thought the Polack must have run out of questions, he went off on a whole new tack. One day, as they hunched under the tarpaulin on their mid-morning break, the Polack started asking about the local customs.

'Customs are what foreigners have,' said Billy, raising his voice against the splattering of the rain. 'We don't have customs here. We have backward thinking.'

'I mean to ask, how people pass evenings . . . Sundays . . . Where they meet. How they spend time.'

'Well, the men go to the pub. The girls . . . their big excitement is going to Taunton, I suppose, though don't ask me what they do there. The rest of them . . . they don't go anywhere much.'

The Polack absorbed this slowly. 'And pastimes? What is it people like to do? To walk? To talk? To go to dances?'

'Dances . . . If you don't mind three old granddads churning out slow waltzes and girls who think they're doing you a big favour by letting you dance closer than six inches apart – then yes, there're dances all right.'

'And this is where young people meet?'

Billy smirked. 'So that's it, is it, Johnnie? You're hoping to find yourself a nice little English girl, are you? Hoping to have yourself a bit of *ro*-mance.'

The Polack shrugged this off with a quick smile, which Billy took as a yes. 'I mean instead,' the Polack said in the tone of someone trying to get the conversation back on track, 'where do young people meet to talk? To discuss?'

'You're getting too technical, Johnnie. Finding a girl in England is no different from finding a girl anywhere else. Probably a lot easier. You take her out a couple of times – to a dance, a film, a caff – you make her feel a bit special, and before you know it, you'll be in there, no trouble. Like fruit dropping off a tree.'

The Polack's features hardly altered, yet Billy had the impression that he had understood his meaning perfectly and had the nerve to disapprove. This whiff of virtuousness had surfaced once before, on the Polack's first day, when Billy had likened a recalcitrant mole wrench to a woman who refused to open her legs, and the Polack's expression had taken on the same distant look.

'Look,' Billy said irritably, 'you might get the weather and the price of potatoes from the men if you're lucky. But the girlies – all they're interested in is frocks and nylons and which blokes are likely to give 'em a good time.'

The Polack turned his cigarette round and examined the lighted end with concentration. 'But for – excuse me, perhaps I have wrong word – *discussion*?' He spoke the word in a Frenchified way. 'Is this in pub, with men only?'

'Blimey, what're you after, Johnnie – a bloody debating society? Well, you won't find anything like that round here, I can tell you now. They already know all the answers, see. And they don't like anyone trying to tell 'em different. But what were you hoping to discuss, for God's sake? Unemployment? Food shortages? The national debt?'

'I wish to learn what people think of politics . . . of social problems . . . of their wishes for future.'

Billy gave a coarse laugh. 'Well, I can tell you – you're in the wrong place for that kind of stuff. This here is the bogs, in case you hadn't noticed. Thirty years behind the times and in no hurry to catch up. No, if you're looking for *debates* and the like you'll have to make for civilisation, or as close as you can get to it. Why don't you ask that schoolmistress, what's-her-name? She might be able—' Seeing the Polack's gaze drop suddenly, Billy peered at him in disbelief before giving a low chuckle. 'So that's where you've set your sights, is it?' The Polack's hasty frown confirmed it, and Billy continued with relish, 'Well, well . . . you don't waste any time, do you? Quick off the mark, I'll say that for you. These books she's been bringing down for you – come with love and kisses, do they? A bit of passion with the grammar.'

'These are books that I ask for,' the Polack said.

'I'll bet they are! No doubt you'll be wanting a whole encyclopaedia at this rate.'

The Polack shook his head vehemently. 'Please. It is not like this.'

Billy laughed. 'You should angle for a few night classes.'

The Polack threw his cigarette into the rain with a sharp flick of the wrist.

'A bit of kissing and cuddling will do wonders for your English.'

Pulling his hat on, the Polack ducked under the edge of the tarpaulin.

'Just a joke, Johnnie,' Billy called after him. But the Polack didn't hear or wasn't listening because he hobbled away without looking back.

At the midday break Billy said, 'Listen, Johnnie, if you're going to stick around, you've got to learn to take a joke. A joke's not serious, right? It's meant for a laugh.'

The Polack gazed at him solemnly. 'I like good jokes, Billy. When I hear them I laugh just plenty.'

At dusk when they hauled the loaded cart back, one to each shaft, Billy didn't stop for the usual breather halfway up the slope to the house but kept going until, nearing the top, the Polack slipped and half fell, only saving himself from the mud by clinging to the shaft.

'You should have got yourself a wooden leg, Johnnie. Less prone to rot.'

Through his breathlessness the Polack laughed. 'This is good joke, Billy!'

'You don't say.'

'I am laughing. See? Ha! Ha!'

'Very funny,' Billy said sourly.

That night after supper the Polack got the old man talking about the local festivals – Wassail Night, the ashen faggot ceremony and the rest of the claptrap – until, unable to bear it any longer, Billy cut short what was normally his favourite smoke of the day and pulled on his oilskins.

Outside, the rain was at its heaviest, sounding tattoos on roofs and empty drums and metal sheeting. He had a job seeing his way up the hill. The lane was streaming with water, he felt the slip and slide of it under his boots, and on the steepest section a small brook must have broken its banks because at one point the water was almost over his feet.

Coming into the village, striding head down under his sou'wester, he was abreast of the church before he realised he could see no lights directly ahead. He slowed uncertainly, peering into the blur. To the right a clear light burned in the pub and another in the house beyond. Only Annie's place was showing nothing, not even a glow from behind a curtain.

He decided she must be in the kitchen or singing the child to sleep or, heeding the government appeals for frugality, was trying to save on electricity.

He went up to the front door and knocked. The sound was rapidly swallowed up by the splattering of the rain and the torrent of a faulty gutter. He knocked again louder, and now the sound seemed to be sucked into the darkness of the house. All kinds of thoughts chased through his mind while he stood in the rain. That it was past the child's bedtime. That if Annie had planned to be out, she would surely have told him. That she'd gone out on purpose, to tease him. That she was seeing someone else, had been all along, that he should have realised, it was so bloody obvious. That he wanted her more than he'd wanted anyone, that his need for her just then was close to torture.

He followed the lane around to the side of the house, but there was no light showing in the kitchen, nor in the lean-to bathroom beyond. Retracing his steps to the front door he stood there for another minute or two before making his way to the George. He was in no mood for clodhoppers' talk, but it couldn't be helped. His feet were wet and he needed a drink.

The pub reeked of wood and cigarette smoke made more pungent by the stench of steaming wool. For once the place was almost busy; there must have been over a dozen customers. Billy looked for his regular drinking companions the Honey-man brothers, but to his annoyance saw only Frank Carr in a party by the fireplace and the usual old codgers in the corner playing dominoes under a pall of smoke, and at the bar two groups of men: four farm workers who acknowledged him with a grunt and a lift of their beer glasses, and beyond them, four men he didn't recognise, two in uniform.

The landlady declined Billy's offer of a drink – she was a bit rushed at the moment, she said – so he drank alone, a Scotch for a change.

The farm workers directed occasional remarks his way, about the rain, or the flood that would surely be coming any minute, or the tractor that had been stuck all day in a ditch, but for the most part they trotted out the same time-worn comments and jokes to each other, and laughed the same booming laughs.

From the end of the bar shouts of mirth also rang out, then a voice that rose above the rest and stayed there, chattering wildly in a chaotic mixture of broken English and the mishmash of tormented sounds that Billy had come to recognise as Polack-speak. Beyond the farm workers, Billy saw a uniform with Polish flashes at the shoulder, and above it an extraordinary face, pale and startlingly thin, with sunken cheeks and protruding bones and deep shadows under the eyes, as though its owner had been badly starved and not seen a square meal since. He was laughing wildly and if he wasn't already drunk Billy guessed he soon would be. With him was another Polish soldier, the same sort of age but with a bit of flesh on him, and two men with the sallow complexion, quick eyes and long unkempt hair of tinkers.

Billy wondered what had brought the Poles here, a good five
miles from their camp, and supposed they had outstayed their
welcome in the pubs around Middlezoy.

Billy ordered another drink. He had forgotten the joys of
Scotch. Scotch didn't make you stupid like cider or stroppy like
ale; it sharpened your wits and heightened your senses. Eyeing
the group by the fire, he waited till Frank glanced his way then
raised his glass in ironic salute. To his satisfaction Frank ran
true to form and, entirely missing the joke, responded with a
slow self-satisfied smirk. 'You great berk,' Billy called out in
a voice almost loud enough to be heard across the room.

Billy tried to spin his drink out for as long as possible, but
when he next looked at the clock it was to find that barely
twenty minutes had passed since his arrival. He longed to go
and see if lights were showing in Spring Cottage, but he didn't
want to risk the inevitable jokes if he had to come back into
the pub again. Best to leave it a while. Or not. The indecision,
like the jittery excitement he always felt at the prospect of
seeing Annie again, formed a knot in his stomach. He ordered
a third drink. The landlady, who was less rushed now, said she
wouldn't say no to a Scotch. It was the last bottle, she said; she
didn't know when she'd be getting any more. The wholesaler
kept his supplies back for his biggest customers and she was
never going to be a big customer, was she? It was typical of the
way the country was going, she complained: one rule for the
rich, one for the poor, and now, on top of everything else,
there was going to be a coal shortage.

Suddenly the room seemed too hot to Billy, he felt he could
hardly breathe, but before he could drain his drink he became
aware of a new stridency in the voices at the bar, a mood of
confrontation. The group at the far end had been getting noisier
for some time, emitting shrieks and yelps and sudden bellows
of laughter, but now the farm workers were sending up a storm
of their own, berating the other group for something, Billy
couldn't immediately make out what. There were yells of
'Watch out there!' and 'Oi oi!' and 'Mind your manners!', then

a jostling, a bumping of shoulders and elbows in what appeared
to be a skirmish, an impression reinforced by the landlady's
shrill appeal for calm and the sudden backward lurch of the
nearest farm worker, who barged into Billy, forcing him hard
up against the bar and knocking the last of his drink over his
hand.

Billy shoved the other man roughly away and sucked the
liquid off his knuckles. When he looked again he realised someone was on the floor, a slouched figure sitting with his legs bent
awkwardly under him and his head bowed over his chest. As
Billy peered through the press of bodies, the figure keeled over
on its side in an untidy sprawl of limbs that managed to entangle
themselves in a number of other people's. The wall of backs
parted momentarily as the farm workers extricated themselves,
then closed again as the argument turned to mockery and deri-
sion. Moving away towards the door, Billy identified through
the forest of legs the figure of the emaciated Polish soldier lying
unconscious or otherwise dead to the world, his mate kneeling
at his side.

Billy wasn't aware of the door opening until he felt a rush
of cold air on his neck, followed by a sprinkling of water as
the incomer brushed rapidly past him.

'Right, men! That's enough! Stand clear!'

The brisk commanding tone was one Billy recognised
instantly: the bark of an officer.

The room fell quiet. Two of the farm workers stopped in
mid-speech and gazed slack-jawed at the new arrival, the other
two looked round vacantly to see what was going on, while
the tinkers stared sullenly. They shuffled clear as the officer
crouched down beside the prone figure and began to examine
him, lifting each eyelid in turn and laying a palm on the bony
forehead. Finally, in a practised move straight from the battlefield, he felt the neck for a pulse.

'You two – pick this man up.'

The Pole's mate and one of the tinkers hauled him up and
propped him on a chair.

'A bit the worse for wear, that's all,' someone scoffed.

'Bring some water.'

One of the farm workers jerked into life as if pulled by strings and shouted 'Water!' to the landlady. After waiting impatiently for her to pour it, he carried the glass with exaggerated care to the officer and presented it obsequiously: anxious to please, eager to serve.

Long live the officer class, Billy thought; what would we do without them? Except this wasn't the real thing, this wasn't one of the gormless toffs for whom it was possible to feel a fleeting pity. This was Lyndon Hanley, farmer's son, promoted by dint of brain and ability: an altogether more dubious animal.

Hanley lifted the Pole's chin and poured some water into his mouth. Most of it spilled down his tunic. Hanley scrutinised him again and bent his ear to the Pole's mouth.

'This man's ill,' he declared.

'He'll be a darn sight iller tomorrow!' someone laughed.

'No – his breathing's low. He needs a doctor.'

The second Pole nodded vehemently and repeated, 'Doctor. Yes, doctor.'

'Where's this man based? What's his name?'

When the second Pole looked blank, one of the tinkers mumbled, 'Middlezoy Camp. Name o' Joe.'

'Surname?'

The tinker snorted as if the idea of knowing a Polish name, let alone pronouncing it, was a great joke.

The officer addressed the question to the other Pole. 'Joe what?' He rotated a palm in the air by way of a prompt.

The Pole understood at last. 'Walczak,' he said. 'Jozef Walczak.'

'Is there a resident doctor at the camp?'

The Pole lifted his shoulders uncertainly.

'At Middlezoy Camp – doctor?'

'One day yes. One day no.'

Appearing to come to a decision, Hanley straightened up and cast around. 'Has anyone got a car?'

Quietly Billy retrieved his oilskins from the hook by the door and began to pull them on.

'I've a van outside,' muttered the tinker. 'But it's loaded with junk.'

From the group by the fireplace someone said, 'I could fetch a car but it'd take a good twenty minutes.'

Hanley's eyes swung round and fixed on Billy. If he remembered their last meeting he gave no sign of it. But then he'd been drunk at the time; now he looked eerily sober, his gaze pale and hard.

Buttoning his jacket, Billy shook his head slowly.

'It'll have to be the van then. Give a hand here.' Three of the farm workers lumbered into action, as did the younger of the tinkers and the second Pole. Perhaps because there were so many bearers they were badly coordinated: as they picked up the Pole they let his head drop back. The officer immediately moved round to support it, cradling it in one hand.

'The door!' he commanded Billy.

Billy, who had been on the point of opening it anyway, paused to give him a slow stare, a delay which forced the bearers to halt before passing through.

The party had to wait again in the pouring rain while the older tinker rearranged the back of the van. Finally they laid the sick man awkwardly over the scrap metal. Hanley took off his jacket and, folding it several times, placed it under the man's head.

When the van doors had banged shut Hanley turned and said crisply, 'Well done, everybody. Now I suggest you all settle down and enjoy the rest of your evening.'

The farm workers shuffled their feet sheepishly and muttered their thanks. Distancing himself rapidly from this abject display, Billy took two steps back, and when that still didn't feel far enough turned on his heel and strode away. If there was one thing that irked him more than a smug officer, it was a smug ex-officer who thought he was still running the show.

Billy had spotted the glitter of Annie's porch light from the door of the pub. Now, as he quickened his pace towards it, he felt a jittery beat of excitement and uncertainty at the prospect of seeing her again. He wasn't sure what he felt for her: lust, need, compulsion, love. But whatever it was, it was strong, like the pull of a drug. Sometimes he veered towards the idea of love because it made him feel he was joining a hitherto closed brotherhood of men who experienced deeper, better feelings; at other times he recoiled from it because, as all sensible men knew, it was a trap.

He had barely knocked when Annie opened the door.

'Oh, it's you!' she exclaimed.

'Why, who else did you think it was going to be?'

'No one,' she said, flashing her eyes in reproof. 'So, to what do I owe this pleasure?'

'Aren't you going to invite me in for a cuppa?'

'Look, I can't this evening, Billy. I'm really behind.'

'But I've come specially.'

'We weren't meant to be meeting till Saturday.'

'But I'm here now, aren't I?' He raised both hands in a gesture of appeal. 'And I'm wet through.'

She gave in with a shake of her head and a low laugh. 'Give me half an hour, then.'

He stepped forward as if to come in, but she blocked his way.

'No. Go for a drink,' she said. 'Then I'll have a chance to sort myself out.'

'I would, but there's been a bit of a commotion in the pub. A bit of a rumpus.'

'No!' She was in turn surprised, amused and intrigued. 'Well,' she declared at last, 'whatever next? You'd better come in then.'

While she was upstairs with the child he made himself at home, hanging up his oilskins, brewing up some tea, fanning the sitting-room fire, which had only just been lit. By the time Annie reappeared, the room was just beginning to warm up.

'Go easy on the coal,' she said. 'I'm getting short.'

'I'll bring you some tomorrow. A sack or two, surplus to agricultural requirements.'

She pretended disapproval but she didn't turn the offer down. 'You'll get me into trouble yet.'

'Chance would be a fine thing.'

She rolled her eyes at the ancient joke. 'So what's been going on in the pub?'

'Some tinkers brought in a couple of Polish lads and there was a bit of a ruckus.'

'Not *your* Pole?'

'Not likely,' Billy declared. 'I don't let him near the pubs.'

'What was it about, the fight?'

'Who knows? But you should have heard them.' Billy put on his yokel accent, the deep Somerset burr he had been so careful to avoid in his youth. '"Don't care where you be coming from, there ain't no call for this 'ere foreign talk."'

'They didn't say that,' Annie protested, stifling a laugh.

Billy put on a look of injured innocence, the honest witness unfairly challenged. 'I swear! Then one of the Poles answered by falling down dead drunk. And then someone pipes up: "This be a shocking sight! Us good Zomerzet folk don't 'old with drunkenness, not in these 'ere parts."'

Annie laughed openly then. She had a beautiful laugh, a soft chuckle that finished on a lingering note, and a way of throwing her head back that made him imagine her in a state of ecstasy.

Having given the fire a last prod, Billy marched into the kitchen and made the tea. Following him, Annie looked surprised when she saw the tray he had prepared, complete with teapot, cups, milk jug and sugar bowl.

'My goodness,' she murmured. 'All organised then.'

He carried the tray into the sitting room and put it on a table. Leaving her to pour because that was women's work, he sat down to one side of the fireplace. It was only the second time he'd got to sit in this room. Usually when he dropped by, Annie kept him standing in the ice-box of a kitchen. In his more sanguine moments he liked to think it was because she didn't trust herself to be in a warm room with him, but in more realistic mood he knew she was sending him a message, that he would be mistaken to think she was going to be easy game. He hadn't minded her holding out; it had added to the anticipation. He minded now, though, because time was running out.

She put his cup down beside him and took her place on the opposite side of the hearth. Sitting there by the fire drinking tea with the rain rushing and gurgling in the gutters outside, they might have been Darby and Joan. The absurdity of the thought made him laugh.

She raised her eyebrows questioningly.

'Nothing,' he said.

'It's never nothing with you, Billy.'

'You wouldn't like it if I told you.'

'In that case, I'm not asking.'

She settled further back in her chair and crossed her legs, and he noticed that she was wearing her best nylons and high heels.

'So who were you expecting if it wasn't me?' he asked lightly.

'No one. I thought my friend must have forgotten something, that's all.'

'Oh? What friend was that?'

She tilted her head sideways. 'Just a friend.'

'Bad friend? Good friend? Old friend?'

She shook her head. Her gaze, though tolerant, contained a hint of rebuke.

He put on his actory voice, which was his guard against being taken too seriously. Rounding his eyes like a film villain, he said in deep melodramatic tones, 'Not a gentleman caller, we trust?'

'You should have been on the stage, Billy.'

'Well?'

She gave him a look of patience wearing thin.

'I could be jealous.'

'But you'd have no right to be, would you? Even supposing there was something to be jealous about.'

He gave a forced laugh. 'Well, that's put me in my place, hasn't it? Good and proper.'

'Come off it, Billy, you're not staying, are you? You made that plain from the start. So there was never going to be any question of us – well, getting serious.'

'But if I *was* staying? What would you say then?'

'I haven't given it any thought.'

'Of course you have. You've thought about it all the time.'

She laughed in protest and disbelief. 'Billy, this may come as a shock, but I've got a lot better ways of spending my time than thinking about *you*.'

'But what we had – it's still there,' he insisted. 'You can't pretend it isn't.'

She said in an altogether more serious tone, 'Things are never that simple, are they?'

'Well, it's either there or it isn't. And if you won't admit it—' Hearing the childishness in his voice, he gave a slow offhand shrug. 'Well, watch it – I might just stay after all. I might just stay because of you.' The words were out before he realised it, and the part of him that feared entanglement wished them unspoken.

'In that case, you mustn't think of changing your mind,' she said easily. 'I'm no reason for you to stay, Billy.'

'Oh? So you're suddenly the best judge of that, are you?'

'You said there were no opportunities for you here.'

He stared at her, momentarily silenced by her practicality.

Annie continued in the same voice of reason, 'If a man's disappointed in his work then no woman's ever going to make up for it, is she? And she'd be a fool to try.'

His anger came suddenly, with a shiver of heat. He jumped to his feet and stood over her. 'You don't need anyone, is that it?'

'I didn't say that.'

'Well, you could have fooled me.'

'I have a child to think of, Billy. I have to keep a roof over my head. What I need comes after, by a long way.'

Reaching down, he grasped her hands and hauled her to her feet. She was tall for a woman and in her high heels her eyes weren't so very far below his. They shone dark and clear, and gazed at him unwaveringly.

'It's still there,' he said. 'You bloody well know it is.' He put his hands on her upper arms and gripped them softly.

Her mouth tasted sweet and salty. For the first second or two the kiss felt strange in a way he couldn't define, a result of his own nervousness perhaps, but then the desire pierced him like heat, and her body was the only body he had ever wanted.

She pushed him away with both hands. 'No, Billy.'

'Come on,' he whispered.

'No.' She moved away into the middle of the room.

He stared at her. For a moment he wasn't sure whether he loved or hated her.

'Step out with me on Saturday,' he said.

She shook her head gently, but her eyes told a very different story.

'Come on. All or nothing.'

Despite herself, she gave a short laugh.

'What have you got to lose?' he pressed.

'Did you say all or nothing?'

'Yes.'

'It'll be nothing, Billy.'

'I'll pick you up at six.'

She led the way to the door and repeated, 'It'll be nothing.'

'I'll take the risk.'

He kissed her on the lips before she had the chance to object, and walked quickly away.

Only when he reached the gate did he realise he'd left his sou'wester on a peg in the hall. By the time he got to Crick Farm the rain had found its way inside his collar and was trickling coldly down the back of his neck.

Chapter Nine

A VIOLENT POUNDING startled Wladyslaw out of sleep, and for an instant he was back in the dark verminous hut in Archangel with bad news beating at the door.

'Out of your pit, Johnnie!' The door thundered and rattled. 'Rise and shine!'

'OK, OK.'

Wladyslaw dressed hurriedly by the light of a candle and stumbled outside, only to stop and stare at the new world that had appeared while he slept. The rain had vanished, leaving a dome of satin that arched high overhead, sharp and clear and immense with stars. Ahead, he could make out the hard black rim of the hills on the far side of the moor, and away to the left some hills he had never seen before, distant and attenuated, a low rippled line against the shimmer of the frosty sky; while somewhere in the darkness in between a solitary pinprick of light glimmered and faltered like a star fallen from grace. On the moor, he fancied he could make out the dark metallic sheen of flood water, and for a while he thought he could hear it too, a body of wetness gently stirring and trembling, a sound so faint that it seemed to come to him, when it came at all, as a faint vibration. If it were a large expanse of water, though, it was a strange one, for there were no stars reflected in it, no haze of stardust. And now that he listened more carefully, the faint indecipherable sounds seemed to come from all around him: a settling of water deeper into the earth, a faint popping of escaping air, an oozing and shifting and general sorting of wet from dry.

He turned his face up to the stars, which were also the stars of Poland, and, basking in their pallid gaze, lifted his arms high and murmured, 'Thank you,' though he couldn't have said quite what he was thankful for, the end of the rain or the glories of the night.

In the kitchen Billy was already pulling on his jacket. Wladyslaw knew better than to speak or keep him waiting. Forgoing his usual cup of tea, he grabbed a slice of bread and a spoonful of jam, and followed Billy up to the shed, where by lamplight they began to load withies onto a trailer. Billy issued no instructions, merely picked up two bundles from the stacks, loaded them onto the flatbed of the trailer, and made no comment when Wladyslaw followed suit. These silences were a feature of Billy's mornings, as though sleep oppressed him and he needed time to regain his equilibrium. Occasionally he showed open irritation, and then Wladyslaw could never make out if he were the cause of this exasperation or merely the target of it; sometimes it seemed to Wladyslaw that Billy barely knew himself.

Today, however, Billy was in a different kind of mood altogether, of preoccupation. When a knot slipped and a bundle of withies unravelled in Wladyslaw's arms, it took Billy a full five seconds to grunt, 'Watch what you're doing.' For some time afterwards he stared into the middle distance, then looked back vaguely, as though he had lost track of time. He didn't speak again for twenty minutes, and then it was to complain mildly, 'No hope of you getting this lot up to the village on your own, I don't suppose.'

The trailer was large and heavy; the idea of one man pulling it was ludicrous. Wladyslaw judged it safest not to reply.

'Well?'

'Give me a horse and I take them anywhere, no trouble.'

Billy looked at him as if he were mad. 'Who said anything about a bloody *horse*? I meant when the bloody tractor arrives.'

'A tractor? OK. You tell me what to do, Billy, and I do it.'

With a sigh of forbearance, Billy grumbled, 'Forget it . . . By the time I explain, I might as well do it myself.'

As Wladyslaw swung away to gather another load, he caught the words: 'Bloody useless.'

Wladyslaw paused. 'You have problem with my work, Billy?'

'Huh?'

'You are not happy with my work?'

Another sigh, and Billy said grudgingly, 'It's all right – so far as it goes.'

'Tell me what I do wrong.'

'Listen, Johnnie, you can't help being bloody useless, all right? It'd take a year to teach you the ropes, and then you wouldn't know the half of it.' Billy stared unhappily at the stripping machine, gleaming silently in the lamplight. He had got the contraption to run with the sweet rattle of well-tended machinery, but it was no use without boiled and softened withies to feed into its jaws, and the ancient boiler in the apple orchard had failed two days ago. Wladyslaw hadn't gathered the exact nature of the defect – a crack in the tank, he thought – but it was a problem that Billy with all his skills had been unable to fix. Now Billy was glaring at the stripping machine as though it were the embodiment of everything that had been sent to frustrate him.

'The boiler cannot be repaired?' Wladyslaw asked mildly.

'Oh, it can be repaired,' Billy muttered. 'But there's not much bloody point, is there?'

Not knowing what he was talking about, knowing better than to ask, Wladyslaw returned to the loading. When the trailer could take no more, they lashed the bundles down with a long rope which they threw lightly back and forth over the top like seasoned wagoners.

When they broke for a cigarette, Wladyslaw strolled out into the yard to look around him again. The stars had faded before the huge glow of light spreading from the east. It was the time just before sunrise when the land is drained of colour and definition. A low mist lay tight on the moor in a grey blur that blended imperceptibly into the darker grey of the hills. Here and there its surface was punctured by willow trees, like islets scattered over a shallow sea. By the time Wladyslaw had finished his cigarette, the first sliver of sun had crept over the eastern hills, turning the mist a milky yellow, making golden skeletons of the trees. Everything was still, except for a flight of geese skimming low over the mist, their cries like distant trumpet calls.

The tractor arrived in a roar, driven by a man who stared at Wladyslaw and did not stop staring until the trailer was hitched and, with Billy and Wladyslaw hanging precariously to the trailer's sides, they started on their way. The tractor howled and belched up the lane, the exhaust pumping out hot bursts of fumes. At one point the hedgerow closed in, and brambles whipped at Wladyslaw's legs and reached out to claw his jacket. The tractor slowed and changed gear to lumber through a deep pothole, then just as it began to gather speed it slowed once more. Wladyslaw couldn't see why until he glanced back and saw a woman step clear of the hedgerow into which she had pressed herself and her bicycle to let them pass. It was Stella. His whoop was drowned out by the engine, so he waved, a manoeuvre which involved taking one hand off the iron post that was his only support and swinging out at an angle, like a trapeze artist taking a bow. Spotting him, Stella waved back, brightly at first, then with what he took to be disappointment. Daring to hope that she had been on her way to see him, he jumped without thinking, and certainly without looking, and found himself dropping towards a ditch partially covered by brambles. He landed with one foot on the edge of the track, the other in the bottom of the ditch, and, allowing his bad leg to crumple under him, fell sideways into the hedgerow, which made for a thorny but safe landing.

'Are you all right?' Stella cried, running up the track towards him.

Extricating himself from the brambles with some difficulty, Wladyslaw clambered out of the ditch. 'Still in one piece, I think!' Rubbing a hand clean, he held it out to her.

She shook it with a quick laugh. 'I never thought you'd jump!'

'I don't wish to miss you.'

She glanced hastily in the direction of the vanished tractor. 'Well, you've missed your ride all right.'

'I will find it later.'

They took a look at each other, she with a quick smile, he with wonder. Her face had all the elements he remembered – the freckled nose, the even teeth, the frank blue eyes – yet his memory had somehow failed to do justice to the overall effect.

Her gaze went to his cheek. 'You're bleeding,' she said. 'Wait . . . I've got a handkerchief somewhere . . .' She reached into her sleeve and pulled out a dainty cotton square with an embroidered border.

'I will damage it.' He knew it was the wrong word and raised his eyebrows, inviting correction.

'Oh, it'll wash all right. You won't spoil it.'

'Spoil,' he echoed. 'Thank you.'

He dabbed at his cheek and looked into the mirror of her lovely face to see how he was doing. A small creasing between the eyebrows and he could tell there was more blood to mop up, a softening of the features and the last had gone.

Her eyes went to the top of his head. 'And you've got a bramble . . .' She indicated the site with a forefinger.

He reached up and tugged the offending object out of his hair. 'There is more?' He lowered his head for her to inspect it.

'No, that's it, I think.'

He shook his head rapidly, like a dog emerging from water, and flicked a hand through his hair to send any last fragments flying. He looked up to find her laughing, and laughed with her.

'I've got a book for you,' she said. 'It's a – Oh!' Glancing down the track, she spotted her bicycle lying where she had dropped it, with the contents of the basket scattered over the ground.

Wladyslaw hurried forward to retrieve it. Fortunately the basket's contents had landed clear of the puddles and the stickier patches of mud, and with some diligent rubbing and dusting a purse and headscarf and various books emerged none the worse for their spill.

With the air of making an offering, Stella held a book out to him. 'It's that grammar I told you about. It's more comprehensive than the other one.'

'I thank you.'

'My mother, along with some of the ladies from the Women's Institute, has been collecting textbooks for the camp and I just happened to see it there in the box. So . . . well, I took it.' Her eyes glinted conspiratorially.

'I am honoured.'

'Oh, and I've been asking about those grammars written specially for foreign-speaking people, but it seems you can't get hold of them at the moment, not for love nor money.'

'Not for love nor money . . .' he echoed.

'It's a saying.'

'This one I understand OK.'

'Not like raining cats and dogs. I'm still trying to find the origin for you, but no luck yet. It's one of those things you say and never think about. And when you *do* think about it, you can't imagine why you've never questioned it before. How's it going with the verbs?'

He pressed his fingertips to his forehead in mock despair. 'Get on, get by, get out, get round, get through . . . I find two, three, *four* meanings for each one.'

'They're the worst,' she conceded. 'But once you've mastered them, you're halfway there.'

'Halfway only!'

She made a show of considering afresh. 'Maybe a touch more.'

They began to stroll up the hill towards the village. He

offered to push her bike for her, but she shook her head firmly, and he could only suppose that pushing a lady's bicycle was reserved for accredited suitors.

'You will go to this dance tonight?' he asked.

'What? Oh no.'

'You don't like dances?'

'Oh, I like to go sometimes. But tonight I'm going to a birthday party.'

'Not *your* birthday?'

'No.' She hesitated a little. 'A friend's.'

The thought of the party seemed to dampen her spirits, and he said, 'In Poland, name days are big occasion for us, not so much birthdays.'

'What's a name day?'

'This is a special day of saint you are named from, saint who is your – I don't know this word – protector?'

'Patron saint?'

'Patron saint – this is it. And on feast day of this patron saint, friends, family send you card, presents.'

'How lovely! And when is your name day?'

'Saint Wladyslaw is in June.'

'*Wladyslaw*,' she repeated carefully. 'I'm sorry – I think I've been saying your name wrongly all this time.'

'You say it fine. I prefer English way.'

'Oh, I'm sure you don't really. You must get fed up with it.'

'Not when it is spoken by such good friend as you, Miss Stella.'

She seemed disconcerted by this, and, colouring a little, concentrated her attention on the track ahead. Not for the first time Wladyslaw reflected on the pitfalls of getting to know English girls, how the most basic compliment, the most sincere declaration of friendship could be taken amiss. He couldn't make out whether this reaction sprang from a suspicion of men in general or Polish men in particular, but in Stella's case he liked to think it came from nothing worse than surprise, maybe even – he dared to hope – pleasure.

For a time the track had been reasonably level, but now it had steepened again, and Stella panted a little with the effort of pushing her bicycle uphill.

She said between breaths, 'The WI ladies have had another idea . . . They thought that with the camp filling up so quickly . . . and so many of the men separated from their wives and sweethearts . . . feeling lonely and cut off . . . that they might like to see how we live . . . to visit English families in their homes . . . and get to practise their English, all at the same time. What do you think?'

Wladyslaw took a moment to answer. 'Sure,' he murmured.

'Just for a couple of hours on a Sunday afternoon – something like that.'

'Afternoon tea, English fashion.'

'Oh, they won't get cucumber sandwiches, not round here. They'll get cake – but plenty of it. So, what do you think?' she asked brightly. Catching his hesitation, she slowed down. 'You don't like the idea.'

'This is fine idea, Stella.'

She searched his face. 'No – tell me.'

He hesitated again. 'It is only – many speak no English, not even one word.'

'No. But they'll be learning, won't they?'

'Yes . . .' he agreed uncertainly. 'But many also – they arrive only just now. They are still uncertain of future.'

'All the more reason to get to know us, surely. To feel they're at home.'

Wladyslaw gave up gracefully. 'Sure.'

She nodded happily, and bent her weight to pushing the bicycle up the last hill.

The lane merged with another before joining the road that ran up to the church. Hitting the metalled surface of the road, the rattling bicycle wheels subsided to a soft whir. Stella was telling Wladyslaw about afternoon tea at its most English – cucumber sandwiches, jam-filled scones, Victoria sponge, doilies,

and fine china – when she suddenly looked at her watch. 'Help!'
she cried. 'I'm going to be late.'

'Miss Stella – one thing I wish to ask you.'

'Yes, Wladyslaw.' She said his name carefully, according to
the Polish pronunciation.

He had prepared his speech diligently, with the help of a
dictionary, and began with confidence. 'I wish very much to
improve my English to the point where I can talk of anything –
everything. I am very grateful for these grammar books you
have given me, but to learn well I need to practise conversation. So I wish to ask, Miss Stella, if you will please give me
classes?'

He thought she would be pleased, but her smile had faded,
she said awkwardly, 'Well, I . . . At the camp, do you mean?'

'I thought, here?' He indicated the village ahead.

'I wish I could help, Wladyslaw, I really do. But . . . well,
I'm not sure I'll have the time, you see. I have school all day.
And I've just agreed to take classes at the camp four times a
week. With all the preparation . . .'

'Sure,' Wladyslaw said, suppressing a sharp pang of disappointment.

In the pause that followed, conflict and uncertainty flickered
over Stella's face, as though his request had stirred up some
deeper, more intractable anxieties. She said, 'I'd suggest an
evening, but . . .'

'It is not any problem.'

She looked away, distracted again, before saying, 'Unless
Sundays were any use to you.'

'Please. I don't wish to trouble you.'

He would have walked on, but she said rapidly, 'But it's no
trouble at all. I could do Sundays easily. The only reason I
didn't suggest it was because I assumed you'd be with your
friends at the camp all day.'

'I go to camp for two, three hours only.'

'Well then, Sundays will be perfect!' She spoke with all her old warmth, the worries forgotten or pushed aside. 'It's settled. Shall we begin tomorrow?'

'Please.'

'Would six suit you?'

'Yes. This suits me well.'

'At my house? It's up past the windmill – ' She corrected herself with a small laugh. 'But you don't know where that is! No, the best thing is to follow the lane to the junction and turn *right* – ' She directed him with neat hand movements interspersed with questioning glances to see if he had understood. 'It's the cottage with the yellow door. And if you get lost anyone will be able to tell you where we live.'

'Thank you.'

She prepared to mount her bike. 'Do you think we should choose the subject for our talk now? So that we have time to think about it?'

'This would help, yes.'

'So, what would you like to talk about?'

He deferred to her with a small dip of the head. 'Please – you choose.'

'Let me think.' She chewed her lip softly, tilted her head to one side and cast her blue eyes skyward, while he absorbed her loveliness like a man who has spent a long time in a dark and desolate place.

'I know!' she declared. 'What about Polish customs?'

'England will be more useful, I think.'

'Of course! English customs then.' She swung one pedal up, ready to start off.

'I study hard before then, like good student.'

She smiled. 'I *will* study hard, like *a* good student.'

He spread his arms wide, his case vindicated, then bowed low in farewell. For this, or something else altogether, he was rewarded with a last smile before she pedalled away, a trim figure sitting erect in the saddle, her copper hair like a conflagration in the thin sunlight.

Wladyslaw watched her until she was lost behind the bend

in the churchyard wall, then, buoyed by an unassailable happiness, set off in the same general direction. Pausing only to admire the solid stone church with its octagonal tower, niched statuary, crenellations and stumpy spire, he followed the lane around two bends into a long stretch with cottages strung out on either side. He didn't know where he was meant to be going, and saw no people and no post office, nor any other sort of place where he might ask. The lane ended in a junction with a similar lane, narrow with a scattering of cottages on either side and no indication as to which way, if any, the village centre lay. For no particular reason, except perhaps that it was the way to Stella's house, he chose to go right, and after some fifty metres came to a cluster of farm buildings. Wandering through the gate, he found himself in the corner of a large yard completely concreted over and bordered on three sides by barns and sheds. It was a withy yard all right – on the side that was open to the fields quantities of hurdles stood in serried ranks, while through the doors of the shed on the far side he could make out stacks of withies – but the tractor and trailer that stood by the shed door weren't right, the tractor shiny blue instead of dusty red, and the trailer with no load.

He was standing at the corner of a long stone building which formed the left-hand side of the yard. In front of it stood two carts with draught horses dozing in their shafts. He moved forward to look along the length of the building, saw an open door, and halted abruptly as a roar of raucous laughter rang out.

From the clamour that followed, Wladyslaw reckoned there were at least ten men inside, maybe a lot more. Too many for comfort at any rate. His distrust of groups had been born during the Russian occupation, confirmed by the journey out of Siberia, and reinforced in Taunton during an evening out from the convalescent home, when a gang of drunken ruffians who outnumbered them by more than two to one had tried to pick a fight.

He was on the point of slipping quietly away when a

cadaverous old man shuffled out of the stone building, and, spotting him, beckoned to him with a loose-jointed wave.

Wladyslaw's instincts urged him to walk away, to take no chances, while his reason argued for calm and confidence. This is the countryside, he told himself, these are friendly people and the world is at peace.

The old man beckoned with another wild scoop of the air. 'Ain't no good stay'n there,' he croaked, swaying slightly. 'The zider's this a-way.'

The argument for confidence won, just.

The babble of voices fell away as Wladyslaw stepped into the doorway. The interior was dark, but in the light at his back Wladyslaw could made out a vaulted room with a huge screw-down press on one side and, standing around it, twelve or more men in the garb of farm workers. There was a strong smell of apples or cider or both.

A voice called what sounded like 'Hurrup!' but it was impossible to tell if this was a salutation or a challenge.

Wladyslaw responded with a 'Good morning.'

There was a stream of 'Mornings'. The men's tone was curious, but not, he thought, unfriendly.

Wladyslaw began, 'I am looking for withy yard—'

'Well, you've come to the right place all right!' someone bellowed. The ensuing laughter was sudden and strident, like a release of tension.

'You be in the right place if you be looking for cider an' all!'

Wladyslaw joined in the general laughter, and found the cadaverous old man swaying at his shoulder, pressing a jar of cider into his hand.

'So where you wantin' to get to then?' called a heavy man leaning against the cider press.

'I don't know name of this place.'

'The name o' this place! Can't say we're too sure neither, are we, lads?' roared a joker. 'Not by this stage o' the day!'

When the laughter had died down, the heavy man said, 'Sounds like you gone and got yerself well and truly lost.'

'I think so, yes.'

'Where you hail from then?' he asked.

Wladyslaw knew perfectly well what he meant, but partly to maintain the jovial atmosphere, partly to postpone the moment of explanation, he answered, 'Crick Farm.'

This was met by another wave of laughter. The joker, a wiry young man with rolling eyes, shouted: 'You got ter find Crick Farm all right then, did yer?'

'They tell me so.'

One man was helpless with laughter, mopping his eyes with a handkerchief, while another was clutching the cider press for support.

Wladyslaw added ingenuously, 'It is very wet place certainly.'

Amidst the roaring and howling, Wladyslaw became aware of an immobile figure on the periphery of his vision. Turning, he found himself looking into a pair of cold eyes set in a fleshy unsmiling face.

'So where you from before that?' the man asked.

The laughter began to subside a little.

'Poland.'

The man turned to the others and raised his eyebrows. 'Hear that, lads? *Poland.*' Then to Wladyslaw: 'Long ways away from here.'

Wladyslaw took a sip of the cider, which was rich and cloudy. 'Yes.'

Laughter continued to ripple around the room, but the mood had became more attentive.

'How long you aiming to stay with us then?'

'I don't know this yet.'

'Like it well enough, though, I'll be bound?'

'Sure.'

''Course he does,' chipped in a cheery voice. 'Can't do

no better than Somerset. Cider and sunshine and bugger-all to
do.'

During the flurry of laughter and comment that followed,
the cold-eyed man continued to gaze at Wladyslaw. He was
short and bull-necked, with wiry fair hair, small eyes and white
lashes, and skin that was pink and blotchy, as though he lived
off a diet of milk and lard.

'You working for Billy Greer then, are you?'

'Yes.'

'What, cutting withies?'

'Yes.'

The man looked down at Wladyslaw's hands, as if to check
for missing fingers. 'Well, if you're with Billy you've fetched up
in the wrong yard. He don't bring his withies here. He goes to
the Honeymans.'

'And where are the Honeymans, please?'

'You're a way out.'

'He not be the only one neither!' offered the joker. 'Us all
be a way out today!'

With a tip of his head, the pink-faced man gestured Wladyslaw towards the door. 'I'll point you in the right direction.'

'I'll be needing some pointing in the right direction myself,
at this rate,' cried the cheery voice.

There were shouts of, 'We'll get you home, Charlie!' 'By
Christmas at the latest!' 'Never lost you yet, Charlie.'

At the door Wladyslaw gave a brief wave and received a
rumble of goodbyes and a couple of raised jars by way of reply.

'Happy fellows,' he remarked as they walked away.

The pink-faced man was staring openly at Wladyslaw's
limp. 'They're marking the apple harvest.' The eyes went up to
the fresh scratch on Wladyslaw's cheek and back to his leg as
if the one might explain the other. 'But then you lot ain't averse
to a few drinks neither.'

'Sometimes, sure.'

'Difference is, you've no 'ead for it.'

The note of truculence was unmistakable and Wladyslaw gave a nod that was deliberately vague.

When they reached the gates, the pink-faced man turned and gave Wladyslaw a narrow sidelong glare. 'Don't go down too well hereabouts, see. Strangers coming and causing a ruckus.'

'A ruckus?' Wladyslaw asked with sinking heart.

The other man was eager to enlighten him. 'Tuesday night, two of your lot come into the George with some gyppos and started an altercation. Fisticuffs and all. But we don't like rough stuff round here, see? We're not that sort of folk. We don't go making trouble, and we don't like trouble coming our way. Best for you lot to stay away. Best for all concerned.' He added in a tone of blatant insincerity, 'No offence.'

Billy had told Wladyslaw about two Poles who'd had too much to drink, but he'd made no mention of a fight.

'I have not heard of this,' said Wladyslaw.

'Well, it was your friends all right.'

'Maybe they are not my friends.'

'What're you talkin' about?' the other man argued indignantly. 'They were in uniform, the Polish marks right there, clear as day.' He jabbed a finger towards the top of his shoulder.

There was something about this man that made Wladyslaw loath to concede more than he had to. 'I'm sorry if these Polish soldiers make trouble,' he said, 'but these are just two men. Most Polish soldiers do not do such things.'

'Well, I'm just telling you, aren't I? I'm just warning you.'

Wladyslaw knew he should leave the matter there, but he heard himself say, 'I do not have the honour of your name.'

'Carr,' the other man muttered after a pause. 'Frank Carr.'

'Well, Mr Carr, I hope that I myself as a Polish soldier will not be unwelcome in your pub.'

The cold eyes were small and sharp and pink-looking in their surround of white lashes. They reminded Wladyslaw of a hog.

'Suit yerself,' Carr said tightly. 'So long as everyone takes care to watch theirselves.'

'I will be sure to watch myself with much attention.'

The white lids blinked rapidly, the cheeks became a patchwork of pink and white.

'And the direction, please, to Honeymans' yard?'

Frank Carr jerked his head up the lane, in the direction Wladyslaw had come from. 'Straight as you go, three-quarters of a mile on your right.'

'Thank you for your help, Mr Carr.'

The small mouth tightened and twitched, before the fleshy head gave a stiff nod.

Wladyslaw walked as fast as he could, but by the time he reached the Honeymans' yard Billy had already unloaded half the trailer. Bracing himself for the sharp edge of Billy's tongue, he was surprised to be met by a raised eyebrow and a sardonic smile.

'Lose our grip, did we?'

'I fell into this hedge.' Wladyslaw touched the scratch on his cheek by way of evidence.

'Pull the other one. I saw the schoolteacher, remember.'

Wladyslaw patted the book tucked inside his shirt. 'She brought me this English grammar.'

''Course she did. And she'll be bringing you a lot more if you're not careful,' Billy said in the voice of doom. 'Like trouble.'

Laughing this off, Wladyslaw set to work unloading. Yet as the two of them crossed back and forth between the trailer and the growing stack of withies, he was aware of Billy eyeing him tensely, with what might have been concern, and a small worm of doubt began to uncurl in his stomach. Finally he demanded, 'What the hell, Billy?'

Billy aligned some bundles against the stack before turning to face him. 'Thing is, Johnnie, she's got a bloke already.'

Wladyslaw felt the stillness come over him that was his defence against bad news.

'She's sold on her cousin, so they say. Name of Lyndon Hanley.'

Wladyslaw saw from his expression that it was true.

'Only heard this minute. Otherwise I'd've told you before.'

Disappointment came slowly to Wladyslaw, in small nudges, interspersed by occasional flurries of denial.

'But I tell you, Johnnie boy, she must have a screw loose if she fancies that berk.' Catching Wladyslaw's frown of incomprehension, Billy tapped a finger to his temple. 'She must be bonkers.'

'Why?'

'Because the man's a pain in the neck and about every other part of the anatomy that you care to mention, that's why.'

'What do you mean?'

'I mean he's a self-satisfied sod who thinks he's a cut above the rest of us. I mean I wouldn't trust him further than I could throw him. I mean he's a nasty piece of work.'

Wladyslaw pondered this statement with rising alarm. 'A nasty piece of work. What is this, please?'

'It's what is says. It's—' But at that moment a hearty voice called Billy's name and a jovial man with a big face shambled across the shed to shake his hand. The man cast a long unabashed look over Wladyslaw before giving Billy a heavy wink of approval. As acquisitions went, it seemed Wladyslaw had been judged a fair buy.

The two men wandered off into the yard. Billy reappeared a minute later to tell Wladyslaw to make his own way home.

If the village had seemed deserted earlier that morning, it was almost busy by the time Wladyslaw started back. First there was a young couple, happy and carefree, who smiled at him. Then a hurrying woman who glared suspiciously and a weather-beaten man on a bicycle who fixed him with a fierce frown. Thinking the older people were simply unaccustomed to strangers, Wladyslaw soon had reason to think again as a couple of farmhands gave him the shortest of nods and muttered under their breath as they strode by, and an elderly couple, avoiding his eye, drew their grandchildren to the other side of the road. These reactions, quite unlike those he'd experienced in Middlezoy not an hour's walk down the road, puzzled him deeply until it came to him with the jolt of the obvious that they knew who he was and had condemned him by association with the troublemakers at the George.

Sometimes on outings from the convalescent home the Polish flashes on his shoulder had made him a target for scorn, but, determined to bear his uniform proudly, feeling he had nothing to apologise for, he had shrugged off the occasional stares and taunts. But now he was a civilian, a working man in a working community, he knew that these things could no longer be shrugged off, that he must accept these people's judgements, however unwarranted, and for the first time since arriving in Britain he felt a small chill of vulnerability.

There were no more people once he turned down the lane to the moor. Reaching the last bend, he saw that the low mist of the early morning had evaporated to reveal drifts of water lying over the moor in sheets, ribbons and ponds. Even where stretches of pasture still showed, the grass glinted and shimmered with wetness. Stopping to stare, it seemed to him that the whole landscape oozed softly, as though the water were seeping up through the thin membrane of the earth from a vast reservoir beneath.

In the absence of any other instructions, he spent the rest of the morning rooting through the clumpy grass in the orchard for the last fall of apples. Stooping, gathering, pushing the loaded handcart up the slope towards the meagre pile of apples, the word *nasty* rang and rang in his brain. It was a word he understood to mean unpleasant, but which took on increasingly dark and oppressive meanings with each push of the handcart.

At midday on his way to the house for food, he stopped at the apple store to look it up in the dictionary. He translated the word back and forth several times to obtain all possible gradations and variations of meaning: unpleasant, offensive, *malevolent*, ill-natured, *abusive* . . . Each sense sent a fresh dart of dismay and bewilderment into his heart.

Emerging from the apple store, he saw that Billy had returned and was disappearing down the drove in the direction of the moor, armed with a woollen hat, a sack of decoy ducks and a shotgun.

Wladyslaw passed the afternoon in the apple store, sitting at his makeshift desk, huddled under a blanket to spare himself the fumes of the paraffin stove, attempting to study but thinking almost continuously of Stella. He found it incredible that she should like, let alone love, an openly unpleasant man, but even supposing for a moment it were true, then he couldn't believe she wouldn't have found some way to let him know she was unattainable. She couldn't have failed to noticed the joy he had in her company, the element of hope; she was surely too honourable, too sincere to allow misunderstandings of such a heartless kind.

He remembered a favourite proverb of his father's: it is a wise man who knows when to give up and a foolish man who falters at the first obstacle. In this case, the obstacles were considerable. Even if Stella were free he had nothing to offer her in the way of money, shelter or worldly goods, either now or in the immediate future. Yet while his logic urged him to accept defeat, his heart ached with wild hope and irrepressible optimism. He could not believe that this wondrous creature had been put into his path only to be stolen away by 'a nasty piece of work'.

At dusk he finally gave up the struggle to study. Going into the farmhouse, he found the kitchen commandeered by Billy, who was filling a zinc tub with hot water from a collection of kettles and pans crammed onto the top of the range. Retreating to the apple store once again, Wladyslaw returned half an hour later to find Billy dressed in a suit and crisp white shirt, combing his hair at the mirror on the mantelshelf.

'You go to the dance?'

'I do not go to the dance,' said Billy, mimicking Wladyslaw's accent. 'The dance is for straw-chewing clodhoppers.' He slid the comb into his pocket and smoothed his hair down with the palms of both hands. 'I go into Taunton with a lady for dinner.' Billy pulled on his raincoat and, with a last smooth of his hair, put a change of shoes into his knapsack and made for the door. 'Don't even think of waking me in the morning, will you, Johnnie?'

'I value my life too much. Have a good evening, Billy.'

He got a rare smile. 'I will.'

Wladyslaw decided against going out that night. There would be no pleasure in going to the pub alone, and he had no appetite for dancing with anyone but Stella. Instead, he played canasta with Stan and listened inattentively to his tales of the flood of 1929.

'Saw pigs swimming,' Stan chuckled. 'Right there in Athelney, just by where Billy was living. And chickens perched in trees. And cider barrels floating about, ready for the taking. Oh, it was a lovely time, it was! A cracking time! Never seen anything like it in all my life.'

'Billy – he lived there with his family?'

'Yes, yes, in Athelney. That's where the worst of the flood was. That's where the banks broke right open. Whoomph! Bang! In the middle of the night.'

'But did people die in this?' Wladyslaw asked.

'Not on account of the flood, they didn't. Most of them, they knew what was coming, see. They only had to hear the wind and the rain, and the force of the water in the sluices, and feel the quaking and quivering through the walls – well, it was obvious then, wasn't it? No, no one died from the flood. But after three months stuck upstairs with no work and plenty of cider? Well, I wouldn't be surprised if there weren't a few who went off their heads and no one the wiser!'

'People lived in their houses still?'

'You bet they did! They got food fetched in boats, cooked it on the fires upstairs. And then there was charity from the city folk in Bristol. Clothes and food and all manner of stuff. Yes, people managed all right. Only ones that needed rescuing were Billy and his dad. But then some said it was high time Billy was rescued anyways, flood or no flood.'

'He had no mother?'

'Mother? Goodness, *no*. She were long dead by then.'

'Ah. And this flood, it was not usual?'

The old man said with a touch of irritation, 'Like I've been telling you – there's regular flooding, and there's the other sort. It ain't enough to have the rain, see. Not even weeks and weeks of the stuff. No, you've got to have a storm too, and from the north-west, so as to push the water over the wrong side of the Tone and wash the whole bloody bank away. That was the trouble, see – the wind blew so blooming hard it wouldn't let the flood water slop onto Curry Moor. Kept blowing it over the *other* bank. And it were soft soil on that south side, soft as buggery. So soft they was growing vegetables in it. Well, soil like that's never going to be any bloody use for holding up a whole bloody river, is it?'

For seven days and nights the villagers patrolled the banks, shoring up the weak points with sandbags, Stan recounted. Then the sandbags ran out. After that, he said cheerfully, it was only a matter of time. In the early hours of the Saturday morning, as another surge of water came down from the hills, the bank above Mrs Miller's cottage gave way, and with a roar that could be felt at the top of the hill, a great wave fifteen feet high leapt clear over Mrs Miller's garden shed to the other side of the road, flooding every house thereabouts, buckling walls, causing a couple of cottages to collapse altogether.

'Billy and his dad lived right there, not two doors from Mrs Miller's,' Stan chuckled. 'They'd never had much in the way of furniture or china or ornaments, but they had a bloody sight less once the water'd gone through, I can tell you!'

'So what happened to Billy?'

But Stan was bent on telling the rest of the story, how after a week or more of the floods the farmers on the far side of the

Parrett began to guard the banks. 'Not against the banks giving way – oh no,' chuckled Stan, 'but against the banks getting *cut* in the dead of night, accidentally on purpose, if you understand my meaning. Getting cut by the people who were fed up to the back teeth with their homes being flooded and wanted to see the water spread a bit more evenly, you might say. The farmers on the far side of the Parrett, their land were dry, see, dry as a bone, and they didn't want no wet, not at any price, so they walked the banks with loaded guns. Yes indeed! And I've no doubt they'd've used 'em too.'

'What happened to Billy?' Wladyslaw prompted again.

'Billy . . . Well, he and his dad, they moved back in, didn't they? Soon as the water went down a bit. Weren't no good, though. Billy had to be rescued all the same, must have been a year later. Not getting fed. Left on his own too much. That father had holes for pockets. Couldn't earn a ha'penny that he didn't go and spend it on beer and horses.' He added in a low knowing voice, as if it explained everything: 'But then he worked on the railways, see. That's how he fetched up here in the first place. Irish, of course. Come with the railway.'

Sunday morning. Wladyslaw allowed himself an extra hour in bed before setting off for the Bennetts'. In a dark dawn under low scudding skies the church bell drew him up the hill, a slow tolling on a single note that ebbed and spiralled on the racing air before descending to a muffled clang as the steeple came in sight. Lights glimmered behind the stained-glass windows, the doors were closed, but if there were people inside they must have been at prayer because he heard no chanting or singing.

Following the doctor's directions, he turned right past the George and took a long looping lane between low hedgerows up to the ridge road.

Lights were showing in the Bennetts' windows, but reluctant to disturb them so early Wladyslaw tiptoed across the gravel drive. He found the bicycle where the doctor had promised it would be, in a shed attached to the side of the house. Wladyslaw was wheeling it to the gate when he heard a door opening and the doctor's voice called out, 'Wladyslaw! Hello there! Would you like some breakfast?'

Wladyslaw wheeled the bicycle up to the door. 'Thank you, Doctor, but I think I will go directly to the camp.'

'Perhaps you'd like to drop in on your way back then? For a cup of tea?'

It was the first time Wladyslaw had seen the doctor in anything but formal clothes. He was wearing baggy corduroy trousers, a threadbare shirt, and the long shapeless knitted garment the English call a cardigan, worn lopsided and, it appeared, incorrectly buttoned. Absorbing this, it was a moment before Wladyslaw registered the heave and fall of the doctor's chest as he laboured for breath.

'Thank you,' he said. 'I will drop in later.'

The doctor came down the step onto the gravel. Close up, Wladyslaw could hear the rattle and rasp of his lungs.

'Wladyslaw, I wonder if you would do me a favour while you're at the camp?'

'Yes. Of course.'

'I attended a young Pole from the camp a few nights ago. A friend of yours, I think. Jozef Walczak.'

'Jozef? Is he OK?'

'He'd suffered some sort of collapse when I saw him. As for how he is now – that's what I was going to ask you. Would you find out and let me know? I'm concerned that his friends might have put him straight to bed and failed to alert the medical staff.'

'He is in sick bay?'

'That's the thing – I'm not sure. I saw him here at the house, you see. Some people brought him in a van from the George.'

'The George?' Wladyslaw gave a harsh groan and swore in Polish, before saying in despair, 'Idiot. Crazy man. I hear about this fight.'

'Fight? No one mentioned anything about a fight.'

'Sure! I hear good about this,' said Wladyslaw, his grammar rapidly deserting him under pressure. 'Fight at George pub. Tuesday. Two Poles.'

'But I found no injuries on Jozef. No cuts or bruises. I was told he'd simply fallen ill. Unless I missed something,' the doctor added doubtfully.

'I go see Jozef all right. Sure! But it's possible I kill him – me myself!' Wladyslaw tapped a finger to his chest. 'If he is not too badly sick already.'

'Don't be too quick to believe everything you hear, Wladyslaw. You know what gossip's like. People are always getting the wrong end of the stick. No, I'm certain Lyndon would have told me if there'd been any sort of fight.'

Wladyslaw stared at him.

Misunderstanding his silence, Bennett repeated, 'I'm sure he would have told me.'

'Sorry. Who is . . . this person?'

'Lyndon Hanley. He brought Jozef here. He took him on to the camp.'

'Ah.'

'Stella's cousin.'

'Ah yes . . . yes.' Wladyslaw glanced away as a keen wind came gusting round the side of the house and bowled into them. He became aware of the doctor shuddering reflexively.

'You will catch cold, Doctor.'

'Yes.'

'Remember – plenty raw onions.'

Bennett's chuckle was lost in a wheezing cough. 'Thank you, Wladyslaw. I'll try not to forget.'

The bicycle was ancient and upright, and Wladyslaw set off at a wobble.

The doctor called after him, 'Careful on the bends. The tyres are a bit worn.'

The warning would have been better aimed at the brakes, whose shortcomings became apparent as the ridge road descended in a long downward slope towards the River Parrett.

Fortunately there was no traffic about as, out of control, Wladyslaw shot across the road at the foot of the river bank, and, taking the escape route offered by a track on the far side, rattled chaotically over its rough surface and skidded to a halt. Laying the bike on the ground, he strolled up an earth ramp to a wooden bridge and found himself gazing down on a high wind-scuffed river held tight between muddy banks, bordered on the near side by brushwood, poplar and birch, and on the far side by a path and a drop to a wide water-streaked moor. The wind off the moor was strong and blustery, it drove angry cat's paws over the river and flecked the surface with dancing metallic flashes. Only under the bridge was the water oily-smooth and dark, the colour of earth and dung. It moved slowly but resolutely on its secret way.

He was turning back when something caught the edge of his visual map, a shape that didn't belong to the river or the moor or the brushwood. Looking hard, he made out what appeared to be a military beret showing over the grassy rim of the far bank some thirty metres away. As he watched, the beret moved a little, then a soldier in British army uniform got slowly to his feet, hauling a rifle onto his shoulder. The soldier put some field glasses to his eyes and scanned the moor, then turned to speak to someone out of sight to his right. After a moment a second soldier stood up, also with a rifle. The second soldier glanced up the length of the river, then over his shoulder, and saw Wladyslaw. Wladyslaw remained very still and so did the soldier. They continued to stare at each other for several seconds until the soldier, eyes still on Wladyslaw, said something to his mate, who jerked round and peered fiercely at Wladyslaw.

Wladyslaw turned away and walked down the track to his bicycle. He glanced back once, just before the gradient and the brushwood hid the soldiers from view, and saw them walking purposefully towards the bridge, faces turned his way. He mounted the bike and began pedalling down the road. He had nothing to fear, yet his nerves juddered and his back crawled, and until he had got safely round the first bend he might have been back in Italy again, caught in the cross hairs of a sniper's sights.

Approaching the camp, he saw people strung out in twos and threes coming over the fields from Camp C, making their way down the lane to Camp B for Mass. Cycling past them, he went to the post room to find it firmly locked and no indication of when it might open.

Worshippers from the first Mass were streaming out of the chapel and mingling with the crowd waiting for the next service. Through the open doors of the corrugated-iron hut Wladyslaw could see candles burning on the altar and the shadowy figure of the priest passing in front of the flames like a giant moth. For a brief moment he felt a nostalgic pull for the ritual and solace of the Mass and the memories of home and family it would bring him. But he had determined to stay away, and he was not going to let emotion undermine his resolve now. His dispute with God had begun in Archangel, deepened in Uzbekistan, and rumbled on with varying degrees of intensity ever since. He could no longer accept the idea of a loving, all-powerful God who stood aside and allowed the innocent to suffer and the wicked to triumph in the name of free will. The promise of justice and retribution in the next life wasn't nearly enough. In the beginning this argument had caused him the sort of misery he'd felt on quarrelling with his father when he was seventeen. But while he had been quickly reconciled with his father, his dispute with God had proved more intractable.

Among the line of people making their way into the chapel Wladyslaw recognised the solid form of Jozef's honorary god-mother Alina, followed by the equally unmistakable Danuta. And, obscured at first, then becoming clearly visible, the sharply etched profile of Jozef. Wladyslaw hurried forward but before he could attract Jozef's attention a tall figure detached himself from a nearby group and stepped into his path. It was Major Rafalski.

'Ah, Malinowski,' he said. 'How's the farm labouring?'

Wladyslaw watched Jozef disappearing into the chapel. 'Fine, thank you.'

'Not too arduous?'

'I have no complaints.'

'And the people – have they made you feel welcome?'

'Oh yes. They've been lending me books. Asking me into their homes. Helping in all sorts of ways.'

The austere face registered mild astonishment. 'Really. And what about the conversation? Do you find enough to talk about?'

'Plenty,' Wladyslaw replied, thinking of Stella.

'Then they must have hidden qualities,' the major said dubiously. 'I find them impossible myself. Warm and jovial one minute, stiff and insincere the next. And so very coarse. Don't you find them coarse? Their jokes are really disgusting.'

'I ignore the jokes.'

'Their attitude to women is dreadful – disrespectful, callous. And then they have the effrontery to accuse Polish men of being gallant and well-mannered, as if it were unsporting in some way.' The major scanned the horizon like a man undergoing a long and futile siege, searching for the relief force that would never come. 'You'll be staying on then, will you?' he asked.

'All being well, yes.'

'Well, careful how you go. A British patrol took a potshot at one of our people yesterday. They were looking for two escaped German POWs and got their nationalities, not to mention their uniforms, mixed up.'

'No one was hurt?'

'Fortunately not.'

'I think I saw them,' Wladyslaw said.

'Who, the Germans?'

'No, the patrol.'

'You were lucky, then,' the major said wearily, 'that they didn't take you for an enemy.'

The chapel was filled to capacity, the overflow clustered around the open door. As soon as the priest's voice began to incant the first prayer, Wladyslaw excused himself and made his way to the canteen. There was a long queue for breakfast, but the wait was worth it. He emerged with a full plate of fried eggs, bacon, sausage and fried bread, with toast and jam to follow. At first glance it seemed that every seat in the canteen was taken but then Wladyslaw spotted a place at a table near the door, opposite a man bent low over some papers. Only after Wladyslaw had put his plate down and pulled the chair out did he take a proper look at the man, and then it was too late to find another place.

'Oh, hello, Grobel.'

Grobel stared at him. Then, in the manner of someone who likes to nail his facts, he stated, 'Malinowski.'

'How are you?'

'You're a civilian then?' said Grobel, ignoring the question.

'I'm working on a farm a couple of villages away.'

'How is it?'

'Not so bad.' Brandishing his knife and fork, indicating with a cheery gesture that he intended to concentrate on eating, Wladyslaw attacked his food.

'Will you be coming to the meeting at eleven?' Grobel asked in his toneless voice.

Wladyslaw finished his mouthful before answering. 'I hadn't heard about a meeting.'

'We're voting on a motion requiring the authorities to segregate traitors and collaborators from the rest of us. To put them in a separate camp.'

'Ah. But now I'm living elsewhere I don't imagine I'm qualified to vote on such an issue.'

'I don't see why not.' Grobel extracted a slip of paper from the stack in front of him and slid it across the table. 'Come and vote anyway.'

The slip was headed: 'Important Meeting!' Wladyslaw glanced over it while he ate.

'So long as everyone comes along and casts their votes then the authorities will have to take notice,' Grobel declared. 'Anyone who doesn't – well, they'll have to look to their consciences! They'll have to live with the responsibility of leaving the rest of us in an intolerable situation!'

Wladyslaw nodded sagely, and continued to nod as Grobel rumbled on through his old grievances, adding a few new ones for good measure, which seemed to revolve around the injustices of the American and Canadian immigration policies and their bias towards single men and other undeserving types.

Finally, as Wladyslaw mopped up the last of his egg, Grobel fell silent.

'Have you had news of your family?' Wladyslaw asked dutifully.

'Yes.'

'Are they all right?'

'Yes. But there's no hope of a transport before April.'

'I'm sorry to hear it.'

After a pause, Grobel said, 'Uganda's a thousand metres above sea level, you know. It makes the climate bearable, even in summer.'

'That's something.'

'It's summer there now.'

'Ah.'

'They're living in mud huts with thatched roofs.'

'But adequate for the climate, I would imagine.'

'The authorities have built a school for them. There are two qualified teachers among the women, so the children are getting proper tuition.'

'That's good. They'll have made up for lost time.'

'It's made of mud, the school, like the huts. They're short of books.'

Wladyslaw prepared to stand up. 'Well . . . April's not so very far away.'

Grobel glared at him. 'But they won't stick to it, will they? You don't imagine the British will keep their word, do you?

You don't imagine Polish women and children will be given anything but the lowest priority? No, the British will let us down, like they always do. No, April . . . September. What do they care?'

With the angry frown of a man who finds he has been unwittingly distracted from more pressing matters, Grobel made a dismissive gesture and, bending over his sheaf of hand-written notes once more, began to scribble.

Wladyslaw escaped with relief and made his way back to the post room to find it was still firmly shut. A clerk in the administration block told him it was most likely to open after second Mass, at ten o'clock. Wandering in the direction of his old quarters, Wladyslaw was hailed by two acquaintances from the Italian campaign and spent a pleasant half-hour talking about old times over lemon tea and English biscuits named after Garibaldi.

He got back to the chapel a few minutes before Mass finished and caught Jozef as he came down the steps.

'How are you, Jozef?' he asked. 'I heard you were ill.'

'It was nothing,' Jozef replied airily.

'I was told that you'd collapsed in the pub. That there was a fight.'

Jozef, sensitive to the slightest criticism, assumed his dark, depressed look. 'I was just ill. But if you don't want to believe me . . . well, don't!'

The rebuke Wladyslaw had prepared died on his lips. It was impossible to look at the gaunt features, the unnaturally tight skin, the angular cheekbones and darkly shadowed eyes, without feeling an illogical responsibility.

'Well, are you all right now?'

'Never better.'

'Dr Bennett was worried that you might not have had the necessary medical attention.'

'I was in the care of my mother hens.' Jozef tipped his head towards Alina and Danuta, who were chattering to some women nearby. 'They kept me in bed for two days and fed me broth and stewed apple.'

'And we sang to him too,' called Alina, who had overheard. 'Like two old witches.'

'There promises to be some rather better singing at Camp C this afternoon,' said Danuta. 'Songs from the Tatra Mountains by some lads from the Tank Brigade. Will you come, Wladyslaw? It's at four.'

'Sadly, no. I have to get back before dark.'

'There's another event at the same time,' said a young woman on a tentative note. 'A visit to an English home for tea.'

There was a short but decisive silence.

Alina said apologetically, 'Until I can speak English better I would feel embarrassed to attempt conversation.'

But it seemed to Wladyslaw that she and the rest of the inmates were held back by more than language. While they would undoubtedly find a great deal to interest them at an English tea party, in their hearts they could see little point in making any attempt to assimilate. They had long ago acquired the mentality of wanderers. They saw no value in putting down roots which would only be torn up again. Each new country, each new camp was simply another staging post on the long and arduous journey home, or if home were temporarily barred to them, then to some Little Poland in another land. England had been a diversion more unexpected than some, but, after the twists and turns of the last six years, experience told them it was unlikely to be the last.

'Will you at least take some refreshment with us, Wladyslaw?' said Janina, adding in a heavy whisper, 'We've managed to acquire some decent vodka.'

'I'd love to. In an hour or so, if that's all right.'

'Where are you heading?' Jozef asked as Wladyslaw began to move away.

'To the post room.'

'I'll come with you.'

Jozef glanced over his shoulder a couple of times as they walked away. Finally he said in a low tight voice, 'Listen, Wladek, I've decided to get out of this place. I'm going away.'

Slowing, Wladyslaw shot him a questioning look. 'What do you mean?'

'It's all set,' Jozef said, striding on doggedly. 'I'm leaving tomorrow. First thing. I just wanted you to know.'

Struggling to catch up with him, Wladyslaw demanded, 'But where are you going, Jozef? And why? What's brought all this about?'

Jozef shook his head as if to ward off further questions, before offering reluctantly, 'I'm going to London.'

'But what will you do in London?'

'Who knows? It can't be any worse than hanging around here waiting for nothing to happen.'

'But I thought you liked it here. You said you'd never been happier.'

Jozef hunched his shoulders. 'It was the relief of getting out of that stinking sanatorium, that's all.'

'Have you got permission to leave?'

'What do you think?'

Wladyslaw sighed. 'For God's sake, Jozef, can't you at least wait for a proper discharge?'

'What's the point?'

'It would avoid being posted absent without leave, for a start.'

'And what are they going to do if they catch me? There's no glasshouse here, in case you hadn't noticed. We're only playing at soldiers now.'

Reaching the post room, they paused at the door. Jozef's gaze shifted restlessly, studiously avoiding Wladyslaw's eye.

'So, what will you do when you get to London?' Wladyslaw demanded. 'How will you live?'

Jozef thrust his hands into his pockets. 'I'll get work, of course.'

'But Jozef, you don't speak English. Your health is shit. You have no . . . well . . .'

'Skills? Thanks for reminding me.'

'Look, I'm only trying to knock some sense into your thick skull. I'm only trying to stop you from stabbing yourself in the back,' said Wladyslaw, grabbing the nearest metaphor. 'There are no jobs for us in London, Jozef. Not for Poles. The most you can hope for is scrubbing floors. Is that what you really want?'

'A friend's going to get me started.'

'And where's it going to lead?' Wladyslaw went on insistently. 'You'll be completely on your own. No help from the army. No help from the welfare people. You can say goodbye to a visa for America or Australia. You'll be burning your boats – and for what?'

With a stubborn expression Jozef thrust his hands deeper into his pockets and looked away over his shoulder.

Wladyslaw muttered, 'For heaven's sake . . .' Then, trying one last throw: 'What do your godmothers say? Or haven't you told them?'

Jozef's frown gave him his answer.

Wladyslaw said dejectedly, 'Well, if you're not going to listen to reason, then at least promise me one thing. That you'll let me know if you run into trouble. That you'll send me a telegram.'

Jozef's mouth twitched. 'OK.'

'Here . . .' Wladyslaw led the way into the post room and, cadging some paper off the postal clerk, printed out the address for Crick Farm. Folding the paper twice, he slid it into the breast pocket of Jozef's tunic. 'Don't lose it,' he said sternly.

Jozef touched a hand to his pocket. 'Sure.' Then with a tilt of his head towards the post rack, he muttered, 'I'll just wait, eh?' It was a gesture of solidarity. During their months at the convalescent home they had both mastered the art of passing the letter rack without a glance, of resisting the urge to look for letters that never came.

This time, however, when Wladyslaw gave his name, the postal clerk reached unhesitatingly into the pigeonhole and handed him a letter.

Jozef let out a low exclamation of excitement.

Wladyslaw stared at the envelope before turning it over to read the name on the back. 'It's from my sister.'

'Well, you'd better open it.'

Retreating to the window, Wladyslaw examined the envelope once again before opening it. The letter ran to four sheets. He skimmed the first few lines hungrily, then read them again slowly.

My dear Wladek,

I received your letter with the greatest relief and joy! It was in May that I heard you had survived the war – the news arrived via a cousin of Tadzio's wife – but of course I had no address for you, no idea even of which country you were in, so I could only wait and hope for confirmation. It is wonderful to have received it at last. I am so glad to know that you have got through these terrible years unscathed.

Aware of Jozef's intense gaze, Wladyslaw said happily, 'Yes, it's her! She didn't know where I was. She didn't know how to find me.'

Your other news brought me confirmation of an altogether sadder kind. Confirmation because I managed to learn the fate of our family some months ago. This was thanks to the unstinting efforts of Stefan, my husband, who undertook to find out what had happened to them. Using every possible means, going to endless trouble, Stefan managed to establish what had happened to Father, then (after some months) to Krysia, then, through the Polish community in Isfahan, to Mother. Enzio's fate was more difficult to determine because of the lack of records, but Stefan is not someone to give up easily. Through a

contact in Teheran he found a record of Mother and
Janina's arrival in Persia, but no mention of Enzio. The
conclusion was only too sadly obvious. My only solace
came from a piece of news Stefan unearthed shortly
afterwards, that you too had arrived in Persia with the new
Polish army, and could therefore – with God's blessing –
be hoped to be alive.

'She already knew about our family,' Wladyslaw recounted
with puzzlement as he turned to the next page. 'Her husband
seems to be a man of great resourcefulness.'

Before posting the above, I received your second and
third letters. I have found it almost unbearable to read of
everything our beloved family endured. Such suffering.
Such anguish. I thought I had no more tears to shed, but I
was wrong. Don't misunderstand me – I'm glad you told
me. It is always best to know the worst, because however
terrible it is there is an element of relief, I feel closer to
them in spirit, and can only pray, as you do, that they rest
in peace at last.
   Before going any further, however, I feel I must correct
you on one important point regarding Aleks's death. That
he was murdered at Katyn seems beyond doubt, I agree,
but I am mystified as to why you should imply (no – state
accusingly) that the Russians were responsible when it is a
matter of historical record that the SS carried out this
terrible crime.

'God Almighty!' Wladyslaw exploded in fury. 'Historical
record?' He flung the words at Jozef with a fierce glare.
'According to whose history? Whose records?'

   It is well documented that the Polish prisoners of war
held in the Ukraine were alive and well until the German
offensive of 1941. To suggest otherwise is, if I may say so,
to fall victim to reactionary propaganda. I can only think
you have been relying on questionable sources for your

information. Like the reactionaries of the old regime in exile, perhaps? The diehards who have an exceptionally large axe to grind?

Jozef prompted anxiously, 'Wladyslaw? What is it?'
'Nothing.' The heat had died in Wladyslaw as suddenly as it had come. 'Nothing at all.'

> While speaking of accuracy, I should also point out a couple of salient facts regarding Father's death. Stefan went to a great deal of trouble to investigate the events surrounding Father's murder, and one thing became clear, that there was total chaos at the time. He discovered that there were four, possibly five, illegal militias rampaging around our neighbourhood with complete impunity. Indeed, the authorities didn't reckon they had restored law and order until well into December – that is, many weeks after Father's death. So your talk of conspiracy and collusion with the authorities has left me baffled and not a little distressed. Can't we just stick to the facts and grieve for Father as a victim of lawless thugs? Why make things worse by going into the realms of fiction and wild accusation?

Shaken by a wave of indignation and loss, Wladyslaw turned towards the window for a moment, and stared unseeing at the hut opposite. When he returned to the letter it was with grim fascination.

> There are other matters on which I believe you are mistaken, Wladek, but this is not the time to go into them, except to say that the political difficulties you quote are very real, though I would suggest they are more on your side than ours. While the original Russian occupation was harsh – I would never pretend otherwise – it's foolish to carry a sense of grievance forward indefinitely, if only because it ignores everything that the Russians have done for us since. You didn't live through the Nazi occupation, Wladek. You can't imagine the scale of the death and

degradation. Russia fought to free us, and in so doing starved as we starved, died as we died, in their millions and millions. If freedom has had a difficult birth, it does not make the child any the less precious.

Jozef had moved to the wall and was leaning against it, watching Wladyslaw out of the corner of his eye.

'It seems I'm guilty of small-mindedness,' Wladyslaw announced. 'Of not giving credit where credit is due.'

Now, with Russia's help we have the prospect of building a better world in which all citizens will enjoy the same privileges and opportunities, the same right to justice under the law. We fervently believe that this prize can and must be wrested from the ashes of our country, indeed that it is the only prize worth having.

'The only prize worth having,' growled Wladyslaw. 'Such certainty, Jozef. Imagine – no doubts at all!'

I cannot help you decide your future, Wladek, I can only tell you that people who cling to the old ways will find it difficult here, while those who are keen to make a genuine contribution will feel entirely welcome. Life is hard, I wouldn't pretend otherwise, but we feel we are aiming for a worthwhile goal.

Yes, I'm a wife now. I work as a medical secretary at the hospital. I also do some voluntary work. Stefan is a lecturer at the university and an active force in the Workers' Party, which keeps him very busy. I try to help him out as much as I can with typing and so on. We have a tiny apartment in the old town, complete with leaking roof, but we're happy here.

I will say goodbye now, and wish you the best in making your choice.

With all my love,
Helenka

Wladyslaw folded the letter slowly and slid it into his pocket. Aware of Jozef's intense gaze, he murmured, 'I'll be off now.'

'You're not coming to Alina and Danuta's?'

'No. Apologise for me, will you? Tell them I was called back to the farm.'

'In that case I'll say goodbye. And . . .' He mumbled something about thanks.

'What?'

'I'm leaving. Remember?'

'For heaven's sake, of course you are.' Looping an arm over Jozef's shoulder, he embraced him swiftly. 'Take care, old friend. Watch out for yourself.'

'Sure.'

'And if anything should go wrong, you know where to find me.'

Jozef said defiantly, 'I'll be all right.'

Watching the thin, nervous figure walk away, it seemed to Wladyslaw that the chances of him being all right were not terribly good.

Wladyslaw lay on his bed smoking while the wind roared around the apple store, drumming at the door and guttering the candle. His leg was throbbing in what seemed like a new way, in dull rhythmical pulses interspersed with the occasional short sharp dart of pain which leapt all the way up to his hip, as if a sadist were applying a needle to an exposed nerve. He made no effort to massage his leg or alleviate the pain with exercise, but allowed the throbbing to mark the seconds like the beats of a metronome and the jabs of pain to curb his frenetic thoughts.

On the table beside him lay a letter to Helenka. It had taken three drafts before he had managed to say everything he wanted to say and in the way he wanted to say it, each thought articulated with fluency, lucidity and passion, nothing left out, nothing overstated, the arguments perfectly balanced and per-

suasively delivered. It was a masterful letter, and shortly he
would burn it. Having burnt it, he would not write again. One
could not argue with a person in possession of the only facts
that had any value to her, facts that had been discovered with
such selfless dedication by her paragon of a husband. One
could not argue with blind certainty.

With relief he let his mind drift back to the old days. He
didn't need to reach for the photograph above his head to see
it clearly, how each member of the family was placed, the way
they were standing and sitting, the expressions on their faces,
his parents with a blend of pride and anxiety, Aleks and Enzio
solemn and self-conscious, Janina and Krysia vibrant and carefree, and Helenka sitting at one end, already a little on her
dignity in preparation for becoming a doctor, but with a hint
of a smile. This was how he would remember her from now
on, he decided, in the garden at Podjaworka with the plum tree
casting a lace-like tracery over her pale dress and an echo of
old laughter in her eyes.

On the far side of his writing table, beyond the letter, were
some of his scribblings from the previous evening, the results
of his labours on the customs of England. For the time being it
seemed as if these too were destined to remain unaired. At five
thirty that afternoon he had cycled up through the village and,
following Stella's directions, found his way to the gate of a
dark cottage set well back from the road behind a low fence.
The place might have been deserted but for a thread of reddish
light between the downstairs curtains. With fifteen minutes to
spare, he had strolled up and down the lane until, holding a
last match up to his watch, he made his way up the uneven
brick path to the door. The woman who answered was an
older version of Stella, with blue eyes now faded, and wavy
hair turned the colour of frosted sand, and a voice that was
startlingly similar to her daughter's.

'You are Wladyslaw,' she stated simply, before telling him
that Stella had been called away unexpectedly. It was something urgent that could not be put off, she explained. Stella

sent her apologies and would try to arrange another time soon. Wladyslaw nodded and smiled his thanks, but for some reason Mrs Mead didn't seem to think he had understood because she repeated the message again in slow emphatic tones.

Thanking her again, Wladyslaw rode on to the doctor's house. There were lights in the living room but he returned the bicycle to the shed and walked away without calling.

The apple store had grown cold; the stove had run out of paraffin. Now a sudden gust of wind rattled the door and blew out the candle. Wladyslaw felt for a match, only to change his mind and reach for his jacket and boots. He emerged into a raucous wind that whistled in the withy racks and tore at the apple trees, making the branches creak and groan in agony. Bending into the wind, he walked down to the end of the yard and stood at the gate to the drove-road. All was dark except for the occasional star glimmering through a rip in the racing clouds. Around him the grasses rustled and shivered, the trees whimpered and thrashed, while rising up from the darkness below, underlying everything, it seemed to him that he could hear the insistent whispering of the wetland, like the breathing of a giant animal.

A shout, very human, very abrupt, rose above the wind. Looking back, Wladyslaw saw a torch beam playing over the apple store and, half illuminated in its reflection, Billy hammering a fist on the door. 'Johnnie? You in there? Wakey-wakey!'

Wladyslaw hurried up the yard. 'What is the matter, Billy?'

Billy spun round and shone the light straight into his face. 'There you are! Come on – grab your stuff. Quick march! One, two! Left, right!'

'What stuff? Where we going?'

'Look lively! No time to hang about.' Billy was already moving away down the yard, the torch beam dancing wildly over the ground in front of him.

Wladyslaw pulled on a woollen hat and thick gloves. What else he was meant to grab he had no idea. Billy had been carrying something over his shoulder, a roll of wire, or a bundle of hoops, but these gave no clue as to what else might be needed. In the end Wladyslaw took a knife, a hook, and a length of rope.

By the time he started off, the wavering beam was already halfway down the drove and going fast. He broke into an uncertain jog, his leg protesting at each jar of the rough surface. As he gained on the torch beam, he caught above the blustering wind snatches of wild discordant singing, and realised with sinking heart that Billy was drunk.

'Billy – what the hell!' he shouted.

'Come on, or we'll be too bloody late.'

'What for?'

'The tide.'

'The tide,' Wladyslaw grumbled loudly as another stab of pain shot up his leg. 'Sure! What else!'

Approaching the wetland where the darkness was at its deepest, the torch beam vanished suddenly, and Wladyslaw was forced to rely on another rendition of 'It's a Pity to Say Goodnight' to guide him to the side of the old rhyne and a rough path he had never walked along before. Then the singing petered out, and there was nothing to guide him but the bouncing orb of Billy's head against the faint luminosity of the sky and the pollards that loomed up one after the other like cannons targeting the heavens. All around him the wind thrummed and sighed, and from the far side of the rhyne came the sibilant rustle of the withies.

The rhyne took a loop south, a stand of willows blocked out the sky, and all of a sudden Billy wasn't there any more.

'Billy?' Halting doubtfully, Wladyslaw's senses reached out into the darkness, straining for a shape, a movement, among the shifting shadows. Calling Billy's name more urgently, he edged forward. Suddenly a curse rose from close in front of him. Peering downwards he made out Billy's form crouching at the water's edge. A series of grunts and oaths followed as Billy

struggled with the wire contraption. Wladyslaw was just leaning forward for a better look when Billy let out a yelp and
started to flail about.

'Billy, what is—' The words died in Wladyslaw's throat as
he felt something nudge the side of his boot, and it wasn't Billy.

'What the hell?'

But Billy was jabbering to himself, half laughing, half swearing, making no sense at all.

Wladyslaw felt another faint but distinct movement against
his foot. 'Billy, what is—' Then on a rising note of disbelief,
'Milosc Boska!'

The torch flashed on, the ground sprang into relief, and
Wladyslaw flinched with revulsion. The grass was heaving with
snakes.

He would have jumped aside, but the snakes were everywhere, slithering rapidly past his feet. 'What is this things?' he
demanded in a strangled voice.

'They're bloody eels, aren't they?'

Regaining his wits, bending forward a little, Wladyslaw
made out gills and fish mouths and black shiny backs and silver
bellies. He counted four – five – six of them within the torch
beam, with more coming up behind. They were heading for the
old rhyne, where they slipped rapidly over the edge of the bank
into the water.

'Catch 'em if you can!' Billy cried as he lunged for one. At
the third attempt he got a hand over the body of an eel, only
for it to leap free with an insouciant flick of its tail and dive
neatly into the water. Billy was laughing so much he kept
having to gasp for breath. Then, with Wladyslaw aiming the
torch onto the rhyne, he lowered the net-and-hoop contraption
into the soupy water and staked it to the bottom of the ditch.
Even before Billy had driven the last stake into the mud,
Wladyslaw saw an eel swim into the mouth of the trap.

Billy climbed out and lumbered off into the darkness. Wladyslaw found him sitting against the trunk of a large willow
under a vault of shivering branches. Sitting down next to him,

Wladyslaw heard the pop of a stopper and a series of gulps, and then a jar of cider was being pressed into his hand.

'What do these eels do, Billy? Why do they come this way?'

'They're trying to get to the salt water, Johnnie, that's what, and they reckon the old rhyne's their best bet. And once they get to the salt then they swim all the way to the Sargasso Sea, which is . . . dunno 'xactly . . . but bloody miles away. An' you know what for? For a fuck. Their one and only *ever*. Then they're dead. Finished. One leg-over and *that's it*. Talk about going out with a bang.' Billy took another swig of cider. 'But you know what? They've got it easy. Don' have to cope with talking and yakking. Don' have to try 'n work out what the hell women are on about. 'Cos one thing's sure – what they say's got bugger all to do with what they mean. I tell you, when it comes to plotting and planning, we've got *nothing* on them . . . *nothing* . . .'

An unformed thought had been chasing around the edges of Wladyslaw's mind. Now it came to him in a rush that Stella had failed to mention her boyfriend not from any oversight or thoughtlessness but from the belief that Wladyslaw must already know, because the rest of the world knew and couldn't have failed to tell him.

'An' tell me this, Johnnie,' Billy was rambling on. 'How it is that the man who goes and fights for his country comes back 'n finds he counts for less than the bastard who stayed behind? How's that, eh? I'll tell you how – 'cos the bastard that stayed behind got himself all set up and made plenty of money, that's how.'

Another possibility, it seemed to Wladyslaw, was that the boyfriend was a touchy subject for Stella, that she was tired of the criticism and disapproval he attracted, and found it easier not to mention him at all. This thought cheered him up enormously, and he listened to the rest of Billy's ramblings with as much sympathy as he could muster.

After less than an hour the net was almost full. They transferred its writhing contents into a sack. Back at the farm,

Billy hung the sack from a hook under the eaves of the withy shed. As they parted for the night Wladyslaw thought Billy said, 'We'll take 'em up to the smokery first thing.'

But in the morning there was no sign of Billy. Stan said he'd left at five on the milk train.

Part Two

Chapter Ten

BILLY WAS woken by the sting of the cold. At some point in the night his scarf had slipped off his head and like a waiting parasite the cold had bitten into the unguarded flesh of his cheek. The hard wooden floor felt almost gentle by comparison, while the touch of the girl at his back, though diluted by thick layers of clothing, gave off a feeble but companionable warmth.

It was dark, but the luminosity of the snow two storeys below gave definition to the window and suffused the frosted panes with white glimmering light. Hearing no sounds from outside, he thought it must be early, perhaps five or six, but as first one vehicle and then another laboured along the street he decided it was probably later. Both vehicles seemed to stop outside the block, but he put this down to a trick of the snow.

In the next flat someone clumped rapidly across the bare boards, there was the protesting whine of a sash being thrown up, and a woman yelled something. Billy recognised the nasal tones of Carol, a leading member of the action committee. She shouted what sounded like a series of questions – he caught only fragments – and then the window was closed with a bang that sent the counterweights rattling in their shafts.

A door slammed in the corridor, footsteps sounded, and he caught a muffled crescendo of voices. Pushing off his blanket, rearranging it around the sleeping girl, he clambered to his feet and went to the window. At first the ice on the glass stubbornly re-formed whenever he tried to rub it away, but by scratching hard with his nails he was finally able to make out the shapes of two vans parked in the road outside, and, bunched around the entrance gates to the block, five figures, at least three of them with the domed helmets of policemen.

He made his way into the bathroom by touch, only to find that the lavatory would not flush and the taps were dry. At first he supposed that the water, like the other services, had been cut off, but going into the kitchen and finding the kettle full of ice, he realised that the big freeze had saved the landlords the trouble.

Treading softly so as not to wake the girl, he let himself out into the corridor. A vehement discussion was issuing from the open door of the next flat. He could hear the shrill relentless voice of Carol and the deep tones of a man arguing against her.

Turning away, Billy made for a candlelit doorway at the end of the corridor. He found Betty Price in the kitchen, heating some water over a portable paraffin stove which had decorated the immaculate white kitchen tiles with long tongues of soot. Betty was a scrawny woman with gap teeth and prematurely lined skin. She had been in residence with her four children since the start of the squat some ten days before.

'Any chance of a cuppa?' Billy asked.

Usually Betty greeted this request with a suggestive reply, played for all it was worth, 'For you, darlin'? Anything.' But today she said baldly, 'No can do, sweetheart. Barely enough water for the kids.'

'You know we've got company?' Billy asked, jerking his head towards the street.

She rolled her eyes scornfully. 'You'd think they'd have better things to do.'

'They won't arrest anyone.'

'Just let 'em bloody try,' she snorted. 'But then they've no need to bother, have they, now the water's off. No, we're all packed. Can't be hangin' about in this bloomin' climate.'

'Where'll you go?'

'Me sister's till she chucks us out. Then . . .' She blew out her cheeks at the prospect of searching for the kind of cramped overpriced accommodation she'd been trying to escape in the first place. 'Gawd only knows.'

The paraffin stove popped and spluttered, and she fiddled with the knob.

'No more squats?' Billy asked.

'No point, is there? Not when the council don't take a blind bit of notice. Still, we got six days with the heat and the light, didn't we? Could've been worse.'

'What would happen if you went and camped on the council's doorstep?'

She gave a cackling laugh. 'Then I'd get myself arrested no trouble at all.'

'Good luck,' Billy said.

'And you.' With a mischievous gap-toothed grin, she grabbed his face in both hands and gave him a smacking great kiss on the lips.

On his way out, Billy looked into the living room and saw her kids sitting around a candle, chewing on slices of bread and jam. Suitcases and bundles of bedding stood ready to go. The younger children stared blankly at him when he waved, but the two older boys made cheeky faces.

'Seen the coppers?'

They nodded happily. At their age it was all a bit of a lark.

When he got back to the flat to fetch his things the girl called out, 'That you, Billy?'

'Sure is.'

She cried with relief. 'I thought you'd gone.'

He struck a match and put it to a candle stump. She was sitting huddled in the blankets. 'Everyone's getting out,' he told her. 'There's no water, and the police are camped outside.'

'You going too?'

'No point in staying.' He began to pack his knapsack.

'Can I come with you?'

'I'm going to work.'

'But after?'

'Don't know, do I?'

'Please let me come with you.'

He shook his head. 'Might go travelling. Haven't decided yet.'

Her name was Rosie. She had attached herself to him shortly after he had moved in and been trailing after him ever since. She was from Dorset, or it might have been Devon, and was alone in London. He would have shaken her off before now but she was thin and sickly looking and made few demands. When she nestled close to his back at night he was glad of the warmth. He wasn't so much of a fool as to try for more, even supposing he'd fancied her, which he didn't.

'I've nowhere to go,' she said.

'What about that hostel where you were before?' He pulled a ten-bob note from his pocket and thrust it towards her. 'Here.'

'I couldn't.' She was close to tears.

''Course you can.' He plucked her hand free of the blankets and pressed the note into her palm.

'Carol says there's another place we can go.'

He fastened the last buckle on his knapsack. 'I thought Carol was for no surrender.'

'She says it's a nice house with a full coal store. She says it'd be weeks before anyone knew we were there.'

'Go with Carol, then.'

'But I want to stay with you, Billy.'

'No one gets to stay with me.'

Taking the candle, he looked into the other rooms to make sure he hadn't left anything behind. He wouldn't be sorry to leave the place. Even without furniture the flat managed to feel oppressive with its striped wallpaper and ornate radiator housings and ceiling lights made of beaded crystal. The only room he coveted was the bathroom, which had a majestic white basin and lavatory, full-length bath, and heavy chrome fittings. It wasn't just the luxury of the hot and cold running water, nor even the depth of the bath, which let you lie with water up to your chin, it was the brazen extravagance that he loved, the idea of splurging so much money on a room where you bathed and shat and shaved. It had tickled him to sit on a throne surrounded by walls of black and white polished marble, to look in a mirror with bevelled borders that reflected light in all directions, and to operate taps so huge and shiny that you could see your own distorted image in them.

When he went to collect his knapsack, Rosie cried plaintively, 'Please let me come with you, Billy. I wouldn't be any trouble, promise. I'd help out. I'd do whatever you wanted.'

He stood over her. 'I need my blanket.'

As soon as she had clambered to her feet he folded the blanket and, averting his eyes from her mournful face, picked up his things and left.

He glanced through the open door of the adjacent flat as he passed, but everyone seemed to have gone.

On the stairs he followed a bunch of people laden with baggage and screaming children who were fumbling their way down from the upper floors in the darkness. Nearing the last turn the bumping and confusion eased as muted light filtered up from below.

The scene in the entrance hall might have come from a film which had employed the wrong cast. The hall, with its tall ceiling, gleaming mirrors and black-and-white patterned floor, could have come from a Fred Astaire–Ginger Rogers film, while the homeless families who were waiting disconsolately in their heavy layers of clothing worn one on top of another, with their boots and tightly wrapped scarves, their rolled-up bedding and bursting suitcases, belonged to a wartime newsreel, a bunch of refugees trekking across alien lands.

Carol was stationed by the grandiose marble fireplace talking fervently to some of the adults. She was an unlikely figure for an activist. No more than twenty-one or two, slight, with bleached hair and a jutting jaw, you would have taken her for a shop girl dreaming of the next night out or the next man, or both. Billy had met her one Saturday afternoon on his way back to Ernie's house. She was standing outside Hackney Town Hall with five or six other women, handing out leaflets for the

Workers' Housing Committee, pleading her case with anyone who'd stop to listen. Spotting Billy, she came marching over and delivered a quickfire speech on the scandal of the housing crisis. He replied, what housing crisis? which got her well and truly going until she realised it was a joke. After that there was quite a bit of mutual sizing up, ostensibly political but also sexual, before they agreed to meet for a drink later that evening. She turned up half an hour late, fuming over some fresh incidence of official callousness, and it took two gin and limes in quick succession to loosen her up enough to laugh, even to flirt, but not enough, it seemed, to sleep with him. She'd thought about it though, he knew she had, although it was probably just as well things hadn't got that far. She was the type to talk politics in bed, not something that would have stirred his passions.

The Workers' Housing Committee had been formed by a group of housewives who'd led one of the first squats, the now legendary occupation of an empty block of flats in Regent's Park which had culminated in a police siege and a crowd of two thousand homeless people staging a sit-down protest in the road outside. Since then, so far as Billy could make out, the founding housewives had abandoned control of the committee to a number of veteran activists who slipped in and out of the block at odd times, trade unionists and communists who whispered advice into Carol's ear and made the occasional round of the flats, stiffening the communal resolve.

They weren't much in evidence now, however, as Carol faced the families alone and urged them to hold tight till word could be sent to the homeless community, who'd come and lob food up to them through the windows.

'They goin' to lob water up an' all, are they?' said one of the women. 'Come on.'

'Have you looked out the door recently?' added a gravel-voiced man. 'No one's goin' to come out in this lot, are they? Not if they was Scott of the bleedin' Antarctic himself.'

'But if they know we're under siege—'

'The whole of London's under siege, innit?' The gravel-voiced man said this for effect, and got a ripple of wry laughter from the listeners. Encouraged by his success, he went on, 'And tell me what sort of herbert's goin' to chuck food up at my window when there's a shortage on?'

This time the laughter was scattered and uncertain. Food was a worrying issue. The unprecedented series of blizzards had come hard on the heels of a national hauliers' strike, and many shop shelves remained ominously empty.

'All right,' Carol conceded quickly with a splayed hand. 'Maybe people won't manage to turn out in this, maybe we can't expect them to. But we still got the police at the door, we still got a corkin' story for the newspapers. We just got to hold on till the press people get here.'

'What's the point?' said the first woman.

'The point,' Carol said in a voice that rose dangerously, 'is for the council to be shamed into givin' us housing.'

'The council's not shown up this far, so they're not likely to show up now, are they?' growled the gravel-voiced man. 'Not when they've got the police doing their dirty work.'

'Can't hang about on the off chance,' muttered the first woman. 'It's too blithering cold.'

'Look, I'm not askin' for all of you to stay on,' Carol pleaded. 'I know there's some of you that's got to get to work, needin' to get the kids hot food. I know that. But the rest of you – it's just two days I'm askin' for. That's all. *Two days*. We've got a couple of stoves up on the first floor. We've got some food.' She forced her voice onto a lighter note. 'And we'll get some beer in to keep us warm.'

No one looked persuaded.

Carol threw out her hands in a final appeal. 'Come on!' she said cajolingly. 'Where's your fighting spirit?'

'All gone, love.'

The mood had shifted. People were tired of arguing. There was a movement towards luggage and children, and the murmur of general conversation as people discussed their transport and accommodation options.

Carol let out a tight breath and glanced towards Billy. 'Oh, it's you,' she declared dispiritedly. Then, registering his knapsack: 'So, you're off too, are you?'

'Looks like it.'

'Well, there's a surprise.'

'Pardon me?'

'You were never goin' to be a stayer, were you? That was pretty bloody obvious from the start.'

'Come off it, Carol. If I thought the newspapers were going to turn up I'd stick around, no question.'

'And you think they won't?'

'Not while there's a national crisis on.'

'Well, that just goes to show how much you know, doesn't it?' she scoffed. 'Because I had a reporter from the *Sketch* all lined up. Goin' to do photographs, the lot.'

Billy offered her a cigarette, which she refused impatiently. 'Come off it, Carol. The papers aren't going to turn up unless there's trouble, and the police aren't going to let there be trouble, are they? Not when they can get us out the easy way, just by sitting there and stopping food coming in.'

She glared at him because she knew it was the truth.

'The only other thing the papers might come for is a bit of light relief. If the story was going to give people some laughs.'

'*Laughs?*'

'Yeah. Like at the beginning. Like with that siege at Regent's Park.'

'You think that was funny?'

'You bet it was. It was the best value ever. Seeing the police and the government looking like total berks, held to ransom by a bunch of women and children sitting in the street. The lads in my camp laughed their heads off. Everyone did. That's what got the country on your side. The entertainment value. But now — well, people aren't in the mood for fun and games, are they? Not when they're busy trying to keep body and soul together.'

'I'll have that fag after all,' Carol declared, thrusting out her hand. She inhaled hard, and glowered at the noisy ragtag horde in front of her as though she'd gladly swap them for a fully equipped guerrilla army. 'All for nothing,' she sighed.

Billy swung his knapsack onto his back. 'Nah. Nothing's ever for nothing. And it's only one battle, isn't it?'

He gave her a kiss on the cheek and, spotting Rosie nearby, purposefully avoided her stare and marched briskly across the hall to the door. His move stirred some other people into action: they began to pick up their bags.

Stepping outside, Billy felt the full onslaught of the wind and the cold. The night's snowfall was ankle deep. The policemen were stamping their feet and hugging their hands, but at the sight of him they pulled their shoulders back and stood stock still.

As Billy approached, one of them bade him an ironical, 'Morning, sir.' Then, as he drew level: 'I trust we are not intending to return.'

Billy paused. 'Well, you'll just have to hang around and find out, won't you?'

Picking his way along the pavement, enjoying a small glow of satisfaction, Billy didn't spot the tall figure in peaked cap and greatcoat until he was a few feet away. His first thought was that the army had been called in to break up the squat, that things might turn nasty and he should stick around after all. But then he realised there were no lorries and no soldiers. The officer was alone.

The tall figure moved towards him and said, 'Excuse me, could you tell me what's happening?'

'What's it to you?'

'Well, I've rented a flat here, you see, and I was rather hoping to move my family in later this morning.'

'I wouldn't count on it.'

'You don't think they'll let me in?'

'Not if you're renting one of their flats.'

'Oh.' The logic clearly puzzled him. 'Do you know how long they're planning to stay?'

'Couldn't tell you.'

The officer hesitated. 'Is the place all right inside? They haven't done any damage, have they?'

'*They* haven't done anything,' Billy said pointedly. 'But I'd speak to the landlord, if I were you, about the pipes.'

Again, the officer wasn't too quick off the mark. 'The pipes?'

'They're frozen solid.'

'Ahh.' It was a heavy sigh of defeat. 'Back to the drawing board, then.'

The dawn had brought a heavy metallic gloom. The wind was bitter, the coldest Billy had ever known. A flurry of needle-sharp flakes darted back and forth on the air, advancing in sudden stabbing motions. The pavements were impassable, a deceptive combination of soft snow and sheet ice, so he walked down the tyre tracks in the middle of the road where the snow was crisp and compacted. There was almost no traffic, just the occasional car moving at a crawl.

Until the snow arrived Billy had walked to work or ridden on a bus platform, but now he took the underground from St John's Wood. The atmosphere in the tunnels was warm and dry, the blast of the approaching train brought an illusion of fresh air, but it did little to quell his incipient panic. Once the doors shut behind him there was no escaping the press of bodies, the closeness of the air, the damp cigarette-fuelled fug, and the cloying scent of women's perfume. By the time he had changed trains and endured a crowded lift at Great Portland Street, his ears were roaring, his lungs were tight, and he emerged onto the street ready to do violence to anyone who got in his way.

The local café, though hot and humid, held no fears for him. The door was never more than a step away and unlocked, while the stink of frying fat, the streaming windows, the slap of the plates landing on the counter brought memories of the NAAFI canteens in which he'd whiled away the early years of his military service.

He ordered egg, bacon and sausage, to be told that the

bacon was off. Yesterday it had been the eggs. He took a seat by the window and glanced at his neighbour's newspaper. It was just four pages long and full of doom and gloom. Carol was living in cloud cuckoo land if she thought that a story about twenty families trying to get a leg up the housing ladder was going to find space anywhere near the headlines *Three Million Laid Off. Power to Be Cut to Homes*. The smaller headlines told of twenty-foot drifts blocking railway lines, of coal not getting through, forcing five major plants to close in a single day. Worse, the government had ordered beer production to be halved, which seemed to Billy to be a crass error. You could ask people to put up with almost anything, cold, even hunger, so long as they could get pissed at the end of the day.

At eight he reported to the showroom behind Warren Street to find it locked and no sign of life. The showroom was George Gibbon's gesture to respectability. Beneath a sign that read 'Gibbon Motors – Jaguar Cars by Appointment' was a double garage fronted by glass-panelled concertina doors through which could be seen a 3.5-litre drop-head coupé in racing green. The car was in mint condition, polished and gleaming, but for all its attractions it never quite sold. This was because George relied on it too heavily for his trips to the greyhound tracks of London, the racecourses of southern England, and his weekend excursions with Mrs Gibbon, whose health benefited greatly from spins in the country. According to Dave the chief mechanic this wasn't the only reason it never sold. The failure of such a beautiful motor to shift even at a knockdown price was kept as proof for the tax inspector, should proof be needed, that trade was truly dire, the worst ever.

Billy waited another twenty minutes until his feet and nose had lost all feeling, then picked his way over the ice ridges of the Euston Road, past a large bombsite blazing white with snow and into the ice-locked streets to the west of Euston Station. The workshop was situated in a grimy mews, largely uninhabited, with at the far end a deep bomb crater fenced off by corrugated iron which the kids had long since breached.

The workshop was poorly lit and poorly heated; he might have been stepping from one winter landscape into another. The only bright light came from the rabbit hutch of an office, where Fred the bookkeeper sat behind a glass panel, bent over his desk, fag stuck to his lower lip, ashtray overflowing. His lugubrious gaze swivelled towards Billy and registered his arrival without interest.

Parked in the paint bay was a Jag that hadn't been there the day before, a maroon 2.5-litre saloon. Dave was nowhere in sight but he was clearly planning a respray because he'd removed the registration plates and begun taping the chrome-work. Dave did all the resprays. Sometimes the job involved just a panel or two, but as often as not it was the whole works, sometimes on cars with no more than a couple of scratches. That was the trouble with your average Jag owner, Dave explained proudly, a bloody sight more money than sense.

Billy donned his overalls and switched on the electric wall heater. Since the heater was mounted a good six feet up the wall most of the heat went into the roof, but the glowing bars gave a passing illusion of warmth. Billy was fixing up an old SS2. The paintwork was patchy, the front offside wing dented, but the engine was shaping up well. He'd fitted a new head gasket and some valves cannibalised from a wreck. After tweaking up the timing, he'd got the engine running sweetly the previous afternoon. He would be sorry to see the job finished, not least because George had no more work for him.

He dropped down into the inspection well to remove the greenhouse heater he had left under the sump overnight and found himself standing in a recent oil spill. Swearing, he switched on the inspection light and, examining the gearbox and sump plate in turn, discovered a bolt with a faulty thread. He replaced it, then hunted through the workshop for some fresh oil. Finding only drums of sump waste the colour and consistency of tar, he went over to the rabbit hutch and flung open the door, to be confronted by George Gibbon in characteristic pose, propping up the wall beside Fred's chair, his face partially obscured by a cloud of cigarette smoke.

George looked up with a benign expression. 'Ah, Billy. Just the lad.'

To Fred's left was a man Billy hadn't seen before, dressed like George in a velvet-collared coat and trilby. With the briefest glance in Billy's direction the man resumed his scrutiny of Fred, who was counting a pile of notes or coupons, deftly flicking the corners with a rubber fingerstall.

'I waited for you at the showroom,' Billy said to George.

'I was unavoidably detained due to forces beyond my control,' said George, who was partial to a well-turned phrase. 'Close the door, sport. It's a bit nippy out there.'

Normally Billy would have taken this as an instruction to make himself scarce but George was gesturing him inside with quick, scooping motions of his cigarette. Billy hesitated. He was never comfortable being party to other men's business. He could never shake off the suspicion that things would turn sour and that somehow or other he would be held to blame.

George's beckoning motions became increasingly impatient. 'Don't hang about!' he said with an exaggerated shiver. 'It's brass monkeys out there.'

Stepping inside, Billy was careful to keep his eyes off the desk. He didn't want to see what Fred was counting, and, even more importantly, he didn't want the others to witness him seeing it. He looked directly at George and, when George talked to the other man, he crossed to the back wall, and stared intently at the jumble of notices and girlie calendars pinned there.

'Thanks, Lennie.' George was ushering the other man out of the office. At the door to the mews, they shook hands warmly, cracked some kind of joke, and gave each other a comradely pat on the shoulder.

Marching back into the office, George said, 'How you doing with the SS2, Billy?'

'All right.' Billy couldn't bring himself to call George 'guv', so he didn't call him anything. 'Two more hours should do it.'

George lit another cigarette. Holding it between forefinger and thumb like a dart, he sucked in the smoke with a greedy rasp. He was fifty or so, with a large face, spread nose and pitted skin, a taste for expensive suits with stripes and wide lapels, and a fondness for eau de cologne.

'Good,' he said. ''Cause I've got a punter for the silver saloon and I need you to take care of it.'

'The silver saloon?'

George stabbed his cigarette towards the only silver car in the place, tucked away in the back of the workshop.

'But it needs a new gearbox.'

'Not now it don't.'

'But it's not ready to go—'

'Everything's ready to go at the right price, son. This punter, he's coming to the showroom at three. Just polish up the bodywork and get it down there, will you? And should I find myself unavoidably detained by the bleeding snowdrifts that pass for roads, then give him the patter, will you? Take him out for a gentle spin.'

'It's like an ice rink out there.'

'Like I said – gentle.'

'And if he wants to drive the car himself?'

'Tell him it's too dodgy. Nothing personal.'

'What about the gearbox?'

George narrowed his eyes against the smoke. 'I don't quite follow, son.'

'What happens if he twigs?'

'Well, he's not going to, is he?'

Billy must have let the doubt show in his face because George lifted a finger and said, 'Listen, son, look at it this way. Is the gearbox seized? Is it without cogs? Is it without gears in either the forward or reverse direction?'

Billy stayed silent.

'That's all I'm saying, ain't I? This gearbox is doing the business. This gearbox is in working order.'

'I'm not going to feed him a line.'

George threw out a hand like a showman appealing to a wider audience. 'And who is asking you to? Is there anyone here in this room who is asking you to feed this geezer what you call a *line*?' George looked around as if to garner his audience's response, before jabbing two fingertips softly against Billy's shoulder. 'Let us not forget, my boy, that we are in the business of selling motors. Let us not forget that business is presently diabolical owing to this bleeding awful climate and the rationing of petrol. Let us not forget that this geezer wishes to part with his money in exchange for a vehicle of his choice. You're with me this far?' He turned up a palm, he cocked his head to one side, his eyebrows shot up. 'Let us not forget that if we do not flog him this motor there is every chance that he will fall foul of one of the villains at the unforgiving end of Warren Street, those to whom value has no meaning. And in buying from them, tell me this – is he going to end up with a superior motor? Is he going to end up with a gearbox that will serve him for the rest of time?' With an emphatic shake of his head, George laid a paternal hand on Billy's shoulder. 'Just tickle up the car, son. Get Dave to help out. He's a king with the chrome. And if I'm detained elsewhere, start the gentleman at two hundred and thirty, hold out for two twenty, and settle for two fifteen.'

'And if he doesn't go for it?'

George laughed indulgently. ''Course he'll go for it. You'll make sure he does, won't you? But if push comes to shove . . .' His large face folded into an expression of calculation. 'Two ten. Absolute minimum. But hold out for more, Billy, my lad. My bones tell me he's good for two twenty.'

'Right-o.'

'Now, son . . .' George took another pull on his cigarette and let the smoke trickle over his lip and into his nostrils. 'As of tomorrow we face a problem in the form of there being no work for you.'

'You told me.'

'It's this diabolical weather – no one's trading.'

'Like I said, I could take time off till things improve.'

'Could be a long wait, the way the country's going,' he said gloomily. 'But look, son, I've got something to tide you over the next couple of days. A spot of delivery work. Romford, Dagenham, a few points north. You can use the SS2, give it a bit of a spin.'

'Delivering what?'

'Just light stuff. Fred'll give you the gen. Won't you, Fred?'

Fred's head, bent low over the desk, lifted slowly and turned into quarter profile. His reptilian eye swivelled towards George's face and drooped in agreement.

George flicked ash off his lapel. 'Just drop off and collect. Dead simple.'

Billy said, 'OK.'

'Good lad.' With a jaunty waggle of his cigarette, George tipped his hat forward and went out into the workshop.

Billy watched him cross the floor to talk to Dave, who was back working on the respray. 'What am I meant to be delivering?' he asked Fred.

Turning his melancholy face towards Billy, Fred held up a fat brown envelope. Billy didn't ask what was in it.

At a quarter to three Billy drove the silver saloon cautiously down the mews and across the Euston Road to the showroom. It was snowing again, an intense fall of small flakes, and the sky had a twilight gloom. Billy felt sure the punter would fail to show. He passed the time smoking and wondering where to bed down for the next couple of nights, whether to beg some floor space off Ernie or rent a cheap room in a travellers' hotel in King's Cross. What he refused to do was pay a week in advance for a poky back room in a lodging house run by a cow of a landlady. The last one had demanded quiet at all times, no flushing of the toilet after eleven, and baths according to a timetable so rigid and inconvenient that all the lodgers forked out to go to the public baths instead. And of course no female visitors; that went without saying.

At half past three a taxi emerged through the falling snow and pulled up behind the Jag. Billy climbed out and saw a shadowy figure paying off the driver. The man who approached Billy through the uncertain light was thirtyish, with a round boyish face under a bowler. The office-gent impression was confirmed by a rolled umbrella and briefcase.

'Wasn't sure you'd show up in this,' he said cheerfully.

'Me neither.'

'Bentley.'

In the instant before the man held out his hand Billy thought it was some sort of parlour game in which he was meant to say, 'Jaguar.'

'Greer.'

Bentley leant down to look at the car. 'What a beauty.' He passed a gloved hand over the roof and walked forward to gaze at the front. 'Always wanted one of these. Actually, I always wanted the 3.5-litre sports, but I knew I'd never be able to run to that.' He gave a hearty laugh, and Billy had the impression he laughed at a great many things.

Billy said, 'Want to jump in?'

As Bentley settled into the passenger seat, Billy added, 'Won't be able to go far.'

'God, no. Don't want to risk a prang before we've even started.' The abrupt laugh seemed very loud in the confines of the car. At first Billy had thought army, but for some reason he couldn't quite put his finger on he changed his mind to navy.

When the engine fired, Bentley said admiringly, 'Nice and smooth.'

As they moved into Warren Street Billy managed to engage second gear with the minimum of barging and grinding. Fortunately the poor visibility ruled out any question of reaching third.

'Blimey!' exclaimed the voice at his side. 'Not the sort of weather you expect in dear old England.'

'It's our punishment,' said Billy, 'for thinking life was going to get easier.'

He was aware of the other man glancing at him curiously. 'I don't think anyone was expecting miracles, were they?'

'They were expecting to have enough coal. They were expecting a government that had some clue as to what it was doing.'

'But this won't last.'

'Oh, I think it's going to last a long, long time.'

A reproachful chuckle. 'That's a bit pessimistic, old chap.'

'Is it? We're on our own now, don't forget. No more American aid. No more handouts. Just British cock-ups.'

'Oh, well,' came the relentlessly cheerful response. 'At least we know where we are with a British cock-up.'

The snow swirled and dodged in the headlights. It seemed to be falling more thickly than ever. The streetlights blurred and faded, and Billy began to lose all sense of space and distance until an illuminated shopfront loomed up, marking the junction with Tottenham Court Road. As he began to turn, he suddenly caught the scissor movement of a women's stockinged legs scurrying straight into the beam of the headlights. 'Christ—' He only just managed to stop in time.

'Close shave,' Bentley remarked calmly. 'Why don't you turn us around, old chap? And if I could just drive her back, we'll call it a day.'

Billy kept close to the kerb while he looked for the next left turn. 'Steady as you go,' came the unruffled voice of command. 'Parked vehicle dead ahead. All clear now. Left turn coming up. No, as you were – it's just an entrance.'

Once they were pointing towards Warren Street again, Billy stopped the car.

'Well navigated,' said his passenger as he climbed out.

'Thanks, Captain.'

The loud laugh was swallowed up by the deadened air as they moved around opposite ends of the car and got back in.

'Is it captain?' asked Billy.

'Nothing so exalted, I assure you.'

'Commander, then?'

'It's plain mister, so far as I'm concerned. Can't take these fellows who try and pull rank in civilian life. The war's over, isn't it?'

Billy watched his hand reach for the gear stick and jiggle it around in search of first gear.

'Bit of a knack, eh?' came the jolly voice.

'You might need fewer revs.'

'Right ho.'

With lower revs, much stabbing of the clutch and a crunch of the gears, the commander finally found first and they moved off.

'What a beauty!'

The snow eased off a little, the visibility crept forward a foot or two, but the commander continued to drive with great caution. At one point he tried second gear. Only after double declutching two or three times at varying revs and wiggling the gear stick into the furthest reaches of the gearbox did he finally admit defeat. 'Come back to that another time,' he said brightly.

Billy recalled Dave's suggestion, to say that the best gearboxes were like the best woman, always a bit on the lively side, but couldn't bring himself to voice such rubbish aloud.

They drew up in front of the showroom and the commander let out a sigh of relief. 'Back in one piece!' He fished some cigarettes from an inner pocket and offered one to Billy. 'Tell me,' he said as they lit up, 'what do you make of her?'

'Pardon?'

'The car. What do you reckon?'

'I'm just the mechanic.'

'That's what I mean. You know better than anyone.'

'I couldn't say what it's worth. I have to go by what the guv'nor tells me.'

'But the engine?'

'The engine,' Billy repeated so there'd be no misunderstanding, 'is in pretty good shape.'

The last glimmer of what passed for daylight had been sucked away by the swirling darkness, and the only light came from a streetlamp which cast a pale diffused rectangle over the lower half of the commander's face.

'The gearbox seems a bit hit and miss.'

'It takes some getting used to.'

'But it's all right?'

Even as Billy prepared to answer, several conflicting thoughts went through his mind. That if George had only let him fit another gearbox then all this could have been avoided. That a fool and his money were soon parted, and it was no concern of his if the commander got a bad bargain. That his only duty was to himself and his next wage packet. That George should have come and done his own dirty work.

'It's serviceable.'

'So it's worth the price then? Two hundred and thirty?'

'That's what the guv'nor says.'

'What about you?'

But Billy wasn't ready to play that game. 'I told you – I couldn't say.'

The commander chewed on his lip. 'Look, do you think your boss would accept two hundred and fifteen? Even then I'd be scraping the barrel. The briefcase is just for show, you see. Haven't actually landed a job yet.' He gave a rueful laugh. 'Always hoping.'

Billy tried to read the other man's face through the gloom. If the commander was spinning him a line then he was making a good job of it.

'The thing is, I always promised myself a Jag, all through the war. Promised I'd treat myself as soon as I got out. You've got to have something to look forward to, haven't you? Otherwise you'd go barmy.'

He seemed to expect a response, so Billy said, 'All I thought about was women.'

'Ah, there was that too. But the chances always seemed rather remote. Not much leave, you know. And, well – not much luck. Can't say things have been that much brighter since I got back. At least with a car there's no fear of being turned down, if you know what I mean.'

Billy gave a short laugh. 'Yes,' he said, 'I know what you mean.'

The commander blew out his lips. 'Blimey, it's perishing. If the pubs were open I'd suggest a brandy. How about a cup of something hot instead? Is there a café nearby?'

'Not far.'

Billy led the way to George's favourite caff on the Tottenham Court Road, a place frequented by car dealers from both ends of Warren Street. They found a free table near the counter, close to the hiss and crackle of the frier.

In the light the commander seemed at first glance absurdly young – with his smooth skin, round pink cheeks and unruly hair he might have arrived fresh from the school sports field – but the eyes with their sallow whites and pink rims and web of fine lines told another story.

'You wouldn't have any real coffee, would you?' the commander asked the waitress, who glared at him as if he were mad.

When the tea arrived the commander produced a flask from an inner pocket. Uncapping it in one seamless movement, he tilted it questioningly towards Billy's cup. 'A stomach warmer?'

'Why not?'

'Better with coffee of course. But beggars, and all that.' He poured a liberal measure into Billy's cup, leaving only a dribble for himself.

'You've left yourself short.'

'Had a liquid lunch.' He gave a conspiratorial chuckle. 'Cheers.' He lifted his cup.

'Cheers.' Tea and brandy made a strange brew, but Billy wasn't complaining.

The commander remarked, 'Kept me going, brandy, through the war.'

'I thought it was rum in the navy.'

'Or gin. But my grandfather left me three cases of Napoleon brandy and it seemed a pity not to polish it off while I still had the chance. Brandy's a miracle worker when it's brass monkeys. Really hits the spot.'

'Where did you get to in the war?'

'The Med for a while. Then the North Atlantic. Convoy duty, Newfoundland to north Norway. Two years. Two *winters*. Not so different from this, but twice as cold.' He blinked with embarrassment, as if the suggestion of hardship had been bad form, and said quickly, 'What about you?'

'Tanks. Up through France and Belgium into Germany. Got as far as Hamburg.'

'And before that?'

'I ran the family business.'

'Really? My goodness! What sort of business?'

'Willow growing. Basket production. Hurdles.'

'Goodness,' the commander said again, looking genuinely impressed. 'You haven't thought of going back?'

'Oh, they wanted me to. Begged me to in fact. But I'm not interested.'

'What, no future in it?'

'Oh, there's money to be made all right. Plenty of demand. But I'd go off my trolley in the back of beyond.'

'Would you? God, I couldn't think of anything better myself,' the commander said wistfully. 'I love the country. Everything about it – the life, the quiet, the people. But there aren't many jobs in the middle of the country, not for the likes of me. Not without capital or know-how.' He shook his head in wonder. 'And to be able to run your own show. God, if I had an opportunity like that I'd grab it like a shot.'

Billy pushed his cup to one side. 'Well, the grass is always greener, isn't it?'

'Anything would be greener for me, old chap. You see, the alternative is to go into *my* family business, and I'm not sure I wouldn't rather shoot myself.' He gave a thin laugh that didn't extend to his eyes. 'It's a printing works in Manchester. Oh, printing's all right – quite interesting actually. But my father and uncle have run it since time immemorial, and my brother and cousins are all set to take over. There isn't really room for me. Oh, I'd be given a desk all right, but heaven only knows what they'd find for me to do. Counting paperclips, or worse.'

'What would you do if you could choose, then?'

The commander gave his great bellow of a laugh. 'I'd be a farmer.'

'You've had a go at it, have you?'

'No,' he admitted cheerfully. 'But I wouldn't care how long it took to learn or how many mistakes I made, so long as I could be my own boss.' As the remoteness of the prospect came home to him, he said dolefully, 'The nearest I've got to a job so far is an interview for secretary of a bridge club.'

'Blimey. What does that involve?'

'Keeping ladies of a certain age topped up with gin, I think.' He looked at his watch. 'Speaking of which . . . I have to go and meet my aunt.' He pushed his chair back a little before casting Billy a diffident sideways look. 'The car . . . Do you think your boss might accept two hundred and fifteen?'

'Tell you something – he'll accept two ten. But for Christ's sake don't tell him I said so.'

They shook on it. The commander said he would telephone the next day as soon as he'd arranged to draw the cash.

When Billy got back to the workshop, he left a message for George. *He was a bastard. Wouldn't budge an inch over £210.*

The house was boarded up, but it was number three all right, and when Billy climbed the front steps he found the door slightly ajar. The hall was dark and reeked of dust, the grit crunched under his feet, and when he called hello all he got was an echo. Then, just when it seemed there was no one there, a distant voice from above launched into a familiar rendition of 'Whispering Grass'.

Climbing the stairs, Billy called out, 'You're a bloody broken record, Brandon! Give us a rest!'

The voice laughed.

The nearest door had a splinter of light under it. Pushing it open, Billy was met by a blast of warm paraffin fumes, the glare of a hurricane lamp, and the sight of Ernie perched high on a stepladder in front of a half-plastered wall.

'Wotcha, mate!' With a wide grin, Ernie stretched out both arms in greeting, before resuming the sweep, sweep of his trowel. 'Long time no see.'

'God help us, Ernie. What the hell're you doing?'

'There's no end to my talents, Billy boy. Sky's the limit.' He was plastering over a ragged circle of exposed brickwork with apparent competence, smoothing the edges into the remains of the tattered floral wallpaper with deft scoops and twists of the trowel.

Billy dumped his knapsack on the floor. 'Since when did you learn plastering?'

'Picked it up as I've gone along, haven't I?'

'Pull the other one.'

'Honest to God. Watch and you will see. Ask and you will be told. I went and found a lovely old geezer and asked for a few tips. Only too glad to help, bless his dear old heart. Falling over himself.'

'I thought you were a chippie.'

'That's the day work, ain't it? Just till I'm set. But this here is Ernie Brandon, General Building and Repairs. That's where the bunce is, Billy boy – in repairs. I could hire myself out ten times over and still have them beating a path to my door. Give me another week or two and I'll be coining it in.'

'You're setting up on your own?'

'Just got to get genned up on the slates and tiles, and then I'm away.'

'You never told me.'

Ernie twisted round. 'Didn't know myself, did I? Not till I

saw the ways things were going.' With a clownish grin, he returned to his trowelling.

Warming his hands at the stove Billy noticed more bomb damage in the form of an ugly crack reaching down the back wall from the ceiling to the corner of the window, and how the window itself seemed to have been knocked skew-whiff, though that might have been a trick of the broken architrave that hung at an odd angle.

'Blimey, Ernie. Hope you know what you're doing.'

'Nothing to it.'

'That wall looks a bit dodgy to me.'

'Bloody hell. I'm not going to leave it like that, am I, you great berk. I'm going to fix a bloody great strap across it and chop in a new lintel.' He rolled his eyes in mock offence. 'No bog-ups here, mate.'

It was a saying from their tank days, and Billy gave his customary scornful laugh. 'So, this roofing business – that's going to be a doddle as well, is it?'

'You betcha. Most of the demand's for patch-up work, see. After cracks and plasterwork, it's all slipped tiles and missing slates. Bloody millions of them all over London.'

Ernie deftly slapped more plaster onto the last of the brick-work, spread it rapidly in quick strokes and skimmed off the excess. A few more passes of the trowel and he declared the job finished.

Sauntering up to the wall, Billy cast a critical eye over the plastering. There were no obvious bumps or blemishes. 'Well, stone the crows,' he said.

Ernie climbed down off the ladder and, scooping up his packet of smokes, tapped one clear and offered it to Billy. 'I tell you, me old mate – nothing to it.'

'So what happens when the whole bloody lot falls down?' Billy asked facetiously. 'You'll do a runner, will you?'

Ernie struck a match and they lit up. 'Nowhere to run on this one.'

'No? They got your number, have they?'

'In a manner of speaking.' Ernie spread a hand like a showman. 'You have before you the one and only E. Brandon, esquire, man of property.'

An odd chill settled on Billy's stomach. 'Oh yeah?' he said lightly.

Ernie stabbed a finger towards the floor. 'This here gaff will be mine before the year's out.'

'How come?'

'Done a deal with the landlord, haven't I? He owns the whole terrace, right? Fifteen houses. I get to do this place up, I doss down here rent-free while I get the rest of the terrace spruced up and ready to rent out. All at a price that suits him and suits me. And the icing on the cake? I get to purchase this gaff at a knockdown price.'

'I don't get it.'

Cigarette jammed on his lip, Ernie began to scrape the last of the plaster out of the bucket onto some newspaper. 'What don't you get, you great git?'

'How're you going to do fifteen houses?'

'Easy.'

'What, on your own?'

Laughing, Ernie broke into 'Me and My Shadow'. 'Nah. I'm never going to do it on my tod, am I?'

'You said you were.'

'What I *said* was, I was going to set up on my own. Run my own show.' Catching Billy's expression, he explained, 'Listen . . . we do three houses at a time, right? I get to do the heavy work, then I call in my mates the plumbers and the sparks, and when they're done, I call in the decorators, see? Meantime, I'm on to the next three houses, and then the next, and on we go down the road – same taps, same sink units, same bleeding wallpaper for all I care. I reckon we'll be out by the summer and on to the next job. I tell you, Billy boy – pure bunce!'

'So where's the catch?'

'There ain't no catch!'

'There's got to be a catch or everyone'd be doing it.'

Ernie tapped a finger to his head. 'You forget, it ain't everybody that's got the nous. It ain't everybody that's got the contacts. And it ain't everybody that's prepared to put in the sodding hard labour either. No – I'm goin' to die stinking rich or bloody perish in the attempt.'

Billy gave a bright laugh, and thought: Of course he'll die rich. It was so obvious Billy couldn't imagine why it had never struck him before. During the advance through Europe they had ribbed Ernie for his relentless pursuit of comfort – the hunt for the best billet, the gathering of dry wood for a fire, the stalking of a stray chicken for the pot, the painstaking search for the last unbroken bottle of booze in the ruins of an inn. But what had passed as enthusiasm for a good challenge was, Billy saw now, something more elemental: the determination to come out on top, the need to win at all costs. It had been the same under fire, he realised with a second jolt of understanding. Ernie had been fearless, often to the point of lunacy, not because he valued his own skin any less than the rest of them, but because he couldn't stomach the thought of someone, let alone the Jerries, getting the better of him. Billy felt a squeeze of envy for the nature and reach of Ernie's ambition, which put his own vague aspirations into the shade.

'Blimey,' Billy said. 'Best not get in your way then.'

Ernie stepped out of his overalls and bundled them into his bag. 'If you weren't such a bloody useless git, I'd get you to come and lend a hand. But an oily rag's no sodding use to me, is it?'

'A bloody sight more use than a numero-uno bog-up merchant like you, you great pillock.'

They grinned at each other, Billy awkwardly.

Ernie fiddled with the knob on the stove and ducked down to inspect the flame. 'Uncle George looking after you all right, is he?'

Billy shrugged. 'Business is a bit thin.'

Ernie gave a yelp of laughter. 'The day business gets to be good for George, that's the day we'll know he's in real trouble.'

'He's asked me to make some deliveries for him.'

Ernie dusted off his hands. 'Well, better than a kick in the shins, eh?'

'Looks like petrol coupons.'

'Oi, oi,' Ernie said with a low chuckle. 'The old devil. A case of ask no questions, eh?' He tapped a waggish finger to the side of his nose. Then, with a last inspection of the stove, he picked up his jacket and gestured towards Billy's knapsack. 'Needing some floor space, are you, old cock?'

'If it's all right with your mum.'

'Course it's all right, Billy boy. Course! She never minds you staying. But when I say floor space – it's floor space. Our Vince's come back home. Got chucked out by his old lady. Says he's not the same man as before the war. What the bitch means is she's been carrying on with another geezer and hasn't the bloody nerve to tell him.'

'He's well shot of her then.'

'Ha! Try telling him that. Stupid sod keeps getting pissed and going round to beg with her. Can't see it. Can't see that she's a first-class cow, always was. One of the tight-knees brigade. Held out for a wedding ring before she'd let him get his greens, and then started having it off with this other bloke the moment Vince'd gone to the war.' Ernie shook his head in pity and disgust. 'You and me – we could've told him where he went wrong, eh? We could have told him that if you can't get it in one place, then you go and get it in another. You don't bloody *marry* them, do you?'

'No.'

Ernie gave Billy a friendly punch on the arm. 'Come on, mate. Let's get a pint before the bleeding pubs run dry.'

London pubs were all the same to Billy. He would have chosen the first they came to, but Ernie wouldn't hear of it and they tramped through the ice and snow for another ten minutes before entering a noisy place with tiled walls and bare wooden floors. Seeing Ernie's eyes lock onto a gaggle of girls sitting in one corner, Billy realised they hadn't come out of their way for a better class of beer.

'All right,' Billy sighed as they eased their way through the crowd to the bar. 'Which one is it?'

Ernie grinned. 'The redhead. Bit of all right, eh?'

Billy should have guessed. She was just Ernie's type, pretty, self-confident, with a hint of challenge. And from the way she smoothed her hair back and tilted her head artfully and pretended not to notice Ernie it was clear he was in business.

'Whatever happened to what's her name?'

'Lizzie? Asked me home to meet the parents. Well . . .' Ernie turned his mouth down and gave a mock shudder. 'Couldn't be doing with that, could I?'

They ordered pints of bitter, and lit cigarettes.

'So, what d'you reckon on her friend?' Ernie said, his narrow gaze sliding in the direction of the corner again. 'The dark one on the right.'

Billy didn't bother to look round. 'I'm not in the mood.'

'What?' Ernie gave a short laugh of surprise. 'Come on, Billy boy. What's with you? Where's your sense of adventure?'

'I'm knackered. I just want to grab something to eat and get some sleep.'

'But we're all set up.' Ernie indicated the two girls with a swivel of his eyes.

'Another time.'

'At least help a mate out, eh? Get me in there with a chance.'

'Not tonight.'

'What's got into you, Billy boy?'

'I told you – I'm not in the mood.'

'Not hankering after your lady-love, are you? Not yearning for a bit of *amour*, Somerset style?'

Billy gave a weary groan. 'For Christ's sake.' He had long since regretted telling Ernie about Annie, not the least because, being rather drunk at the time, he had got carried away with the facts, boasting that Annie was crazy for him, implying she

had demonstrated it in the best possible way. He'd been trying
to play down the idea ever since, without success.

'Come on, then' – Ernie jerked his head towards the girls –
'we're wasting valuable time.'

Billy gave in with bad grace. 'All right. But ten minutes at
the most. Then I'm off.'

Ernie led the way through the crush and, in a well-practised
manoeuvre, drew the redhead and her friend away from the
rest of the group and bought them a drink. As Ernie began his
routine – 'Know what? I dreamt about you all last night' –
Billy eyed the redhead's friend without enthusiasm. Her name
was Irene. She was short and hard-eyed and drank gin and
lime. She told him she worked in a nearby clothing factory.

'So what's your line of work?' she asked in a bored tone.

'The motor trade.'

'Mechanic?'

'Buying and selling cars.'

'Oh yeah?' Her shrewd eyes looked him up and down, and
she raised her eyebrows sceptically.

Billy threw the question back with a stare.

'You've got dirt under your fingernails.'

'So what?'

'So . . . strange sort of buying and selling.'

'Just goes to show – you can never judge by appearances.'
Noticing that her hair looked none too clean, catching under
the cheap scent a faint hint of the unwashed, he thought: Then
again, sometimes you can.

'Sell many cars then?'

'Enough.'

'Got one yourself?'

'Are you always this nosy?'

'Just asking.'

But she wasn't just asking; she was sizing him up, deciding
if he was good for another drink or two; even, if all went well
between her friend and Ernie, a proper night out as a foursome.

'Sorry,' he said. 'You're out of luck.'

She retorted swiftly, 'And why would I want to be in luck?'
'You tell me.'

She glared at him. 'You think I was *begging* or something?'

Billy looked around for somewhere to dump his glass before fighting his way out through the crowd.

Irene hissed, 'You're all the bloody same. Big-headed bastards. Thinking you're God's gift. Well, I've got news for you – I'm not in the market for more troubles. I had a bloke, didn't I? Waited for him all through the bloody war. And the moment the bastard got back, he only went off with someone else, didn't he?'

'Bad luck.'

She eyed him uncertainly, trying to gauge the spirit of this remark. 'Yeah, well . . .' Another look, more trusting this time. 'Don't suppose I was the first to fall for a bastard.'

Fearing her trust more than he feared her venom, Billy leant towards Ernie. 'I'm off.'

Ernie hissed in his ear, 'Come on, mate, another round—'

'Nope.'

'I'm *asking* you.'

'No. I'm off.'

Ernie seemed on the point of anger, then the tension went out of him and, slapping Billy on the shoulder, he said in an odd tone, 'Watch yourself, eh?'

It was only as Billy got out into the street that he realised Ernie had spoken to him in a tone of pity.

Chapter Eleven

THE TRACTOR clawed its way up the steepening slope, until, meeting a drift, it strained and juddered, and seemed to hover, even to lift its nose, as if it might rear up on its hind wheels at any moment. Hastily, Stella stamped on the pedals and the tractor rocked back against the brakes with a violent jerk that caused the trailer to dip sharply under Wladyslaw's feet.

Stella flung a backward glance at him, her eyes in the gap between hat and scarf alive with comment. He gestured for her to take her time, a slow damping motion of one hand. She nodded and let the tractor roll back a short way before heaving on the gear lever with both hands and attacking the snowdrift from a different angle. This time the tyres bit and held, and with a violent roar the tractor ground up the slope and lurched over the rim of the drift. Reaching more level ground it surged calmly through the deep soft upper layers of snow like a boat through water.

They were nearing the last stop on their supply round, a cottage in a snow-filled gully. Through the fast-falling snow Wladyslaw thought he could make out the occupants trying to dig their way along the track, but if so they still had a long way to go. Stella swung the tractor through the gate and charged at the drift, but the snow banks rapidly closed around them in soft impenetrable walls and she reversed out before yanking on the handbrake. Wladyslaw clambered off the trailer as she jumped down.

Her eyes were bright with exhilaration. 'That hill was a bit steep.'

'I had absolute confidence,' said Wladyslaw, lifting his eyes to heaven and pressing his hand against his chest in an exaggerated pantomime of heartfelt relief.

'I should hope so too!' she declared.

'Your hands,' he said solemnly.

Obediently, she took off her gloves and held her hands out to him.

'They don't feel dead any place?' His concern was practical but also self-interested because it gave him the opportunity to take her hands and rub them and hold them tightly between his own.

'Nose is OK?' He prodded it with his finger.

She wriggled it and laughed.

They moved round to the back of the trailer and began to sort the load.

'Are you sure I can't bring anything tonight?' she asked.

'No.'

'Not even cake?'

'No.'

'Cider?'

'No.'

'Would it be safe to assume that the evening is to have a Polish theme?'

He dragged the last bag of coal to the edge of the trailer. 'It is safest in this life to assume nothing.'

'I'll take that as a yes.'

'You are a woman of impulse.'

'Yes!' she declared. Tilting her face up to Wladyslaw's, she repeated with a triumphant laugh, 'Yes!'

He shook his head at her, barely able to contain the surge of agonised happiness that swept through him. Her joy thrilled him not only because it mirrored his own, but because it gave confirmation to what was happening between them, and seemed at last to have put paid to the past. For weeks the shadow of the cousin-lover had lain between them like a sword. Stella never spoke of him and Wladyslaw certainly never asked, but often he would catch a look on her face that he learnt to dread, an expression of bafflement and loss that cast a chill over his heart. According to Dr Bennett the cousin had left soon after Wladyslaw's arrival and was believed to be in London. It was said he was planning to go abroad, a prospect that seemed almost too much to hope for until, in one of Wladyslaw's more tormented moments, it struck him that travel might lend his rival a spurious aura of romantic endeavour.

'This evening,' Wladyslaw said, 'there will be a theme, yes. But not Polish.'

'No?' Stella narrowed her eyes at him. 'Am I allowed a clue?'

'No clues. You must wait.'

She pretended to put her mind to it, to see if she could second-guess him, but it was only a game, she was happy to wait.

The people from the cottage arrived just then. Wladyslaw helped them to carry the supplies down the leeward side of a hedgerow where the snow wasn't too thick. It was the third time the family had been cut off in six weeks, and now their water pump had frozen, forcing them to draw water direct from the well. Before Wladyslaw left, they offered him some brandy called applejack and laughed when he drank it like vodka, in a single gulp.

By the time he got back to Stella she had reversed the tractor out into the lane, and they set off immediately. A sharp wind met them on the ridge road and Wladyslaw shouted and mimed to Stella to pull her scarf up over her nose. Then he hunched low in the trailer, but not so low that he couldn't watch her with proprietorial pride, the way she drove like a veteran, swaying her body in counter-movement to the more violent lurches of the tractor, gripping the juddering wheel, tolerating no opposition from the gear stick. If the effect was slightly marred by her need to extend her leg beyond its natural reach to operate the clutch, it in no way detracted from the overall impression. He loved her determination and her panache, the way she refused to be deterred. She had taken a couple of driving lessons when the blizzards closed the school, and had been rattling around on her uncle's tractor ever since.

All around, the snow fell swiftly in swirling blurs of fine flakes that blotted out everything but the occasional tree and the hedgerows reeling past on either side, their branches caked with huge unwieldy clots of snow. At one point their way seemed blocked by a drift that had formed opposite a gate, filling the road and completely submerging the leeward hedgerow, but by creeping close to the gate and keeping momentum Stella managed to push through.

Coming into the village, approaching a fork in the road, Stella swivelled round and catching Wladyslaw's eye jabbed a finger left. He nodded vigorously and she turned down the hill towards Athelney. As they bumped over the level crossing Wladyslaw found himself looking to left and right as if for trains, but there had been no trains for more than two weeks and the track was buried under parallel bulges of snow.

They passed through the next string of cottages and turned onto a low road that rose to cross the Tone just above its junction with the Parrett. Stella halted on the bridge. The scene was of unrelieved whiteness. Snow drooped on the trees and billowed in frothy waves over the riverbanks, while all around the flakes kept falling and falling. The two rivers were locked in ice that was for the most part snow covered, but in places scratched and scathed by the wind and the myriad criss-crossings of bird tracks. Stella peered upriver and down, searching for two young Bewick's swans that had failed to escape to open water when the freeze set in. She had been feeding them regularly at this spot, but the previous day the one she called Merlin had disappeared, and now there was no sign of Lancelot.

'I can't see them,' she called.

'Maybe they both have flown together,' Wladyslaw suggested.

Her fretful glance declared she thought this unlikely.

On the far side of the bridge she turned the tractor round and drove back along the road below the Parrett, scanning the high banks, diverting up any track and wider pathway that offered the smallest view of the meandering river.

At a place named Oath she turned through a gate and parked below the high mechanism of a sluice gate. Without waiting for Wladyslaw she jumped off the tractor and scrambled up the bank. Reaching the top she made an exclamation, whether of relief or disappointment he couldn't tell until she called out, 'I think it's Merlin!'

Joining her, Wladyslaw saw the swan floating in the pool of ice-free water just below the sluice.

'I'm pretty sure it's him,' she said. 'What do you think?'

'Definitely.'

She had brought bread and vegetables and threw the scraps down piece by piece. 'Look! Look!' She laughed. 'Greedy thing!'

'He's hungry all right.'

'You really think it's him?'

'Yes, I do believe. Or I would not say this.'

She looked at him and said, 'It's true. You wouldn't.'

'He is like me. A simple creature.'

She laughed. 'I'm not so sure about that.'

When the food was gone, they stared wordlessly into the pool. Around them the flakes fell swiftly in a veil, the deep snow-filled silence was mute and unresonant; they might have been lost in a secret world. He went and stood behind her shoulder, almost touching it. Slowly she inclined her head towards his in a gesture that sent a whisper of joy into his heart. He looped an arm around her waist and drew her gently against him. Standing there in the unearthly silence, with her body resting against his, he felt he was caught in a fantastic dream. Only the icy encrustations of her hat against his cheek seemed to have an edge of reality.

She moved, and the dream broke. All his senses were alert to the need to speak. The moment had been of such significance that he felt it must be acknowledged, revered, affirmed. He decided to say some of the things he had intended to say that evening.

'Stella?'

She turned to face him. Close up, her nose was very white, the cartilage like carved ivory; her cheeks under the freckles were dappled with delicate patches of colour, her eyes damp and bright from the bitter air.

'I wish to tell you this – that I have decided to stay in England. Definitely. To make my life here.'

'Oh, Wladek . . . I'm so pleased.' She put a gloved hand to his upper arm. 'So pleased. I hope you never have reason to regret it.'

He smiled down at her. 'I think this is impossible. I also tell you that I have received yesterday papers to apply to London University.'

'Oh.' Then, as it sank in, she exclaimed, 'Oh, that's wonderful, Wladek!'

'It is not ideal, because London is long way from here. But they have quota for Poles and, who knows, maybe they take old fellows like me.'

'*Old,*' she rebuked him. 'But what will you study?'

'This is where I require your advice, dear Stella. This is one thing I ask of you tonight, if I may.'

'I'll be glad to help all I can, of course I will. Though I'm not sure I'll be too much use if it comes to choosing between history and philosophy.'

'I thought also of law.'

'Oh . . .' She tried to hide her bewilderment, and failed. 'Why law?'

He wished he'd never mentioned it now, because it had detracted from his main purpose, it had spoilt the mood.

'More practical, I think.'

'But if your heart's not in it . . .'

'Ah, my heart, Stella . . .' Suddenly the mood was restored, and he determined not to let the enchantment slip away again.

Moving a little closer to her, he removed his glove and touched the back of his hand softly to her cheek. 'Yes, my heart must be my guide. This is why I must say to you, there are two reasons I go to study. One, to build a good life. Second, so that I can hope to be near to you, Stella. Because without you, this life will be nothing for me.'

She stared at him. 'Oh.' She sighed again. 'Oh.' Her eyes filled suddenly, she looked down and clamped her lips together.

Not sure what to make of this, but feeling it wasn't entirely negative, he pressed on. 'You give me hope for future, Stella. You give me purpose in this life. I feel that if I can be near to you then my future will be rich and full of happiness.'

She looked up again, her gaze tearful and bright. Her mouth, strongly shaped and well delineated, was parted slightly as if in hesitation. With infinite slowness he bent to kiss her. Her lips were cold, but they were soft and they exerted an unmistakable answering pressure against his own, a pressure that grew and shifted, until her lips were moving under his.

When they drew apart, her eyes flickered open, she breathed, 'What you said . . . that was the most lovely thing anyone has ever said to me.'

'I speak from my heart, Stella.'

Her eyes brimmed again, she gave a light laugh. 'I don't know what to say.'

'Say only that I may live in hope.'

She gazed at him while the snowflakes danced and dithered and spiralled between them. 'Yes,' she said shyly. Then, with a small smile: 'Yes, you may.' Then a last time, with growing confidence: 'Yes.'

'Then I am happy man.'

The snow was easing off, the sky seemed to have lifted a little as they rumbled back along the river road. Coming to the tip of the long tongue of land that dissects the wetlands, they turned onto the ridge road, its surface smooth and icy from the scouring wind. The road rose steadily for a mile or so before dipping towards a bridge over a railway cutting. At first the bridge was partially obscured by a bend, but Wladyslaw caught a glimpse of two lorries parked there, both of them military. As they drew closer he saw a third military lorry parked opposite by the start of a drove-road. Stella took the tractor slowly onto the bridge and stopped. The lorries were empty. Stella stood up in her seat to peer over the side of the bridge. 'There,' she said. Going to the edge of the trailer, Wladyslaw looked down into the steep-sided cutting and saw a gang of men strung out along the railway tracks, shovelling at the voluminous snowdrifts. Their uniform greatcoats and caps identified them as German POWs. There must have been guards too, but he couldn't see them.

Wladyslaw said, 'Good job for them, I think.' But Stella wasn't listening. She was looking up the road towards a car coming from the direction of the village. She flung Wladyslaw a questioning look over her shoulder. At first he thought she was concerned about the speed of the car, which was fast for a vehicle travelling on snow, but then he realised it was the car itself she had recognised.

Approaching the bridge the car braked abruptly and began to skid, its back end slowly swinging out to one side, until the driver wrestled the steering the other way, when, with a brief counter-lurch, it straightened up again and at a more sedate pace turned across the road to park behind one of the lorries. Arthur Hanley climbed out and glared at them, his face set in a mask of fury. Going to the boot he pulled out a shotgun and, wedging it over one forearm, came marching towards them. He shouted something to Stella, which Wladyslaw couldn't catch over the rattle of the tractor, and followed it with an impatient flicking motion of one hand.

Stella climbed out of the driving seat and dropped down onto the road. She tried to say something, but her uncle was already shouldering past her to mount the tractor. In the time it took Hanley to get into the seat and wedge the shotgun against the mudguard Wladyslaw vaulted out of the trailer. He had barely landed before it moved off with a jolt.

He remembered that Stella's aunt had been ill with pneumonia, and said immediately, 'Is it your aunt, Stella? Is she not well?'

'No, no! It's the Germans' – she indicated the cutting – 'he says they've been stealing from him.'

The tractor swung wide around one of the lorries and disappeared down the drove-road.

Wladyslaw began to follow at a brisk hop of a walk. He called back to Stella, 'You stay here, OK?'

He set off down the drove-road as fast as the snow and his leg would allow. Ahead, the tractor was steaming rapidly down the hill, the trailer rocking frantically in its wake. Suddenly Wladyslaw's foot hit ice and he almost fell. By the time he had regained his balance and re-established some sort of stride, the tractor had reached the bottom of the hill and was turning across the snowfield. Wary of more hidden ice he kept his eyes firmly on the path in front of him, registering the tractor's progress only as a movement on the periphery of his vision.

When he finally reached the level ground, he saw the tractor standing by the railway embankment and Hanley clambering up the slope onto the track, the shotgun in his hand. Following the path of compacted snow left by the tractor, Wladyslaw began to run.

As Hanley neared the entrance to the cutting the first group of prisoners stopped shovelling and stared at him. There seemed to be some conversation, or possibly some shouting, because the next group of prisoners also lowered their shovels and looked round. Still talking, or at least gesticulating, Hanley marched away from the first group and began to harangue the second bunch of men. The hectoring voice was muted by the snow, a faint disjointed sound. The rest of the prisoners had been concealed inside the cutting but as Wladyslaw scrambled up the embankment he could see them spread out beyond Hanley, twenty, maybe thirty of them, their uniforms dark against the wall of whiteness. They had stopped working and were looking towards the scene of the shouting. For some reason there were no guards in sight.

Limping hurriedly along the track, Wladyslaw heard Hanley's voice lift in a roar. 'Don't pretend you don't know what I'm talking about!'

The first group of prisoners gave Wladyslaw a cursory look as he went past. One of them was lighting a cigarette, another smiling slyly as if at a joke.

The second group, some seven or eight strong, had fragmented, drawing back into a ragged semicircle, leaving an impassive man of about forty to take the brunt of Hanley's onslaught, which consisted of the same speech repeated with a bully's emphasis, the enunciation exaggerated, the consonants delivered with a shower of spittle and vaporised breath, the message underlined by a furious jabbing finger. 'Don't go pretending you don't know what I'm talking about! You were seen taking them away! You were seen in broad daylight! And I'm not leaving till you get them back to where they came from. You hear me? I'm not budging from this spot!'

The impassive German gave a slow shrug, a lifting of both shoulders and an outward turn of a gloved hand.

'Don't give me that, you piece of vermin!' Hanley's voice hammered out. 'Don't pretend you don't know what I'm talking about. You're guilty as hell, the lot of you!'

The German turned down his mouth in an expression of disdain or incomprehension or both.

His face contorted with rage, his mouth twitching uncontrollably, Hanley grasped the shotgun in both hands and swung it up to point at the German's chest. 'You think this is some kind of joke, do you? You think this is funny? Well, I'll teach you otherwise.'

There was a collective pause, a freezing of all sound and movement, which no one seemed inclined to break until Wladyslaw stepped forward and said quietly, 'Maybe he does not understand.'

Ignoring him, Hanley lifted the shotgun higher. 'Answer me, you devil!'

Smoothly, showing no flicker of expression, the German uncurled the fingers of one hand from the shovel and, leaving a thumb looped around the hilt, spread his fingers in a fan of surrender, while raising the other hand lazily to shoulder height. As a gesture of submission it was almost farcically relaxed; as a gesture of indifference it was defiantly accomplished.

Quivering with rage, Hanley jabbed the gun forward. 'Answer me, do you hear?'

At that instant it seemed to Wladyslaw that Hanley's finger curled and tightened on the trigger. With a sense of having left it too late, his nerves steeled against the impending blast, Wladyslaw stepped forward with what felt like impossible slowness and, grasping the twin barrels in one hand, quickly pushed the gun up until it was pointing at the sky.

Hanley gave a grunt of surprise and fury before trying to wrench the gun free. Wladyslaw clapped his other hand to the barrel and held on as Hanley yanked it backwards and sideways with violent jerks and twists. After some particularly fierce tussling, Wladyslaw thought the older man's grip was loosening, that he would relent, but then Hanley's shoulder came barging into his, a raised elbow cracked hard into Wladyslaw's nose, and he realised that the lull had marked nothing more than a change of tactics. If Hanley was stronger than he looked, he was heavier too, and, thrown back onto his bad leg, Wladyslaw almost lost his balance. Getting his good leg down again, he twisted round and managed to thrust the gun barrel up once more, pushing it higher and higher until Hanley, holding on tenaciously, was forced to lurch backwards. At once, instinctively, Wladyslaw saw his opportunity to hook a foot round Hanley's ankle and pull him off-balance. To get his foot that far, however, it was necessary to swing it back and get some momentum behind it. By chance and ill fortune he was perfectly balanced as he took aim, his good leg solid beneath him, his bad leg swinging forward with plenty of weight behind it. By the time he realised that Hanley was shifting the leg he was aiming for it was too late to pull back, and his boot crashed into Hanley's shin with a solid crunch.

With a sharp bellow Hanley staggered back and let go of the gun. Wladyslaw barely managed to get a safe grip on the barrel before his own leg became a shaft of fire. The pain made him want to retch, a mist seemed to cover his eyes, and it was some moments before he was able to call to Hanley, 'You OK?'

Hanley was bent over his leg, nursing it. His cap had fallen off his head onto the snow and Wladyslaw limped across to pick it up.

'The kick was accident,' he gasped, holding out the cap to him. 'Sorry.'

Hanley glared at Wladyslaw in disbelief, his eyes bulging, his skin damp, his lips pulled back in a wide grimace. His bared teeth were yellow in the bleached light, his skin an unhealthy grey, and the falling snow was forming a white down on his dark hair.

Wladyslaw was still holding out the cap. 'Now . . . if you wish . . .' he panted. 'I will make enquiries.'

When Hanley didn't respond Wladyslaw dropped the cap onto the snow just beside him and turned to the impassive German. '*Sprechen Sie Englisch?*'

The German had relaxed again. He was leaning on his shovel. '*Nein.*'

Wladyslaw threw the question out to the rest of the group and got a general shaking of heads.

Wladyslaw's German was poor, barely a few words; he asked if anyone spoke Polish. People glanced at each other, then a voice from the semicircle shouted across to the first group of prisoners. The man who lifted his head and turned round in response was the one who'd been lighting a cigarette when Wladyslaw passed by, a square-jawed character with a badly broken nose.

'Would you translate?' Wladyslaw called to him.

'So long as it doesn't get me shot,' he said in excellent, virtually unaccented Polish. Drawing on his cigarette, he strolled forward until he was within easy earshot.

Wladyslaw turned back to Hanley. 'So,' he said in a tone of conciliation, 'what is problem exactly?'

But Hanley was still glaring at Wladyslaw as if he hated him.

'I can try for answer,' Wladyslaw said with something like gentleness, 'if you inform me of problem.'

Finally, with a terrible effort, Hanley hissed, 'Give me my gun.'

Wladyslaw glanced rapidly around in the hope of seeing some guards, but saw only Stella standing a short distance behind him, wearing an expression of misery and disbelief. Turning his back on Hanley, he hobbled over to her.

'I'm sure he didn't mean it,' she whispered. 'I'm sure he wouldn't have done anything.'

Not knowing how to answer this, feeling a sudden weight of responsibility, Wladyslaw said, 'Look after these, please.' Breaking the gun open, he removed the cartridges from the twin barrels and placed them in her hand. She shook her head gently as she grasped them.

Wladyslaw walked back and gave Hanley the empty gun.

'You'll pay for this,' Hanley said with cold antagonism. 'First thieving – now assault. I'll get you locked away. And your friends – the whole lot of you.'

'These are not my friends, Mr Hanley.'

Hanley's mouth quivered and twitched.

'These are not my friends,' Wladyslaw repeated. 'These are German prisoners.' Realising that further explanations were useless, he said, 'But I will ask for the information you wish. If you tell me, please, what they have stolen.'

'They know what they've stolen all right!' Hanley said, his agitation bobbing back to the surface. 'They've stolen my gates, that's what!'

For a moment Wladyslaw thought he must have misunderstood. 'Gates?' he echoed.

'Gates!'

Wladyslaw delivered the accusation to the man with the
broken nose, who relayed it in German like a parade sergeant,
in a tuneless chant at the top of his voice.

The impassive German began to reply, but was interrupted
by a couple of the men behind him. Some sort of disagreement
followed, Wladyslaw couldn't tell what it was about.

Finally the impassive man overruled the others and delivered
a message for relay into Polish.

'We are freezing in our barracks,' intoned the broken-nosed
man. 'There is no fuel. The men were desperate for wood.'

Wladyslaw said, 'You admit to stealing the gates then?'

The man with the broken nose seemed to think this unworthy of translation until Wladyslaw urged him on with a flick of
an upturned hand.

'They thought the gates were abandoned,' came the reply.

'Where are the gates now?' Wladyslaw asked.

'Back at the barracks.'

During these exchanges Hanley had become increasingly
restless. 'What're they on about? What're they saying?'

'It appears that they have knowledge of these gates,' Wladyslaw said with great politeness. 'Now I try to discover what
has happened to them.' He said to the Polish speaker, 'Can
they be returned?'

There was some delay before the translator reported, 'We
smashed them up ready for burning.'

Wladyslaw took a long breath before saying to Hanley, 'I
think maybe you will want to apply for payment for these gates
from British authorities.'

Hanley's expression was scathing. 'What! You can tell your
friends they're not going to get away with it as easily as that.'

'The gates are in pieces.'

'I don't care what state they're in,' Hanley said, the quiver of righteousness resonating in his voice. 'I want them back. Every single bit of them!'

Wladyslaw said to the Germans, 'Will you be prepared to return the wood?'

The attitude of the impassive man grew weary at the question. He issued his reply in a tone of infinite boredom, leaving long pauses between sentences, and not simply for the purposes of translation.

'It will be difficult to return the precise wood . . . The men spend all their available time collecting many kinds of wood . . . If we have to return the wood we will go cold tonight . . . Not only is this contrary to our rights as prisoners of war . . . but we have volunteered for the job of clearing this railway . . . It will not go down well with the men if the wood is taken from them . . . Also, we would point out that the gates were in a bad state when we found them . . . They were not the gates of a good farmer.'

Wladyslaw was deciding how much of this, if any, it would be wise to relay to Hanley when a shout sounded on the deadened air, and he saw four guards hurrying along the railway track with the bustling officiousness of men who know they have been found wanting in their duty and are about to take it out on everyone else.

'At last!' Hanley cried in savage triumph. Armed with an expression of high moral purpose, he went forward to meet them.

When Wladyslaw glanced back he found himself exchanging a look with the impassive German. He was about to turn away when the German said in English, 'To live through the war only to die *now* . . .' and gave an audible snort of disdain.

Wladyslaw found Stella holding the cartridges stiffly in one hand.

'Best thing I walk back to the farm,' he said.

'You did the right thing, Wladek,' she said unhappily.

He gave a light shrug. 'It is done now.' He looked into her face, searching for confirmation that everything that had passed between them at the sluice was not entirely forgotten, and saw only anxiety. 'We will meet at seven?'

She nodded dumbly.

He offered a small smile. After a moment's hesitation she returned it. Reassured, he began the long walk back.

Since the arrival of the snows Wladyslaw had missed only five days' work on the moor, three when the blizzards were too thick to see in front of his face, and two when he was bed-ridden with a cough and mild fever. Otherwise it might have been Siberia again, a fact not entirely lost on him as he bent to the back-breaking labour of cutting the withies. Sometimes, when the wind was particularly keen, he would try to find a bed where the existing withies gave the impression, probably illusory, of a lee. At other times the snow was so thick on the ground that it was a job to find a bed where the base of the withy stocks was showing through. Even then, it might only be an outside row or an irregular patch where the wind had scoured the snow away. Whatever the conditions, the yield was at best mixed. Some beds were full of the bent and horny stems that Billy had called spraggle, others were festooned with shrivelled but tenacious weeds that had to be pulled free, yet more beds produced little but hurdle wood which fetched next to nothing at Honeymans' yard. Whatever the harvest, the cart was useless in the snow, and he had to carry the bundles back to the farm strapped to his shoulders, four at a time. On some days he had to make three journeys from one end of the moor to the other, and then the work seemed very hard.

Now, feeling he should do some work before preparing for Stella's arrival, he broke open the bundles he had cut the previous day and, spreading the meagre harvest over the floor of the withy shed, began to sort through it.

Somewhere in a far corner of the shed a rat scuffled, and he made a mental note to put poison down. The sound came again, but this time it was more of a scraping noise, too substantial for a rat. Letting his bundle drop, Wladyslaw listened carefully before walking softly past the stripping machine towards the dark corner where the corrugated-iron sheets, fence posts and lengths of timber were stored. In the gloom he saw a man getting up off a pile of sacking. It was Jozef.

'Dear Lord,' Wladyslaw exclaimed with an involuntary laugh. 'What the hell are you doing here?'

Jozef pulled his mouth down, partly in greeting, partly in a grimace, as if his bones had seized up in the cold. He was wearing a fur cap and thick woollen donkey jacket, and his bony face seemed very white as he came forward into the light. 'I was waiting for you,' he said.

Wladyslaw gripped his shoulder delightedly. 'For heaven's sake, how are you?'

'I'm all right.'

'Where have you been? Did you get to London?'

Jozef gave a bitter sigh. 'I got to London all right.'

'Ah . . .' Wladyslaw murmured sympathetically. 'It didn't work out?'

'It worked out fine!' Jozef cried sharply, as if they'd just been arguing the point. 'It was great, OK?'

Wladyslaw stood corrected. 'I'm glad to hear it. You found a job then?'

'Listen, have you got a smoke? I'm desperate.'

Wladyslaw led the way to the work area and, extracting two cigarettes from his packet, threw one to Jozef. When they had lit up, they sat side by side on a wooden trestle, facing the yard and the falling snow.

Wladyslaw asked, 'So, tell me, what sort of a job did you get?'

'In a shop. A department store.'

'Good Lord!' Wladyslaw exclaimed, genuinely impressed. 'And what did you do there?'

'Oh, loading, unloading. Maintenance,' Jozef said carelessly.

'Was it hard?'

'No! Easy.'

'And otherwise? Where did you live? What did you do?'

'What I did was to have a great time!' Jozef clamped his lips together and blinked rapidly as if to contain some powerful emotion, then Wladyslaw saw to his astonishment that his eyes were shining with bitter tears. 'I've never had such a great time in my life. Never! London's a wonderful city, and anyone who says different is just trying to fool you. We never stopped, not for a minute. We had a car and we went all over the place, trying different pubs every night. It was crazy! Eating fish and chips. My God, I think we had fish and chips every night for a month!' He gave a wild laugh as if the craziness of it still excited him.

'Who were your friends? Workmates?'

'God, no. No, they were crazy fools like me. Poles on the loose.'

'Really? And had they found jobs as well?'

'Sure! It's easy. This talk of no work – it's just to keep us away. I tell you, there's plenty of work.'

'You astound me,' Wladyslaw said.

He would have asked what kind of work these friends had found, but Jozef had begun to talk with a strange mournful excitement about the sights he had seen, the visit they had made to a place called Brighton, the shop they had discovered in the Soho area of London which sold Polish sausage and cheese and pickles, as well as vodka. 'Not Polish vodka, of course, not even Russian, but good enough to have some crazy nights. My God, we had some crazy nights! One time we ended up driving to the flower market at dawn and drinking beer till midday.' He slapped a hand against his forehead as if in remorse, but really in pride and bravado at having lived to the hilt.

'I bet you had a hangover.'

'And how! The best ever! My head was like an anvil. My

eyeballs like sandpaper. I slept for a whole day. Yes, truly magnificent.'

'But you've survived. You look well enough at any rate.'

Jozef made no effort to answer. His strange euphoria had evaporated, leaving him morose and inert.

'You found a place to stay all right, did you?'

It was a while before Jozef responded. 'Mmm? Yeah . . . with friends.'

'Was it a rented place?'

Jozef gave a dismissive shrug.

'I only ask because I'm thinking of going to London myself and I was wondering how hard it was to find lodgings.'

But Jozef had given up all pretence of listening. Sinking deeper into his preoccupations he drew on his cigarette and began to kick his boot at the floor with short stabbing motions.

'So, what brings you back, Jozef?'

Again he seemed not to have heard, but the moment Wladyslaw began to repeat the question Jozef sprang into a fury as sudden as it was violent, throwing up both hands, jamming his eyes shut, trembling and shivering with rage.

Taken aback, retreating to safer ground, Wladyslaw took a long breath and asked in a tone of mild enquiry, 'Are you here for long?'

Jozef gave another shiver and breathed, 'Not if I can help it.'

'What's the problem, old friend? Is there something wrong?'

'Just leave it!'

'I was merely asking,' Wladyslaw said reasonably, with the smallest hint of reproach. Taking refuge in practicalities, he asked, 'Have you anywhere to stay?'

Jozef shook his head.

'Well, you could probably sleep in the apple store for tonight. It used to be my place before I moved into the house. I'll have to ask permission from the old people, of course, but they won't mind, I'm sure. Would that be any good to you?'

Jozef nodded.

Wladyslaw stood up. 'Come. I'll show you.'

Jozef collected his kitbag and followed Wladyslaw down to the apple store. Stopping on the threshold, he stared at the bare white room as if it were a prison cell.

Wladyslaw lit the paraffin stove and explained how the controls worked and how it mustn't be moved any closer to the door or the draughts would blow it out. 'Are you all right for food till six?' he asked. 'I can bring you something hot then.'

Jozef seemed reluctant to come further into the room. When he finally moved, it was with the shuffle of a man entering solitary. 'Sure,' he said, lifting his kitbag onto the bed.

Wladyslaw placed the matches by the bedside candle and checked there were spare candles on the shelf above. When he looked back, it was to find Jozef unscrewing a bottle and taking a long swig. Exhaling with a small shudder of pleasure, Jozef passed the bottle over. It was vodka, and not bad at that. They sat opposite each other, Jozef on the bed, shoulders slumped, Wladyslaw on the rickety wooden chair, upright, watchful. For a time Wladyslaw talked lightly about the news from the camp, the arrivals and departures, the celebrations and feuds, the British government's grudging recruitment of a few dozen Polish miners for their struggling coalmines, with, it was rumoured, more extensive recruitment to follow, until the bottle had been back and forth several times and Wladyslaw detected a mellowing in Jozef's expression.

He offered Jozef another cigarette and, holding a light to it, said in a compassionate tone, 'Look, I'm glad you felt you could come to me. I'm glad to be able to help out. But in return I must ask that you confide in me. That you tell me why you're here.'

'I wish I could!' Jozef retorted bitterly. 'I'd like to know myself! I'd like to know why I was forced to leave London and come back to this dead-end place.'

Wladyslaw gazed at him quietly through the drift of cigarette smoke, letting the silence urge him on.

Shifting to the edge of the bed in a jerky movement, Jozef

thrust his forearms onto his knees and, head hanging low, gaze fixed on the floor, growled, 'They tried to say I did something wrong, they tried to say I was a thief. But it was a complete lie. It was just an excuse to get rid of me. I was an easy target, wasn't I? A Pole. A foreigner. I was always going to get the blame if things went wrong. It was a forgone conclusion, right from the outset.'

'What were you meant to have stolen?'

Jozef threw a sharp upward glance at Wladyslaw before resuming his examination of the floor. 'They said some boxes had gone missing from the loading bay. Six cases of Scotch whisky. They said I was the only person who could have taken them. But where was I meant to have put them? Up my shirt? Under my arm? Down my throat? I'd have had to drink the whole lot in ten minutes flat. And where was I meant to have hidden the bottles? Up my arse? No, it was a set-up. They picked on me because I was an outsider, because the other workers didn't like me, because I couldn't speak the language. They decided they'd blame me, and that was that. No argument. No discussion. No one interested in hearing my side of the story. It was just: Clear off or we'll call the police.'

'At least they gave you the choice.'

'But I *wanted* the police,' Jozef argued fiercely, with a wild outward fling of one palm. 'I wanted to clear my name and stay in London. As it was, I was dragged away, I was made to look guilty as hell.'

'Your friends dragged you away?'

'No – Linder!' Jozef exclaimed. 'Linder panicked me into leaving before I had the chance to think. He told me I was about to be arrested. But it was a lie – I know it was a lie! He was only saying that to get rid of me and save himself trouble. That was all he cared about – how it looked for him. He rushed me into leaving, he made it look as though I was running away. He made me look guilty. And now, *now* – ' Jozef's voice rose in anger and self-pity, he clutched a hand to his forehead.

'Who is this' – Wladyslaw hesitated over the name, thinking he might have misheard – 'person exactly? This Lin-whatever?'

'Linder. *Linder*,' Jozef repeated impatiently, as if Wladyslaw were being particularly stupid.

'Do you mean *Lyndon?*' Wladyslaw enquired carefully.

'That's what I said – Linder.'

'Hanley?'

When Jozef nodded, Wladyslaw began to struggle with a number of conflicting thoughts, all of them disturbing. 'I don't understand – how was he involved?'

'Oh, he got me the job. For which *big* thanks, I don't think! *Big* favour, for which he can go to hell! He never even listened to my side of the story. No, well, they were *his* friends, weren't they?'

'Who were?'

'Him and the store owner's son. War comrades. So I never had a chance, did I? A nothing Polish boy from nowhere.'

'And you honestly cannot think of why you should have been accused?'

Jozef clapped a hand against his chest. 'On my heart – there was no reason! I did nothing wrong, I swear to you.'

Wladyslaw stubbed out his cigarette in the saucer that served as an ashtray, and kept stubbing it long after the last spark had been extinguished. Eventually he stood up. 'I'll bring some food at six then,' he said. 'The old man cooks well enough. You won't be disappointed.'

The mare had one pace, slow and steady. Bennett had long since decided that this was just as well. Both of them were rather long in the tooth for anything more adventurous, even on the rare occasions when the weather and road conditions might have allowed it. The mare had been lent to him by a farmer immediately after the first snowfall, and within the space of two days he had discovered the joys of riding high above the hedgerows in rare sunshine with a wide unimpeded view of the snow-drenched landscape, and the misery of a fierce blizzard taken head on, with a wind that cut straight through his waxed coat, and no reference points to guide him on his way.

Early this morning he had ridden through swirling snow to a remote farmhouse on North Moor to attend a breech birth which gave him several anxious hours until he was able to deliver the baby buttocks first. It was a boy for the farm, and the parents wept with joy. On his way back through Burrow-bridge he called on two elderly patients to find both tucked up in their cottages with fires blazing and enough food to keep them going until the neighbours brought more supplies. Then, hungry and thirsty, he stopped at the King Alfred pub under Burrow Mump and treated himself to a couple of whiskies with a plate of bread and cheese.

It was almost three by the time he set out again. A sulphur-ous sky had brought an early dusk, while a hard wind ruffled the mare's mane and sent whorls of snow skittering across the packed surface of the road ahead. A scattering of flakes flew on the rushing air, marking the end of the last storm or the start of the next.

Taking the road towards home, the mare's pace seemed to pick up a fraction in anticipation of her stable, and Bennett felt duty-bound to lean forward and tell her, 'Not quite done, old girl. One last call to make.'

Riding into the Hanleys' yard, Bennett led the mare into the shelter of the tractor shed before going to the front of the house and ringing the bell. He heard the closing of a distant door and the approaching steps of Arthur Hanley. Preparing for the small talk that was always something of a trial for him, Bennett was taken aback when the door opened to reveal not Arthur Hanley but his son.

Lyndon Hanley ushered him in with a lift of one arm. 'My father said you might be coming.'

They shook hands.

'Good to see you back,' Bennett said. 'How are you?'

'Fine.' Dispensing with further niceties, Lyndon took his coat and hat and said, 'You'll let me know how she is? My father's out at the moment.'

'Of course.'

'You know the way?'

'Yes, thank you.'

Bennett went upstairs to the draughty front bedroom to find Janet Hanley deeply asleep in the old-fashioned brass bed, her face drained of colour, her lips dry, her hair stuck to her forehead. When he spoke her name she opened her eyes and muttered a faint greeting. She had been seriously ill with pneumonia but even before he examined her he could tell that the fever had gone and the worst was over.

'It'll be some time before you get your strength back,' he told her when he had finished listening to her chest. 'You'll have to take things gently for quite a while.'

'My son . . .' she murmured. 'Is he . . .?'

'He's downstairs.'

She breathed fretfully, 'Did he say if he was staying?'

'I don't know. He didn't tell me.'

'He's going away again. I know he is.'

'Well, he's here now. I'm sure he'll be up to see you shortly.' Bennett put a hand over hers, but she drew no comfort from it.

He helped her to drink some water, then sponged her face with a flannel from the bathroom. She was asleep before he left the room.

Lyndon Hanley was waiting for him at the bottom of the stairs. 'How is she?'

'The fever's passed. But she'll need a long period of convalescence. Several weeks at least.'

'Is there anything I can do?'

'Can you cook?'

'Badly.'

'Well, she'll need invalid food. Chicken broth, stewed apple, rice pudding, that kind of thing.'

'I can but try.'

'And look, it's awfully cold up there. Might it be possible to light a fire?'

'I'll see what I can do. But my father doesn't usually allow fires in bedrooms. He thinks it's unhealthy. Fancy a drink, Doctor?'

'A bit early for me.'

'Tea?'

'That would be lovely, thank you.'

They went into the kitchen. Bennett sat at the table while Lyndon filled the kettle and plopped it onto the stove with a crash.

'When did you arrive?' Bennett asked.

'A couple of hours ago.' Lyndon leant back against the stove rail and, heaving his shoulders high, crossed his arms and squeezed them against his angular body as if he were very cold or very tense. With his unruly hair and penetrating gaze, he was an uncomfortable presence; his mind seemed altogether too sharp, his senses too raw.

'You didn't come on the Norton, did you?' Bennett asked.

'There aren't any trains.'

'Of course. I'd forgotten about the trains. You must have had an interesting ride.'

'Oh, it wasn't too bad till we got onto the smaller roads.'

Bennett noted the 'we' in passing, and half supposed he was referring to the bike. 'Well, I hope you don't feel you were summoned unnecessarily. Your mother gave us real cause for concern a couple of days ago.'

'That's the thing – I never got my father's telegram. He sent it to my club, but I haven't been there for ages. I didn't know my mother was ill till I got here.'

'Good heavens. So you'd decided to come anyway?'

'I was intending to come in a couple of weeks. Then . . . well, I changed my mind. I decided to come earlier.'

'Extraordinary. But then these things happen all the time, don't they? And the more they happen the more one suspects they can't always be put down to coincidence.'

'Of course it was coincidence,' Lyndon said firmly. 'Come on, Doctor, you can't believe all that claptrap about intuition.'

'When I was young I would have agreed with you. I thought it was complete poppycock. But then – well, a couple of things happened to me on the Front to make me think again.'

'I would have thought war was the last thing to make you believe in the possibility of benevolent forces.'

'Ah yes . . .'

'Well? What happened?'

'The first time was soon after I arrived in Flanders. I was put in charge of a dressing station a short distance behind the front line. When I arrived the men had got the main tent half erected. But I had this extraordinary conviction that we should move it somewhere else. Tents, staff, supplies, the whole damn show. Well, you can imagine how popular that was. I dreamt up an excuse about insanitary conditions – but that was all it was, an excuse. Luckily my CO wasn't around. He was further up the line and didn't return till the next day. By which time we'd moved a hundred yards away and the original site had been blown to smithereens during the morning bombardment. Nothing but a crater.'

'The site was too close to the front line,' Lyndon declared. 'It was just common sense to move it.'

'But the second site was no further away, just further to the west. And the shell that fell on the first site was the only one to fall so far behind the lines.'

'I don't care. There must have been something wrong with the first site, something that you logged subconsciously, that your mind never articulated. Perhaps you realised that the place had been used before, as a divisional HQ perhaps. Something that was an obvious target. No, I'm sorry, Doctor – that one won't wash.'

For the sake of argument, Bennett conceded with a turn of one hand.

'And the other experience?'

'That was even more striking. It was about six months later.

I was assigned to a casualty clearing station near Maricourt.
I'd come off duty after a twelve-hour stint and gone back to
my billet to get some sleep. I was dog-tired, but try as I might I
couldn't sleep. I kept thinking about my family – my parents
and two brothers. Nothing unusual in that, you might say, but
I'd only been married a short while and it was usually Marjorie
who was in the forefront of my mind. My family were rather
more – well, not in the background exactly, but less conspicuous. Anyway, I tossed and turned for a couple of hours before
I felt this compulsion to return to the clearing station. It had
never happened before, I couldn't explain it at all, yet I felt
absolutely no doubt that I must go. When I got there it was
about five. The bombardment had started earlier than usual
that night and large numbers of casualties were arriving from
the dressing stations. I walked into one barn – there were three
to choose from, but I knew exactly which one – and went
straight up the middle, looking to my right. Not to my left, but
to my right. And there, second from the end, was my younger
brother.'

At Lyndon's back the kettle was hissing noisily but he
ignored it.

Bennett added, 'I knew he was somewhere on the Front of
course, but I thought his regiment was much further to the
west, near Thiepval. I had no idea they'd been moved to our
section.'

Finally Lyndon reached back to slide the kettle off the
hotplate. He stared intently at Bennett before saying, 'I'm glad
you found your brother, Doctor, but I cannot accept your basic
proposition, that you were guided to him by some extrasensory
force. I imagine you were working long hours under appalling
conditions. I suggest that in the hubbub and confusion you
overheard someone mentioning your brother's regiment, and
that this information stayed buried in the back of your mind
until you tried to sleep, when it came to the fore, and you made
the connection between the regiment, your brother and the

beginning of the bombardment, which alerted you to the possibility of his being in danger.'

'I hadn't thought of that.'

Lyndon pulled out a chair and sat down. Leaning forward, he spread an emphatic hand palm down on the table in front of him. 'I cannot explain why you should have gone straight to the right barn, except for the obvious reason, that there was always going to be a one-in-three chance of getting it right. But if you want to call it intuition – well, that's up to you.' His long fingers flexed and lifted off the table, his eyes glittered. 'But I can't accept the idea that a force can be both benevolent and arbitrary. It's a total contradiction. Any force that picks and chooses, that warns you of one bullet but fails to warn you of the next – which by definition is the one that's going to kill you – is at best fickle, at worst sadistic, because it's toyed with you, it's given you the illusion of protection. No, the idea of forewarning, of intuition, is just another form of voodoo. Another tyrannical deity to add to all the rest.'

Bennett wondered if Lyndon was an atheist or an agnostic, and decided atheist. Though not without a struggle, he suspected; not without doubts.

'And if this force relies on some sort of telepathic communication, some sort of magic *waves*' – Lyndon drew some contemptuously in the air – 'then why doesn't it function when we really need it? Why doesn't it work when the people closest to us are in danger? How can such a force let us believe that someone we love is just close by' – the arc of his hand indicated a point behind his shoulder – 'safe and sound, when in fact they've vanished, gone for ever? How can it let us think everything's all right when at that very instant this person we love is being subjected to the most appalling suffering?'

Something in Lyndon's expression made Bennett stay silent.

'How is it' – and now Lyndon took his time, choosing his words with care – 'that we can have an extraordinary affinity with someone, that we can feel so highly attuned to them that we can almost read their thoughts – and your force fails to scream and shout and rage at us when they're in pain?'

Lyndon's gaze sharpened, inviting a response.

'I cannot answer that,' Bennett said.

'Of course you can't. Because your force doesn't exist.' Lyndon sat back in his chair and said in an altogether brisker tone, 'No, Doctor, it's all a matter of luck. Good or bad. Nothing more. The mistake is to start wondering why you had the luck to survive when other people didn't. That way guilt and religious conversion lie.'

'I certainly wouldn't argue with the idea of luck. We all need it now and again.'

Lyndon looked as though he might say something else but appeared to think better of it. Glancing around at the kettle, he made to get up.

'No, please don't worry,' Bennett said. 'I should be getting back anyway.'

'Are you sure?'

'Absolutely.'

Lyndon led the way into the hall.

'Are you here for a while?' Bennett asked as he pulled on his coat.

'For a few weeks. Till I start my new job.'

'Ah. And what's that?'

'Colonial Office,' he replied without enthusiasm. 'Burma.'

'How exciting.'

'I rather doubt it. The work's going to be boring as hell. And the diplomatic life – well, I've glimpsed it. I've no illusions on that score. Cocktail parties. Snobbery. Petty politics.'

'There'll be compensations, I'm sure.'

'Yes, I'm hoping to get upcountry now and again. To get right away. It's very beautiful there.'

'So I've heard.'

When Bennett had wrapped the last scarf around his chin, Lyndon opened the door and they shook hands.

Lyndon said, 'Your younger brother, the one you found . . . Did he . . .?'

'He died. There at the clearing station.'

'You were with him?'

'Yes.'

'He had some luck then, at the end.'

The roof had not been designed to resist blizzards blown in by gale-force winds. The snowflakes, fine and sharp, found their way up through the overlaps of the tiles, emerging in puffs of white dust to settle over the floor of the loft in a series of ridges and corrugations. It took Wladyslaw ten bucket-loads and five journeys up and down the stepladder to clear it, but this was as nothing compared to the first snows, when large areas of the loft had been knee-deep in drift.

With the last bucket-load deposited out of the window, he closed the trapdoor and put the ladder away. He lit the fire in Stan and Flor's room so that it would be warm by the time he brought Flor up from the kitchen, then went down to the unused parlour and made up a fire of coal and kindling which he would supplement with apple wood just before Stella arrived. He shook out the rugs and dusted the furniture and swept the floor and put fresh candles in the candleholders, two of them brass, the rest improvised from cored apples.

At six he went into the kitchen to find Stan ladling stew and potatoes into a bowl and Flor propped up in her easy chair, a napkin round her neck, an apron draped over her lap, a spoon clutched in her hand. At the sight of Wladyslaw, she stretched out a gracious hand; but for the spoon, she might have been a famous beauty demanding homage. He bowed over her hand and kissed it, as he always did, and saw her face break into a delighted smile.

'Does this Joe eat like you?' demanded Stan. 'Like a blithering horse?'

'He will pay for his food, Stan. OK?'

'*Joe*. What sort of a name is that? It's bloomin' English.'

'Like Stan is also Polish.'

Stan scoffed emphatically, though he never tired of Wladys-law bringing up the idea so that he could shoot it down in flames. 'Stan-*ley*. I keep telling you: Stan-*ley*. English as they come.' Then, as he handed Wladyslaw a bowl of beef stew and potatoes: 'Question is, does this Joe play cribbage or does he not?'

'I will ask. But I think he is too tired tonight.'

'No use to me then, is he? And you neither, with your English lessons.'

'I play cribbage with you tomorrow, Stan. OK?'

He grumbled, 'Don't have much option, do I?'

Wladyslaw carried the bowl of stew up to the apple store to find the place in darkness and Jozef fast asleep. It took a lot to wake him, and even more to get him to sit up and eat. Wladyslaw didn't have to look for the empty bottle to know he had finished the vodka.

After supper Wladyslaw lit the fire in the parlour and took a bowl and a kettle of hot water up to his room to wash. The room was at the end of the house and very cold. Ice glittered on the inside of the window and his breath emerged as vapour. Quickly, before the cold had time to bite, he stripped and scrubbed himself energetically from head to toe. He had no suitable civilian clothes so he put on his army shirt and trousers over some clean underwear he had washed and dried the previous day. Combing his hair in front of the patchy mirror, feeling his body smart from the cold, he felt great lurches of agonised happiness. It seemed incredible that this amazing woman should even now be making her way to him through the snow, that she should be coming not just as a friend but as a lover, the unquestioned owner of his heart. He saw her before him in the falling snow at the lock, the brilliance of her gaze, the pallor of her carved features in the bleached light, the sudden unexpected upwelling of tears; he felt again the touch of her lips, the way they had moved softly against his; he heard the confident joyful 'Yes' that told him she had begun to love him in return; and his optimism surged, he felt that his poverty and lack of prospects would not after all be an impossible barrier. He knew only that he had told her the truth, that his life would have no purpose if he couldn't be near her, that all his happiness lay in seeing and hearing her.

Hurrying down to the kitchen, he went up to Flor and lifted both arms wide in a gesture of regret. 'I must take you up early tonight, dear lady, because I have English lesson.'

Smiling, she put down her crossword puzzle and reached up to loop an arm around his neck. He lifted her easily, lightly, swinging her up into his arms like a lover, and perhaps it stirred a memory because, though their progress up the stairs was necessarily ponderous because of his leg, there was a wistfulness in the tilt of her head, a certain dreaminess in her eyes. When he placed her carefully on the bed, however, the dreams had gone and she fixed him with a look that was sharply maternal, a blend of affection and wonder at this, her most unexpected foundling, the son of the wild winter, blown in with the wind and the blizzards from God only knew where.

They bade each other goodnight in their customary fashion, she with a wave and a cracked smile, he with a hand to his chest and a short bow.

It was just before seven when he placed some apple logs on the fire and lit the candles in the parlour. He arranged the chocolate biscuits he had bought from the village shop on a plate alongside two teacups and saucers, and laid out the information from London University on the desk flap, with a pad and pencil to make notes. For the finishing touch, he fetched the picture postcard of London he had borrowed from a comrade at the camp and propped it up on the mantelpiece, angled to catch the light from the nearest candle.

By the time he had finished, the apple wood was sending up bright flames and giving off its sweet seductive scent. While he waited for Stella, he searched through the papers from the

university, looking for information about money, his most
immediate concern. So far as he could gather he had the option
of a student grant or taking extended leave from the Resettlement Corps on normal pay, from which he concluded that the
value of the two must be about the same. But whether the
money would cover the cost of rented accommodation they
didn't say. A student hostel was out of the question, not only
because of his age, but because it would rule out any chance of
starting married life. And he could not contemplate so much as
a year, let alone two, without Stella.

By twenty past seven he had lost all concentration and was
staring into the fire. By half past he was listening to the wind
buffeting the window and berating himself for letting Stella
refuse his offer to collect her. He saw her slipping on ice, lying
helpless with a broken leg. He saw her falling into a ditch,
twisting her ankle. Five minutes later he pulled on his jacket
and hat and went out into the night. The snow seemed to have
stopped, though the blustering wind was sending sprays of
powder off the roof and scuffles of snow along the packed
surface of the yard. He started up the hill, his eyes scanning the
whiteness, his ears reaching out to catch the slightest sounds
above the hissing and skittering of the wind, and castigated
himself again and again for not having gone to collect her.

He had reached the steepest part of the lane when he saw
someone emerging from the pale gloom ahead. The figure was
moving lightly along, it could only be Stella, and he shouted
her name. She waved, and in his joy he quickened his pace.

She began to speak while she was still some distance away.
'Wladek, I'm sorry, I'd have come sooner to tell you but – well,
something's come up, you see.'

He grasped her shoulders and laughed with relief. 'Here you
are! I thought something had happened. I thought you were
lost or fallen or . . .' Something in her manner or her silence
made him pause.

'I'm sorry,' she repeated.

Only then did he understand that she wasn't coming.

'Your aunt is not well?'

'No. It's . . .'

Her hesitation made him nervous. 'What?'

'It's my cousin. He's come home. And – well, I have to see him. I have to.' She murmured again, breathlessly, 'Sorry,' and this time the word was like a stake driven into his heart.

Chapter Twelve

As THE train lumbered clear of the hills Billy saw in the first light of dawn a low ground mist stretching away towards an indistinct horizon, and close under the track the dark glint of waterlogged fields and overflowing streams. Twice in the night the train had slowed to a crawl for what seemed many miles, and twice it had stopped altogether in the middle of nowhere. The guard had said there was a broken-down train ahead, but during a halt at Frome the ticket collector told him it was the flooding.

A dark hill rose up and the train roared through a tunnel and a series of cuttings before slowing for the last stop before Athelney. While Billy was still alone in the compartment he stood up and, knees braced against the seat, spruced himself in the high-set mirror, smoothing his hair back with long passes of the comb, setting his jacket square on his shoulders and straightening his shirt and tie. The suit had cost him all he had, but despite the occasional misgivings about the style, which in his more critical moments seemed uncomfortably reminiscent of George Gibbon's, he considered it money well spent. No one in the village would have anything to match it.

Sitting by the window again, he thought about the day ahead. Until as recently as yesterday he had intended to go straight to Annie's, partly because he would be passing her door and nothing would be more natural than to stop and say hello, partly because he wanted her to see the suit so she would realise that he'd made some money while he was away and wasn't coming back out of desperation. But now he was having

second thoughts. To call on her even before he'd dumped his
stuff at Crick Farm would be to appear too keen, never a good
idea. Better to wait till the evening when the suit could be
explained by a late meeting or some other important business.
Now, more than ever, he wanted to strike the right note with
her, to underline the fact that his postcard, sent a few weeks
ago, was no joke. It had taken three attempts and two wasted
cards to get the message right. *Don't say I didn't warn you.
I'm coming back to start a new business.* The bit he'd got
wrong was the signature. To avoid the soppiness of *Love, Billy*
or the flatness of plain *Billy* he wrote *Guess who?*, which he'd
regretted the moment he dropped the card into the box. He'd
taken care to put Ernie's address at the top of the card,
however. He told himself it was for news of the farm, but really
it was a test to see if she was still interested.

Her card had arrived three days later. *Dear Billy, What
news! Can't wait to hear about it. Everything fine at Crick
Farm. Love, Annie.* He set store by the 'Can't wait'; a woman
wouldn't write something like that unless she meant it.

The train stopped and some people climbed into his compartment, three youths with the threadbare coats and frayed
shirt cuffs of junior clerks, and a couple of chattering shop
girls. The girls flicked him appraising glances, and for a while
he eyed them right back.

Starting off again, the train seemed to launch itself off the
edge of the town onto a wide sea. As the row of high-backed
houses fell away, the watery wilderness of Middle Moor
opened out to the north, wetter than Billy had ever seen it, and
then Aller Moor, completely flooded, with the Parrett wandering aimlessly alongside, just two banks snaking along the
surface. If the drove-roads were still afloat he couldn't see
them.

Then the train squeezed past Oath Hill and began its
ambling journey across the corner of West Sedgemoor, the
greatest ocean of them all with nothing but water on either
side, and just the occasional willow and stubbled oblong of

uncut withies to indicate the pattern of the beds and rhynes beneath, and marking the edge of the moor a long line of pollards like lampposts fringing a winter beach.

The ridge rose up, returning them to dry land. Then the train panted through the cutting and they were at sea again on Stan Moor, where the flood was so high it seemed to have swallowed up some of Burrowbridge and possibly some of Athelney as well.

As the train began to slow for Athelney Station, Billy pulled his kitbag off the rack and lowered the window, ready to turn the handle. There were perhaps ten people waiting on the platform, standing expectantly or moving towards the train. He paid them no attention until he had got off, when he looked up and noticed a smartly dressed woman reaching for a door to the next carriage. Her neat figure, her slim legs, her stylish clothes and jaunty little hat would have marked her out in his sight at any time, but when she swung the door open and the back of her hat gave way to a striking profile he realised with a leap of surprise that it was Annie.

He called her name and saw her hesitate and look over her shoulder to scan the platform behind her. Her gaze swung round and she finally spotted him striding towards her.

She gave a wide smile. 'Well, if it isn't "Guess Who".'

Her skin was white and smooth in the morning light, her lips a shiny red. She seemed both extraordinarily familiar to him and unnervingly foreign.

'We wondered when you were coming.'

'Didn't I say?' he remarked with mock astonishment.

She shook her head.

'Maybe I forgot.'

'Maybe you did.'

She laughed easily, her eyes dancing. She seemed exceptionally happy. While he wanted to believe that his arrival had something to do with it, the part of him that doubted his judgement in matters of happiness, that automatically cautioned against the risk of humiliation, told him it might not be so. He tried to read her face, to get some key to her thoughts, but saw only the bright confident gaze.

'Where are you off to?' he asked.

'To work.'

'You found a job then?'

'It's only three days a week and the pay's nothing to write home about – but yes.'

'Enough to keep you in hats?'

She laughed. 'Just about.'

A whistle blew.

'So what's this business you're starting up?' she demanded.

'That would be telling.'

'A secret, is it?'

'Not if you're free for a drink' – he pretended to work out the best day – 'tomorrow? Or another day,' he added casually, to show he was in no particular hurry.

The whistle sounded again on a high insistent note, but she took no notice. It was one of the things that had always attracted him so much: she answered to no one.

'Can't do tomorrow,' she said. 'Don't laugh, but I'm helping at the village hall.'

'Why would I laugh?' he said.

'Because it's the sort of thing our mums used to do.'

Or not, he thought.

'It's an evening in aid of the war memorial.'

'I thought we already had a war memorial.'

'There isn't enough room on it. They've got to buy a plinth.'

The engine sent out a whoosh of steam. Finally she got into the carriage and he closed the door behind her. She lowered the window and stuck her head out.

'What about tonight then?' he said.

She gave a slow smile. Her eyes were dancing again. 'All right.'

'Seven?'

'Seven.'

On the level crossing the gates clanged shut across the road.

'So?' she said with a tilt of her jaunty little hat.

'So?' he replied, tilting his head in parody, mimicking her smile, having the reward of another rich laugh. In that moment it seemed to him that a look of understanding passed between them, that her eyes told him she knew what he was thinking, and that she was thinking the same, that it was all on between them. His mood soared; he almost laughed aloud.

The train clunked into motion. He was about to ask where she'd like to go that evening when she cried, 'Oh, I must tell you – those Poles have been amazing. Working through the snow and the floods.'

'Poles?' he queried, walking alongside the train.

She nodded emphatically. 'Never stopped for a moment, any of them.'

He was walking fast now, the train starting to outpace him. He called, 'How many are there, for God's sake?'

She said something he couldn't hear, and then it was too late, she was speeding away from him. He stood and watched as she gave a bright wave and ducked back through the window.

A section of road on the far side of the level crossing was flooded. A couple were waiting for a lift on a van or lorry, but, risking a touch of mud, Billy hitched a ride on the trailer of a passing tractor. The farmer took him up the hill as far as the crossroads. Walking briskly through the village, Billy's mind veered erratically between thoughts of Annie and the Poles. *Never stopped for a moment, any of them.* He had a vision of a gang of Poles slashing their way down the withy beds. He could imagine all too well how the situation had come about. Polack Johnnie had found the work too hard and too lonely and had talked Stan into hiring some of his comrades to keep him company, and Stan, gullible and pig-headed, hadn't thought to count the cost. Visions of the satchel being raided at weekly intervals drove Billy on at a brisk pace.

He began his audit as soon as the moor came into sight, sweeping the sheen of water for the stubble of uncut beds and

finding none. Rounding the bend in the lane, he noted the gate
to the track solid on its hinges, the fences in one piece, the
orchard . . . He slowed for a moment, thinking his eyes were
playing tricks, but there was no mistake – the apple trees had
been pruned back to a few stunted limbs. The job seemed
unnecessarily savage until it occurred to him with a spark of
anger that the Poles had probably been taking the branches for
firewood.

He scoured the yard ahead. The floor was clean, the area
tidy. A few withies stood propped against the first line of
drying rails, a dense line of hurdles against the next, while on
the edge of the pasture wisps of smoke rose from a smouldering
pile of spraggle. In the withy shed stripped willows were drying
beside the stripping machine, and when he touched the motor
casing it was still warm. Next to the wall was a stack of baskets
and wicker trays. At first Billy thought they must be locally
produced stuff, samples perhaps, but when he looked closer he
realised the designs weren't in the usual style. One tray had a
fluted edge of a type he'd never seen before, one basket was
oval with a handle running from end to end.

Going back into the yard, he heard a voice somewhere
behind the shed and followed it round into the orchard. He
saw smoke coming from the boiler chimney before he saw the
boiler itself and Wladyslaw balanced on the side wall, loading
withies into the tank with the help of a man standing below.

Wladyslaw glanced up and, taking a harder look, raised a
hand in salutation. 'Billy! Hello there.'

'Don't let me disturb you.'

'I just finish.' Wladyslaw took a bundle from the other man
and manoeuvred it into the tank with a deft prod of his stick.
Clambering down, he limped over and, wiping a palm on his
leg, held his hand out. 'How are you, Billy?'

'Couldn't be better,' Billy said brightly, shaking hands. 'So
how's it all going?'

'Not so bad.'

'Been keeping busy, have you?'

'Sure. The snow, the floods haven't been so good, you know.
But we manage to stay working.'

'We? How many are you exactly?'

Wladyslaw touched a hand to his chest in a gesture of
apology. 'Forgive me, please. This is Jozef. He has been working here since January.'

Billy felt certain he had seen the bony face and fierce eyes
somewhere before, but he couldn't immediately place him.

'How many are you?'

'Just two.'

Billy grinned. 'Try again, Johnnie.'

A flicker of puzzlement crossed Wladyslaw's face before he
said, 'You mean Polish Stan?'

'I don't know, do I? That's why I'm asking.'

'Polish Stan comes from the camp maybe two, three times
each week to make baskets.'

'Does he now?' Billy said in the same lively tone. 'Well,
well. Quite a little industry then.'

Catching the note of sarcasm, Wladyslaw's eyes turned
narrow, a wariness settled over his features.

'Everyone been earning good money, have they?'

Wladyslaw replied calmly, 'I earn same as before. Jozef, he
does same work but on lower rate. Polish Stan, he asks only a
few pence each basket.'

'Very modest. And they just turned up, did they, your
friends? Offering to help out?' No sooner had Billy asked the
question than he withdrew it with a gesture of amused scorn.
'No – spare me the details. I think I can guess.'

'There was much work to do, Billy.'

'I'll bet.'

'After we fix the boiler we reckon that we get best money if
we boil withies and make baskets and hurdles ourselves.'

'And have you?'

'Sorry?'

'Got the best prices?'

'Not so bad, I think.'

'Where d'you sell them?'

'The baskets in Taunton.'

Billy gave a bellow of derisive laughter. Selling baskets in Taunton was like flogging cheese in Cheddar, you could barely give the stuff away. 'God help me,' he spluttered pityingly.

Wladyslaw took a handkerchief from his pocket and with concentration began to wipe his hands.

'Taunton . . .' Billy muttered with a benevolent shake of his head. 'Well, I think we might *just* be able to do better than that. The boiler – how d'you fix it?'

'Mrs Bentham, she found this welder. The cost was not great.'

'Mrs Bentham?' He felt a quiet thrill at speaking Annie's name. 'And it's fixed good, is it? No leaks?'

Replacing the handkerchief in his pocket, Wladyslaw regarded Billy with a steady gaze. 'No leaks.'

As Billy ambled over to the boiler, he remembered where he'd seen this Jozef before. In the cold morning light the fellow looked even worse than when he'd been lying unconscious on the floor of the George. With his skull-like head, sunken cheeks, and staring eyes he might have come out of a Boris Karloff film, one of the living dead.

Billy cast a cursory eye over the boiler before wandering back to Wladyslaw.

'This basket-maker of yours . . . is he any good?'

'Sure. He's old chap, you know. From lakes of Poland. He makes baskets all his life.'

'That fancy stuff I saw in the shed – that's his, is it?'

'Yes.'

'He can do large stuff as well, can he?'

'This I don't know.'

'Because that's what we're going to produce, Johnnie.' Billy gave him a comradely slap on the back. 'The large stuff. Laundry baskets. Haulage baskets. Porters' baskets. Going to send them direct to London. I've got it all set up. Fifty of each, just for starters.'

Wladyslaw tried to speak but Billy was still talking.

'We can use up a lot of the hurdle wood that way. Bash 'em out quick.'

'Billy—'

'I might even be able to keep your friends on,' Billy added in a spirit of generosity. 'We'll see how it goes.'

'Billy, listen please. I must tell you that I am leaving. And Jozef also.'

Billy felt the cold plunge of betrayal. 'What, you're buggering off, are you?'

'We wished to leave weeks ago. We wait only because we hear you are returning and we don't want to leave Stan and Flor alone.'

'So . . . you beg for a bloody job, you take the money for as long as it suits you – and then you just bugger off.'

'But the cutting season is almost over, Billy. You always said—'

Billy stabbed a finger at Wladyslaw. 'Don't tell me what I said! Don't talk to me about the cutting season. You can just bugger off right now, both of you! Go on! Just get the hell out of here!'

He stalked off, only to turn on his heel and come straight back, the anger still crashing in his ears. 'I could have you arrested – you know that?' he said wildly. 'You're meant to give proper notice. That's how we do it in this country – everyone works out their notice, fair and square. But you wouldn't understand that, would you, coming from where you do? From where they treat workers worse than muck.'

By the time Billy had run this argument back through his mind for flaws, Wladyslaw was saying, 'But you never wished me to stay, Billy. You always said this. You always said . . .' Reading Billy's expression he abandoned the argument with a dip of his head and half turned towards Jozef as if to consult about something. Thinking better of it he looked back and said, 'If you wish me to stay for one week more, then I will do this.'

'Wait a minute, wait a minute,' Billy said, in a tone of sudden enlightenment. 'I get it. You've had a better offer. You've been promised more money.'

Wladyslaw gave Billy the look that had always irritated him so much: the quiet stare with the hint of reproach, the air of moral rectitude. 'It is not money, Billy. I will go to university to study. And Jozef, he will try for building work in Bristol.'

'You've got it all worked out then.'

Wladyslaw was silent.

'Well, you can go to hell, both of you. And you can go right now. Go on – bugger off!'

Wladyslaw's calmness finally deserted him. He said with a spark of anger, 'Sunday is first time we can leave. Nothing is possible before Sunday.'

'Please yourself.'

'You wish us to stop now, or finish these withies?' Wladyslaw threw a hand towards the boiler.

'I told you – do what the hell you like.'

Billy marched down to the house and entered the kitchen with a bang of the door.

Stan was standing in front of the table as if he'd been waiting for him. Flor was propped in a chair by the range, weeping, a handkerchief pressed to her eyes.

'What's she crying for?' Billy demanded.

Stan shook his head. 'It was the schoolmistress.'

'What're you talking about?'

'Wladislaw wouldn't be going if she hadn't thrown him over for that Hanley fellow. He'd have stayed till autumn-time.'

Billy dropped his bag onto the floor. 'Well, he's not staying, is he? So you'll have to make do with me.'

Annie answered Billy's knock almost immediately and stepped out with a smile. Before closing the door she called a farewell to someone called Margaret, presumably the babysitter.

At the gate he offered her his arm and she looped her hand

easily through his elbow. She seemed as self-possessed as ever, yet beneath the surface he thought he could sense an edge of tension not unlike his own. She was, after all, publicly stepping out with him, she had gone to the trouble of arranging a babysitter; it was a statement of, if not intent, then at least strong possibilities.

'You don't mind the George?' he asked as they started down the road.

'Course not.'

'When I get some transport we can try some other places.'

'*Transport*.'

'Don't get excited. It'll be a van, second-hand.'

She laughed. 'Well, so long as it goes all right.'

'Oh, it'll go all right. With me around, it won't have much option.'

There were four people in the saloon bar, none he knew. He chose a table in the corner, away from curious eyes that might peer round the edge of the partition separating them from the public bar. Annie asked for a dry sherry while Billy treated himself to a double Scotch from the solitary bottle on the shelf behind the bar. They sat on a settle, Billy swivelled sideways in his seat so as to see her better.

He said, 'So what's been happening while I was away?'

She made a show of racking her brains. 'Ohh, you know how it is – nothing much happens round here.' She was teasing him, throwing one of his more arrogant remarks back at him. 'No, we were cut off for quite a while in the blizzards. No trains, no buses, only tractors could get through. And no electricity in the afternoons, of course. The school closed down, and then we had no post for a while. But you know how people are here – they like a bit of a challenge. They like to feel they can cope with anything.'

'What about you?'

'Me?' she echoed innocently, understanding his meaning all too well but choosing to ignore it. 'Even less happening with me.'

He questioned her anyway, about the child, going into the sort of detail he hoped would please her, and the new job, and what she'd been doing; and all the time her tone, her looks and gestures were sending the message he wanted to hear, that there was no one else, that she was here for the same reason he was, to give it a go between them.

He bought another round. With the second drink the last of his tensions ebbed away, he felt a quiet, insistent elation. She was the right one for him, she always had been. Over the rim of his glass he drank in the sight of her long white neck, the curve of her breast under the woollen cardigan, the way her hair glinted with beams of colour, and the dark slant of her eyes looking across at him, sending their message.

Finishing her news, she said with pretended annoyance, 'I warned you there was nothing to tell. I want to hear about you and this business of yours.'

So he told her, first in outline, then in detail, about his idea to make large utility baskets to order for some of the bigger customers in London and the major cities, and deliver them direct to their doors, cutting out two sets of middlemen. 'It's just a matter of making the right contacts,' he said, 'and offering the right price. I've already got some interest from a laundry that looks after some of the big hotels. And an introduction to this bloke at Billingsgate Market.'

'It's a wonderful idea, Billy.'

'Course it is. It's going to make me rich.'

She choked back a bubbling laugh. 'It is, is it?'

'Well, there's no sense in working yourself half to death without making money, is there?'

'None at all!' Then, on a thoughtful note, she added, 'I'll say this . . . if anyone can do it, it's you, Billy.'

He wasn't used to votes of confidence; his chest swelled, his throat jammed, and he reached busily for his drink.

Misreading his silence, or understanding it too well, she said, 'I mean it.'

Not knowing what to say, he took refuge in practicalities.

'Can't get the thing off the ground without basket-makers, though.'

'Well, you've got Polish Stan, haven't you?' she said immediately. 'There's bound to be more where he came from. The Middlezoy Camp's full to busting.'

He wasn't sure it was going to be as simple as that, but her confidence swept him forward all the same. She made him feel everything was possible. On an impulse he told her so.

'It's because I believe it.'

He laughed, he couldn't have said why, and leaning forward said in a low voice, 'If you're not careful I'll rope you in to help.'

'Will you now?' she breathed. 'Well, I wouldn't say no to the work.'

'I couldn't pay much.'

'I can wait till you're rich.'

As he leant slowly towards her she held his gaze, closing her eyes only at the last minute. He kissed her softly, and felt her lips part under his. Drawing back a little, he whispered, 'So, Annie?'

'So,' she murmured.

They walked back to the cottage arm in arm. A low moon cast long strips of pale light across their path. He felt her shoulder press against his, and squeezed her arm closer. When they reached the porch he drew her to one side. He said through the thickness in his throat, 'You know, don't you – it wasn't just the business I came back for.'

Her face, pale and moon-washed, tilted up at him. 'No?'

He shook his head.

She murmured, 'What else was it then?'

'You know all right.'

She said nothing, but reached up and touched his hair.

He prompted, 'You're glad I came back then?'

'Yes, I'm glad.'

'We're on then, are we – you and me?'

She tilted her head to one side. 'So long as . . .'

'What?'

'You don't want to own me.'

Barely listening, he kissed her lightly. 'Own you?'

'Stop me working. Having my own life. I couldn't take that. I'd go mad.'

'Can't have you going mad.' He slipped his hand round her waist but exerted no pressure. 'So – we're on, are we?' He needed to hear her say it.

She swayed closer and said in a low voice, 'Yes, we're on.'

She began to say more but he stopped her with a kiss. Their tongues met, they kissed greedily, and she made a sighing sound. Her thighs came up against his and he felt a shudder of lust. Pulling at her coat he reached for her breast, but she drew back and gasped, 'Wait round the corner while I get rid of Margaret.'

As soon as the babysitter was safely out of sight, he slipped back to the door and she drew him inside. In the light from the landing they kissed hungrily again, before half falling into the darkened living room. Dragging at each other's clothes, they staggered to a settee before sliding down to the greater freedom of the floor. But he didn't want it to be hurried, unsatisfactory. He waited a moment, his mouth just above hers, breathing her breath, and watched her eyes open, liquid and black in the dim light. Sitting up, he pulled her up beside him and slowly removed the last of her clothes, kissing each new area of flesh as he did so. Then, dragging some cushions from the settee, he laid her on them and went slowly down her body with his lips and tongue, exploring the contours of her breast, the smooth belly, the dark secret places.

'We need to be careful,' she whispered as he finally rose above her.

But he was prepared. Nothing, however, had prepared him for the joy he felt when the moment came, the sense of rightness, of coming home after a long time away.

*

When Billy got down to the kitchen next morning Flor was already in her chair by the range and the breakfast cleared away.

He bent down and gave her a smile. 'How are you, Flor?'

She reached for his hand and gripped it.

'No more tears?'

She shook her head.

'Was it the lifting up and down stairs you were worried about? ''Cause I can do that just as well, you know.' He curled his arm in an impression of Charles Atlas. 'Big and strong, that's me.'

She gave her crazy lopsided smile, and on impulse he kissed her papery cheek.

On his way up to the withy shed he saw Stan leaning over the side of the pigsty emptying the contents of a bucket into the trough.

He called, 'What you got in there then?'

'Well, what in hell do you think? A weasel?'

Billy laughed aloud, and was amazed at this elation that had not dimmed or soured overnight.

He found the Polacks in the withy shed, lounging around, talking to an old round-shouldered man sitting on the floor with his back against the wall, in the process of making a basket.

Jozef glowered at Billy's cheerful greeting, while Wladyslaw gazed at him curiously.

'And you must be Polish Stan?'

The old man smiled and gave a casual salute.

'Can he make large baskets?' Billy asked Wladyslaw.

'You wish me to ask him?'

'Please.'

The two men talked in Polish, then Wladyslaw asked, 'How large is large?' After Billy had explained, they talked some more. 'He says yes,' Wladyslaw announced at last. 'But he would be slow. It is trouble in his bones. Large baskets will be difficult for him.'

'Does he know any other basket-makers in the camp?'

Further consultation. 'He knows one, maybe two, but after so long they try other things. One man is going to Canada soon. The other, he tries for work on fishing boats.'

'I'll pay a good wage.'

A last burst of Polish, then Wladyslaw said, 'He will ask. But it is best if you go to camp and ask the administrators. They will know if there are more basket-makers.'

Billy clapped him on the arm. 'Good man!'

Wladyslaw looked at him as if he were slightly mad, and perhaps he was just then.

Billy spent the rest of the day dismantling, oiling and reassembling the stripping machine. At six he bathed and put on his new suit. After downing a quick glass of cider he went up to the village hall, a place he had visited only once before at the age of seventeen, under considerable protest.

The woman on the door said proudly, 'We're sold out.'

'That's all right,' Billy said, handing over his one and six. 'I'll stand.'

Inside, a tinny piano was thumping out the accompaniment to a man and woman singing an old-fashioned duet. Billy combed the audience for the head of dark shining hair but couldn't see it. He wandered up the side, examining each row in turn. Then, just as he was beginning to think she wasn't there, she emerged from a room on the other side of the hall and crept into a seat in the second row. Moving forward, he leant against the wall where she couldn't fail to see him when she glanced round.

On the platform the end of the duet seemed a long time coming as the stolid couple warbled over and around the melody like two people forever in search of the right notes. When the applause finally sounded, Annie looked across and spotted him. She waved, then made a teasing face as if she couldn't believe he'd actually come.

He shook his head as if he couldn't believe it either.

After that the show seemed very slow. A choir came on and

sang interminable songs in an unwieldy harmony of bass and treble that reflected the singers' ages, old or very young with nothing much in between. Those in their twenties, Billy hardly needed reminding, were in the pubs. The choir was followed by a pianist performing a medley of popular tunes. And then, just when Billy thought the show must surely be coming to an end, a large woman wearing a lacy dress with a panel that hung over her ample bosom like a lampshade strode onto the platform and announced she was going to sing 'They Call Me Mimi' from the opera *La Bohème*. Billy had no way of telling if her voice was up to scratch – anything in this vein sounded like a screech to him – but her mannerisms caused a gurgle of laughter to rise perilously fast in his chest. The coquettish tilt of the head, the girlish hand pressed to the bosom, the coy, fast-fluttering eyelashes had him clamping a hand to his mouth to choke back explosions of laughter. He didn't dare look at Annie until the song was over. From the way she was biting her lip he guessed she had been battling too.

The raffle was drawn, everyone stood up to sing 'Jerusalem', and then at last it was over. As the audience began to move, Annie stationed herself with some other women behind a line of trestle tables and began pouring tea.

'You nearly had me going there,' she hissed in mock anger when he reached her side. 'That lady came all the way from Bridgwater to sing for us.'

'Best entertainment I've had in a long time,' Billy said truthfully.

'You're a bad influence,' she said.

'I do my best.'

Her eyes laughed at him. 'Would you like some tea?'

'I'd prefer a beer.'

'And while there's no beer?'

'Then I'll have tea.'

She was kept busy after that. He watched her fetching a fresh pot, measuring milk into the next line of cups, finding

extra sugar for an old boy who swore that anything short of
three lumps gave him a turn. He saw with pride that she had a
natural way with people, that even the old codgers couldn't
help but warm to her, and he felt a fresh surge of astonishment
and well-being at the thought that this woman could be – *was*
– his.

During a lull in her tea pouring she told him she would have
to stay and help clear up afterwards. 'I might be a while,' she
said. 'Why don't you go off to the pub and have a drink?'

'Trying to get rid of me?'

She gave her slow, wide smile. 'I don't want you saying
you've been deprived, that's all.'

'There's only one thing that could make me feel deprived.'

'Is that so?' she murmured. 'In that case you'll just have to
make do with the cider from my kitchen, won't you?'

She was called away then. Wandering off, he was drawn
into a group of old boys complaining about the floods and the
need for more pumps. No sooner had he escaped them than he
was cornered by Stan's neighbour from Sculley Farm blathering
on about fencing and vermin. Barely listening, he was all the
time alive to Annie's presence just a few feet away, to the fact
that she too was counting off the minutes till they could slip
away to the cottage. Every so often he stole a glance at her.
Twice, she caught his gaze and he felt a surge of excitement
and longing at what was to come.

When he next looked round she had disappeared. At first he
thought she must have taken a tray of dirty cups away, but
when she hadn't reappeared after five minutes he went looking
for her. In the side room a band of women were washing and
stacking teacups, but Annie wasn't among them. She wasn't
among the group shifting the piano either, nor the people
stacking away the rows of chairs. He wandered onto the stage
but the threadbare curtains concealed nothing but bare walls.
He made his way down the hall to the entrance lobby where
the ticket seller was counting the takings. He saw the door

marked Ladies' Toilet and feeling foolish realised where Annie must be. Not wanting to embarrass her he began to retreat, only to hear the door open and see a strange woman emerge.

People were drifting away in twos and threes. An elderly couple turned to speak to him but he kept moving, making another circuit of the hall before looking into the side room once again. The washing-up squad had dispersed, and he saw on the far side of the sink an outside door he hadn't noticed before. It was ajar and he pushed it open wider. The light spilled out to illuminate a strip of grass and a bushy hedge. He peered down the side of the hall towards the road but there was no one there. He was turning back when he caught a muffled sound coming from the darkness behind the open door. He went to look round the door, but at the last minute stopped short and waited, he couldn't have said why. After a moment or two he heard a man's voice speak in a low insistent tone, the words inaudible. Then came a woman's voice, anxious, pleading. Annie's voice.

He shoved his head out and saw them standing four or five yards away. In the darkness only their faces and hands were visible. The man was agitated, his head bowed low over hers, speaking fast and gesticulating with both hands. Annie was shaking her head slowly and rhythmically. Then she cried in a tone of distress, 'No, no, please don't, *please*,' and reached out to touch an imploring hand to Lyndon Hanley's face.

Billy felt something deadly strike at his heart. For an instant he was lost in a hot mist, he could neither see nor hear. He turned away, only to swing straight back and blunder towards them. Annie spotted him and stared dumbly. Following her gaze, Hanley shot Billy a brief glare before hissing something at Annie in an undertone. His words or the way he spoke them caused her to give a sharp unhappy gasp and beg, 'No, wait—'

If Billy hadn't known what he was going to do when he started towards them, he certainly knew now. But before he could get at Hanley, Annie had stepped between them and grasped his arm.

'Billy – no!' She clung to him doggedly as Hanley walked quickly away into the darkness. 'Billy – leave him! Leave him!'

He gave up with a shudder of undischarged anger and cried, 'What the hell was that about?'

'Nothing.'

Billy drew her towards the light and said thickly, 'Well, it looked like a hell of a lot to me.'

'He was just . . . upset, that's all.'

But it seemed to him that she was the one who was upset, that she was the one feeling – it came to him like another blow – hurt, maybe even – the thought made him sick – regret.

'Oh yes?' he said scornfully. 'And what was he upset about?'

She shook her head.

'I'm asking – what was it about?'

'I can't say.'

'Can't or won't?'

'Oh, Billy,' she sighed heavily.

'Oh, Billy, *what*?'

'Don't be like this.'

'I'm not being like *anything*. It's *you* who's being—' Unable to find the right word, he snapped, '*stupid*.'

He stepped back from her in an agony of uncertainty, longing for her to tease and cajole him back to her side, desperate for some small sign of reassurance. Instead, she stared at him and said, 'So little trust, Billy.'

'Well, what do you expect? You sneak outside with him, you cosy up—'

'*Cosy up?*'

'I saw you all right – touching him, pawing his face.'

She shook her head wearily and moved towards the door. 'Why don't you go and calm down, Billy? I can't talk to you like this.'

But his anxiety was running hot and high; he could not leave it alone. He put out a hand as if to hold her back. 'Was it *him* that was bothering *you*, then? Because if he was, I'll make bloody sure he doesn't do it again.'

'No, Billy, no.'

'What, then? *What?*'

'I've told you – it was nothing.'

'Give me a plain bloody answer!'

'I already have,' she declared, and disappeared into the hall.

He walked at a furious pace for many minutes until, coming abreast of her cottage, assailed by vivid memories of their love-making, he halted in a rage of longing. The plunge from sweet lustful expectation to misery overwhelmed him. He thought of waiting for her, but he was in no mood to endure the jollity of the pub; nor did he relish the ignominy of hanging around on her doorstep like some lovelorn idiot. In the end the sound of revellers spilling out of the George drove him away. Tucking his head down, he hurried across the road, rounded the bend in the churchyard wall and headed out of the village. Even then, he didn't feel safe until he had turned down the lane towards Crick Farm. He was hardly aware of his heels chiming on the stony surface until, nearing the brow of the last rise, he caught the sound of voices ahead. He trod more cautiously until, making out some high-pitched words in Polack-speak, he speeded up again. Gaining on them rapidly, he heard the deranged one's voice rise in a long screech of accusation and injury, followed by Wladyslaw's steady calming tones. They stopped at his approach and did not speak again until he was striding past, when Wladyslaw murmured, 'Hi, Billy.'

At the farm Billy went straight to the larder and, pulling out a jar of cider, took it to the table. He drank the first mugful in three gulps. At some point Wladyslaw came in and muttered goodnight before climbing the stairs to his room. Billy barely looked up. He was struggling with the image of Annie with Hanley. The scene when her hand reached out to caress his cheek kept flashing up like a picture on a cinema screen, bold, larger than life. He told himself that in the poor light he might have mistaken the gesture, that she had made it not from

affection but pity. But even as he began to persuade himself
of this, he saw again Hanley's aggressive stance and felt a
sickening conviction that something important had happened
between them.

When the drink did nothing to calm him, he went out again
and walked quickly back to the village.

Chapter Thirteen

———

MARJORIE STOOD by the wardrobe watching Bennett button his cardigan and said anxiously, 'Please don't go.'

'But I must.'

'You're not well.'

'I'll take an aspirin.'

'But you should be in bed, you know you should. Please, darling – just tell them you can't go. It's only a dead body, after all. It can wait till daylight. It can wait for another doctor, come to that. Why does it always have to be you?' Even as she said this, she took another cardigan from the wardrobe and put it on the chair in front of him.

'It won't take long,' he said.

'These things always take much longer than you think.'

He eyed the second cardigan uncertainly.

'No – wear both,' she said. 'Put it on top of the other one. There's a terrible wind.' Then, with a sigh of resignation she went downstairs, and he knew she would be heating some soup for the Thermos flask.

The man waiting in the hall was someone Bennett knew only by sight. 'Good morning, Mr – ?'

'Elkin.' He was about forty, and dressed in waterproofs and waders.

'Have the police been notified?'

'We went and told the constable at North Curry. It was him that said to come and fetch you.'

'The body was found in the Parrett, was it?'

'No, the Tone.'

'Well, if you wouldn't mind guiding me there, I'll be with you shortly.'

'No hurry, Doctor.'

Bennett went to the surgery and checked his bag for his report pad and pencil. He put in a spare pair of spectacles and a small torch to supplement the large torch he would pick up from the hall table. Then, more to assuage Marjorie than from any real hope of benefit, he swallowed two aspirin washed down with a gulp of the iron tonic he kept for his convalescent patients. When his bronchitis had flared up three days before, he had begun a course of the new antibiotic M&B, but either the antibiotics were having no effect or he had a viral infection because his head was pounding, his mouth dry, and he didn't need a thermometer to tell him he was running a fever.

Back in the hall, he asked, 'Will I need gumboots or waders, Mr Elkin?'

'Gumboots should do you, Doctor.'

He took some waterproof trousers as well; there was usually quite a bit of kneeling involved.

It was quarter to five by the time they set off. Bennett drove, with Elkin in the passenger seat, while Elkin's fishing companion followed in a van. A near-full moon glowed under a thin veil of racing cloud. It was meant to be the start of spring, but the wind was from the north-east and sharp as a lash.

'Where are we going?' Bennett asked.

'Hook Bridge. And then it's a short walk along the Curry bank, just on the bend there.'

'How did you find the body?'

'Well, we were just sitting there on the bank waiting for the elvers. You know – waiting for the top of the tide. But Walter, he decides to try his luck early. He stands there with his net, oh, a good half-hour before the tide turns. We keep telling him he's wasting his time, but he's a born hoper, is Walter. He don't take no notice of what anyone says. He stands there, net out, and all the elvers way out in midstream with not a thought of heading for the banks. So when he shouts that he's got something, well, we think he's having us on. But then he yells to bring the lamps close, and we know something's up. Whatever he's got, it's something heavy. Too heavy to lift without breaking the net, so we take the lamps closer and we look down into the water and we see what looks like a bunch of rags. Walter says, it's a person, but I says no, never. And then Brian, he says there's only one way to find out, and he wades in with his hook and drags the object into the bank. Well, then we see a hand, o' course, we see a head, and we realise what we've got. We pull him up onto the bank a ways, we take a look at him, but he was long gone. I'm no expert, Doctor, but I'd've said he'd been dead a while. As cold as cold could be.'

'Did you recognise him?'

'We all had a look, best we could, but none of us reckoned we'd seen him before. But then we're from the other side of Curry Moor, Doctor. We're from West Lyng.'

Drownings were a feature of the Levels. Bennett was called to at least one a year, sometimes as many as three, while in the county newspaper one read of perhaps four or five more. Some were the result of drunkenness, a stumble crossing a bridge on the way home from the pub, a wrong turn on the path; some were accidents, men poling their way home across flooded moors on the flimsiest of craft at night; some were suicides, though where no note was found the coroner was inclined to record the deaths as accidental. For some reason the drunks and suicides always seemed to end up in the Parrett. In fact Bennett couldn't remember the last time a body had been found in the Tone. Perhaps this was because the Parrett had a couple of sluices to catch the bodies coming down from Langport, perhaps because the Tone, in disgorging its waters into the Parrett at Burrowbridge, covertly disgorged its human cargo at the same time.

Elkin directed the doctor off the Athelney road into a lane which quickly gave way to a rutted drove-road. Bennett navigated with increasing caution as the glint of water appeared close on one side and then the other. They trundled over the

boards of Hook Bridge, and Elkin said, 'Best stop here, Doctor.' Bennett needed little encouragement. Just a short distance
ahead, the drove-road dipped down and vanished beneath the
flood waters of Curry Moor.

Climbing out of the car, Bennett met the full force of the
wind. It tore at the tails of his coat and forced him to drag his
cap tighter onto his head. On the moor the moonlit flood
waters were corrugated with ripples of black and silver, and a
crooked tree gave the look of a boat darkly sailing. Some way
down the river a cluster of lights winked and dipped at the
water's edge, and he guessed it was there they were heading.

They walked along the path in single file, Elkin lighting the
way with the big torch, his fishing companion bringing up the
rear. Small waves hissed and slapped at the river bank, and in
the aureole of the torch beam Bennett saw that the water was
angry and wind-torn.

At one point the flickering lights ahead seemed to dim,
almost to retreat, but it was only a trick of the wind, and soon
Bennett could make out two, then three figures waiting by the
hurricane lamps.

'Doctor?' The local bobby loomed up in uniform and
helmet.

'PC Longman, is it?'

'That's right, sir.'

'Are you ready for me to verify the death, Constable?' The
question was a formality; it was his only function in such cases.

'If you would, sir.'

The body was lying under a groundsheet just above the
water's edge on a steep bank that glistened blackly with mud.
Bennett went down cautiously, testing each step before trusting
his weight to it. PC Longman followed and, drawing back one
end of the groundsheet, shone his torch onto the body, which
was lying on its front, the face turned away towards the river,
one arm stretched out as if to touch the water.

Bennett took off a glove and put two fingers to the side of
the neck. It was ice cold, with no discernible pulse.

'I'll need him rolled over.'

'Right-ho.'

Bennett stood back while Elkin and PC Longman removed the groundsheet and attempted to turn the dead man over. The job was harder than it looked. Elkin pulled on one shoulder while PC Longman stood at the dead man's chest trying to get a grip on his clothing. At one point Elkin slipped and sat down abruptly, while the constable had to gouge his boot into the mud to get a firmer foothold, but finally, with a last heave, the body rolled over with heavy reluctance, the outstretched arm describing a wide arc in the air, the hand swiping across Elkin's face. Elkin jerked back and hastily wiped the mud from his cheek with rapid flicking movements.

Bennett knelt down and directed PC Longman to shine his torch from above and slightly to one side of the head.

Except for a strip of bare skin down the side of one cheek, the dead man's face was daubed in glutinous layers of mud which filled one eye socket, obscured the other, and imposed a dark abstruse landscape over the contours of the nose and mouth. Even so, there was a familiarity to the features that caused Bennett to utter a deep sigh.

PC Longman moved the torch a little. 'All right, Doctor?'

'Yes. Thank you.'

Bennett went through the necessary procedures, feeling for a pulse on the wrist, holding a stethoscope to several points on the chest, before closing his bag and standing up. 'What about washing some of the mud away, Constable?'

'I was going to suggest the very same thing, sir.'

One of the fishermen produced a bucket. Another waded into the river and, scooping up some water, poured it gently over the head of the dead man. The layers of mud bled slowly away to reveal a sculpted face with a long nose and deep-set eyes.

The constable slanted the torch at a different angle. 'Hello,' he said. 'I know this lad.'

'I think you'll find it's someone called Lyndon Hanley.'

'Indeed it is. Yes, that's precisely who it is. Arthur Hanley's son.' He sucked in his breath with an audible rasp. 'Dear me.'

There was a solemn pause during which the fishermen looked down at the white face with new respect. This was no drunk from Taunton, no suicide from Bridgwater; this was someone from the ridge, virtually one of their own.

'All right to move him now, Doctor?'

But Bennett was crouching down to look more closely at a wound on Lyndon's left temple. 'If you could shine the torch this way, Constable?' he asked politely.

On the curve of the frontal bone there was an area of laceration perhaps three inches by two, but it was the underlying indentation to the skull that held Bennett's attention. The skull was hard to crack, and even harder to stave in. This injury could only have been caused by a massive blow.

'Have you notified your superiors yet, Constable?'

'I'll be reporting to them directly I reach a telephone, Doctor. I don't go reporting to no one until I've seen the body in case it's a false alarm, if you understand me. I've been called out to a dead pig before now.'

'And your superiors will contact the pathologist straight away, will they?' He knew they would, but he wanted to impart a sense of urgency to the constable.

'They will indeed,' said the constable on a gruff note of rebuke, as if Bennett had impugned his own professionalism as well as that of his colleagues. 'And the coroner too. That goes without saying. Oh yes indeed, without delay.'

As if to bear this out, PC Longman briskly commanded the fishermen to help lift the body onto the top of the bank. 'Steady as you go!' he ordered, though it was he himself, stationed at the dead man's left shoulder, who let one arm fall and drag over the lip of the path. Once the body was on the path, they drew the groundsheet over it and weighted the corners down against the wind.

Unusually, Bennett offered to wait while PC Longman cycled home to make his calls. It wasn't that he doubted the fishermen's ability to keep watch, or that after so long in the profession he felt a sudden urge to keep company with the dead, who were as ever beyond loneliness; it was for Stella's sake that he felt he must wait, and for the parents', in the unlikely but not impossible event that they should ask.

Leaving Bennett to his vigil, the fishermen took their lamps and moved along the river to start fishing at a respectful distance. As Bennett stood alone on the path, the moon vanished behind a bank of denser clouds, sending a flurry of darkness racing over Curry Moor towards him, covering the silver-flecked sea with deep shadow. Ahead of the cloud came a blast of wind so strong it almost knocked him off his feet. Retreating, he went and sat on the grass close under the lip of the path where there was a little shelter, and, resting his arms on his knees, hunching his shoulders against the wind, settled down to wait. For a while he gazed at the fishermen moving about in the lamplight, hauling in shivering netfuls of elvers. But soon the rush and bluster of the night filled his ears and weighed on his eyelids, and he fell into a troubled doze. A confusion of images mingled with the buffeting of the wind and the ache in his lungs. He was returned to the darkness and rain of France, trying to organise the hurried evacuation of the dressing station. There was great urgency; the enemy had advanced and a bombardment was about to begin. But the transport failed to arrive, no one could tell him why. He felt the desperation of foreknowledge. He kept warning the orderlies to prepare for an attack, but they looked at him pityingly and took no notice. And then the foul air was upon them. He felt it catch in his lungs, and began the long painful struggle for breath.

Waking with his forehead slumped on his folded arms, he jerked his head upright. The asthma attack might yet be averted if he breathed slowly and systematically. He was always telling his lung patients to resist the urge to snatch at their breath, to try to ignore the sense of suffocation and panic and concentrate

on a single calming image, but he knew as well as any of them
how easy this was to say and how difficult to achieve.

Around him the darkness was lifting, the fishermen and
their lights were gone, and the river was in turmoil, coursing
away on the fast-falling tide, the wind kicking against the flow
in angry ruffles and peaks. He fixed his eyes on the far bank
and counted his breaths in and out to the image of the men
who had built and maintained the bank over the centuries and
the lives they had led.

The attack passed, but from habit and prudence he kept
counting. At some point he must have drifted into another light
doze, because the next thing he knew he was waking to the
sound of approaching voices and the sight of PC Longman looming up to offer him a hand up. Behind the constable were two
other uniformed policemen and two detectives in plain clothes.
The senior officer was a trim, wiry, businesslike man of forty-
odd who introduced himself as Detective Inspector Shearer.

When PC Longman had removed the groundsheet, Inspector
Shearer crouched down to scrutinise the body. After a while,
he said, 'Any thoughts, Doctor?'

'I'm no pathologist, Inspector.'

'But the injury here – it's serious?'

Bennett got down on one knee to take another look at the
strong young face. The indentation in the skull was both deeper
and longer than it had appeared in the torchlight: probably
three-quarters of an inch deep and some three inches long,
extending at an angle from the eyebrow to the hairline. The
skin was lacerated along the length of the injury, and was
completely split at the deepest point, exposing some brain
tissue. 'Yes, it's serious.'

'A possible cause of death?'

'I really couldn't say.'

'Don't worry, Doctor, I won't quote you. Strictly off the
record. For my ears only.'

'Very well. In my opinion it would almost certainly have

been fatal. Not necessarily instantaneously, but within a few hours, a few days at the most. After such an impact the brain swells, a great deal of pressure builds up inside the skull, and the brain tissue not immediately destroyed by the blow becomes irretrievably damaged.'

In the cold flat light Bennett saw some marks he hadn't noticed earlier: a cut on the right cheekbone surrounded by an area of bruising. This bruising was well-established. It served to emphasise what he had already seen but not fully absorbed – that there was almost no bruising around the indentation in the skull. The implication of this was unmistakable – that the blow to the temple was virtually simultaneous with death.

He said, 'He could have drowned first, of course.'

The inspector gave him a long pensive stare. 'Yes indeed. Any thoughts on how long he'd been in the water?'

'I couldn't begin to speculate, I'm afraid. I can only tell you that when I first examined the body it was quite cold.'

'That's the trouble with water,' said the inspector cryptically.

'You've arranged a pathologist?'

The inspector nodded. 'The forensic expert from Bristol.' With a last squint at the head injury, he straightened up and began to look up and down the river with his quick, eager eyes.

Bennett stood up more slowly. He volunteered, 'The river was high when the body was found.'

Shearer gave a preoccupied nod. 'Indeed?'

'And the tide still coming in. Though quite slowly, I believe.'

Shearer glanced down at the racing torrent before resuming his survey of the further reaches of the river. 'Yes . . . thank you, Doctor.' His eyes still on the horizon, he called sharply to one of his men. 'Willis?'

The second plain-clothes man stepped forward. 'Sir.'

'We'll be needing a map marked with the places that offer access to the river, both above and below this point. Access and *near* access. Bridges, paths, roads that finish at or near the river. Got me?'

'Yes, sir.'

'And, Willis?'

'Sir.'

'Nothing that's currently under water, if you don't mind.'

'Sir.'

Sighting PC Longman, the inspector beckoned him over. Before the two men had a chance to speak, Bennett said, 'If you've no more need of me, Inspector?'

'Of course, Doctor. Thank you for your assistance.'

'The family – you'll be notifying them soon?'

'Within half an hour.'

Bennett hesitated. He knew there was something he should mention, something that followed on from a recent train of thought, but the idea hovered on the periphery of his consciousness, refusing to form. Defeated, he said weakly, 'Well, good-bye then.'

The inspector offered him a fleeting professional smile before fixing his eager eyes once more on the task ahead.

Bennett slept for an hour and woke feeling hot and weak and troubled. The fever was still on him, there was a sharp catch in his lungs, he had the Hanley family to visit, and the unformed thought still pressed on him, just out of reach on the edges of his mind. Marjorie brought him tea, which he followed with a cup of coffee made with the best part of a week's ration. But neither the tea nor the strong coffee did much for his fatigue, still less his head. It was a struggle to get through his morning visits, and when he set out for the Hanleys he broke into a damp sweat, his stomach constricted with the threat of nausea, and the daylight seemed unbearably bright.

There were two cars outside the Hanleys' house and two more in the yard. It was a job to decide where to park. Manoeuvring at last into a corner of the yard, he pulled on the handbrake and looked up to find himself gazing at the tractor shed. It might have been the sight of the empty space where

Arthur Hanley's car normally stood, or the memory of Lyndon opening the front door to him, or a blend of other half-realised images, but the elusive thought finally slid into his mind. It was so obvious that he sighed aloud. It was, of course, the matter of the motorbike. He should have told the police about Lyndon Hanley's motorbike so that they could start to search for it. After more thought, he gave a softer sigh, this time of relief, as it came to him that they would certainly know about it by now, indeed would probably have found it, and that his responsibility, such as it was, was over.

The front door was answered by Stella's father George, a large man with a florid complexion who in the long summer afternoons batted at number eight. George gave an awkward smile. 'Good of you to come.'

On the far side of the hall Stella's mother appeared briefly in the living-room doorway to see who had arrived, while another woman looked out of the kitchen before shyly retreating again.

'How are they bearing up?' Bennett asked.

The language of grief did not come easily to George. After some searching, he muttered, 'Janet's taking it pretty bad.'

'And Arthur?'

'I don't think it's sunk in yet. He's been too busy. Didn't get back from the police till eleven, and now he's gone off to see them again.'

'Any news on how Lyndon got into the river?'

George shook his head. 'Nothing yet.'

'Have they found the motorbike?'

'Not that I've heard.'

From the living room Bennett could hear the soft murmur of female voices and, rising over them now and again, a low moan. 'Janet's in there, is she?'

George nodded and, gesturing briefly for Bennett to go ahead, took a small apologetic step towards the kitchen to show that he would not be going with him.

As Bennett started across the hall he heard light feet on the stairs and looked up to see Stella coming rapidly down. Her eyes were fixed urgently on him as though she'd heard his voice and was coming specially to see him, an impression reinforced by the staying gesture she made as she covered the last few feet between them, a lift of one hand, a single shake of the head, to forestall him from speaking.

George had paused to see what was happening, but as Stella drew Bennett further into the hall he ducked his head and vanished into the kitchen.

Stella's face was very white, her eyes swollen from crying, the area around her nostrils inflamed from the chafing of a wet handkerchief. She said rapidly in a voice that shook a little, 'Doctor, please – they're going to get completely the wrong idea unless you go and tell them. It's that fool Frank Carr. He came here with some story about a fight – wanting to know if he should go and tell the police. And of course Uncle Arthur couldn't *wait* to go and tell them. Longing for a reason, you see. Longing for someone to blame. And now they've gone to the police in Taunton. Please, Doctor,' she pleaded breathlessly. 'Please go and tell them – before it gets out of hand. Tell them you know Wladyslaw. Tell them he'd never harm a soul.'

Bennett had already put a hand on her shoulder. Now he said, 'Slow down, Stella. Just slow down.'

She took a ragged breath and nodded vehemently.

'This fight that Frank's talking about – who was meant to be involved?'

'Lyndon and Wladyslaw. And Jozef as well. I think so, anyway. I only heard the end of it, but I think that's what Frank was saying – that it was the three of them.'

'And when was this meant to have happened?'

She gave a fierce sigh. 'Last night.'

'And the reason?'

'Oh, no reason! How could there be any reason? No – there was no reason.' Her eyes brimmed with sudden tears. 'Please, Doctor – make them understand this is *madness*. Make them realise there's no one to blame. Lyndon's dead and nothing's going to bring him back. Nothing.' Her face contorted and reddened.

'But Stella, I'm not sure quite what I can do.'

'Oh, please.' She dragged on his arm like a child.

'The police will make whatever enquiries they want to make. I can hardly ask them to stop.'

Dropping her head, Stella pressed a hand over her eyes and began to sob.

He gazed at her helplessly. 'I could try to find out what's happening, I suppose. I could go and talk to them.'

She lowered her hand to her mouth and looked at him through her tears.

'That's all I can do, Stella.'

She nodded dumbly and in a swift movement laid her head against his shoulder and embraced him untidily, before hurrying back towards the stairs.

Bennett did not stay long with Janet Hanley. Sometimes the bereaved wanted to reminisce, sometimes to ponder the mystery of death and the chances of eternal life; but sometimes they simply wanted to be left alone with their families. When Janet Hanley failed to respond to his questions and finally gestured him away, he bowed to her wishes and, leaving a sleeping draught for the night, said he would return next day.

He set out for Taunton in the odd state of light-headedness that exhaustion and illness can bring. His lungs were hurting, the daylight seemed to beat hard on his brain, and a cluster of shifting dots had began to dance menacingly in the corner of his vision. His sense of time and distance became spasmodic, so that the journey seemed to progress in strange leaps, with landmarks looming up out of nowhere and the intervening terrain lost to consciousness, even memory.

At this time on a Sunday there were few cars on the streets of Taunton and even fewer people. Inside the police station, however, it could have been a weekday in a busy firm. As

Bennett announced himself to the uniformed desk officer he heard phones ringing and the murmur of voices and the clip of heels hurrying along corridors. A part of his mind registered the thought that this level of activity was unexpected for a Sunday. It didn't occur to him to connect it with Lyndon's death, the idea would have seemed out of all proportion.

'If you'd like to wait in there, sir.' The desk officer indicated a side room painted cream and brown with a narrow window and a line of wooden chairs and the occasional cigarette-scarred table pushed hard against the walls. An unkempt woman with glaring eyes appeared to be the only occupant until, stepping inside, Bennett saw a man sitting in the near corner. It was Frank Carr.

'Well, I never!' Frank cried, getting hastily to his feet. 'Hello, Doctor!' Then, in a great dawning of understanding, he said in a low conspiratorial voice, 'You must be here for the same reason as I am.'

'I expect so, yes.' Bennett indicated the chair next to Frank's. 'May I?'

'By all means!' Frank waited attentively until Bennett had taken his seat before perching on the edge of his chair and pulling a packet of Player's from his pocket. 'Cigarette, Doctor?'

'No, thanks.'

Tapping one out, Frank announced, 'Don't usually partake myself, but in the circumstances – thought it might calm the nerves.' He struck a match and held it to the cigarette with childlike concentration before turning his eyes avidly on Bennett's. 'Shocking business, eh, Doctor? Shocking.'

'Yes. Yes, it is.'

'Saw him in the George only last night, large as life, enjoying a pint or two, having a joke with the rest of us. You just never know what's round the corner, do you? Here one minute, then—' He pulled down his mouth in an expression of doom.

Bennett nodded sagely.

'You, er – know how he was found, do you, Doctor?'

'Yes. I attended the scene.'

Frank looked at him with awe. 'Oh, forgive me, Doctor. I hadn't realised. Yes, of course . . . Yes. In which case you *know*, then. You know how it was.'

'I don't know anything, Frank. I prefer to leave that to the police.'

'Oh yes, indeed. Yes . . . We can only play our part. We can only make our contribution.' With a glance at the unkempt woman on the other side of the room Frank lowered his voice confidingly. 'That's the reason I'm here, see, Doctor. 'Cause I saw something last night, this *incident* which might just have a bearing, if you understand me.'

Bennett coughed and felt a pain shoot up under his ribs. 'Oh yes?'

'I wasn't sure what was best to begin with,' Frank commented. 'I mean, you don't want to go stirring up trouble where it's not warranted, do you? But seeing as someone has *died* and those Poles of Stan Thorne's were involved – well, I felt it wouldn't be right to let the matter rest. I felt—'

Bennett coughed and gasped and could not catch his breath. 'You all right, Doctor?'

'Fine,' he spluttered. 'Please – do go on.'

'I didn't feel I could go to the police though, not straight off, not without getting Arthur's say-so. So when I went to pay my respects, I asked him. I said, this is what I saw, Arthur – what do you think I should do? Should I go and tell them? Well, he had no doubts, none at all. In fact he brought me here himself. Yes, it was a weight off my mind, I can tell you, knowing he was with me on this. Oh yes – a weight and a half. And of course, the police – they listened all right. They took a statement from me. It's evidence, see. Evidence.'

A tight band had settled around Bennett's lungs, usually the harbinger of an asthma attack, and he tried to concentrate on his breathing. 'Frank, the cigarette – would you mind? Just till I get over this coughing.'

'Course, Doctor. You should have said.' He turned away and stubbed the cigarette out in the nearest ashtray.

Bennett took a slow breath. 'So, what was it you saw, Frank?'

'I saw a fight, that's what I saw! Yes, right outside the George. I came out and there they were, having a set-to, fists and all.'

'They being?'

'Those Poles! Yelling and shouting they were, before wading in and punching Lyndon to the floor.'

'And it was both the Poles, was it? Both were fighting?'

'Ohh, yes. Each as bad as the other.'

'You could see in the dark? It *was* dark, wasn't it?'

Frank frowned at the slant Bennett's questions were taking. 'There was the light from the pub, and no mistake.'

'And you're sure the other one was Lyndon Hanley?'

'I know what I saw,' Frank said stiffly, taking offence. 'It was Lyndon all right. I wouldn't mistake a thing like that. Saw the whole thing, clear as day. Poor devil never had a chance, they were on him so quick.'

There was a discrepancy in the story somewhere, but Bennett didn't feel he could press Frank any further. 'So how did it end?'

Frank stated self-righteously, 'I stopped it myself, that's what. I yelled at them to lay off.'

'And they did?'

'Ohh yes, they stopped all right.'

'And then? What happened after that, Frank?'

But Frank's eyes had shifted to a point above Bennett's head. Following his gaze, Bennett turned to see Arthur Hanley standing in the doorway. Getting to his feet, Bennett went and shook his hand gravely, before drawing him towards the relative privacy of the front lobby. 'I'm so very sorry,' he said in a low voice. 'Please accept my condolences.'

'I told you it was a mistake to let them into the country,' Hanley said with cold rancour. 'I told you what would happen.'

Bennett almost said something, but thought better of it.

'They're brutes. Vermin. The lowest of the low.'

Bennett chose his words with the sense of picking his way through a minefield. 'But Arthur . . . can we be certain they were involved? Do we know—'

'They killed my son. They killed him, and I'm going to see 'em hang for it.'

For a moment Bennett could only stare at him. When he finally spoke, it was gently, in a tone of concern. 'Perhaps . . . don't you think . . . it might be best to wait until the police have finished their investigation before—'

'Wait?'

'Yes. For their findings.'

Something in this was the undoing of Hanley. 'For God's sake!' he howled, pushing his fists down to his sides and shaking with fury. 'They killed my son!' His face turned crimson and the veins stood out from his temples in tight bunches. 'They – killed – my – son!'

Bennett made a gesture of retreat. 'I understand,' he said rapidly. 'Please don't distress yourself. Would you like some water? Shall I—'

'They *attacked* him and then they *hit* him when he was down.'

Bennett was careful to make no response.

'His *head* was stove in.'

Still Bennett said nothing.

'They treated him worse than an animal, because they're worse than animals themselves! Vermin!'

And then it was over as quickly as it had begun. Hanley exhaled with a shudder and screwed his eyes shut while he hauled himself back from the brink.

During Hanley's tirade Frank had appeared from the side room and Inspector Shearer from the corridor.

Bennett murmured, 'See him home, will you, Frank? Tell him I'll call in later.'

'Yes, Doctor.'

Bennett stood on the step and watched them go. When he came back into the lobby, Shearer was waiting with the look of a man who is pressed for time.

'Doctor? You wanted to see me?'

Bennett mustered his story. 'Yes, Inspector. Yes . . . The motorbike. You know Lyndon had a motorbike?'

'Yes.'

'Well, I think you should also know that he used to drive it very fast, not to mention dangerously. And that he occasionally – no, *more* than occasionally – used to drive it while under the influence of drink.'

The inspector absorbed this slowly, with a series of small nods. 'Indeed?'

'I patched him up once after an accident.'

'Did you now?'

'He hit his head flying over a wall. Lucky to have escaped without serious injury.'

'Indeed?'

'And he'd certainly had a few drinks on that occasion.'

'Well . . . I'm most grateful. Thank you for letting me know, Doctor.' With a flash of his bleak professional smile, the inspector prepared to move off.

Bennett detained him with a move of one hand. 'And, er . . . I wasn't sure if you wanted any information on tides, river flow . . . that sort of thing. It was an equinoctial spring tide last night . . . very high . . .' He trailed off indecisively.

'Thank you, but we have someone to advise us on these things.'

'Ah. Of course.'

There was a pause while Inspector Shearer waited to see if Bennett had anything more to say and Bennett wondered how best to broach the subject of the Poles.

'Obviously Arthur Hanley is deeply shocked,' Bennett said.

'Obviously.'

'He seems to have got the idea that Lyndon was attacked and killed.'

The inspector's expression did not alter.

'And that the two Poles in the village were somehow to blame.'

The inspector tucked in his chin and crossed his arms in the stance of a man who is about to be subjected to an opinion he does not need and does not want.

'But I feel sure he's got quite the wrong end of the stick, Inspector. I happen to know Wladyslaw Malinowski extremely well, and I can vouch for him without reservation. He couldn't possibly have been involved in something like that.' Bennett halted, aware that he was arguing against the available evidence. 'I gather there was some sort of dispute last night,' he continued awkwardly. 'But I'm sure you'll find it was just a harmless scuffle, an excess of high spirits after an evening in the pub. Wladyslaw is an extremely peaceable chap, a bookish sort of fellow. He'd never resort to violence, and I'm certain he would never encourage anyone else to do so either.'

At the end of this speech the inspector's expression had if anything grown harder, and for a moment Bennett imagined the men of the Polish Corps as this seasoned policeman might see them, as volatile foreigners with ungovernable temperaments, battle-hardened campaigners from war-torn lands who, far from abhorring violence, retained a dangerous taste for it.

Bennett switched to firmer ground. 'But surely Lyndon's death was an accident anyway?' he said. 'Surely he just crashed into the river?'

The inspector lifted his chin and raised his eyebrows in an expression of absorption. 'Something to consider, I'm sure. Thank you for your thoughts, Doctor. Most grateful.'

Bennett watched the inspector walk briskly away with the feeling that he had argued his case badly, indeed that he might have done better not to have spoken at all.

Chapter Fourteen

THE BICYCLE chain had developed a habit of slipping on the
uphill stretches and there was a strong headwind on the ridge,
but by pedalling hard and taking the downhill section of the
ridge road at breakneck speed Wladyslaw managed to reach
Middlezoy in under fifteen minutes. Skirting the village, he did
not take his usual turn to Camp B but stayed on the top road
and sped into Camp C through the main gate. Keeping off the
main paths, he wove through the accumulation of chocked-up
cars, cannibalised vans, and makeshift sheds that had grown up
around the squatters' huts, and emerged into the Polish sector
near the bottom of the camp. It was a long time since he'd visited
the godmothers and reaching the third avenue he slowed down
until he recognised a familiar bunch of dried flowers through
the misty bottle-glass of a front window. Dropping the bicycle
on the grass, he rapped briefly on the door before going in.
The communal area was empty, the hut silent. He paused uncertainly. It was the time on a Sunday afternoon when there were
no organised activities in the camp, and people might be anywhere, playing cards or visiting friends or out for a walk.
Or – as he turned to leave he caught a muffled snore from the
passageway – taking a doze. He called Alina's name softly, then
Danuta's, before remembering he had no time for politeness.
Calling again in a peremptory tone, he heard the creaking of a
bed and a woman's voice grunting a drowsy hello.

He said, 'It's me, Wladyslaw.'

Eventually a door opened and Danuta put her head out.
'Well, well, what a surprise,' she sang in slow rapture.

'Danuta, I'm looking for Jozef. Have you seen him anywhere?'

Something in his tone made her pause and peer at him sharply. 'One minute.' She went back into her cubicle and shuffled about before emerging with her blouse half buttoned and wisps of hair sticking out at odd angles. 'Jozef? No, Wladyslaw, I haven't seen him for – oh, it must be two weeks now. Why do you ask?'

'I hoped he might have come here, that's all.'

'Not a sign. And, apart from going to Mass first thing, I've been here all day.' Danuta swept some loose hair back from her face and fumbled with an unfastened button. 'Why, is there something wrong?'

'I'm afraid so, yes.'

She tutted anxiously. 'He hasn't been drinking too much again, has he? Making himself ill?'

'It's not that.'

'What, then? A squabble?'

'Worse. He quarrelled with this man, and now the man's dead.'

Danuta abandoned her buttons and searched his face. 'Dead? I don't understand. Are you saying Jozef was responsible?'

'No, not at all. It's what other people might say that worries me. And what Jozef believes they will say.'

'He thinks he'll be blamed?'

Wladyslaw gave a heavy sigh. 'There was a bit of a skirmish last night. Jozef was rather the worse for drink and got overexcited. Before I could pull him away, the stupid idiot swung a wild punch at this fellow. The blow wasn't hard, more of a tap really, but it drew some blood. And it was seen. That's the point – it was witnessed. And now I must find Jozef before he does anything foolish.'

He moved towards the door, but Danuta flung out a hand to restrain him.

'But who was this man? What was the quarrel about?'

'It was the fellow who got him the job in London, the one he fell out with over—'

'You mean the *Lyndon* man?'

'Yes.'

'Oh, my Lord!' She clapped a hand to her breast and exhaled in a long, slow shudder of dismay. 'He's dead?'

'Yes.'

'How did he die?'

'His body was pulled out of the river, that's all I know.'

Danuta uttered a succession of sighs on varying notes of anxiety and disbelief before muttering distractedly, 'I always said he was trouble, that fellow. Right from the beginning when Jozef had that collapse and he brought him to our door. Oh, he showed great solicitude and concern. Yes, one couldn't fault him on that score. Coming to see if Jozef was all right. Encouraging him to think he had a friend. But all the time filling his head with ideas about London. Taking no account of Josef's ability to cope. Ignoring his precarious state. No, he was a bad influence, that man. I always said so. And in death too, it seems. But, Wladyslaw, what are you telling me? That Jozef has run away?'

'He disappeared soon after we heard the news. Whether he's actually gone . . .' Wladyslaw gave a rapid shrug. 'But you know how he is – quick to believe the worst.'

'Running away won't look good.'

'No,' he agreed as he opened the door. 'But it's not the accusations that worry me, Danuta, it's what he might do if – when – they try to catch him. It's his mental state that concerns me.'

'Yes – you're right! Yes! He'll take it badly. Oh dear, oh dear! What can we do, Wladyslaw?'

But he couldn't answer that and, when he waved from the bottom of the steps, he saw that Danuta was weeping softly.

He cycled across the fields to Camp B and went to the administration block. On Sundays there were few staff on duty and he half expected to find it closed, but the door was

unlocked and a clerk was sitting at the reception desk, pretending to look busy.

'Major Rafalski's unavailable,' he said.

'But he's here?'

'He's occupied.'

'Could you tell him it's urgent?'

'When he's next available, I could mention it, yes. If you'd
like to wait.'

Wladyslaw turned away as if to take a chair but walked on
and entered Rafalski's office with the briefest of knocks.

There were three of them, all standing. Rafalski was behind
his desk, arms crossed, a knuckle resting pensively against his
mouth, the British liaison officer was opposite, his hands on
the back of a chair, and a junior Polish officer was by the side
of the desk, virtually at attention. Whoever had been talking
stopped instantly, their heads turned and they stared at him.
The silence that followed was oddly charged. Rafalski slowly
dropped his hand from his mouth, the liaison officer lifted his
eyebrows in mute comment, and the junior officer looked from
one to the other while he tried to work out what was going on.

'Ah,' Rafalski murmured at last. 'Come in, won't you,
Malinowski?'

At the mention of Wladyslaw's name the junior officer
glared at him askance and Wladyslaw had confirmation, if
confirmation were needed, of what had been under discussion
when he entered the room.

Rafalski said to the young officer, 'Please convey my thanks
to Captain Robertson and ask him if he would be kind enough
to excuse us.'

When the junior officer had translated this into English,
Robertson gave a nod and with a last glance at Wladyslaw left
the room. Rafalski ordered the young officer to follow, then,
gesturing Wladyslaw to a chair, sat at his desk and regarded
him solemnly over steepled hands.

'The British police were here,' he said. 'They want to

question you and Jozef Walczak about the death of a local man.'

'Yes, I was rather afraid they might.'

'Well? What do you have to say?'

'Neither of us had anything to do with it. You have my word.'

Rafalski nodded, unsurprised. 'What reason might they have for thinking that you did?'

'Oh, Jozef had argued with the fellow, and took a swing at him. That was all there was to it, I assure you. One weak punch.'

'And you?'

'Me?'

'You had no argument with this man?'

'No.' Even as Wladyslaw said this, it occurred to him that losing out in love might be seen as more than enough reason for hostility.

'So it was just Walczak?'

'Yes.'

'What was the argument about?'

'Oh, the two of them had been friends at one point but had fallen out, and Jozef still felt angry about it. He can get rather hotheaded on these occasions, especially when he's got a few drinks inside him.'

'Hotheaded?' Rafalski gave a small frown. 'I would avoid that word when talking to the British police, if I were you, Malinowski. It's not likely to help his case.'

'Excitable, then.'

Rafalski's frown deepened. 'From what I have observed, the British distrust excitability almost as much as they distrust emotion, which is saying something. No, I'd keep it to an excess of drink, if I were you. That's something the British understand well enough. Where's Walczak now?'

'I don't know. I came here to look for him.'

'Do you think he's gone on the run?'

'It's possible.'

Rafalski gave a weary sigh and rested his fingertips lightly against his temples. 'What on earth would possess him to do that? How could he imagine it would help?' He lifted his head and fixed Wladyslaw with a narrow gaze. 'Or was he already in trouble? Was that why you failed to tell me he was working with you at the farm?'

'I didn't want to put you in a difficult position.'

'You didn't believe I would exercise my judgement?' Rafalski asked in the tone of a disappointed parent, only to dismiss the question with a twist of one hand. 'What was he in trouble for?'

'He was blamed for some petty theft at his workplace in London.'

Rafalski gave a bitter sigh. 'This is how it ends for us. We drift away like a rabble army, reduced to begging for the lowest jobs and distrusted for our trouble. We are treated like thieves and vagabonds, like the vanquished instead of the victors. But don't get me started on that subject!' He straightened his back and pushed his hands flat on the desk top. 'So . . . will you give yourself up, Malinowski? Or will you wait for them to find you?'

Wladyslaw was startled by his choice of words. 'Good Lord, you make it sound as though they're going to arrest me.'

'I really couldn't say what they intend.' The major's tone suggested that anything was possible with the British. 'But they made it clear that they wanted to speak to both of you as soon as possible. If you decided to go and see them now I could arrange for a liaison man to accompany you.'

'Thank you, but no,' said Wladyslaw, getting rapidly to his feet. 'I must try to find Jozef first.'

'As you wish. But, Malinowski? When you do get to see the police, I would advise having a liaison officer and interpreter present. To avoid misunderstandings.'

On the return journey the wind was strong on Wladyslaw's back, pushing him like a giant hand. Yet he couldn't go fast enough. He kept seeing Jozef's expression when Stan had told them the news of Lyndon Hanley's death, how he had been very still at first, then as Stan recounted the sparse details – the body found in the River Tone, 'bobbing down' with the tide – conflicting emotions had begun to chase over his face. Confusion and doubt, what might have been remorse, but most of all a bleak understanding: that he was fated to attract suffering, that he always had done in the past and, now it seemed, always would, that a new country, peace, and relative freedom counted for nothing because the fault lay deep in himself and could never be eradicated. Disaster oozed from him like a body smell; he felt himself hopelessly contaminated.

Reading this in his face, Wladyslaw said earnestly, 'It was an accident, I'm sure. It was that motorbike.' But Jozef was beyond such easy remedy: Wladyslaw could read that in his face as well.

While Wladyslaw gave half an ear to Stan rambling on about bodies in the River Tone, he watched Jozef go to the door of the withy shed and pull out his cigarettes. When Wladyslaw glanced round a moment later, he was still there, exhaling a stream of smoke. A minute or so after that and he had vanished. Suppressing instinctive alarm, Wladyslaw put his head into the apple store and the house. He searched the outbuildings, the orchard, and the meadow. With increasing urgency, he scanned the wind-ruffled flood waters, the semi-submerged drove-roads and boggy footpaths along the moor-land edge. Returning to the apple store, he found everything in its usual chaotic state, Jozef's oilskins strewn over the unmade bed, his gumboots across the floor, while at the foot of the bed his open kitbag spilled spare clothing and old Polish-language newspapers. Wladyslaw attached little significance to the presence of the clothing – it would be typical of Jozef to abandon it – but delving deeper into the bag he took heart from the discovery of Jozef's most treasured possessions – the family photograph in its heavy frame, an antique locket, and a small metal box containing postcards and letters and dog-eared snapshots. He told himself that Jozef would not leave these things behind, that he was bound to return for them sooner or later. Unless he had taken fright in a very big way. Unless he had decided to run for ever. Unless— But some thoughts were too depressing to pursue, and when he remembered the god-mothers he seized avidly on the idea that Jozef would go there, that it was the obvious place for him to go. Even when he failed to overtake Jozef on the road to Middlezoy he persuaded himself that Jozef had managed to hitch a lift.

Now, as Wladyslaw peddled back over Stanmoor Bridge, he considered taking the low road to Athelney Station to see if Jozef was waiting for a train there, only to rule it out almost straight away. Jozef would be too impatient and too unorgan-ised to settle for a train. If he had decided to get away, he would simply have started walking.

With a sense that he had wasted his last chance of finding Jozef, Wladyslaw started up the ridge road, then, for the sake of covering another route, cut down onto a footpath that meandered along the pastures bordering the moor. It was hard going in places, the path sometimes muddy, sometimes laid with rough stones, and twice he had to lift the bicycle over gates. One pasture was divided by the railway line, another was dotted with sheep, but there were no people, and no Jozef.

Approaching Crick Farm, the path rose diagonally across a broad pasture towards the farm's upper boundary. The angular withy shed was visible from a long way off, as was the roof of the house, but a slight undulation in the contours of the slope hid the body of the house and the two cars almost concealed behind the racks of hurdle wood until he was relatively close. Only a section of one car's bonnet was showing and even less of the other's roof, but both were black, and both, he had little doubt, belonged to the police.

He pedalled hard up the last of the slope and along the boundary fence at the top of the meadow before turning in through the gate. Coasting down the track, he saw Stan standing in the yard with two men, and below them, coming up the drove-road, a bunch of uniformed policemen in tight formation. At first Wladyslaw couldn't make out what locked them together, then he saw Jozef's head jerk up from their midst and his legs flailing uselessly. One moment Jozef seemed to struggle, the next to collapse, so that the policemen were drawn tighter together by the effort of dragging him along. Lastly came Billy, with a shotgun over his shoulder.

Halting in a judder of brakes, Wladyslaw ran over and shouted, 'Jozef! Are you all right?'

Jozef's head lifted, but the timing was coincidental: his eyes were jammed shut, his teeth bared; he wasn't seeing anything and he wasn't hearing much either. He struggled again, a twist of his shoulders, a wild swing of his head, and Wladyslaw realised his hands were manacled. As one of the uniformed men opened a car door, another pushed Jozef's head down, and they bundled him head-first into the back seat.

Wladyslaw said to the approaching plain-clothes officers, 'This is not a violent man.'

'Are you Wladyslaw Malinowski?' asked the older one.

'This is not a violent man!' Wladyslaw repeated forcefully.

'He resisted arrest, sir. We were forced to restrain him. Now, if I might ask you to accompany me to the police station?'

'Yes, yes!' Wladyslaw cried impatiently. Then, on a note of reason: 'But, Officer, I tell you – he knows nothing of this man's death. And me also. We were here last night, both of us. Billy – he will tell you—'

But when he turned to look for Billy, it was to see him walking rapidly away towards the house.

'I'm sorry about Hanley.' Billy was panting hard from his bike ride up the hill; his words arrived in a rush.

Annie was standing in the doorway wearing a coat; coming or going he couldn't tell. She was waiting for him to say more, but when he tried to speak again his tongue felt thick, it seemed to stick to the roof of his mouth; the words came with painful slowness. 'And I'm sorry . . . for what I said . . . to you.'

She dropped her eyes momentarily, but her expression told him it wasn't enough.

'I wasn't thinking straight.'

'No.'

Again it was a wrench to speak. 'It was because of . . . the way I felt about you – *feel* about you. It made me . . .' He made a gesture, helpless, conciliatory, but still she offered no help. '. . . stupid.'

'You can say that again.'

Impatient with himself, aware that he must not waste this opportunity, he said boldly, 'You're the only one for me, Annie. Always were. Always will be.'

She dipped her head rapidly to look at her feet. When she looked up again, it was with a slow nod, a glimmer of a smile, which gave him a jolt of absurd happiness.

She stood back to let him in and he saw the child standing there, also dressed to go out. Taking off the child's coat, Annie asked her to go and play for a while.

In the kitchen they embraced silently, before she moved away to fill the kettle. 'They're dragging the river at Stanmoor Bridge.'

Relief made him slow on the uptake. 'What for?'

'The motorbike. They reckon that's where it must be. Something to do with the tide – I don't understand exactly. But Stanmoor Bridge makes sense all right. That's the way he would have gone. And there's a slight bend there, just before the bridge, enough of a bend for him to miss it, the stupid bloody idiot.' She said it fiercely, with affection and sorrow.

'They think he might have crashed, then?'

'Of course,' she said, an odd note in her voice. 'What else would he have done?'

He felt he must be missing something obvious. 'It's the police who're dragging the river?'

'Yes. Constable Longman, with some Burrowbridge men.'

'And it was an accident?'

Again, the strange look. 'Yes. Why do you keep asking?'

'Because the Taunton police seem to be thinking a bit differently. They've just arrested the Polacks and hauled them off for questioning.'

'Wladyslaw? Jozef? But why?'

'They didn't say.'

'To do with Lyndon's death, though?'

'Yes.'

'But what . . .?' She pressed a hand to her forehead while she ordered her thoughts. 'Oh, for heaven's sake . . . Not that stupid fight . . .' She explained fretfully, 'Lyndon and Jozef – they had a scrap last night. There was nothing to it. Nothing. But that was why he came to find me. He always did, you see, when he needed to talk.'

She stood in the doorway to the sitting room, watching the child drawing pictures at a table under the window. From time to time she called encouragement, once she went over to applaud the child's progress, but for the most part she leant back against the door-frame and recounted her story in a low voice.

'Lyndon found this job for Jozef in London,' she began. 'But it all turned sour. I don't know how or why exactly. But Jozef went and blamed Lyndon, as if Lyndon had done it on purpose or something. Lyndon was hurt . . . disappointed. He'd only been trying to help.'

Billy leant back against the opposite door-frame, watching her closely, both because he could not get enough of her and because he wanted her to see that he was listening attentively.

'Jozef was a difficult sort of person, of course. But that was why Lyndon felt a duty to try to help him. He knew what it was like to be an outsider because he was an outsider himself. Oh yes,' she insisted, as if Billy had been about to argue the point. 'He never really fitted in, did Lyndon. Not at school, not at home, not in the army. He felt he marched to a different tune, that he was always on the outside looking in. The only place he felt happy was at the university because he had a couple of good friends there, and no one cared if he read all day and did no sport and didn't join in. It was the only place where he felt no one was looking over his shoulder.'

While she turned to give the child a few words of encouragement, Billy battled to stop a fresh surge of jealousy from showing in his face. 'He wouldn't be the first to feel he didn't fit in.'

'No, he wouldn't. But he had it so bad he could never settle. He was always searching for something, and he never knew what it was.' She sighed. 'But this fight last night – well, it was the last straw. He was already in a high old state about taking the job with the Colonial Office. Is that its name? Colonial Office? Well, whatever it's called, he knew he should never have taken the position there. He knew it was a mistake. But his father was proud as Punch, expecting him to rise to whatever you rise to in the Colonial Office. And his mother was fretting about him going overseas, sure she'd never see him again. And Stella – well, Stella was being Stella, hanging about in hope, waiting for the day he'd ask her to marry him. All of them wanting him to be something he wasn't, couldn't be.' She stopped abruptly and gazed at the child in an unfocused way. 'So he came to find me, like he always did when he needed to talk. We could always talk, see, right from the start.' She slid Billy a warning look. 'Now don't go getting the wrong idea again, Billy. We were drawn to each other all right, but not in *that* way. Never in *that* way. Which was why we could talk. Why things were so easy between us.' Once she was satisfied that he had absorbed this statement, she added with a touch of pride, 'He knew that I went by my own opinions, that I didn't give a toss for what he was meant to be, past, present, or future. That whatever he was, it was all the same to me.'

The child began to hum tunelessly as she laboured at her drawing, and Annie tilted her head to catch the sound. Then she murmured almost to herself, 'No, they both came out of the war badly, him and Jozef. That's what brought on the trouble.'

'Well, the war wasn't too easy for anyone, was it?'

'No,' she agreed quickly. 'No, of course not. But with Lyndon—' She gazed at Billy before coming to a decision. 'Well, he lost his best friend in Burma, you see. I don't know how exactly – he wouldn't say – but he couldn't get it out of his mind. It was like—'

A sudden clatter from the living room made them look round. Annie went to retrieve the drawing pad from the floor and say something to the child. When she returned, she said in a murmur, 'I couldn't swear to it, but from a couple of things he said I think his friend was captured by the Japanese and badly treated. And that somehow Lyndon heard it happening. They were in the jungle, you know. And somehow he heard it . . .'

In the silence that followed, Annie straightened up and went into the passageway. When she returned she was wearing her coat again.

'I must get Beth to her friend's then go to the police. Do you think I should try to find Constable Longman? Or go to Taunton, to the police station there?'

'I don't know. What're you going to say?'

'Why, that I saw Lyndon right as rain after the fight. That he drove off on his bike afterwards. That the Poles were nowhere about.'

'I'll come with you then.'

She looked pleased. 'You will?'

''Course.' He kissed her lightly on the mouth, and the memory of their row receded like a bad dream. 'And for what it's worth I'll tell them I saw the Polacks making their way down the hill from the pub, and that they got to the farm a short time after I did and went straight to sleep.'

'When was this?'

'After you sent me away with a flea in my ear.'

'And before you came and stood under my window?'

'Didn't know you'd seen me.'

She gave a small smile. 'Oh, I saw you all right.'

'Well, it was before then, yes.'

'You didn't think of knocking?'

'Didn't dare.'

'I only wanted you to cool off a bit.'

'I did that all right. Chilled to the bone I was. Teeth rattling.'

'In that case you'd better knock next time, hadn't you?'

Chapter Fifteen

———

BENNETT WASN'T aware that the phone had rung or that Marjorie had answered it until she shook his shoulder and dragged him from sleep. Even then, he wasn't entirely sure if her voice was real or belonged to the strange confused dream that clung so heavily to him, a dream in which he had something vital to do, a life to save, only to find himself in a hospital bed, bound tightly by massive bandages and unable to move. Even as he struggled to free himself, he felt the temptation to succumb, to let himself slip towards a warm and beguiling place where he would be undisturbed for ever.

'Darling, wake up. He says it's important.'

As he rolled onto his back, the pain around his lung was sharp as a knife.

'It's Captain Robertson from Middlezoy Camp.'

Bennett had left a note for Robertson that afternoon. He'd driven to the camp as soon as he heard about Wladyslaw's arrest, only to discover that he'd missed Robertson by a matter of minutes. After some language-based confusion, he'd established that Robertson had gone to the police station in Taunton with Major Rafalski and an interpreter and possibly a lawyer, though no one was quite sure about the lawyer. Feeling he could achieve nothing useful by waiting, he had left a note for Robertson and come home, where he had slept like the dead for an hour before calling on two patients and returning to sleep again. At some point Marjorie had give him chicken broth. Now, as he hauled himself back from sleep, he knew only that he had slept for a long time and his mouth was parched.

Marjorie's bedside light was on, but as she handed him the receiver he had the impression that dawn was breaking in the world beyond the curtains.

'Hello?'

'Sorry to bother you, Doctor,' came Robertson's voice, 'but I thought you would want to know.'

In Bennett's groggy state he heard a Polish name that was surely Wladyslaw's and the word 'dead', and his heart seized, he had a sense of disconnection from the room, his ears roared with anguish and repugnance. Grief blocked his throat, and he thought his chest would burst. It was a long moment before he became aware of Marjorie calling anxiously to him and Robertson's voice repeating a name in the earpiece.

'Walczak?'

There was a baffled pause from Robertson. 'Yes?'

'It's *Walczak* who's dead?'

'Yes.'

'Not Wladyslaw?'

'No, no. Walczak.'

Heat pricked at Bennett's eyes. He heard a long shuddering sob of relief, and realised it had come from his own mouth.

'I'm all right, thank you, dear,' he said to Marjorie as he rang off, but it was a good two to three minutes before he felt steady enough to get up.

An hour later, Bennett followed Detective Inspector Shearer down a corridor and through a pass door into a reception area rather different from the one that greeted visitors to the front of the police station. Here there were no windows, just overhead lamps that cast a baleful light over chipped green walls and a floor of worn grey lino. The air was filled with the smell of disinfectant and cigarette smoke and what might have been fried bacon. A uniformed sergeant stood at a high counter, filling out a logbook. Behind him, in an office area, two constables sat at a table with mugs of tea, while another leant against the open flap at the far end of the counter.

As the two men came through the pass door a heavy silence

fell. One of the officers at the table clambered to his feet and the other joined him. Their eyes travelled with scant curiosity over Bennett before fixing watchfully on Shearer.

The sergeant said, 'Dr Tring's in there now, Inspector.'

Shearer nodded and said, ostensibly to Bennett but more to the whole room, 'We've always had a good record, a very good record. Just two in the last three years, isn't it, Sergeant?'

'Sir.'

'Both of them accidental?'

'One natural causes, one inhalation of vomit, sir.'

'And none recently?'

'That's correct, sir.'

The inspector gave a vexed sigh and, crossing the room to a heavy door with a wire-reinforced window, held it open for Bennett. They entered a passage with more bleak lighting and green paint. There were eight cells, four on either side, with heavy metal doors and shuttered Judas holes. Some of the doors were open, spilling a dull glow of natural light into the passageway. Voices sounded from a cell on the left.

Shearer murmured, 'You know Dr Tring, the police surgeon, do you, Doctor?'

'Slightly.'

Bennett had in fact met Tring on several occasions, and had learnt to avoid him whenever possible.

At the door, Shearer gestured Bennett to go ahead. Inside the cell Captain Robertson was standing next to a uniformed police officer, while Tring's broad back was bent over the body on the metal-frame bed.

The uniformed man, a tall sergeant with a drooping face, straightened his shoulders and looked past Bennett to the inspector. 'He used a bedspring to rip up the blanket, so far as I can make out, sir. Though for the life of me I still can't fathom how he managed it without us seeing.'

Bennett moved forward and gazed down at Jozef's body. The young face looked virtually unaltered, as pale and worn and haggard in death as it had been in life. Bennett had never subscribed to the belief that a man's final emotions remained etched on his face, yet Jozef's forehead seemed to be corrugated in a frown of despair.

Tring glanced up. 'Bennett! Hello, old boy, what brings you here? Not one of yours, is he?'

'He was a patient for a while, yes.'

'Well, well. Been doing a bit of War Ministry work on the quiet, have you?' He gave a soundless chortle, which had the effect of spreading his several chins. When Bennett failed to respond, Tring nodded towards the dead man. 'Always mentally unhinged, was he?'

Bennett immediately recalled why he disliked Tring. It wasn't just the sweeping judgements, but the mocking, boastful contempt he showed for the hapless creatures he was called to examine in the course of his police work.

'Not in my opinion, no.'

Tring raised his eyebrows. 'Really? He seemed pretty far off the rails when I saw him last night.'

Bennett's anger came from nowhere and caught him by surprise. It was all he could do not to bark: *Then why didn't you have him put on suicide watch? Why didn't you have him admitted to a place of safety?* If he had thought Tring worth a second more of his attention he might have added: *Because you're a pompous self-satisfied idiot who's unworthy of the job.*

Tring said, 'I gave him a bromide to quieten him down, but he probably spat it out the moment I left.' He leant down to snap his bag shut. 'Alcoholic, was he?'

'Why do you say that?'

'Because he showed all the symptoms of DTs, old boy. Rapid pulse, agitation, sweating, and trembling.'

'He'd suffered a lot of war damage.' Bennett wasn't sure why he chose an expression normally reserved for buildings, but on reflection decided it was entirely appropriate. 'He was badly injured in Italy. His head took a crack, and I think you'll find he was left with only half a stomach.'

Another mirthless chuckle from Tring as he got to his feet. 'Not for me to find anything of the sort, thank God. Leave that to the pathologist.' He added in the tone of someone getting to the crux of the matter, 'So, a neurasthenic, was he?'

Bennett realised that Tring was planning his report, looking for a diagnosis that would absolve him of any suggestion of dereliction. But Bennett wasn't prepared to play that game, certainly not with neurasthenia, a disparaging diagnosis used to imply that nervous disorders without obvious cause sprang from lack of backbone. 'Not neurasthenia, no,' he stated firmly. 'I would say that he was a brave young man for whom the battle simply went on too long.'

Tring threw him a dubious glance. 'Indeed, indeed,' he said briskly, making for the door. 'Well, thank you, gentlemen. Thank you.' The inspector left with him, the rumble of their voices fading down the passageway.

In the silence that followed, Bennett pulled the blanket up over the dead man's face.

On entering the cell he had glanced at the barred window and just as quickly glanced away again. Now he took in the height of the window and the ragged makeshift rope fastened to one of the bars, and the severed end from when they had cut him down.

'Must have taken him hours,' the sergeant remarked, following his gaze. 'We checked regular as clockwork every half-hour through the night, but we never caught him tearing up the blanket, let alone shifting the bed under the window. He seemed to know exactly how to go about it, I'll say that for him.'

Robertson's voice said, 'He gave no sign of what he was intending?'

'Depends what you mean by sign,' the sergeant replied, a touch defensively. 'There's some that yell and shout all night, and there's some that stay quiet. It doesn't mean much. They usually perk up just the same after a good breakfast. This one, he was quiet when we began our shift. Then, about nine, he started making a commotion. First, we put it down to him being foreign, if you know what I mean. But when he didn't calm down, we called Dr Tring. After that, he was quiet again. Looked like he'd gone to sleep. Nothing to tell us he was planning something like this. Nothing at all.'

Bennett asked, 'When was he found?'

'At five a.m., sir. He must have done it right after the four-thirty round, because by the time we discovered him he was long gone.'

Bennett pictured Jozef feigning sleep as the officer looked in through the Judas hole, waiting for the footsteps to fade before shifting the bed and reaching up to the window to tie the makeshift rope to the bar. What would go through a man's head in those last moments? Did he think of his family? Of his God? Did he look forward with joy and anticipation to the release from his agony? Was he filled with longing for the freedom to come?

Robertson asked, 'Did he have any family, do you know?'

'I believe he had a mother in Poland, but best ask Wladyslaw. He's aware of what's happened, I presume?'

'I believe so.'

'Yes, he knows,' confirmed the sergeant.

The sergeant escorted them to a cell at the end of the passage and unlocked the door.

Wladyslaw was sitting on the bed, his forearms resting on his knees, his hands clasped in front of him. He turned his head unhurriedly, without interest. Only when he saw Bennett did his eyes sharpen in greeting. Getting up, he grasped Bennett's hand and sat him down solicitously on the bed next to him.

Bennett said, 'I'm so very sorry, Wladyslaw.'

He gave a minute shrug. 'With Jozef it was always big problem to keep him alive in his own thoughts.'

'But this business.'

'Yes. This was not good.'

Robertson offered Wladyslaw a cigarette, which he took with a brief nod. Inhaling slowly, he said, 'He believed that

bad things were following him. That he had no hope of a better
life. I told him there is no evidence, but he did not listen. All
the time I shouted across to him, calm down, calm down, it
will be OK, but nine, ten o'clock he went crazy for a while.
Then after the doctor comes he is quiet. I ask police to leave
the thing open' – he mimed the sliding shutter over the Judas
hole – 'and I called to him all the time, you OK? Then at one,
two o'clock he said he wished to sleep.' Wladyslaw spread a
palm in a gesture of impotence. 'He had made his decision by
this time. I listened in the night, I called two, three times, but I
heard nothing. Nothing at all.'

After a suitable pause, Robertson said, 'He had family in
Poland, I believe?'

'He had his mother and three sisters.'

'Where would I find their address?'

'At the farm. There are letters in his kitbag. You will not
tell them how he died?'

'I've no doubt Major Rafalski will find some way round it.
Influenza, something like that.'

'You will leave me a copy of this address, please? And tell
me what caused his death when you know, because I will write
also.' He scoffed, 'If – when – I get out of this place.'

Bennett said, 'They can't hold you much longer, Wladyslaw.'

'They say I killed Hanley because I lose Stella to him. They
say I am mad with jealousy. Because Poles are passionate crazy
people who go mad with jealousy all the time for no reason.
We know this well.' He looked from Bennett to Robertson and
rolled his eyes in silent comment. 'I tell them, next time I kill
someone, it will be for better reason than this. Like they are
Russian soldiers. But they don't think this is too funny. They
sure don't smile.'

Bennett could imagine how well this had gone down with
Inspector Shearer and his colleagues, for whom talk of other
enemies and other wars would be deeply suspect.

In the same tone of exasperation, Wladyslaw added, 'I ask
them why I wish to kill Hanley when the lady has made her

choice. I ask them why I wait three, four weeks to do it. I ask them how I get Hanley into the river.' He made a question of this with a wide swing of his cigarette. 'They have no answer.'

'They can't hold you for more than twenty-four hours without evidence, Wladyslaw. Isn't that right, Robertson?'

The captain nodded. 'Thirty-six at the most.'

But Wladyslaw had cocked an ear to the sound of approaching voices outside the cell. He said, 'One thing, Captain. You will find a priest for Jozef?'

'Well . . . of course.'

'Some priests, they won't say prayers for people who die this way. If the Polish priest won't do it, you will find an English priest?'

'Of course.'

'Despite all the things that happened to Jozef in his life, he believed still in God. He has a bad bargain, I think, if he does not receive prayers at the end.'

The bolts sounded and the door opened. Inspector Shearer appeared, with the sergeant at his shoulder. 'Mr Malinowski?'

Wladyslaw dropped his cigarette onto the floor and ground it out before looking up.

'You are free to go.'

Bennett gripped Wladyslaw's shoulder in triumph before climbing to his feet. 'He's completely in the clear?'

'Yes.'

'There!' Bennett cried. 'What did I tell you?' Then, to Shearer, 'You've discovered it was an accident?'

'We have reason to believe so, yes.'

'You found the motorbike?'

'Yes. It has been retrieved from the River Tone at Stanmoor Bridge.'

'And it had crashed?'

'It would seem so. The, er, forensic expert believes he has found a point of impact on the bridge.'

'There!'

'Also, two witnesses have come forward on behalf of Mr Malinowski regarding his whereabouts.'

Robertson murmured, in the tone of someone wanting to get things absolutely straight, 'On behalf of Mr Walczak as well?'

'Him as well,' the inspector agreed.

Wladyslaw asked, 'This was Billy Greer?'

'Mr Greer was one of them, yes.'

Wladyslaw seemed quietly pleased at this. He gave a slow nod.

It was a week before the burial could take place. The turnout was larger than Wladyslaw had expected. From the camp came not only Major Rafalski, Captain Robertson and two other administrative officers but the godmothers and six of Jozef's comrades from the Third Carpathian Rifles, who bore the coffin to the grave before forming an honour guard. To one side of them and some way back stood Billy with Annie Bentham. Only Dr Bennett was absent.

The cemetery lay on the edge of a moor beyond Middlezoy in what was little more than a field. No trees grew there, and the large area not yet taken up by graves was covered in rough grass. The plot allocated to Jozef was in a remote corner not far from a number of unmarked graves, presumably those of paupers and vagrants. Yet for a young man who had once dreamt of running a smallholding it was an appropriate spot, for just beyond the iron boundary fence cattle grazed, and when the Polish priest began to intone his prayers it was to the accompaniment of soft ruminating and the swish of hooves passing through long grass.

After the priest had finished, Rafalski spoke. 'This soldier fought bravely for our freedom. Now he has given his soul to God, his body to foreign soil, and his heart to Poland.' After a moment's silence Rafalski stepped forward to cast the first earth onto the coffin.

Wladyslaw walked down to the gates with the godmothers. Danuta dragged a handkerchief across her eyes and said, 'So you're leaving us too, are you, Wladek?'

'Yes. I've decided on Canada.'

'Oh dear, oh dear.'

'It's meant to be a great country.'

'I know. But it's so far away. Everywhere's so far away.' Dabbing at her eyes again, she made for Robertson's car.

Alina kissed Wladyslaw on both cheeks then touched her fingertips wistfully to the side of his head. 'Maybe we will follow you, Wladek. Who knows?'

Wladyslaw waited for Robertson and Rafalski to come through the gates. As they approached, Wladyslaw was surprised to hear Rafalski talking in broken but passable English.

As Robertson hurried off to organise the transport, Rafalski reverted smoothly to Polish. 'Ah, Malinowski,' he murmured in his abstracted way. 'You're off now, are you?'

'Yes.'

'Whereabouts in Canada was it?'

'Toronto, hopefully.'

'Ah . . .' The note of faint bewilderment sounded again. 'Well . . . what can I say except good luck? I'm off myself at long last. I should be in Paris by the end of next week, in time for my sister's wedding.'

The image of the family celebration gave Wladyslaw a twinge of envy and longing. He said, 'I wish your sister all happiness.'

'Thank you.' A rare smile lit Rafalski's austere face. 'It's extraordinary, but she's marrying an old friend of mine from military college. They met in Paris. Such a small world. But then it's bound to be, I suppose, when you live abroad.'

Billy and Annie gave Wladyslaw a lift back to the village in Billy's new acquisition, a tall-sided van painted chocolate brown with the name of a Taunton baker and the legend *Bread – Cakes – Pastries* in spindly cream lettering on three sides.

Because of its dodgy clutch Billy had beaten the baker down and got it at a bargain price.

Stopping outside the Bennetts' house, Billy said, 'Sure you don't want us to wait and take you to the station?'

'Thank you, but I am OK to walk.'

They got out and Annie gave Wladyslaw a farewell kiss. 'You've been a wonder,' she said. Then, as Billy went to the back of the van to collect Wladyslaw's kitbag, she said, 'Don't worry, I'll keep an eye on Stan and Flor.'

'And on Billy too, eh?'

She laughed. 'Looks like I'll have to.'

Billy dropped the kitbag onto the ground and said, 'Not too late to change your mind, Johnnie. Stay and make your fortune with me. Won't find too many withy farms in Canada.'

'I'm not sure this makes me so sad.'

'All that skill gone to waste.'

Billy looked as though he was going to slap Wladyslaw on the shoulder, only to change his mind and thrust out his hand. Swinging up into the van, barely waiting for Annie to climb in the other side, he fired the engine with a roar. 'Bye, Johnnie. Watch out for the wolves, eh?'

The door was answered by Mrs Bennett, her eyes dull, her face etched with weariness. 'Oh, it's you, Wladyslaw,' she said on a note of relief.

'I wondered if it was possible, for just a few minutes, to say goodbye.'

She looked at his kitbag, she put a hand to her forehead in a gesture of forgetfulness. 'Oh goodness, it's today that you're leaving, isn't it? Yes, of course.' She stood back hastily. 'Come in, Wladyslaw. He'd hate to miss you. He's been asking after you.'

Entering the hall, Wladyslaw became aware of other people in the house: the rustle of a newspaper followed by the low murmur of a man's voice; from the kitchen the muted rattle of a cooking pot. Passing the living room, he saw a young woman glance up anxiously from her chair and knew from photo-graphs that it was the daughter. From another chair a man's head craned into view to stare at him and Wladyslaw guessed it was the son-in-law. Moving on, he heard a woman speak in the kitchen and a second one answer.

Mrs Bennett started to lead the way upstairs, only to pause on the first step and ask, 'When were you last here, Wladyslaw? Was it Friday?'

'It was Saturday.'

'Ah yes,' she said, climbing again. 'Well, he's had a couple of better nights since then.'

'Yes?' said Wladyslaw in a tone that echoed hope with hope.

'His breathing doesn't seem to trouble him so much. And the fever's finally gone down.'

'I am very glad.'

At the far side of the landing she stopped outside the half-open door. 'He still gets very tired, though.'

'I will not stay too long.'

She hesitated, as if to say more, but thought better of it.

The room was flooded with light. The doctor lay propped up in bed, his head turned towards the window, his eyes closed and his mouth slightly open. Even as Wladyslaw waited by the door he could hear the rasp of his breathing.

Mrs Bennett bent over the bed. 'Darling? Wladyslaw's here.'

For a moment the doctor didn't seem to hear. Then he cried hoarsely, 'Wladyslaw!' and turned to look for him.

'Hello, Doctor.'

'You're here! On your way to the station!'

Wladyslaw took his outstretched hand and pressed it warmly between his own before pulling up a chair. As he sat down he tried not to notice how much flesh had gone from the doctor's face, and how poor was his colour.

'I'm sorry I couldn't get to the cemetery, Wladyslaw. How did it go?'

'It was very fine. A soldier's burial.'

'I'm so glad. And there was a Catholic priest?'

'Yes. It was agreed that Jozef died from the shock of war, which is not so much of a—' With a rotation of his hand Wladyslaw searched for the lost word. 'What is the sin beyond saving?'

'A mortal sin?'

'Exactly! It was a lesser sin than this.'

'So there were proper prayers, that's the important thing.'

'Yes.'

'And who was there?'

'His two lady godmothers from the camp. The administrators and senior officers. And six comrades from his regiment. Also Billy.'

'Ah. He came, did he?'

'With Annie Bentham.'

'They're together, are they, those two?'

'I think for sure. Billy smiles early in the morning. He says good things about everyone, even Polacks. Yes, I think they are together.'

'Well, he'll do all right with Annie. More than all right.' Bennett coughed long and low; his chest heaved with the effort of regaining his breath. When he spoke again, it was in short bursts, on snatches of exhaled air. 'And you, Wladyslaw? Don't forget that London isn't so far away . . . You must come and visit us often . . . You know you'll always be welcome . . . to stay here with Marjorie and me. Any time at all. Why don't you come in a couple of weeks? The wild flowers will be out by then. All the summer birds will have arrived . . . wagtails and warblers and buntings and . .' The names of the other birds seemed to escape him, he lost momentum. 'Yes, it's really quite magical in May. You'd hardly recognise the place. And today isn't such a bad start, is it?' He turned his head towards the window. 'A bit of warmth in the air at last.'

'Doctor, I must tell you – I have finally decided to try for Canada.'

Bennett turned back. 'Canada?'

'Please, do not think it is for any bad reasons. It is not that

I wish to leave this country so much. It has been a good place
for me. Everyone had been most kind. It is more that I feel it
would be better to try for somewhere new.'

'So . . . you won't be taking up the college place in London?'

'No. I am going to apply instead for this course in Toronto
where it is possible to study English and work for teaching
qualifications at the same time. I go for my visa next week.'

'Teaching, Wladyslaw!'

'Yes!' he laughed. 'I think in my heart I always wished to be
a teacher.'

'Well, for what it's worth, I always thought so too. All those
ideas of yours. All that talk about the purposes of education. I
think there was no escaping it.'

'It is possible they will not like my ideas, of course.'

'Maybe so. But just stick to your guns. Don't let them put
you off too easily.'

'I will try my best.'

Bennett said, 'We'll be sorry to see you go, Wladyslaw.
More than sorry. But you must go to Canada. You must make
the most of your opportunities.'

'It is not just the opportunity, Doctor. It is also a matter of
geography. To be a long way from Poland is better for me, I
think. If I cannot go back, then it is better to be far away in a
new country where everything is different and new. Here the
war is still too close.'

'Yes.'

'And you know, when I arrived in England, I travelled
through Athelney on the train, through water on each side like
an ocean. I told you once, I think?'

'Yes, you did.'

'Well, my leg was in bad shape then. Full of infection. I
thought that I would lose it finally. I thought the doctors would
take one look and—' He made a short scything motion with
the edge of his hand. 'But one doctor at the military hospital,
he said, no, let's try one more time with this fellow, and I
thought then, if I keep my leg I will have no reason to complain

in my life again. So when I leave on the train today, when I
pass through the ocean once more, with my leg in one piece,
and with my life and my health, I will resume my journey
without complaint.'

Bennett gripped his hand. 'Go safely, Wladyslaw.'

'I will write often.'

'Go now or you'll miss your train.'

'I thank you for everything you have done for me, Doctor.'

'Goodbye, Wladyslaw.' Suddenly the doctor seemed desper-
ately tired. With a lift of one hand, a sketchy wave, he turned
his head towards the window and closed his eyes. By the time
Wladyslaw reached the door he had slipped into a deep,
unhealthy-looking sleep.

Wladyslaw did not allow himself time to stop or think until
he had said goodbye to Mrs Bennett and hurried away into the
road. Then his vision blurred, his throat seized, and he almost
walked into the hedge. Stopping, he cried, 'My friend, my
friend . . .'

Eventually he wiped his eyes with the back of his hand and
walked on. He barely noticed the figure bicycling towards him
until she was quite close. It was Stella. She braked and dis-
mounted in front of him.

'I was coming to find you,' she said.

'Well, here I am.' Not knowing what else to say, aware that
his eyes were still damp, he started on his way again.

She turned her bicycle round and walked beside him.
'You've been to see the Doctor?'

'Yes.'

'How is he today?'

'Not good.'

She gave a soft groan of dismay. 'I thought – we all thought
he was getting better.'

Wladyslaw did not believe in offering false hope. He said,
'He will not get better.'

Stella faltered and covered her face with one hand. He
waited attentively while she found a handkerchief and blew her

nose, then they walked on again in silence. After a time she said, 'I was very sorry about your friend, Wladyslaw. I would have written but . . .'

'Sure.'

'I know my uncle didn't help, making those accusations, but he didn't mean it on purpose, you know. He really didn't. He was just – overcome.'

Unable to offer any useful response to this, Wladyslaw said, 'I wish to say that I am sorry about your cousin also.'

'Thank you.' She added in a tone of resignation, 'I thought I was the one person who could persuade him to drive slower and drink less. But I couldn't. The Doctor said no one could, and I'm trying very hard to believe he's right.'

A tractor came round a corner and they pulled in to the side.

When it had passed Stella cast him a thoughtful glance. 'I wanted to ask you something, Wladyslaw.'

'Of course. But I am leaving today, Stella. I am leaving now.'

'Yes, I know. That's why I came. You see, I wanted to ask if I could write to you.'

The combination of grief and surprise had lowered his defences. Despite everything, he found his heart lifting. 'Stella . . . I don't see . . . why . . .'

'I so want us to keep in touch.'

He said bluntly, 'I'm going to Canada.'

But she seemed to know about that as well. 'Oh, but I'd love to hear about it,' she said warmly. 'I'd love to know how you're getting on.' Then, more tentatively: 'And, well . . . there are things I wanted to say, Wladyslaw . . . to explain. Things I can't explain now.'

He came to a stop, and Stella stopped as well. Gazing at her clear eyes, her bright hair, her open face, he remembered all too vividly why he had fallen in love with her.

'Stella, it is a good thought, but it is not necessary. What is past is past. My heart is mended,' he lied. 'I will always think of you in friendship and wish you all good fortune for the future.' He took her hand and kissed it formally.

She stepped closer to him, and the bicycle lurched precariously. 'For the sake of friendship then, Wladyslaw – let me write. It would mean so much to me.'

He could find no argument to that, and perhaps he didn't want to. He smiled at her. 'So long as you don't try and correct my English.'

She said, 'It's a promise.' Then, gesturing for him to rest his kitbag on the saddle, she allowed him to take charge of the bicycle, and they walked through the village and down to the station, talking of Canada.

Historical Note

FOLLOWING THE Soviet invasion of eastern Poland in 1939, some 1.6 million Poles were deported to prisons and forced labour camps in the Soviet Union. Of these, roughly 500,000 were civilians taken from their homes. The remainder consisted of captured soldiers, political prisoners and those caught attempting to flee the country. Within a year, half were dead.

In July 1941, soon after Germany's attack on Russia began, the Soviet Union agreed to grant amnesty to Polish prisoners and slave labourers, and subsequently to allow for the formation of a Polish army on Soviet soil. Only 115,000 men and dependants reached the new army, however, partly because so many Poles had already perished, partly because the Russians broke their word and failed to release large numbers from the camps. When the Russians proved reluctant to feed and equip the new army, the exiled Polish government, with Churchill's support, negotiated the army's evacuation to Persia and thence to the Middle East, to serve under the British.

At the end of the war, only 310 of those who had emerged from the Soviet Union to join the Polish Second Corps opted to return to Soviet-dominated Poland.

In Britain the belief that the exiled Poles were unreasonably anti-Soviet persisted until 1948, when Russia's iron grip on Poland and the rest of Eastern Europe became glaringly apparent.

As a result of trade union opposition, the placing of Poles in employment was at first painfully slow, and it was not until mid-1947 that significant numbers began to find work. Even then, almost all the jobs were unskilled. For those who aspired to skilled and professional work, emigration remained the best option.